SHERIFF JOE

C. J. PETIT

TABLE OF CONTENTS

PROLOGUE

Fremont County, Wyoming
May 28, 1881

"Son of a bitch!" Joe shouted as the ground eight feet behind him exploded and was immediately followed by the echo of a Winchester.

Joe immediately dropped from his gray gelding, pulling his repeater from the scabbard, and led the horse toward a small group of boulders as he scanned for the telltale cloud from the shot. It didn't take him long to find it when another shot rang out and the .44 caliber bullet buzzed past his head.

"Damn! Damn! Damn!" Joe muttered as he dropped to the ground still ten feet from the protecting boulders. He brought his own Winchester to bear and fired at the cloud's base, about a hundred yards away.

As soon as he did, another Winchester fired from a spot just fifty feet to the right of the last one. Then, a third rifle began to shoot at him from a hundred feet further to his right.

"At least that means all three of you bastards are up there," Joe said to himself as he laid in the prone position on the ground.

He was in a bad position and knew it. Even if he made it to the boulders, he'd be pinned down and one of them could just swing through those trees on the right and get a clean shot.

Joe knew he couldn't stay here and be the victim. He needed to get on their flank, not the other way around.

Joe endured three more .44 volcanos within six feet of his position when he suddenly hopped to his feet, feinted toward the boulders and then suddenly spun and ran away from their safety, sprinting toward the trees sixty yards away.

The Hobson brothers, Al, Johnny and Ben all opened fire when he had first jumped to his feet but had expected him to head for the boulders and led him in that direction, but as soon as he made his sudden bolt for the trees, they all quickly changed their aim and began firing again.

Joe still ran toward the trees as they adjusted their fire and all he could do was to vary his speed, running in a herky-jerky fashion so they couldn't lead him accurately, but with three of them firing, the odds were he'd be taking a hit soon, even though he noticed that only two of the shooters were anywhere close to being accurate.

"Keep firing!" shouted Al, the oldest Hobson brother, as if they were going to let up.

Each brother was rapidly levering in new rounds and firing at Joe as quickly as they could, but Ben had his eyes closed and was firing willy-nilly.

Joe was just fifteen yards from the trees when he felt the first hit, a deep graze across the back of his left butt. He didn't waste the energy on cussing at the damage but put on a surge to reach the safety of the trees as lead kept whizzing past.

Suddenly, he was among the trees and everything changed. Now, he would turn them into the targets.

He took a couple of seconds to feel his butt and wasn't rewarded with any blood. He pulled out his wallet and found out that it had taken the abuse and not his behind. It was a good tradeoff, he reckoned as he began trotting through the trees.

"We gotta get outta here!" Johnny shouted, "he's gonna get behind us!"

"No, he ain't!" yelled Al, "just get behind them rocks and cover those trees. He's gotta show himself!"

Al then turned back and trotted back to the rocks he had mentioned and set up position while Johnny and Ben followed suit. Soon, they were all established in their new positions and had their three Winchesters aimed at the edge of the trees where they expected the sheriff to appear.

Ben looked over at his two older brothers and felt sick. They were trying to kill Sheriff Joe!

Joe knew he couldn't just pop out of the trees, sure that the Hobsons didn't just keep standing where they were, so he angled toward the right and headed for the hill where the trees ended. He began a slow climb up the rock-strewn hill and kept glancing to his left to see if he could spot the three brothers.

He was well out of the trees now and wondered where they were. Joe finally stopped to catch his breath and do a thorough scan of the ground where he expected them to be and only then, did he spot the three barrels resting on rocks pointing at the trees. They were so intently monitoring the trees that they hadn't even seen Joe when he began his climb. Now, he had to keep it that way as he slowly stepped up the hill to gain some height advantage. If he was able to get another twenty feet up that hill, he'd be able to reach behind their rocky cover with his Winchester.

He climbed slowly, but still keeping a wary eye on those three rifle barrels. Then, their heads came into view and then their shoulders.

Joe finally stopped climbing and crouched behind a small boulder. The range was less than eighty yards and those boys were all dead if Joe decided to pull the trigger.

But as he aimed his sights at the Hobson to the right, he couldn't just fire.

Keeping his rifle's sights on his target, he shouted, "Drop 'em, boys! I've got you all under my Winchester!"

Al whipped his head and then his rifle at the shout, followed by Johnny, but Ben froze and pushed his rifle over the rock, letting it clatter to the ground on the other side.

Ben had realized that they didn't have a chance and threw up his hands. It was the smart thing to do. Al and Johnny both thought they had a chance if they fired up the hill at the sheriff and tried their luck.

As soon as Joe saw the two rifles swing in his direction, he opened fire. His first .50 caliber bullet spun out of his Winchester's barrel, crossed the two-hundred-and-fourteen feet and punched through Johnny Hobson's chest just below the left clavicle, ripping through lung and blood vessels before exiting his chest and burying itself in the ground. He never got a shot off.

Al Hobson fired his Winchester at Joe, the bullet ricocheting off the boulder the sheriff was hiding behind, as he levered in a second .50-95 Express cartridge and fired his second shot at the shooter.

Al felt the punch of the massive round as it hit in almost exactly the same spot as it did on his younger brother with the same results. Al fell over backwards and died just four seconds later from the extreme damage done by the bullet.

Ben then stood with his arms outstretched and his eyes closed, expecting to be shot any moment. The panicked fear had caused him to empty his bladder, but he didn't care. He knew he was going to die.

Joe quickly left his boulder and slid and scrambled down the hill toward the one standing Hobson brother. When he reached level ground, he kept his muzzle pointed at Ben Hobson as he walked closer.

He was going to tell him to get on the ground, but knew it wasn't necessary. As he drew closer, he not only noticed that he had wet himself, but that Ben Hobson couldn't have been sixteen years old.

Joe reached the base of the rock where Ben's Winchester still rested, picked up the carbine and leaned it against the side of the rock. Then he sidestepped around the left side of the rock, looked down quickly at the two dead Hobsons and then approached the youngster. He pulled the boy's Colt from his holster and tossed it onto the chest of Al Hobson.

"Okay, son, you can put your hands down now," Joe said.

"You ain't gonna shoot me?" Ben asked, his eyes still tightly shut.

"Why would I shoot you? You're not armed anymore. You can open your eyes now, too."

Ben slowly opened his eyes and looked at the sheriff.

"I…I didn't mean to hit you when I was shootin', sheriff. I was aimin' high."

"It doesn't matter, son. Shooting at a lawman at all is a serious offense. A lot more serious than robbing a stagecoach. You and your brothers were only looking at five years until you decided to make a fight of it."

Ben then began to cry. He tried not to, but he couldn't help it. He closed his eyes in his shame for wetting himself and now crying. He was supposed to be a man now!

Joe sighed and let Ben do what he had to do and began gathering weapons from the two dead brothers. He then removed Ben's gunbelt while he still sobbed.

Once all of the gunbelts and Winchesters were in one spot, Joe walked back to Ben and said, “Sit down, son.”

Ben wiped his face with the back of his hand and took a seat on one of the shorter rocks.

“Now, I’m not planning on taking your brothers’ bodies back to Lander. It’s too far and they’d be in bad shape by the time we got there. I don’t mind digging a grave for them, but I can’t have you at my back while I do it. So, here’s the deal. You help me dig your brothers’ graves and I won’t hogtie you. I want your word that you won’t give me any trouble. I don’t want to have to shoot you. Will you do that?”

Ben nodded and said, “Yes, sir.”

“Okay. Now, let’s head over to my horse. I have a small shovel that I keep with me for this kind of thing.”

Ben stood and followed Joe as he walked back to his gray gelding a hundred and fifty yards away.

As they walked, Joe asked, “Why did you boys decide to knock off a stagecoach? It’s not like any of you were criminals or anything.”

Ben replied, “It was Al’s idea. He told me and Johnny it would be easy to get some real money, and nobody would get hurt. I didn’t want to go, but he’s my big brother.”

“Well, he had that all wrong, didn’t he? Luckily, the driver was only wounded and not murdered, but you sure scared the hell out of those folks in the coach. I assume their loot is still in your saddlebags?”

“Al has it all in his. It was Al who shot the driver. He didn’t need to, either. The driver was steppin’ down.”

“I know. I talked to him when he drove the stage into Lander. He wasn’t happy about it, either.”

They reached Joe’s horse and Joe grabbed his reins and they headed back to the bodies.

“What’s your name, son?” Joe asked.

“Ben. Ben Hobson. Al was the oldest and Johnny was two years older than me.”

“Do you still have parents?” Joe asked as they plodded along.

“Yes, sir. Well, I have my mother. My father died four years ago.”

Joe grimaced then asked, “So, you left your mama alone to go and rob a stage?”

“Not alone, sheriff. She was with my sister, Margie and my younger brother, Harry.”

“How old are your brother and sister?”

“Margie is seventeen and Harry is thirteen.”

“How old are you, Ben?”

“I’ll be sixteen next month.”

Joe shook his head, then asked, “Is your mother Abby Hobson who lives on a small spread near Baldwin Creek west of North Fork””

“Yes, sir? Do you know my mother?”

“I’ve never met her, but I’ve heard the name.”

They reached the bodies and Joe pulled out the small shovel from his bedroll.

“You can start digging, Ben. I’ll watch and when you get tired, let me know. Just dig one hole.”

“Yes, sir,” Ben said as he accepted the shovel.

As he began to dig, Joe asked, “Why were you three riding northeast? If your ranch is west of North Fork, you were going in the wrong direction.”

Ben kept digging as he replied, “Al wanted us to join up with some gang up in Cooperstown. I think he said the leader’s name was Bob Jones.”

Joe’s eyebrows rose as he asked, “Hanger Bob Jones?”

“I think so. Al said we could join his gang because we were white.”

Joe pushed his Stetson back on his head and asked, “What has that got to do with it?”

“Al said that there are three gangs in Cooperstown, one white, one half-breed and one with Frenchies who claim to be mountain men.”

“And they’re all in Cooperstown? That place was abandoned six years ago.”

Ben continued to shovel dirt aside as he said, “Yes, sir. But Al said they were turnin’ it into kind of an outlaw town.”

Joe just realized that his job had gotten much more serious now if what Ben was telling him was true. He knew about Hanger Bob Jones and his band of cutthroats, but the Frenchies were new and so was the group of half-breeds. He’d have to do some research when he got back to his office.

Ben finally signaled he was tired, and Joe handed him a canteen. He had slid his Winchester into its scabbard on Boomer and would have to keep an eye on it as he dug.

Ben just took a seat and watched as Joe began to dig. He thought he was going to hang now and thought about making a break for the sheriff’s rifle, but he didn’t because he had given his word. He remembered that his father had always told him that a man’s word was better than a piece of paper and if he broke his word, then he wouldn’t be a man at all.

It took almost half an hour working in shifts to get the grave dug, and then Ben and Joe dragged the two bodies into the grave and then took turns shoveling the dirt back on top and covering the mound with rocks.

When they were done, Joe asked, “Do you want to say anything, Ben?”

Ben shook his head and said, “No, sir.”

“Okay, let’s get your horses and we can start heading back.”

“Yes, sir.” Ben said dejectedly.

Forty minutes later, Joe and Ben were riding side-by-side. Each horse was trailing another. Joe had emptied a Winchester and left it in Ben’s scabbard and placed the other two still-loaded rifles in the trailed horses’ scabbards. The gunbelts were in the saddlebags along with the stolen loot.

After they’d been riding an hour, Ben asked, “Aren’t we going in the wrong direction, Sheriff?”

Joe didn’t look at him, but replied, “Nope.”

Ben swiveled in his saddle and wondered why they were riding west and not south.

An hour later, Ben began spotting familiar terrain, and after they crossed a north-south road, Ben suddenly knew where they were headed.

“Why are we goin’ to my ranch?” he asked.

“Because, Ben, we are going to talk to your mother,” Joe answered.

Ben was startled and ashamed. When he and his brothers had gone off to rob the stage and then join up with a gang, he had been excited at the idea of adventure, but it hadn’t turned out the way he expected at all. They had bought the Winchesters using almost all of the household expense money and then, there was the confrontation with the driver that had terrified him, and he had been aghast when Al had fired his Winchester into the man. After they had taken all of the passengers' valuables and ridden off, he was sure that the driver was dead. He knew his life was over and he didn't want to be a criminal anymore. Then, they had been trailed by Sheriff Joe and Al had convinced him and Johnny to drygulch the lawman. Now, he was going to hang, and the sheriff was going to tell his mother what they had done, which was almost worse.

The ranch came into view as the sun was low on the horizon and Joe spotted a boy running toward them. Joe assumed that was thirteen-year-old Harry.

As they approached the access road, Harry waved at Ben, who didn't return the greeting, but hung his head in shame.

By the time they reached Harry, the front door of the small ranch house had opened, and Joe assumed that it was Mrs. Hobson standing on the front porch with her hands on her hips. A young woman stepped out behind her.

"Where's Al and Johnny, Ben? How come you're with the sheriff?" Harry shouted as he jogged alongside the small caravan.

They reached the front of the house and Joe asked, "Mrs. Hobson? I'm Sheriff Joe Brooks, and I need to talk to you, if I may."

"Please step down, Sheriff," she replied as she looked at Ben, who finally raised his eyes to look at his mother.

"Step down, Ben," Joe said as he dismounted.

Ben slowly stepped down from his horse, then took the reins and followed the sheriff's lead in hitching the animals.

"Mrs. Hobson, I was on the trail of three men who had held of the Overland Stage and shot the driver. I caught up with them after trailing them for a day and they attempted to ambush me, but I wound up getting the drop on them. I told them to throw down their weapons, but two chose to shoot it out and they were both shot and killed. Ben and I buried your sons Al and Johnny where they fell. I'm sorry to have to tell you this."

Abby Hobson closed her eyes; her worst nightmares having come true.

She asked quietly, "And Ben? Is he going to hang?"

"No, ma'am. I believe that Ben here isn't like the other two. He threw down his rifle and surrendered. He gave me his word that he wouldn't try anything, so we could bury his brothers, and he kept it. Now, I've been talking to him since then and I decided it would serve no purpose for anyone if I brought Ben back to Lander. I'll write in my report that all three perpetrators were killed. That means I'll have to return with at least two horses and their weapons. I can leave one horse and say it was shot in the melee, but that's the best I can do."

Abby opened her eyes and looked at the sheriff, "Why would you do such a thing, Sheriff Joe?"

Joe shrugged and said, "If I brought him back, some jury would probably want to hang him. What good would that do? I think you need Ben here helping you more than the ground needs him. I won't even write the name Hobson in my report. You've suffered enough, ma'am."

Ben had been listening to the sheriff and couldn't believe it. *He was just going to stay home?*

Abby wiped a tear away from her right eye and said, "I can never thank you enough, Sheriff. I'll make sure that he never does anything like this ever again."

"I don't believe he will, ma'am."

Then, he turned to Ben and said, "Ben, I'm going to take those horses and guns with me, but I'm going to leave you with my shotgun, which is a useful weapon for a rancher. Now, I know your mother believes you'll stay straight from now on and so do I, but I want to hear a promise from you that you'll never break the law again."

Ben replied, "Yes, sir. I promise that I will never break the law. I won't even bend it."

Joe smiled and said, "That's good. Now, you remember that promise until you're old and gray."

Ben smiled back and said, "Yes, sir!"

Joe then turned back to his mother and said, "Well, I've got a long way to go to get back to Lander, ma'am."

"Can't you stay for dinner, Sheriff?" she asked.

"I'd like to, ma'am, but I really need to be getting back."

She quickly stepped down, walked up to Joe and kissed him on the cheek.

"Thank you, ma'am," Joe said before he mounted his gray, then reached over, pulled the shotgun from his left scabbard and handed it to Ben. He didn't ask for the Winchester.

But he did unhitch the trail rope from Ben's horse and attach it to Boomer before he waved at Mrs. Hobson and her three children, then wheeled his horse and rode away from the ranch house to head back to Lander.

CHAPTER 1

June 3, 1881
The Harper Ranch
Twelve Miles Northeast of Lander

Wilbur Harper pulled the wire tight and grunted to Billy, "Bang that nail in, son!"

Billy swung the hammer and the head slammed against the heavy wire nail, mashing it into the fencepost, securing the now tight barbed wire.

Wilbur released the tool and said, "Good job, Billy. That's one strand of wire that's not going anywhere."

Billy grinned at his father and said, "No, sir. It's stayin'!"

"Now, how about you and me going back to the house and see if your mama could give us two hard-working men some lemonade?"

"Okay, Papa," Billy said as he picked up the can of U-shaped wire nails.

The two hard-working Harper men began to walk toward the ranch house a half a mile away.

Billy noticed it first and asked, "Papa, what is that dust cloud out west?"

Wilbur took off his glasses and wiped them on his shirt before putting them back on and looking west.

"I don't know, Billy. It's a bunch of riders, I think. Let's get back to the house faster."

"Okay, Papa," Billy said as they began to jog back to the house.

By the time they were halfway there, the dust cloud had resolved itself into a large group of riders. Wilbur estimated at least a dozen and that many men riding that fast couldn't be good news.

As they moved, Wilbur said, "Billy, drop the hammer and nails. When we get to the house, I want you to go into the barn and climb up into the loft. You have my old shotgun up there, don't you?"

Billy tasted the bile of fear in his mouth as he replied, "Yes, Papa."

"Good. I want you to keep an eye on what is happening, but don't fire the shotgun unless you have to. It's only loaded with birdshot. Got that?"

"Yes, sir."

They crossed the back of the barn and Wilbur and Billy separated, Billy running into the barn as the large group of riders turned onto the access road.

Wilbur reached the back of the ranch house and ran quickly inside.

"Emma! We have trouble! A lot of riders are coming in!" he shouted as he rushed to the pantry where he kept his new shotgun, but it was loaded with birdshot as well. It was too late to worry about it now as he trotted down the hallway.

Emma Harper was cleaning out the fireplace with her sixteen-year-old daughter Annie while fifteen-year-old Mary stood nearby holding the bin for the ashes. When they heard Wilbur's shout, Emma and Annie both stood quickly, and Mary dropped the bin on the floor as they all jogged to the windows and spotted the men all arriving before the house in a cloud of dust. It didn't take long to know that they were not good men.

Wilbur entered the main room and said, "Emma, get the girls out the back now!"

Emma said, "No, Wilbur! I'm staying! They are not going to hurt my children!", then turned to Annie and said, "Annie, go! You and Mary run out into the pastures and keep running!"

"Yes, Mama!" Annie said as she took her sister's hand and they both sprinted out of the room.

Wilbur cocked both hammers of his shotgun as the front door suddenly exploded open and slammed against the wall.

Wilbur shouted, "Get out of…", but his threat was interrupted by three simultaneous booms as three of the outlaws all fired their Colts.

Wilbur's eyes went wide, and he fell forward, the shotgun falling to the floor without going off. He had barely hit the wood when the room was suddenly filled with outlaws and Emma turned to run, but never even got three steps away before she was grabbed by clawing hands and thrown to the floor.

She knew what was going to happen to her and she just closed her eyes, but it didn't. Instead, she felt rough hands pulling her hands behind her and pigging strings being wrapped around her wrists. Then, more hands tied off her ankles. She was being groped as they tied her, but that was all they did after making sure that she was subdued.

Then one shouted, "Out back! They ran out back!"

Another man yelled back, "Jimmie and Hank will run 'em down!"

"Okay, let's get that wagon!" the first voice commanded.

Emma wanted to scream but they were all suddenly gone. *What was going on?* Now, her biggest concern wasn't for her own safety, but that of her three children.

Annie and Mary had sprinted out of the house, crossed the back porch and did as their mother had told them and began to race across the pastures. They had heard the gunfire and Mary was already crying as they left the dirt of the back yard and reached the grass. Annie was holding back her tears as fear filled her. *They had to reach the far trees!*

Billy had climbed up into the loft and was hunting for the shotgun when he heard all of the gunfire from the ranch house and knew that his parents were dead. He found the shotgun and wanted revenge for their loss, so he walked to the open loft doors while cocking both barrels. He stood looking at the house and was watching when Annie and Mary both bolted from the house.

He was about to shout to them when he saw two riders suddenly come charging around from the front of the house. He leveled the shotgun at them and squeezed the trigger. He was rewarded with a loud click when the two hammers hit empty chambers.

He stepped back into the loft and cracked open the shotgun and saw two spent shells. He suddenly remembered having fired the shotgun at some quail a week earlier and hadn't reloaded. The problem was that all of the shells were in the house. Now, he was completely defenseless and couldn't help anyone.

Annie and Mary had only run sixty yards into the pastures when they heard the thunder of hooves behind them, and both turned as the two riders were almost upon them. Annie screamed as the riders dismounted while their horses were still running and chased after them.

Mary added her scream as the outlaws reached the girls and threw them to the ground. Like their mother, they knew what was going to happen to them and fought to prevent it. But again, they were just thrown onto their stomachs, felt knees pressed against their backs and felt their wrists being bound with leather strips.

"Let's get back to the house, ladies," one of the men said while the other laughed.

Annie and Mary were both crying as the men roughly marched them back to the house while they led their horses with their free hands.

Billy watched his sisters being taken to the house and wondered what he could do. He began to pace in the loft and knew that if he went down to the house, he'd be dead and that wouldn't help anyone. He needed to get help.

But before he could even think about leaving the barn, he heard voices heading for the barn and quickly fell to his stomach and crawled into a dark corner.

The voices grew louder as they entered the barn.

"That ain't much of a wagon, Bob," said one voice.

"It'll have to do. We might be able to pick up a nicer one later anyway."

"We got plenty of room, though. Those three women won't take up too much space and their food and other stuff probably won't even fill it."

"Don't forget, we've got two more places to visit," said the first voice.

The second one laughed and then said, "Yeah, but they've got wagons, too, boss."

"Let's get this thing harnessed and moving. We got a lot of travelin' to do."

"Okay, boss."

Billy could barely breathe as he stayed motionless under the barn's eaves. They hadn't killed his mother after all. They weren't going to kill his sisters, either, but they were taking them somewhere and using the family's wagon to do it. Then they were taking the food, too. *What was going on?*

Then the non-boss voice asked, “Wasn’t there a boy here too?”

The boss replied, “I don’t care where he is. If you see him, shoot him. He ain’t gonna know anything.”

“Okay, boss.”

Then there was a bunch of creaking noises and he heard the wagon being rolled out of the barn. Billy didn’t dare move as he listened to the sounds of their horses being harnessed.

Over the next twenty minutes, he heard the sounds of men laughing and talking as they were moving things out of the house and being put into the wagon. Then, his stomach flipped when he heard his sisters and his mother being taken from the house. His mother was telling them to leave her daughters alone when he heard a loud slap and his sisters wail. Then it was silent again.

Billy finally began squirming his way across the floor until he reached a crack between some boards and looked outside. He could make out the back of the wagon and saw that it was loaded with things that surprised him: mattresses and blankets, lamps, dishes and food, and then his sisters and his mother. All three were tied and their dresses torn. He was filling with deep anger as he looked at them but knew there was nothing that he could do but wait for them to leave and then go and get Sheriff Joe.

Then the wagon began to move and one of the men shouted, “Let’s go get more women!”, which was greeted with a bunch of laughter and catcalls. *They were going to do this again?* Then he recalled the line about making two more stops today. They were going to do it twice more today.

Billy kept his eye pressed to the crack as the wagon disappeared from his sight, but he was able to spot some of the men. One of them was wearing a black eyepatch. He just looked evil and seemed to be in charge. He counted eight men but knew there must have been some he didn’t see.

He marked their horses, so he wouldn't forget and even noted the number of rifles that they carried, knowing that the sheriff would want to know. But could the sheriff and his deputies chase after so many bad men? He didn't know about the deputies, but he trusted Sheriff Joe.

Forty minutes after they'd gone, Billy finally climbed down from the loft and trotted to the front of the barn. He stopped and peeked out of the doors to make sure that they were all gone, then quickly ran across the yard and into the house. He stopped dead in his track when he reached the kitchen. It was empty except for the cookstove, kitchen table and chairs.

Then he ran through the house, stopping in each room and finding them empty as well. He checked the drawers in the bedrooms and found that all of his mother's clothes and his sisters' clothes were gone, but his were still there.

He hurriedly threw his clothes into a burlap bag and carried it out to the kitchen, avoiding the main room after seeing his father's legs lying motionless on the floor. He then began pumping and cupping his hands under the water and slurping it to quench his thirst.

Then he left the house to go and find a horse to ride into town but wasn't surprised to find all six horses gone. He'd have to walk all the way to Lander.

Billy then began his long journey, glancing to the north to make sure that none of the men would come back. He soon reached the road and picked up the pace, alternating jogging and walking as fast as he could.

The wagon holding all of the Harper's things as well as the Harper women trundled north as Billy walked south.

Emma Harper had her eyes closed and feared more for her daughters than herself. She was a widow now and her life didn't matter. Three things bothered her about the raid: the gang stole things that a gang normally wouldn't bother stealing, they hadn't made any attempt to hide their faces, even now, and she had heard the shout of 'let's get more women!', which meant they were only the first. *To what end?*

Then, there was Billy. *What had happened to her son?* She knew that he had been out mending fences with Wilbur, but she hadn't seen him since he left that morning. She assumed they must have killed him and that thought made her drop into even a deeper despair.

Hanger Bob was at the front of the group of riders and had assigned Lou Brown to drive the wagon, and Jean Martin and Willie Gray to watch the wagon while he and the rest would ride to the Riley ranch three miles northwest.

Ten minutes later, Bob Jones led his remaining twelve riders away from the Harper wagon and headed for the second ranch of the day, expecting no problems.

John Riley was out in the pasture with his two sons, sixteen-year-old Bob and fourteen-year-old James. They were culling the small herd to select the twenty-five cattle they would be driving down to Lander for sale.

John had just moved a steer to the culls when he spotted the cloud coming along the road from the south and shouted, "Bob! James! We have visitors, and I don't like the looks of it. Let's get back to the house and pull your rifles!"

"Yes, Papa!" they shouted in unison as each yanked his repeater from his scabbard.

None of them wore sidearms.

John set his horse to a medium trot toward the house flanked by his two sons. His wife, Jennie and his two daughters, Clara and Cora, were hanging laundry behind the house and didn't notice either group of riders descending on the house.

"We got men with rifles comin' down from the pastures, boss!" shouted Sorry Ferguson.

Bill yelled back, "They're just ranchers, Sorry. They don't know how to use those things."

Sorry wanted to argue but didn't.

They turned down the access road and Bob Jones waved over his head, causing the riders behind him to spread apart, making them a more difficult target. All of them had their repeaters in their hands.

John Riley knew now that his was going to be a losing battle and noticed that his wife and daughters were still hanging laundry, oblivious to the oncoming threat. He raised his Winchester to his shoulder, cocked the hammer and fired a shot toward the oncoming riders to alert his wife.

Jennie Riley and the girls suddenly looked up, saw the family males riding toward them with their rifles then turned in unison toward the access road and saw the mass of riders.

"Run!" Jennie shouted, as all three women lifted their skirts and ran north away from the house, but not toward the Riley men. Jennie knew they needed a clean field of fire, but also knew they didn't stand a chance against that many men. It was like a small, invading army.

Once John had fired, all thirteen men returned fire at two hundred yards. No one on either side was hit, but that would soon change as the gap between the two groups decreased.

The jostling and bouncing of the moving horses kept the damage down as they closed to a hundred yards, both sides firing rapidly creating a huge cloud of gun smoke over the ranch.

The first casualty was when a .44 fired by Bob Riley struck the horse ridden by Fred Argyle. The horse went down taking Fred with him.

Then, the serious hits started when John Riley took two .44s almost simultaneously; one in the left thigh and one in the gut. He dropped his Winchester and bent over at the waist.

"Papa!" shouted James as he saw his father's stomach flood with blood.

The shout had barely left his lips when a shot fired by Louie Bouton struck James in the neck, knocking him from his horse. He bounced once on the dirt and rolled to a stop, leaving only Bob Riley still on his horse. He was still firing and managed to wound Jean Martin in the left forearm before a hail of .44s killed him seconds later. He slowly rolled off the back of his horse and smashed into the dirt.

Without a command from Hanger Bob, the whole group then turned to chase after Jennie, Clara and Cora Riley who had only managed to run a hundred and fifty yards before they were winded and struggling to keep moving.

Just like Emma Harper, Jennie Riley thought she knew what would happen when they reached her and her daughters, but again, was confused when they were herded like cattle and brought to the barn where they were tied and moved to the wagon. Then the wagon was trundled out of the barn, and men quickly harnessed the wagon and began running to the house.

She was mystified when they began stripping the house of food, kitchenware and bedding. Then came other household items and then they grabbed all of the horses, including her dead husband's and her sons'. She was so numb from the sudden change from a normal laundry day to total terror that she didn't even cry. She couldn't hold her daughters close to comfort them as they both wept uncontrollably.

If she was confused by what she was witnessing, she was thoroughly baffled when the wagon was driven out of the ranch and joined up with another wagon with her neighbors, Emma, Anna and Mary Harper in back along with their household things.

SHERIFF JOE

Jean Martin had patched his forearm injury and Fred Argyle had replaced his shot horse with one of the Riley's animals as the newly enlarged caravan moved north to their last target of the day.

"Joe, you can't be serious. You can't leave! Where the hell would you go?" asked frustrated Fremont County Deputy Sheriff Charlie Wheatley.

His fellow deputy, Ed Smith, sat nearby not saying anything, leaving the arguing to his senior deputy.

"It's time, Charlie. I've been doing this job too long. I'm getting too soft-hearted. Five years ago, I would have arrested that kid or shot him. Now, I just take him home to his mama and tell him to be a good boy."

"No, you wouldn't. You've always been soft-hearted, Joe. What's really put the burr under your saddle?" Charlie asked.

Joe exhaled and said, "I don't know, Charlie. It just seems kinda pointless nowadays. I just shot two kids the other day. Neither one was over twenty."

Charlie thought he knew the reason and said more quietly, "Joe, they were shooting at you. You told them to drop their weapons and they didn't. Would you rather have been shot yourself?"

Joe didn't say what he really wanted to say, but replied, "I suppose not. But I'm still leaving, Charlie. I'll stick around for the rest of the month and then I'm pulling up stakes and moving on."

"Where will you go, Joe? You don't even have a house."

"I know that, Charlie. I've got a good amount saved up over the years and can buy one if I wanted to, but I don't want to. Maybe I'll go someplace warm like Kansas or Texas."

"Kansas isn't that much warmer, Joe, and Texas and Kansas both have tornadoes."

"Everyplace has something, Charlie. Just relax for a while and get used to the idea of being the sheriff. You've got the experience. You'll do a good job and it pays another thirty dollars a month, too. Betty will sure appreciate that."

Charlie shrugged and said, "Yeah, I suppose she will, but she won't appreciate me going out of town so often, either."

Joe laughed and then said, "Hell, send Ed out there. He's still unattached."

Ed finally spoke up saying, "Not for long, Joe. You know I'm courtin' Charlotte Peterson."

"You're not married yet, Ed," Joe said as he grinned at the young deputy.

His real reason for deciding to leave the job was much more complex. Joe's thirty-fifth birthday was coming up soon and he realized that his life was more than half over and he had nothing. Or, more accurately, he had no one and the reason he had no one was his own fault and he knew it.

———

Billy Harper had walked five and a half miles and had stopped to drink from a creek while twelve miles northeast, the two wagons carrying his mother, sisters and the Riley women along with their household belongings rolled along.

The women were all thirsty, hungry and still fearing for what awaited them at the end of the journey, wherever it was. None of them had spoken since they had left the Riley ranch after Jennie Riley had been struck with a backhand when she had asked for water. It was a lesson well learned.

Without any fanfare, most of the escorting riders suddenly set off at a fast trot, leaving four of the men behind in addition to the two drivers. The women all knew what it meant. They were going to hit another ranch, and they all knew it would be the Foster spread.

Sarah Foster was just setting plates of food down for her husband, Mike, and their only son, Abe. Her daughters, Katie and Rachel were helping before they would all take a seat and have their noon meal.

After Mike took a biscuit and spread butter on top, the others felt it was okay to eat as well.

The nine men led by Hanger Bob Jones trotted down the access road rather than making a lot of noise because they hadn't been spotted yet and didn't see anyone out in the fields.

Bill held up four fingers and waved to the back of the house, and the first four men behind him peeled off and slowed their horses to a walk as they approached the house. They continued to walk their horses to the back of the house as the remaining men all dismounted at the front porch.

Abe Foster was the first one to hear any of the outside sound of hooves.

"Papa, I think someone is outside," he said, a forkful of beans still in the air before his mouth.

Mike Foster stopped chewing and listened but heard nothing.

"I don't hear anything, son. Maybe it was just the chickens arguing about who was going to be in the pot on Sunday," he said with a smile.

Abe began to rise when the kitchen door suddenly flew open and four men rushed inside, their pistols drawn and cocked.

Everyone at the table popped out of their chairs, and Mike began to protest when all four men fired. Three aimed at the man, and one fired at Abe. The massive sound reverberated through the room as the acrid smell of gunsmoke filled the kitchen.

Sarah and her two daughters all screamed as they watched the paterfamilias slam against the wall, then fall on top of his chair, knocking it over and collapsing on top, leaving blood splattered everywhere.

Abe Foster added his scream to his sisters' and his mother's as the .44 caliber bullet from Charlie Smith's pistol drilled through his chest and exited his back before punching through the thin kitchen wall. He dropped to his knees, and his screaming stopped when he fell face forward to the floor.

Charlie then shouted, "Shut up!", and the room went silent.

Sarah reached for her daughters as more men suddenly appeared from the hallway, one wearing a black patch over his left eye.

"Let's get moving. We don't have a lot of time!" he shouted as he replaced his unused pistol.

Sarah shouted, "You bastards! Murdering bastards!" and was rewarded with a hard slap to her face by Charlie Smith.

"I said shut up!" he growled as he glared at her.

Then the men began to pull out pigging strings from their pockets and Sarah felt like a rag doll as she was groped and grabbed while being trussed up and watched helplessly as her daughters were similarly treated.

Then she, Katie and Rachel were marched out of the kitchen and were pushed into a sitting position on the back steps while they watched the family wagon being pulled from the barn and hurriedly harnessed to their draft horses. They were then yanked back into a standing position and walked to the wagon, placed in the bed and had their ankles tied with more pigging strings.

Like the two other families' women, they were all confused about what was going on as they watched a line of men carrying household goods and food from the house and loading them into the wagon with them. Other men ran to the corral and formed a long trail rope, led the five horses from their corral and saddled three of them with the family's saddles.

Soon, one of the men leapt into the driver's seat, flicked the reins and the wagon began moving across the yard, heading for the access road.

Sarah soon spotted two other wagons with strings of horses trailing. They each had three women and stacks of household goods in the cargo area. She recognized her neighbors, the Rileys and the Harpers. *What were these men doing?*

———

Billy Harper had resumed walking and couldn't keep up the pace that he had used when he started as his left calf had begun to cramp. He was still five miles out of Lander when the wagons, horses and riders all rode out of the Foster ranch and turned northeast. They were heading to their new home with their day's booty.

———

Deputy Wheatley had given up arguing with Joe and still didn't understand why he seemed so hell bent sure about quitting the job. He'd been the only sheriff that Fremont County had for twelve years now. Granted, the entire white population of the county wasn't even three thousand, but all of those ranches, especially the small ones, really depended on Joe. Joe may have given him a vote of confidence, but Charlie Wheatley was honest enough with himself to know that he couldn't do what Joe did, nor did he wish to try. He'd take the sheriff's job, because, as Joe had said, his wife would appreciate the added financial rewards, but there was the added danger. Joe Brooks was a wizard with his weapons, but more importantly, he just had a head for figuring out how to avoid getting shot.

Even when dealing with serious trouble, Joe defused many more potential gunfights than the ones that resulted in lead flying everywhere. It was one of the reasons he was so well-respected in the county and elsewhere. And despite his earlier protests, everyone knew he was soft-hearted beneath that gruff mask. Letting that Hobson boy go was just the latest example. He and Ed Smith were the only two who knew the full story including the names of the perpetrators. The victims were just tickled to get their property back and the county prosecutor was glad he didn't have to have a trial.

Joe walked out of his small office with a stack of wanted posters and stood by the front desk, laying the posters on the desk in front of his two deputies.

"Charlie, here are the wanted posters I could find on the members of Hanger Bob's gang and I think that Frenchie gang Ben Hobson mentioned is Pierre Le Tour's gang. I'm really sketchy on the half-breed band that he talked about, but it might be Charlie Smith's bunch. I didn't know he was a half-breed, though."

Charlie and Ed began perusing the stack, and Ed asked, "Why would they be going to Cooperstown, Joe? There's nothing up there. It's a ghost town."

Joe rubbed his lightly stubbled chin and said, "I don't have a clue, unless they were planning on using it as a hideout of sorts. If they're all together, that's a real mess. I guess they'd have between a dozen and eighteen men, and all of them dangerous."

"I've never heard of three gangs getting together before, Joe," Charlie said, "too many bosses kinda makes that hard to work."

"I know. If they are together, Hanger Bob Jones would be in charge. He's older than the others and has kept his gang together the longest. He's a nasty piece of work, too."

Ed Smith asked, "Do you know where he got the moniker, Joe?"

"He was sentenced to hang for two murders down in Laramie six years ago. Had the noose around his neck and was just seconds away from having that trap door open when his gang showed up and shot the place to ribbons and cut him loose. One of the stray bullets cost him his left eye, though, when a splinter from the scaffold punched into it. Since then, when he has the time, he'll hang his victims to let them know he's still unhappy about having that rope around his neck. He's never been in Fremont County before, and if he's really here we've got problems. If he's really here with those other two bunches, we have serious problems."

"Then how can you leave us, Joe?" Charlie asked.

"I won't until I make sure they're either not here or they're gone," Joe replied as he began to collect the wanted posters.

Charlie and Ed breathed a sigh of relief at Joe's decision.

———

The parade of wagons, trailed horses and thirteen mounted men continued northeast, still following the roadway.

Hanger Bob Jones was in the lead and then shouted, "Let's pull over and get something to eat. Get those women off the wagon and let 'em get something to drink and use those bushes over there."

There were murmurs of consent as the entire column swerved to the right and then stopped near a creek. The thirteen riders all walked their horses into the creek and let them drink while the slower-moving wagons still creaked forward.

Jean Martin rode up to Bob Jones and asked, "Do we cut 'em loose so they can do their business?"

"Just three at time and then tie 'em up again after they're finished eatin'," he replied, then paused and added, "Hold on. I want to go and talk to 'em first so they know what's gonna happen to 'em."

Jean grinned and said, "This oughta be fun," then wheeled his horse around and walked his gelding behind the boss.

Hanger Bob walked his horse to where the wagons were finally being brought to a stop and then stopped nearby and eyed the first wagon of women, the Harpers.

"You women!" he shouted, "I'm Bob Jones and I'm the boss of this group of fine gentlemen. We are what you good folks call outlaws. Altogether, we've murdered over fifty men, raped more than a hundred women, and stolen more than you can count. Now, we got ourselves our own town. It used to be called Cooperstown but now, we renamed it Lawless. Lawless, Wyoming, and I'm the mayor. We have two councilmen, Pierre Le Tour and Charlie Smith."

You women will be doing the cooking, cleaning and laundry for our new town, and you'll be keeping our gentlemen satisfied. As long as you cooperate, you'll stay alive and won't be harmed. If you sass back or fail to service any of us when we ask you to, you will be beaten. It's no different than what you did before, so I don't want to hear any whining. And in case you think you're gonna be rescued somehow, you can forget it. No lawman is gonna come anywhere near our town and live. Now, we're gonna cut each of you loose, so you can eat, drink and use those bushes, but we're gonna do it in threes. One young girl from each family, then the second young girl, then the mamas. Then, you'll all be put back on the wagons and we keep riding toward Lawless. We're gonna have to stop for the night and that's when you'll start providing services for the boys. Just lay back and enjoy it."

He grinned and then wheeled his horse away from the wagons.

On the wagons, each of the three mothers was feeling the same sense of doom and total fear for their daughters. Their daughters were all just horrified at the thought of being ruined by such evil men.

Yet, as they were taken from the packed wagons, none said a word in fear of the retribution that they knew would be coming if they reacted.

———

SHERIFF JOE

Billy was off to the side of the road just three miles from Lander and rubbing his calves. He realized he had made a mistake earlier by jogging and walking too fast. If he had kept just a slightly faster pace, he'd almost be there by now. He'd keep that pace when he started up again and guessed he was a little more than an hour out of town.

Joe sat at his desk, tapping a pencil against the edge as he thought about his decision to quit. He'd been thinking about it for almost a year now. He was thirty-four years old and all he'd ever done was to carry a badge. He never knew his parents, having grown up in an orphanage in Kansas City. He left when he was eighteen and headed west; an ignorant kid with big dreams. He kept drifting until he stopped in Cheyenne, Wyoming where he became a deputy sheriff and found he was good at it.

Then, he left Cheyenne and took on the sheriff job in Fremont County. He was the only lawman in the county back then and it was a wild country. It still was, but there were more good folks here now.

Somehow, the years just slipped by and before he knew it, here he was close to thirty-five years old and still living alone in Underwood's Boarding House. His room and board were paid for by the county, and he'd made quite a bit on rewards over the years as the county still allowed him to keep the money for wanted criminals believing it to be a wise investment, so he had a significant balance in his account at the Lander National Bank.

What he didn't tell Charlie or Ed was that he was incredibly lonely. When he had returned Billy Hobson to his mother, he was tempted to take Mrs. Hobson up on her offer for dinner to get to know her better. She was still a handsome woman, although she looked to be about forty, but he hadn't done so because he felt he would have been taking advantage of the situation. At least that's the excuse he used at the time, but he knew the real reason.

His problem had surfaced as soon as he left Kansas City. It had never been a problem for one clear reason: he had very little contact with women. Once he became a deputy, it took close to a year before he could even carry on a reasonably normal conversation with a woman.

By the time he had become the sheriff of Fremont County at the age of twenty-one, he could talk to women without any problems unless it involved something that might lead to romantic involvement. The first time it really mattered was when he had been smitten by a pretty redhead named Mary Sheehy. She obviously knew that he was taken by her and let him know that any advances would be welcomed, but the more she warmed up to him, the more withdrawn Joe had become. She finally got totally frustrated with the young sheriff and married the butcher and it had devastated him.

The decision to quit was driven by his failed romantic life because it meant he'd stay a bachelor for the rest of his life. He saw himself going gray while sitting in a rocking chair on the boardwalk in front of his office waving as folks walked past. It would be a lonely life and he'd leave it the way he came into it, with not a soul caring one way or the other.

The caravan was moving again, still rolling northeast toward the newly-christened town of Lawless.

As he rode in the front of the long line, Hanger Bob was flanked by Pierre Le Tour and Charlie Smith.

"We are going to need a lot of hay for that many horses, Bob," Charlie said loudly.

"I know. We've got three wagons and after we get settled back in Lawless with the women, I figure we leave six men in town to keep an eye on 'em while we head southeast to that McClellan farm and fill 'em up with hay. We can add another wagon, maybe two and pick up two more women while we're there, too."

Pierre laughed then said, "Always thinking, Bob. That's what I like about you."

Bill didn't smile but replied, "We're gonna strip this county bare, Pierre. By the time we're finished, Lawless will be the only town in the entire county."

Charlie then said, "What about the law, Bob? They ain't gonna take this lyin' down."

Bill did smile this time when he answered, "Yeah, they will. What do they have out here? Three of 'em. Do you think three badge-toters are going to take on sixteen heavily-armed men who would just as soon shoot 'em as look at 'em?"

Charlie then replied, "There's always the army, Bob, if we get too noticeable."

"If the army shows up, we hightail it out of here with our loot, but they won't do that for a few months and then, it'll be winter, and we'll be all nice and snug in Lawless with our supplies and our women."

Bill's answer seemed to assuage Charlie Smith's concerns and they continued to ride.

———

"I'm going to do rounds, Charlie," Joe said as he picked his hat from the peg on the wall.

"I'll get the south side, Joe," Charlie said as he stood quickly to grab his own hat.

"I'll watch the office," Ed said with a grin.

"I figured as much, Ed," Joe said as he pulled on his hat and headed out the open door, turning left to walk to the north side of town.

Charlie exited right behind him and headed in the opposite direction.

———

Billy was limping as he approached Lander but was grateful for the sight of the buildings. Soon, he'd tell Sheriff Joe about what had happened, and he'd go after those bad men. Billy had only met the sheriff twice when they'd had a few head of cattle stolen. The sheriff had returned the cattle in just two days and brought the two rustlers back to Lander where they were tried and hanged. Billy had been impressed with the big lawman and even though he was only one man, didn't doubt for a second that he'd be able to get his mother and sisters away from that large gang of bad men.

He turned into Lander and before he even looked for the sheriff's office, he spotted Sheriff Joe walking straight at him. He waved wildly over his head and began shouting, "Sheriff Joe! Sheriff Joe!"

Joe had seen Billy as he walked into town and was curious why he was afoot. He recalled the young boy, but couldn't remember his first name, just that he was a Harper. When Billy began waving and calling to him, Joe started jogging toward the youngster.

Billy saw Sheriff Joe trotting toward him when his legs gave out, dropping him to the boardwalk.

Joe quickly reached Billy and knelt down next to him, "What's wrong, son?"

"They came this mornin' and killed my father and took my mother and sisters and a lot of other things and all the horses, too," he replied rapidly, running words together, almost turning a sentence into one massive polysyllabic word.

"Okay, son. Just calm down and give that to me again, only more slowly so I can understand you. I know you are a Harper, what's your name?"

"Sorry, Sheriff Joe. I'm Billy. Billy Harper. This morning, me and my father were mending fences and we saw this large dust cloud comin' down the road. My papa told me to run into the barn and get my shotgun while he went into the house to warn my mother and sisters that a lot of men were comin'. I was in the loft and saw them go into the house and heard a gunshot. Then, my sisters came running out and headed for the pastures, but men chased them down and caught them before they could get away. After that, they came into the barn and pulled out the wagon and put my mother and sisters into the wagon. They were all tied up. Then they began loading the wagon with food and things from the house. Even mattresses and blankets. I couldn't do nothin', Sheriff Joe! The shotgun was empty, and I just watched them take my sisters and mother away! I'm a coward, a dirty yellow coward, and I didn't do nothin'!"

Joe put his hand on Billy's shoulder and said, "No, Billy. You're not a coward. You're smart and savvy. If you had shown yourself, you'd be dead, and I wouldn't know what had happened. I'm proud of you, son. Now, let's get you onto your feet and we'll head back to my office and get you something to drink and you can tell me the whole story. Okay?"

Billy had been on the verge of bursting into tears when he felt Joe's hand on his shoulder and heard his soothing words. He struggled to his feet and began walking with the sheriff along the boardwalk.

"Are you gonna go and get 'em back, Sheriff Joe?" he asked, "There were a whole passel of bad guys."

Joe had already assumed that the story that Ben Hobson had told him about the three gangs staying in Cooperstown was true and that young Billy Harper had just witnessed their first criminal act in his county.

"Yes, Billy. I'll go and get them back, but I need to get ready. The worst thing a lawman can do is rush pell-mell into something as dangerous as this, but I should be out of here in a couple of hours. Okay?"

Billy understood and nodded as they reached the office and turned inside.

"Ed, get Billy here some water. The Hanger Bob outfit just hit the Harper ranch."

“Yes, sir!”, Ed said loudly as he jumped up and trotted to the back room where the pump was located.

“Sit down behind the desk, Billy and I’ll ask you some questions. Okay?”

“Yes, sir,” Billy said as he took the chair recently vacated by the deputy.

Joe just sat on the edge of the desk, took off his Stetson and asked, “Billy, did one of the men have a black patch over his left eye?”

Billy nodded and said, “Yes, sir.”

“How many men would you say altogether?”

“I was lookin’ through a crack in the barn door and counted thirteen, but I think there were a few more that I couldn’t see, but I looked at them and their horses, so I can tell you more.”

Joe pulled a sheet of paper and a pencil from the box on the desk and said, “Okay, Billy, go ahead.”

Ed returned with a glass of water and handed it to Billy who practically inhaled the liquid and then handed the glass back to Ed.

Before he began, Joe said, “Ed, head on down to the diner and get a plate of food for Billy.”

“I’m on my way,” Ed replied as he grabbed his hat and left the office.

Billy closed his eyes and began reciting the descriptions of the horses that he remembered and the men who were riding them. Joe was writing furiously in his personal shorthand to keep up with Billy.

He was still writing when Charlie Wheatley entered the office, removed his hat slowly and hung it on a peg as he watched his boss writing down what the boy was saying, hearing very good descriptions of men and horses.

Billy finally stopped and opened his eyes, saying, “That’s all I remember, Sheriff Joe.”

“Billy, I’ve never had a witness give me better information, and that’s usually with only one or two bad men. You’ve given me very good descriptions on a dozen. I’ve never heard a better statement.”

Then he turned to Charlie and gave him a quick rundown of the situation as Ed entered with a tray of food and set it down on the desk in front of Billy, who began to eat three seconds after it contacted the desktop.

“I’m really bothered by that two lines that Billy said that one of them had shouted. Billy says that one of them had yelled, “Let’s get more women!’ and he’d heard them say they had two more stops today. That, plus the odd behavior of stealing household goods and food makes it sound like they’re settling in over at Cooperstown.”

Charlie nodded and said, “It sounds like it, Joe. Are we all going?”

Joe shook his head, “No, Charlie. I’ll take this one on by myself. My concern is that they’re not stopping anytime soon. You and Ed need to stay here and be ready for more reports and to protect Landers. A gang this size isn’t going to hesitate to come into our town.”

Charlie didn’t bother objecting, nor did Ed. They both knew he was right. Besides, he was the only one who could even come close to getting the women out of their clutches.

“When are you leaving, Joe?” asked Ed.

“I need to get my weapons ready to go, stock up on ammo, get some food and a few canteens of water and anything else I might need. One other thing, Charlie. If I’m not back in a week, notify the army down at Fort Steele. They’re three or four days away, but it’s the closest we’ve got.”

Charlie nodded and said, “Okay, boss. What if we have to engage them ourselves?”

"If you hear that they're coming, send the telegram and get some of the citizens armed to help. It's the best we can do."

"Okay," said Charlie.

Billy had already finished eating and looked up at the sheriff and asked, "Can I come with you, Sheriff Joe?"

"No, Billy. You stay here in town. I'll head out to your place and then pick up their trail from there. It's a good day's ride to Cooperstown with that wagon, and I won't be getting there until tomorrow."

"I'm going to follow you anyway, Sheriff Joe. Even if I have to walk. They killed my father and took my mother and sisters. I can help."

Joe looked at Billy and wasn't sure he was wrong. He'd shown a lot of guts to not do something stupid when the men were there and then he'd been cool enough to remember those descriptions.

"Alright, you can come along. I'll saddle up a horse for you, which we're going to need anyway for all of the firepower I intend to bring with me."

Billy smiled and said, "Thank you, sir."

"Don't thank me yet, son," Joe said as he stood and walked back to his office.

He entered the small office and opened his gun cabinet. He'd accumulated quite an arsenal over the years, and he felt he'd need most of them now. He took out a Sharps carbine chambered for the .50-70 cartridge, four Winchester '73s, two twelve-gauge shotguns, one with a sawed-off barrel and stock that was only twenty-eight inches long from butt to muzzle, and then he took out three gunbelts. One of them was a two-gun rig. He removed his single-gun setup and donned the two-pistol gunbelt. Instead of Colts, there were two Smith & Wesson Model 3 pistols. He'd lifted them from a would-be stagecoach robber three years earlier and was fond of the guns but didn't wear them often because he didn't want to wear them out. He felt he needed the extra firepower for this trip.

He then began pulling boxes of ammunition from the shelves, two boxes of twelve-gauge shells for the shotguns, four boxes of .44 rimfires for the pistols and Winchester '73s, a box of the .50-70s for the Sharps and two boxes of the .50-95 Express cartridges for his Winchester '76, stacking the boxes on his desk.

Satisfied he had enough weaponry and ammunition, he called Billy into his office.

"Have you ever fired a Winchester or a pistol before, Billy?" he asked.

"No, sir. Just a shotgun."

"Well, you're going to have to learn pretty fast. Here, try this gunbelt on. It was worn by a young man, so it should fit," he said as he held out the gunbelt that had been word by Ben Hobson.

Billy accepted the pistol belt and wrapped it around his waist and buckled it into place.

Then Joe handed Billy one of the Winchesters.

"Hang onto that one, and I'll load up the rest after we get the horses saddled."

"Yes, sir."

Joe then walked around his desk, opened his bottom drawer and pulled out a compass and a set of field glasses then set the field glasses on the desk after slipping the compass into his pocket.

"Okay, Billy, let's get the horses ready."

"Okay," Billy replied as he followed the sheriff out of his office.

Joe grabbed his hat as he passed his deputies and after he and Billy left the office, they turned right and headed for the nearby livery. Joe was lucky that he had three horses in the livery at the moment after he had returned with the Hobson horses and rigs. As it was, he'd need all of his extra scabbards, too. He had a pile of them that he stored in the livery, and knew he'd need a total of eight of them. Two on each of the horses he and Billy would be riding and four on what would be their pack horse.

Back at the office, Charlie Wheatley looked at Ed Smith and said, "Joe is really going to do this, isn't he?"

Ed replied, "He doesn't really have any choice, Charlie. He's right about leaving us here and the army is just too far away, and that's assuming they're not too busy to come here right away."

"I suppose," Charlie said as he stood and walked into Joe's office to look at the guns he had pulled from his armory.

———

Joe and Billy had stopped at Johnson's Dry Goods and picked up some food and other basics for the ride. Joe had his Winchester '76 and a shotgun on Boomer and Billy had his '73 and a second '73 on his left side. The trail horse had the Sharps in his right front scabbard, another '73 in the left front as well as the back left. The sawed-off shotgun was in the back right scabbard, lost in the leather. The trail horse had a set of heavy saddlebags with all of the ammunition. He was also carrying two large bags of supplies hung across the saddle and tied down with cord.

They rode north out of Lander in mid-afternoon and headed for the Harper ranch.

———

The caravan headed by Hanger Bob Jones had crossed two creeks and had exited the roadway and was following a trail toward Lawless, still thirty miles away. He planned on keeping them moving for another four or five hours and then pulling over for the night and letting the men get to know the women. He planned on being first.

———

As they rode, Joe was showing Billy how to fire the Winchester and the Colt he wore. Billy had already been told about gun safety from his father, and Joe was pleased that he knew the rules about handling guns because it saved them time. Billy was a smart boy and picked up the gun handling methods and firing techniques that Joe showed him very quickly.

By the time the ranch was in sight, Billy had already fired both weapons to good effect, which had thoroughly impressed Joe.

"Billy," Joe said as he spotted the ranch house, "I'm going to have to bury your father. Did you want to stay out here?"

"No, sir, I'll come along. I want to see what they did to him."

"Okay, son, it's your right."

They turned onto the access road and five minutes later, were stepping down and hitching their horses to the rail.

They stepped down and walked onto the porch, the smell of death was already hanging in the air as the door was left wide open. Joe walked in first, and spotted Wilbur's body near the door, three bullet holes in his chest and gut. It could have been worse. His face wasn't damaged, but it still wasn't a pretty sight.

Billy walked in slowly and stood next to Joe, looking at his father.

"We have shovels in the barn, Sheriff Joe," he said softly.

"Okay, Billy. I'll pull your father out of here. Okay? You go and get the shovels and a pickaxe if you have one."

"Thank you, sir. We do, and I'll take them to where we need to bury my father."

"Go ahead, Billy," Joe said as he bent over Wilbur's body.

He waited until Billy had gone and then stood and walked to a thin rug and slid it over to the corpse. He then rolled Wilbur Foster onto the rug and wrapped him in the worn fabric, then picked up the body and carried it in his arms across the floor and through the open door. The stench was powerful, but Joe was accustomed to the smell of death and managed to keep his stomach calm.

When he got outside, he saw Billy exiting the barn with two shovels and a pickaxe. Billy spotted Joe carrying what he knew was his father's body, and turned to his right, heading for the pastures.

Joe hoped Billy didn't go too far because his father wasn't a small man.

Billy stopped just after reaching the grass and set his shovels and pickaxe on the ground. He then lifted the pickaxe and began to break the soil.

Joe reached Billy five minutes later and gently laid his rug-wrapped father's body nearby and picked up one of the shovels. He waited until Billy had softened the dirt and stepped back, and then began to dig.

It took him and Billy almost a half an hour to dig his father's grave and then another twenty to lower the body into the hole and cover it with dirt.

When they were done, Billy said, "We'll have a ceremony when my mother and sisters can be here."

Joe just nodded, amazed at the maturity of the boy. He'd already behaved more like a man than most adult males he'd known.

They returned the tools to the empty barn and then soaked their heads in pumped water before bringing their horses over to drink.

"Do we go on right now, Sheriff Joe?" Billy asked.

Joe replied, "We've still got some daylight, Billy. I think we ought to make use of it. I'm particularly worried about the other small ranchers in the area, the Rileys and the Fosters. Each of them had two teenaged daughters and their mothers were still young enough to be kidnapped like your mother."

"I thought my mother was as pretty as my sisters, Sheriff Joe. I didn't think she was that old."

"How old is your mother, Billy?" Joe asked as they boarded their horses, having a good idea, and already fully aware that Emma Harper was a handsome woman, having met her several times.

"She just turned thirty-four. My older sister, Annie is sixteen and Mary is fifteen. I'm almost fourteen."

"If I remember right, the Riley girls and the Foster girls are about those ages, too. I have a bad feeling about this whole thing, Billy," Joe said as they turned their horses to the access road.

"Me, too," Billy said loudly as they picked up the pace.

———

As they rolled along, Billy's mother, Emma, said to her daughters, "Annie, Mary, in a little while, those men are going to rape us all. I know this is coming and you need to know what is going to happen. There is nothing we can do about it and if we fight, as we all want to, we'll be hurt badly, and it will still happen. Please, don't fight what they do to you. I know it will hurt, but it will be over quickly. Don't be ashamed for what is happening to you. Be angry for what these animals are doing to us and pray for salvation. It may not come in this life, my sweethearts, but it will come."

Annie said, "We'll try to be strong, Mama, but I'm so afraid."

Emma replied, "I know, Annie. So am I. Just close your eyes and pray. It's all we can do. I'm sure that Mrs. Riley and Mrs. Foster are telling her girls the same thing right now."

She was right in her assumption as each mother tried to build up their daughters' strength for what they knew would be happening to them all when the sun went down.

Joe and Billy reached the Riley ranch and saw the flock of buzzards circling behind the ranch house, many of them coasting in for a landing. Several coyotes were stalking the area as well.

Joe reached down and slipped his '76 from its scabbard, cocked the hammer and aimed at the coyotes. He squeezed the trigger and immediately began levering in one round after the other, scattering the coyotes and sending the vultures back into the sky.

After his fifth shot, he lowered his smoking rifle and they continued to walk their horses to the back of the house. It was a much uglier sight that greeted the man and the boy when they cleared the house and saw the three mangled bodies on the ground. Between the gunshot wounds and the damage from the scavengers, the three bodies were barely recognizable as human.

Billy leaned over to his right side and vomited onto the ground. Joe again managed to keep his stomach's contents in place, but even he felt a wave of nausea.

"Billy, ride into the barn and see if there are shovels."

Billy didn't answer but turned his horse to the barn and rode him inside before stepping down and trotting to the pump over the trough and quickly stroking its handle until water flowed and he began to slurp and spit the water out to clear the taste from his mouth.

Joe had followed him to the barn and stepped down. He spotted an old, beat-up tarp hanging over a stall and pulled it from its resting place and walked back out to the bodies and covered them with the tarp before returning to the barn.

Billy was standing with his arm on a support post and his head down when Joe returned.

"Are you all right, Billy? I've covered the bodies with a tarp, so they're not visible any longer."

"I'll be okay, sheriff," Billy said.

"I'll get those shovels and start digging. I'll take care of the bodies, Billy. You just wait here."

Billy then raised his head and took his hand from the support as he said, "No, I'll help. I'm okay now."

Joe nodded and handed a shovel to Billy. There was no pickaxe, so they would have to break the ground with the spades.

The sunset was almost gone when they finished the grave and Joe just slid the tarp and the underlying bodies into the hole, but when they fell, one of the boys' bodies fell free and Billy wretched again, leaving Joe to start shoveling dirt into the hole.

Billy recovered quickly enough to help finish the job and then they tossed both of the shovels onto the grave, making a tool cross in the process.

"Let's get the horses unsaddled and get something to eat in the kitchen, Billy."

"Yes, sir."

———

An hour later, they were sitting in the kitchen eating supper and drinking coffee. The lamps and kerosene had been taken by the gang, so the only light was from a candle Billy had discovered in one of the bedrooms.

"We're going to find this at the Fosters tomorrow, aren't we?" Billy asked after taking a sip of his coffee.

"I'm afraid so, Billy," Joe replied.

"Is it always like this for you, Sheriff Joe?" Billy asked.

"Not usually this bad, Billy. Sometimes it's worse, but most of the time it's not this bad. And you may as well start calling me Joe, Billy. It'll save you time and you've earned the right."

Billy nodded and said, "What happens when we find the gangs, Joe?"

"That's the big question, isn't it? The answer is that I don't know. There are too many to take on in a gunfight. We'd lose in less than five minutes. When we get near Cooperstown, we'll swing north before we get there so we can watch the town from the tall hills north of town. They won't be looking that way because the only road into town, it's more of a trail, really, comes from the south. We'll need to figure out where they have all of their captives first, so we can keep them safe. Then, we'll need to come up with a way to get them out of there. I'm going to count on one thing, Billy. I'm hoping that they aren't done getting supplies and they'll make another foray into the county, splitting up their numbers. Some will stay with the captives, but most will go off to raid some other ranches or farms."

"That means we'll have to wait, won't it?"

"Probably. Maybe a day or two."

"Then, they'll hurt my mother and sisters," Billy said dejectedly.

Joe sighed and said, "Billy, you've got to assume that's already happened. They didn't kidnap a bunch of women just to have them do their laundry. All we can do is get them out of there and hope that your mother, Mrs. Riley and Mrs. Foster can help your sisters and the other girls through this."

"I know, Joe. It still bothers me, though."

"It bothers me, too, Billy. It bothers me more than watching a man die. At least they had a chance to defend themselves. Women don't get that chance."

"It's not fair, is it?"

"No, Billy, it's not fair, but it's the way it is."

Billy nodded and continued to eat slowly.

"Did you name your horse?" Joe asked suddenly.

Billy's head snapped up and he said, "I get to name him?"

"Sure. You can keep him and the Winchester and Colt, too. You've earned them."

"He's not quite all brown, but he has that odd blotch on his side. I'm not sure what it looks like, though."

"When I saw it, I thought it looked like a map of Ireland."

Billy smiled and said, "Maybe I'll call him Irish."

"That'll suit him. I just hope he doesn't have an Irish temper."

Billy laughed and asked, "Why did you name your horse Boomer? I heard you call him that today and I was curious. Is it something to do with guns?"

Joe replied, "Not unless you count his personal cannon. When I first bought him three years ago, I was pleased because he's mostly dark gray with just that slash of white on his forehead and was thinking of just calling him Gray or something equally stupid but hadn't decided yet. Well, I was out tracking a horse thief and had caught up with him when he was setting up camp, so I dismounted and was planning on sneaking up on him and got within a hundred feet when Boomer let's go with this enormous horse fart."

Now, I didn't even know they could do that, but he did. The horse thief jumps up from his campfire and starts to whip out his hogleg. I already had my Winchester on him and told him to drop it, but he didn't, so I shot him. He didn't die from the bullet wound, but I felt like shooting my horse for his flatulence. I named him Boomer for that obnoxious noise and smell. He never did it again, but that doesn't mean it can't happen."

Billy was laughing hard by the time Joe finished the story, as Joe knew he would. Billy needed something to put the bad news to rest, at least for the night.

———

The worst fears of the women on the three wagons finally were realized when they watched their captors playing poker for the rights to deflower the six teenaged girls.

One by one, men would throw down their hands in disgust as the winners would jump up and dance around, knowing what they would soon be doing.

When the last hand was won, the six victors approached the wagons and each one grabbed his teenaged trophy and dragged her onto a nearby patch of grass. The mothers looked on in horror as the men lined up to watch the spectacle as the six girls were all laid onto the grass and quickly disrobed.

There was no privacy, just cheering as the men violated the girls who tried not to show any emotion but after several slaps demanding that they stop laying there like mattresses, had to actively participate in their own shame.

When they were all finished, the six men stood back, and the mothers were hastily pulled from the wagons, stripped naked and thrown to the ground. Hanger Bob must have preferred Emma Harper over the thinner teenaged girls and was the first one to rape her. Again, the men demanded that the women show some level of enthusiasm, so they complied.

The girls and their mothers were then subjected to a second round of humiliation when the men who hadn't satisfied themselves took their pleasures. Emma and Jennie Riley were the only two to have to undergo the assault once as Hanger Bob had announced that Emma was now his alone. Jennie Riley had been claimed by Pierre Le Tour, and Charlie Smith took Sarah Foster, but allowed one of his gang to have her once more.

After they allowed the women to dress, they were tied again and left on the grass while the men all prepared to eat.

———

After the levity of the Boomer story, Joe began telling Billy some of the many other stories about his life as a lawman to pass the time.

Billy asked questions periodically, but mostly sat mesmerized.

"Then why are you leaving, Joe? Deputy Smith said you were going to stop being sheriff." he asked.

Joe leaned his kitchen chair back onto its back feet and replied, "I don't know, Billy. Maybe it's just the thought of getting old and sitting there on the boardwalk with a gray beard watching life pass me by that has me spooked. I'm almost thirty-five and all I have is this badge, my guns and some money in the bank. Hell, I don't even have anyone to leave it to."

Billy smiled and said, "You can leave it to me, Joe."

Joe laughed and then replied, "Maybe I will, Billy. Maybe I will."

"I was just jokin', Joe. I don't want your stuff or money. I just want my mama and sisters back."

"We'll get them back, Billy. I promise you that. I'll get them all back or die trying."

"I don't want that, either, Joe. Let's just say we get them back and those bad guys all die."

Joe dropped his chair back to all four and said, "I hope so, Billy. Let's get some sleep. We have a lot of riding to do tomorrow."

"Okay."

There were no mattresses in the place, so they used their bedrolls in the main room.

Thirty-two miles northeast, the women all shivered in the night, all of them snuggled close together for heat. The blankets that would keep them warm were just thirty feet away in the wagons, but none of the men bothered to bring the blankets to them.

Each of the mothers tried to comfort their daughters as they were pressed together, but it was so hard as they all knew that more of this kind of treatment awaited them when they reached Cooperstown tomorrow afternoon.

CHAPTER 2

Hanger Bob Jones had them up and rolling before seven-thirty. The women were granted time to use some nearby bushes then have a cup of coffee and a piece of jerky before they were tied again and put back onto the wagons.

Joe and Billy left the Riley ranch at eight o'clock, having had a good breakfast of bacon and eggs washed down with fresh coffee. Joe had told Billy that it was always a good idea to eat when you could when you were out on a mission because you wouldn't know where or when the next meal would arrive.

They rode for forty minutes before they turned onto the Foster ranch, but this time, there weren't any buzzards circling the place.

"Where are the buzzards? Didn't those outlaws come here?" asked Billy.

"No, they've been here, Billy. You should have noticed the large number of hoofprints on the access road. I think we'll find the bodies of Mike Foster and his son in the house."

"Oh," Billy said as his stomach was already beginning to roll.

"I'll tell you what, Billy, I'll go into the house and you can go and check for shovels and a pickaxe."

"Okay," replied a grateful Billy Harper.

They split up at the barn and Billy rode inside then stepped down. He found one shovel and a pickaxe this time and then walked out of the barn to find a place to dig the grave.

Joe found both bodies in the kitchen. Mike Foster had three gunshots and his son only had one, but the overpowering stench was hard to fight.

He left the room, walking back outside to take some gulps of fresh air, spotted Billy carrying a shovel and pickaxe and stepped down from the small back porch and went to meet him.

"Let's dig closer to the house, Billy. I'm going to have to drag those bodies out of there as fast as I can and don't want to have to go too far."

"Okay," Billy said as he handed Joe the shovel.

Just twenty feet past the back porch, Billy began to swing the pickaxe's pointed end into the hard dirt. Joe started shoveling while Billy leaned on the pickaxe, sweating.

They must have gotten used to gravedigging, because it only took twenty minutes to dig the hole. Granted, it was only four feet deep, but it would be enough.

"Look away, Billy. I don't want you to lose that big breakfast," Joe said as he looked back at the house.

Billy not only looked away but took ten steps away from the hole.

Joe took a deep breath, then rushed into the kitchen, grabbed the boy's shirt and dragged him out of the doorway, still holding his breath.

He pulled him over to the hole and slid the body into the hole. Then he took another deep breath and repeated it for Mike Foster's body. Once they were both in the hole, Joe started shoveling dirt into the hole, and after the bodies were covered, Joe told Billy it was okay, and Billy started shoveling dirt onto the corpses, letting Joe catch his breath.

When they were done, Joe began gathering rocks to cover the earth from scavengers because of the shallower depth.

Two hours after they arrived at the Foster ranch, Joe and Billy were riding back out of the access road. They turned north to follow the wagon tracks.

After riding for another hour, the tracks left the roadway and followed the trail toward Cooperstown.

"Billy, I need to make a short detour here. We'll get back her in less than an hour. Okay?"

"Sure, but what do you need to do?"

"I need to warn the Hobson family. They're about three miles down that way. I don't see the tracks heading that way, but they're close enough, and Mrs. Hobson is a widow with a teenage daughter."

"Oh."

Twenty minutes later, the Hobson ranch popped into view and Joe spotted Ben Hobson tossing some hay into the corral. He waved, and it took a second for Ben to know who was waving at him before he waved back. He left the corral and must have shouted to the house, because when they were entering the access road, Mrs. Hobson, her daughter and other son all appeared on the front porch. They must have been finishing lunch or something, Joe guessed.

When they were close, Mrs. Hobson smiled at Joe and said loudly, "Sheriff, what brings you back here so soon?"

Joe waited until he was close enough to reply without shouting and said, "Mrs. Hobson, let's wait until Ben gets here. It has nothing to do with your family directly, I just swung by to warn you of a threat that's popped up."

Abby's eyebrows went up as Ben trotted over, "What kind of threat?"

Joe looked over at Ben, then back to his mother.

"Yesterday morning, a band of about fifteen outlaws attacked Billy Harper's family ranch about fifteen miles south of here. They also attacked the Riley ranch and the Foster ranch. They killed all of the males in each family and kidnapped the women and teenaged girls. They also ransacked the house of food and household goods. I believe they're setting up an outlaw haven in Cooperstown about thirty-five miles northeast of here. Now, they've already headed that way, and I'm going over there to see if I can get the captives freed. I want you to know about the possibility that they might come back here."

Ben said, "I'll come with you and help, sheriff."

Joe looked down and said, "I appreciate the offer, Ben, but your job is here to protect your mother and sister. You've got that Winchester and a shotgun, but I'd recommend that you keep some horses saddled and ready to go. If you see a big dust cloud coming from the east, all of you just mount up and ride away to a good hiding place. Don't try to be a hero and engage these men. They're all killers. Okay?"

Ben nodded and said, "Okay."

"Billy is coming along because his father was murdered by these men and his mother and sisters are being held captive. He said he'd follow me anyway, so I let him come with me. I don't want to have to chase after your mother and sister."

"Okay, Sheriff," Ben said.

"How can you take on that many men, sheriff?" Abby asked.

Joe smiled at her and said, "Very carefully, ma'am," then tipped his hat and he and Billy wheeled their horses back to the access road and began trotting away.

Abby watched them ride off and knew that he was riding to his grave.

———

Joe and Billy reached the turnoff twenty minutes later and kept riding northeast. They were gaining on the gang and the wagons but were still more than thirty miles behind.

They ate some jerky and drank from their canteens as they trotted along following the wagon tracks.

By three o'clock, they had found where the wagons had pulled over for the noon break but didn't stop.

———

"Another five or six miles," Hanger Bob yelled back to the wagons and riders behind him, "we'll pick up the town in another hour or so."

No one acknowledged him as the wagons trundled along, swaying on the uneven turf.

Emma had Annie leaning on her left side and Mary's head on her right shoulder. Neither had spoken of what they had endured the previous night and Emma was worried about both of them. She wondered how the Riley and Foster girls were doing. She knew that the mothers had to provide the strength for them to survive but didn't know what kind of life was even possible for her girls. Her new worry was now pregnancy. She hadn't conceived since she had a miscarriage seven years ago, so she didn't believe she was at risk, but her girls were, and she knew that nightmare was part of the fear that was filling their souls and torturing their minds.

Mary finally whispered, "We're never going to escape, are we, Mama?"

Emma was torn between honesty and trying to bolster her strength, so she replied, "Just pray, Mary. We have to leave our salvation in God's hands."

Annie then said softly, her head never leaving her mother's shoulder, "I'd like to believe that our salvation is in the hands of Sheriff Joe. He'll come, won't he, Mama?"

Emma said, “If he finds out about it, he will, Annie. All we can hope is that he finds out about it soon.”

Mary then replied, “But even if he brought his deputies, he’d only have three against sixteen, Mama.”

Emma said, “Even if Sheriff Joe came alone, he’d be able to beat them, Mary. You have to have faith.”

Mary sighed and said, “If you say so, Mama.”

———

Over in the Foster wagon, a similar conversation was going on, but it was leaning more to the spiritual, at least in the beginning.

“Mama,” asked Katie, “why did God let this happen to us? Papa and Abe were shot right in front of us and those men did horrible things to us last night. How could God let this happen?”

Sarah replied, “It’s not God who let this happen, Katie. God created each of us with our own free will and if some choose to ignore God’s and man’s law, it is on their soul and they will have to answer for those transgressions. If God put his finger on each of us and made us do as he wished, why create us in the first place? God isn’t responsible for those terrible things and he won’t be responsible for when we are saved from these horrible men.”

Rachel then asked, “Do you really believe we’ll be saved, Mama? There are so many of them and they have so many guns.”

“Yes, they do, sweetheart. But the power of the righteous can overcome such numbers and their guns. I really do believe we will be saved, and that Sheriff Joe will come and kill every one of those evil men for what they did.”

“But Mama, Sheriff Joe doesn’t even go to our church. I don’t think he goes to any church at all,” said Rachel.

Sarah replied, "I know, Rachel, but that doesn't mean he's not a righteous man. You've all heard the stories about Sheriff Joe. He's a good man and he won't stop until every one of those bad men is standing before God and being condemned to hell."

Rachel sighed and said quietly, "I hope it's soon, Mama."

———

The conversation in the Riley wagon was far less religious, but no less vengeful.

"How can we get away, Mama?" asked Clara quietly.

Her mother replied, "We can't on our own, Clara. We'll just have to wait to be rescued."

"Is the army going to come, Mama?" asked Cora.

"Maybe, but they'd have to come here from far away. The only law close is Sheriff Joe in Lander."

"But he's just one man, Mama. He can't rescue us by himself."

Jennie replied, "Now, girls, you both have to believe that Sheriff Joe will figure out a way to get these men and make them pay for what they did. He'll shoot every last one of them and leave them out on the ground for the vultures and coyotes."

The idea appealed to Cora who said, "Don't forget the mountain lions, Mama. The wolves need to eat, too."

Jennie was pleased that they both seemed better and said, "They'll all be able to feast on the remains of those evil men when Sheriff Joe is finished with them."

———

In front of each wagon, the driver heard the women talking and wondered who the hell this Sheriff Joe was. Then, each of them blew off the hopeful comments as nothing more than wishful thinking. Hanger Bob already had told them that there was almost no law in the territory and the army was two hundred miles away and couldn't get there before winter set in. Nope, this Sheriff Joe was nothing more than a mirage.

The mirage in question was still riding northeast with Billy as they followed the trail. They were moving at more than double the speed of the wagons, but still had only closed the gap to twenty-four miles as the sun grew low in the sky.

Then, they reached where the wagons had pulled over for the night, and Joe turned off the trail to examine the campsite to get a better idea of the numbers he was dealing with, not that the difference of one or two would make a big difference, but if they waited until a large body of them rode off to raid another place, he could count the number leaving and know how many he'd have to face that were left in the their town.

He and Billy stepped down and Joe spotted a roughed-up area on a patch of grass and some dried blood. He knew what had happened and hoped that Billy didn't see it, but his hopes were dashed when Billy stopped and looked down at the blood.

"Joe! They shot some of the women!"

Joe walked back to Billy and said, "No, Billy, they didn't shoot anyone. They raped the girls, and they were all innocent."

Billy didn't understand what Joe was saying and asked, "What do you mean, Joe? I don't understand."

Joe felt a bit uncomfortable, but said, "When a girl or a woman has sex for the first time, they bleed. It only happens once. The six girls were all abused here last night."

Billy stared at the ground, knowing what it represented and almost threw up again, but held his stomach instead.

"I'm so ignorant, Joe. Why don't I know these things?"

"Some parents don't talk to their children about what happens when they get older and get involved with the other sex. If you'd like, I can tell you about it as we ride. You should know these things, Billy."

"I think so," Billy replied as Joe began looking at footprints.

Joe spent ten minutes before they returned to their horses, who had enjoyed the creek and the grass while he finally settled on sixteen as the number of men he'd have to deal with.

The climbed into their saddles and kept riding northeast. Joe didn't need to follow a trail now. He knew where they were going.

The newly christened town of Lawless finally came into view as the sun was low on the horizon, and none of the captives were impressed.

The wagons rumbled past a new sign proclaiming the town of Lawless, Wyoming and soon entered the ramshackle town. They rolled down a main street that was already overgrown with weeds and pulled up to a stop in front of what looked like a boarding house. It even had as faded sign that said something to that effect but was missing most of the letters.

The men then all dismounted, and some took the animals down the street to what used to be a livery with a corral that seemed to be reasonably well preserved.

"Okay, ladies, time to make yourselves useful in other womanly ways," shouted Hanger Bob as he approached the wagons.

"We're going to cut you loose and you're going to help unload the wagons and take them into your new residence. We'll be living on the bottom floor and you'll all live on the top floor, where we can keep an eye on you and pay you a visit whenever we feel the urge. We expect to be well fed and have our laundry clean. We even thoughtfully brought your clothes along, so you can dress into something different. Let's go."

With that, the remaining men began to cut their bonds and the women had to rub their wrists and ankles to be able to move, but soon were dismounting from the wagon and began to do what they were told to do and unload their own food and household goods and carry them into the boarding house. All they were allowed to take upstairs was their own clothing. Everything else, including the mattresses and bedding were brought into the downstairs bedrooms.

Emma only counted six bedrooms on the first floor and another six on the second and wondered how sixteen men could manage to fit into just six rooms.

She received her answer when they were shepherded into just three of the upstairs rooms. Three women from each family per room, and the rooms themselves were disasters.

They didn't get to languish long in their rooms, though, as they were all herded back downstairs to the kitchen, which, although messy, still had a cookstove and all of their cookware, dishes and flatware that had been stolen from their homes.

Under the leering eyes of three of the outlaws, Emma took charge and had the girls begin to clean while she, Sarah Foster and Jennie Riley began to cook. None spoke while under the attentive watch of the men. Emma noticed that they were so arrogant that they had left the butcher knives among the things that they had stolen. Maybe it wasn't arrogance at all, each woman knew what would happen to the others if one attempted to harm one of their captors.

While the captive women cleaned and cooked, Hanger Bob was talking to his councilmen, Pierre Le Tour and Charlie Smith in what used to be the parlor.

"Where are we goin'?" asked Charlie.

"The McClellan farm. It's about twenty miles southeast of here and grows the hay for a lot of the ranchers. Like I said before, there are two women to add to our collection in addition to the hay and whatever else we can find. It'll be a good run."

"We shoulda grabbed some of those beef critters from one of those ranches, Bob," said Pierre.

"I know, but we had so many horses that are more useful, it woulda slowed us down even more. We can pick some up on the way back tomorrow. We don't want a whole herd, maybe five or six. There's a cattle ranch just eight miles southeast, but the only woman on the place is about sixty. They've got two hired hands, though. Do you want to risk it just for some beef?"

Charlie said, "Hell, yes, we risk it. We just do it different, that's all. We pretend we're droppin' off some hay because McClellan is shuttin' down. We just don't tell him that we're shuttin' him down ourselves. When we get close and get those ranch hands to help unload, we open up on 'em."

Hanger Bob nodded and said, "I like it, Charlie. We'll do it your way. There's a lot less risk."

Charlie leaned back, satisfied with his suggestion.

"What time do we head out, Bob?" asked Pierre.

"We'll take a day off to enjoy the women a bit more and get things settled. We'll ride out the day after."

"Okay, boss," said Pierre as the three men rose.

———

Joe and Billy pulled over for the night and unsaddled all three horses, led them to drink and hitched them in a grassy area near the creek.

After they had eaten and were just drinking coffee, Joe spent almost an hour telling Billy the facts of life, but his explanation was a far cry from what would have been expected from a father. Joe explained everything as he would to a man his age, and to Billy, it was all a revelation.

“And women really like that?” he asked with his eyes wide open.

“Most do, but some are so caught up in the supposed shame of it that they won’t even admit it to themselves. Now, in the situation that the captive ladies are in, it’s nowhere the same. They’re being assaulted, just like if you or I were being beaten by some big thug, only it’s worse for a woman because it just is.”

“Are my mother and sisters all going to be changed?” he asked quietly,

“Maybe. I don’t know, Billy. I’ve seen some women bounce back quickly and others let it fester inside and they’re never the same again. I think it has to do with two things. One is faith. The women that are true believers seem to be able to push those memories aside. The other is anger. Women who have been raped need to get angry and be able to take their revenge on the men who did it to them. They need their own form of satisfaction. The worst are the ones that go all quiet and just hold everything inside. Sooner or later, they’ll explode. What the result is of the explosion is anyone’s guess. Now, I’ve met your mother, as well as Mrs. Riley and Mrs. Foster. They’re all strong women and I hope they can pass that along to their daughters.”

“Joe, what happens if we get them out of there? I mean, when they come home to the ranch?”

“That’s up to your mother, Mrs. Riley and Mrs. Foster. They’re all young enough to remarry and with the scarcity of women in Wyoming, I’m sure they’ll find a husband quickly if they wish. Your mother is still a very handsome woman, too, Billy. Mrs. Riley and Mrs. Foster are as well, but not as good-looking as your mother. I think they’ll all be fine. I’m more concerned about the girls. The longer they’re in that situation, the harder it will be for them to recover.”

“You think my mother is good-looking?” asked Billy.

"I don't say what I don't mean, Billy. Your father was a very lucky man."

"Why don't you marry her, Joe?"

Joe shook his head and said, "We're getting way too far ahead of ourselves here, Billy. We haven't even found them yet, much less figured out a way to get them free of their captors."

"I know, but still..."

Joe let the subject drop and poured himself another cup of coffee. The last thing he needed now was some distraction like that. He'd admired Emma Harper for years, but that's as far as it would ever go. He knew he'd never be able to talk to her beyond casual conversation.

———

That night, the women were all directed to their rooms and the doors closed after they had entered. Once inside, they used some of their clothes as mattresses and were soon lying on the floor.

Emma had been told by her 'husband', Hanger Bob, that tomorrow would be a day to settle in and the women would all be used again, but he would be the only one to take her, as if it were a bonus. He said that the other two adult women were similarly 'married' to the other gang bosses and only the girls would be servicing the other thirteen men.

Emma then did the math and knew that one of the girls would be assaulted three times tomorrow. She didn't know how long she could take this and as she lay on her back on a folded dress, she closed her eyes and prayed for their deliverance.

CHAPTER 3

Joe and Billy were on the trail by seven-thirty the next morning, moving at a medium trot, even with the trailing armory/supply horse.

"How much further, Joe?" shouted Billy over the loud hoofbeats.

"The town is about twenty miles but we're going to turn north in about fifteen miles, so we can avoid being seen and get to those hills north of the town," Joe yelled back.

Billy was glad that Joe knew where he was going, because he'd never been this far away from the ranch before.

He was still thinking a lot about what Joe had told him last night. He had been embarrassed early when Joe had started talking about the body parts involved, but then, Joe started talking to him like a man and not a boy and he appreciated the difference. Toward the end, he and Joe were joking like old friends and he appreciated that even more.

Billy still had his mother's widowhood on his mind. He loved and admired his father, and knew he loved his mother, but his father was gone, and he didn't want his mother to be lonely. He glanced over at Sheriff Joe and just wondered.

———

Nineteen miles away, Emma, Jennie and Sarah were cooking breakfast while their daughters were cleaning the lower floor. For the first time, no one was watching them, and they were using the opportunity to talk about what had happened and what the chances were of getting away.

"How are your girls?" Emma asked as she flipped bacon.

Sarah replied, "Katie and Rachel are very upset, but I've been trying to keep their spirits up. It's a horrible thing for all of us, but worse for them."

Jennie answered, "My girls are trying to cope with what they have to do, but I don't know how much longer they can take this. I'm not sure I can take it much longer either."

Emma then said, "I know. That monster that claimed me as his wife is so horrible that even the thought of him makes me nauseous. But I don't know what we can do. If we all ran out of the back door right now, even if we were able to get away, the girls are all under their control and they'd have no one to help them through this. All we can do is hope that help comes quickly."

"I was talking that to my girls on the way here, and the only help we can hope for is Sheriff Joe. I told them that he could do it, but it was all just brave talk. The army's too far away to matter, and that's only if anyone knew we'd been taken," said Sarah.

Jennie said, "I told Clara and Cora the same thing, but I don't see how it's possible. There are just too many of them. They even talk about fighting off the army, for God's sake."

Emma sighed and said, "We have to believe in something, or there's no point in going on. I've met Sheriff Joe a few times and if anyone can do it, he can. We simply have to have some faith that he'll try."

Sarah nodded and said, "I agree that we have to have faith, Emma. We don't have any other choice."

Jennie then said, "We're all widows now, you know. John and my boys were shot down as we tried to escape. They're probably all just lying there still, and it hurts so bad. My boys..."

Then she began to cry lightly and shake.

Emma walked over and hugged Jennie and let her cry. Then Sarah thought about Mike and Abe lying on the floor and began to cry herself.

Emma couldn't afford to cry. She still held out hope that Billy somehow survived. She knew she was a widow, but she had to be stronger than ever now. She'd grieve when she was free of this place, if she grieved at all. If she did mourn, she'd feel like a hypocrite.

The women were all huddled together when they heard footsteps and the three gang leaders walked in to see their 'wives'.

The women quickly tried to recover and return to cooking breakfast, but Charlie Smith seemed to take offense at Sarah's tears and stomped up to her and turned her around harshly.

"What are you cryin' for, woman?" he shouted as her tears resumed.

Charlie reached back and slapped her hard across the cheek, knocking her to the floor.

Emma quickly reached down to help her to her feet when Pierre felt that Jennie deserved much of the same for her crying and slapped Jennie even harder. Jennie didn't fall but angrily tried to strike back, which was the worst thing she could have done. The moment she opened her hand and drew back her arm, Pierre quickly gut-punched Jennie, who fell to the floor just as Emma was picking up Sarah.

"Don't you dare raise your hand to me, you whore!" Pierre shouted as Jennie curled up into a ball on the floor holding her stomach.

Emma then shifted her attention to Jennie and knelt over her to keep Pierre from doing any more damage.

"Where's my breakfast, woman," Hanger Bob snarled at Emma.

"I'll bring you your breakfast as soon as I can get Jennie up off the floor."

"You'll feed all three of us right now and leave that bitch on the floor or you'll join her. Get up!"

Emma patted Jennie on the side, stood and walked over to the stove and began to move the bacon and eggs to the plates. Jennie continued to sob in her curled-up position.

As Emma and Sarah moved the food to the table, Hanger Bob and Charlie Smith took seats, but Pierre looked down at Jennie and spit at her. Then he reached down and yanked the front of her dress apart, laughed and then took a seat.

As he sat down, Pierre said without looking at Jennie, "And when I'm finished eating, you'd better satisfy my other appetite, woman."

Jennie was almost beyond caring, but after all three men were eating, Emma again knelt down next to Jennie and whispered in her ear, "Don't let them win, Jennie. I know it hurts, but don't let them win."

Jennie struggled to her feet and then had to fix her torn dress as best she could before Emma guided her to the counter and poured a cup of coffee and handed it to her. She accepted the cup with both hands and began to sip her coffee.

Joe and Billy had reached a point that Joe deemed close enough and turned due north.

"We need to keep an eye to the east to make sure we can't see the town. We need to stay invisible until we're well north of the town."

"Okay, Joe," Billy said.

Joe knew that they were less than five miles from the town, but the topography dictated when they could make their turn as there were some tall hills in the way. They were similar to the row of hills north of Cooperstown that they would use as their reconnaissance location.

They rode for another hour before they spotted the row of hills that Joe wanted.

"There they are, Billy. We'll ride straight for that gap and pass through it, then turn on the other side of the hills and ride another hour or so. Then we tie the horses down and climb the hill to see what's going on."

"How far will it be to the town?" Billy asked.

"About a mile or so. That's why I brought the field glasses."

Billy nodded, and they continued to ride at a good pace.

———

The women had all been victimized again by noon and then sent to their rooms while the men engaged in some poker.

"You know what we need around here?" said Charlie Smith as he dealt.

"Beer and whiskey," shouted Willie Gray from another table.

"And lots of it!" yelled Henry Pleasant from a third table.

Hanger Bob turned to Pierre and asked, "Where can we get some liquor?"

Pierre tossed his cards down and said, "If we send some men a little further south, we can stop at the Shoshone Agency store and pick up all we need."

"Okay, let's do this. We take two wagons with us. One for the hay and the others for a few barrels of beer and a few cases of whiskey."

"Okay. Don't forget about the cattle at that ranch, either."

"I haven't. It'll mean that before we hit the farm, some will head to the agency store and the others, head back north with the hay and get those cattle."

"We can pull it off. Maybe we should only leave four here with the women. It should be enough."

"Okay. We'll leave four and have twelve for the two jobs."

Pierre nodded and looked at his new hand without appreciation and tossed them onto the table.

Joe and Billy had cleared the gap between the hills and turned east behind the row of hills that blocked their view of Cooperstown. Now, it was a question of estimating the distance they'd need to travel.

Joe guessed that each hill was about a mile in diameter and six hundred feet high, so he decided to pass three more hills before they stopped behind the fourth.

It took them another forty minutes, but they finally dismounted and led the horses to a small pond that would probably be gone in another month when the summer heat finally arrived. They didn't unsaddle the horses yet until Joe was sure this is the hill he wanted.

"Ready to climb, Billy?" he said as he pulled his field glasses from his saddlebags.

"Yes, sir!" Billy said enthusiastically, glad to be out of the saddle. He'd never come close to riding this long before.

Joe began to climb the grassy hill with long strides. There were pine trees scattered around all of the hills; not densely enough to be called forests, but enough to provide some cover.

It took them almost fifteen minutes to climb to the hilltop and look down at Cooperstown, less than a mile away. It was actually closer to a half a mile, which surprised and pleased Joe.

"Okay, Billy, let's take a look. I'm sure that they're in that building almost in the center on our side of town. See the smoke from one of the pipes? It's probably the cookstove pipe at this time of year. I don't see any movement anywhere but look at that corral to our right," he said as he handed the field glasses to Billy.

Billy had to focus the glasses and saw what Joe wanted him to see – horses, lots of horses.

"Those are their horses, Joe. I recognize most of them, including the ones they stole from our ranch."

"I know. That means they're all probably in that one building, too. Take a look at the building and tell me what you make of it."

Billy swung the glasses back to the building and stared for a few seconds before saying, "It looks like a hotel or boarding house."

"That was my guess. In a small town like Cooperstown, it probably only had about ten or twelve rooms. But with a kitchen, I'd guess it was an old boarding house."

Billy lowered the field glasses and said, "And my mother and sisters are in there right now."

"I'm sure that they are, along with the other women and sixteen outlaws. Let's go back down and unsaddle the horses and set them up so they can graze and drink from that pond. We'll be eating cold from now on. We can't afford the smoke."

"Okay," Billy said as he took one more look at the boarding house where his mother and sisters were and wished they could go right down there now with guns blazing but knew that it wouldn't be a smart thing to do.

He then handed the field glasses to Joe and they started walking down the hill.

Forty minutes later, they had returned to their chosen observation point near two trees. They both sat with their backs against the trees ten feet apart. Joe had the field glasses with him, but he wasn't using them. They were just watching the town for any sign of movement.

"Why aren't they moving around, Joe?" Billy asked.

"They're all probably inside. They probably only arrived yesterday and are trying to set everything up. See the wagons over there in that livery building? You can see the fronts of the wagons without the field glasses."

"I noticed them earlier. Three wagons, so that means they didn't go anywhere else."

"Not yet. I just don't believe they'll be staying put for very long. They haven't been in this town very long according to Ben Hobson, so they probably need a lot more supplies to last them. They don't have a general store or a feed and grain store to be able to just pick up necessary supplies. They have to forage for what they need and aren't going to walk into Lander and buy things."

"Are you sure that they're all still there?"

"I'm positive. If they're missing any horses, it's only one or two, but notice that they don't have any lookouts, so they think they're safe, and that works to our advantage."

"How are we going to get down there, Joe?"

"We, Mr. Harper, when the timing is right, we are going to just walk down the hill. You'll be carrying your Winchester and I'll have mine and the sawed-off shotgun. They won't be looking this way. Like I said before, we may have to wait a day or two, but when they ride off, hopefully they'll leave less than half of their company back in the boarding house. They probably have the women scared to death and figure they won't do anything to try to escape, especially as they're the ones with the guns. Once they do ride off, we wait for three hours so they'll be far enough away not to hear the sound of gunfire over their hoofbeats."

Then, we walk down the hill. I'm going to want you to go over to where the horses are being held and wait there so they don't escape. Keep your Winchester aimed at the front of the boarding house. Make sure of your target before you shoot. Wait until he gets closer than a hundred feet. If he's a bad guy, don't hesitate or warn him, just squeeze off the shot and lever in a new cartridge right away."

When we reach the bottom of the hill, you'll break off and get to the livery. I'll wait a couple of minutes until you get in position at the livery and I'll walk into the kitchen with my one of my pistols cocked and my sawed-off shotgun in my left hand. I expect to find at least some of the women there, and I'll make sure to have my badge displayed so they know not to shout or anything. At least I hope they won't. Then, I'll ask where everyone is and start making my way through the house. If I have to fire, it'll warn the others, so I'll handle each situation as needed."

It's really important that none of the ones in the building can escape to bring the others back. That's your job. Not one of those remaining outlaws can get out of Cooperstown to tell the rest of the gang – not one. Once I've eliminated the bad men or driven them into your fire, we get those wagons harnessed, get the other horses hitched behind them, then get the women into the wagons and out of here. But before we go, I'm going to set this town on fire, so they don't have a hideout to return to. Once I'm sure that you and the women are safe, I'll chase them down and kill every last mother's son of them."

Billy had been listening carefully and nodding but was startled by his last line.

"You sound like you hate them, Joe."

Joe kept his eyes focused on the town and said, "I do hate them, Billy. I'm sure that you do as well. It's because of what they've done. They've murdered good men, boys, and hurt good women. As far as I'm concerned, not one of them deserves to spend one more day on this earth."

Billy said, "I hate them, too. I hope I can shoot them if they try to get away."

"You'll do fine, Billy. Just try and picture what they did to your mother and sisters. Do that and you'll want them to die in pain."

Billy visualized what had happened to his mother and knew that he'd shoot them without hesitation.

———

"How are you doing, Jennie?" asked Emma as they prepared the evening meal.

"I'm okay. I thought I was going to die, Emma. It hurt so bad, but it's all right now. I can't believe he hit me and then made me…you know."

"I know. But most of them are going somewhere tomorrow and we'll only have a few of them here."

Sarah looked over and asked, "How do you know that, Emma?"

"I heard the eyepatch talking to one of his bootlickers. I think they're going south to get more women and some hay for the horses."

"Do you think we can do anything?" Jennie asked.

"No, we can't, but maybe if Sheriff Joe is watching, he'll know that we only have a few captors and can make his attack. We'll be able to help him when he arrives."

Sarah said, "Emma, you can't be serious. There's no one here but us. Sheriff Joe can't be watching us. It's not possible."

Emma looked at Sarah and said, "Believe what you want, Sarah, but I have to believe he's out there. I can almost feel his eyes on us."

Jennie smiled wistfully and said, "I hope you're right, Emma. I'd love to see him come through that door after they leave."

Emma smiled back and said, “Then we’ll all be happy, Jennie.”

______

The sun was going down, so Joe and Billy walked back down the hill and had themselves some cold beans and jerky for dinner.

“Is your mother a good cook, Billy?” Joe asked before taking a big spoonful of cold beans.

“She’s the best, Joe.”

“Maybe she’ll cook us lunch tomorrow before we all leave.”

Billy looked up and asked, “Do you really think they’ll be leaving tomorrow, Joe?”

“I’d say better than a fifty-fifty chance. They had all day to carouse, but tomorrow they’ll need to get enough food for themselves and the horses. The question is, how many will they leave behind to guard the women after the foraging parties leave. I’d be satisfied with eight, but I’d like it better to be six or even four. I’m actually leaning towards four because men like that don’t think much of women. They’ll believe that four tough men can easily handle nine helpless women and that’s a mistake, Billy. Add it to their list of blunders on this one. They didn’t go looking for you. They didn’t set up any lookouts, and they have all of the women in one building.”

“I sure hope this all works, Joe. I want to see my mother and sisters again.”

“You know, Billy, your mother and sisters probably think you’re dead. I think you’ll make them very happy when they see you again.”

Billy hadn’t thought about it, but the thought of his mother smiling at him made his eyes moisten and he had to sniff.

Joe smiled to himself. He was looking forward to seeing the family reunion himself even more than he was looking forward to putting a few rounds of lead through those bastards, and that was something he really wanted to do.

The women were all in their rooms again, and Emma had told her daughters that she believed that they would be freed tomorrow because most of the gangs were going to be gone most of the day.

"Are we going to use the knives to kill them, Mama?" Mary asked with perfectly innocent eyes.

"No, Mary, we can't do anything because they'll still have guns and would kill all of us if we tried. I just think that after they're gone, Sheriff Joe will come in that door and shoot them all."

Annie quickly asked, "Did you see Sheriff Joe, Mama?"

"No, but I felt like he was watching the boarding house. I don't know why, but I did. It gave me confidence that we'd be on our way home by noon tomorrow."

"What can we do to help, Mama?" asked Mary.

"Just stay out of the way, sweetheart. Fall to the floor when the bullets start flying. If you get time alone with the other girls tell them if they hear guns go off or a commotion somewhere in the house, just fall to the floor and lay flat on their stomachs until it stops."

"Okay, Mama," Annie said, wondering how her mother seemed to know what was going to happen.

CHAPTER 4

Joe and Billy were up in their perches on top of the hill by the trees shortly after sunrise and were peering at the boarding house. There wasn't any smoke from the cookstove pipe yet, so that meant there was no one awake this cool, still-to-blossom morning.

They had been there for less than ten minutes when the smoke started pouring out of the pipe.

"Looks like your mother is making some coffee, Billy. Hopefully in another hour or so, we'll see the bad guys going to get their horses and some wagons. Then, we start counting them and the more that leave that old boarding house the easier our job will be."

"Maybe they'll just tie up the women and all leave," Billy suggested.

"That is a possibility, Billy. But to be honest, I'd like to start thinning their ranks."

"You can do that and not hurt any of the ladies?"

"If I play my cards right, I can shoot every one of those bastards that will be left in there without them getting a shot off."

"How?"

Joe sighed and said, "Because, after the big group rides off, the small bunch that will remain will be bored after a little while and decide to entertain themselves. I don't intend to let them get that far along. We may move earlier than the three hours I had planned for, Billy. If they're over four miles away, and driving a wagon or two, they won't hear the gunfire over the creaking wagons and the horses' hoofbeats, especially if the gunfire is indoors. We have to play the hand that's dealt to us, Billy, but we'll get every one of those ladies out of there in a few hours."

Billy nodded. He was getting excited about the possibility of seeing his mother and sisters in a little while, and just to grinned in response to Joe's comment.

Almost exactly an hour later, they had their first look at the outlaws when four of them walked out of the front of the boarding house quickly followed by another six.

Joe had his field glasses on them and said, "That's ten already, Billy. It's looking good, but I don't see Hanger Bob Jones yet. I wonder if the three bosses are all going to stay in the boarding house and just send out their sycophants."

Billy asked, "Sycophants?"

"A fancy word for bootlickers, Billy," he replied, then paused and said, "There he is! And I believe that's Pierre Le Tour with him, too. I don't know what Charlie Smith looks like, but Pierre has this odd moustache, according to the wanted posters. He really likes that thing and always had some moustache wax with him. It's beyond a normal handlebar moustache, and curls around on the ends, and that man I'm looking at definitely has an odd moustache."

"Now we wait, Joe?"

"Now we wait. But I was thinking, Billy. I think we might bring the horses up here and tie them back in the trees. That way we don't have to go too far to bring them back down. What do you think?"

"I think it's a good idea. Then, when they're all dead, I can run up here and ride them back down the hill in just minutes."

Joe grinned and said, "I had already volunteered you do to that very thing, Billy."

In the boardinghouse, a subdued Emma and her two new adult woman friends were cleaning the dishes and had been joined by all of their daughters after an order from Hanger Bob who wanted them all in one place. Their four guards were at the kitchen table playing poker.

Billy had the field glasses when the first wagon was pulled out of the livery barn and then a second.

"They're really leaving, Joe," Billy said excitedly, "and they're taking two wagons!"

"I can see that, Billy. Now, we just wait."

Billy continued to watch in the early morning sun as the wagons were harnessed and led out into the street. The men were saddling their horses and Billy was finding it hard to contain his excitement. *How had Joe known that they were going to do this?*

So, he asked, "How did you know, Joe?"

Joe was watching intently but replied, "I just guessed, Billy. The need for supplies aside, this is a restless bunch of men and they feel the need to do bad things to keep their level of excitement high. If they weren't, then they'd be just like honest folks who usually do hard, boring work every day, and they'd never be satisfied with that. But you know what's funny about their way of life, Billy? They really don't make much money at all. I'll bet when we go down there and after they're all dead, I'd be surprised if one of them had ten dollars in his pocket."

"Really? I thought they were all rich."

"Ben Hobson's oldest brother thought the same thing and convinced his two younger brothers they could become criminals and make a lot of money. It took the deaths of the two older brothers after they robbed a stage to convince Ben that they were wrong. The total value of the loot they had in their saddlebags wasn't even fifty dollars. None of them make a lot of money, Billy. Hanger Bob has sixteen members of his gang. They can kill and rape their way across the territory, but they'll never have much money at all, and sooner or later, they'll all either die from a bullet or a noose before they reach forty. Add to that they never get to enjoy the love of a good woman or have children to raise and love. Now, you tell me, Billy, who is really rich? The man with a good woman and children, or a criminal with ten dollars in his pocket and a price on his head?"

Billy looked over at Joe and asked, "But you never had a good woman or children, Joe."

"No, I haven't, and I'm insanely jealous of those that do. Some men I know have both and all they do is complain about it. I want to slap them and tell them to recognize the riches they have, but they'd tell me how lucky I was to be a bachelor and can spend as much money as I want on things that they wish they could have. But all I really have are my guns and Boomer."

"Do you have a lot of money, Joe?" Billy asked.

"More than I need. I've been a sheriff here for thirteen years now, and they pay for my room and board and I don't have a lot of expenses other than ammo, and they pay for that, too. I get all the rewards for the bad men who have them posted, too. So, I'm okay."

Billy didn't ask another question as his focus was down in Cooperstown as the men were mounting their horses and drivers were in the wagon seats.

"There they go, Joe!" he almost shouted, making Joe cringe.

"Quieter, Billy," Joe said in a normal voice, making Billy grimace at his mistake.

"Now, let's wait for them to leave town and then we go back and get our horses."

"Okay," Billy said as he continued to watch.

Ten minutes later, the convoy was riding south along a second trail.

"They're heading south this time. Must be heading for the McClellan farm for some hay for their horses, and I think Al McClellan has a daughter and a wife they might try to take back, too. I think we need to cut the time as closely as we can, Billy. Let's go get those horses."

Billy popped up from his sitting position and they quickly walked down the hill.

———

In the kitchen, Emma was deliberately slowing down, so sure was her belief that Sheriff Joe would be walking through the door soon, but the problem was the room was crowded with the girls and the three adult women. The four guards were still playing poker, so Emma needed to come up with some way to get the girls out of the room.

As it turned out, it wasn't necessary. The reason may not have been ideal, but ten minutes later, the four men threw down their hands and one stayed while the other three ordered all of the girls out of the kitchen and down the hallway into their bedrooms, two girls to a room.

The one who remained, Ten Finger Green, one of the half-breeds, sat at the table and watched the three mothers, but knew they were off limits as property of the three chiefs, but still ogled them all, and was thinking about violating the bosses' privileges.

———

Joe and Will brought the three horses up into the trees near the top of the hill and tied them off before walking to their viewing spot. Joe pulled out his glasses and looked down the southern trail for the wagons and spotted them about three miles away.

"We'll give them another half an hour, Billy. That'll put them about five miles out and with the creaking of those wagon wheels, they shouldn't be able to hear any gunshots."

"Okay, Joe," Billy said as anxiety began to creep into his mind.

Joe had his field glasses fixed on the receding column to make sure they didn't turn back, but after hearing Billy's tremulous reply, said, "It's okay to be afraid, Billy. I am."

"You are?" Billy asked in astonishment.

"Sure. A little fear is a good thing. It keeps you on your toes. I can't tell you how many times I've run across men who claim not to be afraid and they freeze up when the lead starts flying. Now, I'm not worried a bit about you, Billy. You'll be fine."

Billy felt immensely better as Joe handed him the field glasses.

While Billy was watching, Joe checked his pistols first, each one with a full load of .44s just in case. Then he double-checked the shotgun's load of #4 buckshot and even his Winchester. He didn't want any surprises.

It was only twenty minutes later when Joe said, "This is close enough, Billy. Let's start walking."

Billy put the field glasses back in the saddlebags before he turned back, then he and Joe began to carefully walk down the hill as if they were out on a Sunday stroll. They headed straight for the boarding house, Joe's badge flashing in the morning sunlight. Billy peeled off and trotted away to the livery as they reached level ground while Joe continued to march toward the back of the boarding house, his gray eyes boring into the building.

In the boarding house, Emma's firm belief of their imminent rescue had her glance out the kitchen window and her heart just about exploded when she spotted Sheriff Joe striding right at her about a hundred yards away. She quickly began to think of ways to help him.

Joe walked until he was near the back of the boarding house and just waited for Billy to get into position. While he waited, he listened for any noises coming from the house and was rewarded with the banging of some pots and pans. That meant at least one of the women was in the kitchen, probably with at least one of the captors. He leaned his Winchester carefully against the wall of the neighboring building and cocked the hammer to his right-hand Smith & Wesson and continued to wait; in another minute or so and he'd make his entrance.

Emma had been banging the pots and pans to let the sheriff know they were there. Then, after putting them away, she glanced at the outlaw sitting at the table, still staring at them with lust-filled eyes.

Then she looked over at Sarah and said, "You know, Sarah, I think you and me and Jennie should all have some Joe."

Sarah and Jennie both looked at Emma curiously, and Emma then smiled at the outlaw and said, "I think you'd like some Joe, too, wouldn't you?"

Ten Fingers grinned and replied, "Maybe. If you're gonna sit on my lap and hold it for me while I keep my hands busy."

Sarah and Jennie still hadn't figured out why Emma was calling coffee 'joe'.

Then Emma looked at Sarah again and asked, "I do like one-star Joe when it's nice and close, don't you, Sarah?"

Then, they both understood, and Sarah replied, "Oh, yes, I do."

Ten Fingers had no idea what they were talking about and was about to ask when Emma walked to the cookstove, took the coffeepot and let it slip, spilling the hot coffee over the floor.

"Stupid woman!" shouted Ten Finger as Emma hurriedly snatched some towels and gave one to Sarah and Jennie.

"Let's clean this up and I'll make more in a minute."

All of the women then lifted their skirts, went to their knees and began to mop up the coffee while Ten Fingers forgot his anger over the spilled coffee and looked at the women's bared legs.

Joe had been listening to Emma and had appreciated the conversation immensely. She was telling the other women and him that she knew he was outside the door. He knew they would be low for a few more seconds, so he tightened his grip around the sawed-off shotgun and took a deep breath as he carefully stepped onto the porch. It was in such a sorry state that he was sure it would either collapse from his weight or at least creak, but it did neither as he neared the door latch. He hoped it was open as he slowly used the fingers of his left hand to lift the latch finding it unlocked.

Once the latch was in the up position, Joe blew out his breath and then just swung the door open and stepped into the kitchen.

He immediately spotted the three women on the floor as their lone captor suddenly jerked his head up and saw the lawman standing there with a cocked pistol in his hand. Joe quickly aimed his revolver at the man and shook his head to tell him to keep his mouth shut.

Surprisingly, Ten Fingers did just that, knowing he was dead if he didn't comply. But he still let his right hand drop from the table as Joe quietly walked into the room, each of the three women staring up at him wide eyes.

Joe had seen Ten Fingers' hand drop to his pistol and knew he didn't have much time. He took two quick but careful strides past the women, pulled his finger from the trigger and slammed the barrel on top of Ten Fingers' head as hard as he could.

Ten Fingers hadn't expected the attack, so his hand never reached his pistol as he slumped forward onto the table as blood rushed from his skull.

Joe quickly checked his carotid pulse, then turned to Emma who had already begun to approach.

"Where are the other three?" he whispered.

"Each one is with two of the girls in the three bedrooms down the hallway. What can we do?" she asked quietly.

Joe already had an answer.

"When I get in position, I'll signal to you, then I want you to scream and go running past me to the front of the house. The other two will need to lay flat on the floor to avoid any stray rounds. Okay?"

"Okay," Emma replied as Sarah and Jennie quickly laid on their stomachs on the dry part of the kitchen floor.

Joe then turned and walked down the hallway on his tiptoes and positioned himself just past two closed doors with the third closed one on his right toward the kitchen. He could hear noises from all three rooms but thought the girls hadn't been taken yet. He then slid to the right side of the hallway and nodded at Emma.

Emma screamed and then ran down the hallway and as she passed Joe, he shouted in a gruff voice, "They're runnin'!"

He only had to wait for five seconds and heard scuffling from the two rooms on his right, and then a half-naked Fred Argyle shot out of the one right next to him and Joe rammed the muzzles of the sawed-off shotgun into his naked belly, folding him over just as Jimmy Preston ran out of the second bedroom closer to the kitchen, shirtless but with his uncocked revolver in his hand.

Joe didn't give him the chance to cock the hammer and fired from four feet, the .44 caliber round drilling through his chest and then racing down the hallway into the kitchen. Before the last door opened, Joe slammed the barrels of the small shotgun across the back of Fred Argyle's head, doing massive damage.

Joe was halfway into his turn back to the last closed bedroom door when Louie Bouton popped out of the room, believing that one of his partners had shot one of the women, only to find some damned lawman standing there with a pistol swiveling in his direction.

He rushed at Joe and slammed him into the wall, his Smith & Wesson clattering away. Louie then lurched to grab the revolver just four feet in front of him.

Joe recovered from the hit quickly and slapped both hammers back on the shotgun just as Louie reached his Smith & Wesson and was beginning to stand, cocking the revolver as he did.

Joe didn't aim the small scattergun, he just pointed it at Louie and pulled the trigger. Even with the shortened barrels, the distance was so short that there was no appreciable spread, and Louie Bouton caught all of the buckshot pellets square in the center of his chest, making a massive hole and sending him stumbling back, tripping over the body of Jimmy Preston, then collapsing in a heap just behind Jimmy's body.

Joe quickly made sure that the shotgun-struck Fred Argyle was dead before retrieving his own pistol, releasing the hammer, sliding it back home into its holster and pulling the hammer loop in place.

Just one minute and fifteen seconds after entering the boarding house kitchen, all four captors were dead.

Joe quickly shouted, "Mrs. Harper, it's safe now. They're all dead, including the one in the kitchen. We need to start moving now. I need you and Mrs. Riley and Mrs. Foster to look after your daughters."

With his announcement, the girls all began sticking their heads out of the bedrooms, fixing their clothing as they did.

Emma came jogging out of the main room as the girls began slowly walking out of the bedrooms into the gunsmoke-filled hallway. Jennie and Sarah rapidly exited the kitchen and were soon hugging their daughters, while Emma hugged Annie and Mary, all of them ignoring the three dead bodies in the hallway. There was loud, excited chattering among them all as they realized they were free and would soon be going home.

Joe let them have a few minutes, knowing that the elation of their sudden release would soon be replaced by their horrifying memories of what had happened to them and what they had lost. There was now only one male member of all three families, and he was in the livery.

Joe finally approached Emma and said, “Mrs. Harper, could you take a minute and stick your head out the front door and tell my backup man to come in from the livery. Just shout his name and he’ll come running.”

Emma looked up at Joe, smiled and said, “I’ll do anything you ask, Sheriff. What’s his name?”

“Billy.”

Emma’s mouth dropped open and then she asked, “Billy? As in my Billy?”

“Yes, ma’am. He ran all the way into town to get me right after they attacked your ranch. If it wasn’t for Billy, I wouldn’t have known about the attack for days.”

Then, without hesitation, Emma and her daughters raced down the hallway and out through the front door.

Joe could hear her shouting, “Billy! Billy!” as she ran and suppressed the smile he felt because of the news he would have to give to the other two widows.

Joe then turned to the other two mothers and said, “Mrs. Foster and Mrs. Riley, I want to let you both know that we buried your husbands and sons before we left your ranches. It was the best I could do. I’m sorry that this all happened.”

Both women looked at Joe with tears in their eyes and nodded.

Sarah then said, “Thank you for that, Sheriff, and thank you even more for saving us.”

“Yes,” agreed Jennie, “Thank you so very much. How can we get out of here?”

“We’ll talk about that in a few minutes. We’ve got to get moving because I aim to burn this town to the ground before we leave, and I have to go and stop those men from hurting more people.”

"Okay. What do we do now?" asked Sarah Foster.

"All of you get your things and then I'll harness the last wagon. We'll load up whatever you want to take back along with enough food to return to Lander, where you'll be safe until I can take care of these men."

"But..." began Jennie, but she was stopped by Joe.

"Ma'am, we need to move now and talk later," he said.

The women nodded then took their daughters' hands and quickly walked past the three dead bodies and hurried up the stairs to their rooms to gather their things. Joe began gathering gunbelts and handguns from the dead men. There were nine women and he wanted to arm as many as possible.

He brought the guns into the kitchen and then began loading some of the food from the pantry into the same burlap sacks that had been used to remove the food from the ranches. He opened a large bag and tossed the still-empty coffeepot and some knives, forks and spoons into the bag as well as a cooking grate, a large frypan and some tin cups. He finally tossed in some tin plates and set the heavy bag aside.

Emma, Billy and her daughters re-entered the boarding house and walked down the hallway when they saw Joe in the kitchen.

When he heard them coming, he stopped packing food and looked up.

Emma was holding onto Billy as if she was never going to let him go, but Joe said, "Mrs. Harper, I need to have Billy go up the hill to retrieve our horses, if you don't mind."

Emma smiled, let Billy go and said, "As I said before, Sheriff, anything you need, just ask."

Billy smiled at Joe and trotted past and out the back door.

Joe was getting ready to explain to Emma what was happening, when there was the sound of snapping wood and a sudden curse as a board in the short porch gave way under Billy's weight. He quickly extracted himself and began his trot up the hill to bring the horses down.

Joe looked at Emma sheepishly and said, "I'm sorry if he learned that language from me, ma'am."

Emma shook her head and said, "No, he probably learned it from me."

"You, ma'am?" he asked.

"Me, sir. I can be downright ornery if it suits me."

"Remind me never to get you ornery then, ma'am. I told the other ladies that I need everyone to take what they want to bring back and I'll harness the last wagon. I intend to burn this town to the ground before we leave."

Emma nodded then replied, "Can we each set a building on fire, Sheriff Joe?"

Joe smiled and said, "It's your right, ma'am."

Emma smiled back and then guided her daughters down the hallway and up the stairs. Joe then took the four gunbelts and carried them out to the front porch and returned for the bags of food and the heavy utensils bag. There were four heavy bags and he figured that would be plenty for the two-day trip.

Then he returned to all of the bedrooms and collected four Winchester '73s and three more boxes of ammunition and brought them out front. Once they were all there, he left the boarding house and trotted across the street to the livery and began to harness the last wagon.

By the time he had it ready to go, Billy was riding into town on Irish and trailing Boomer and the spare horse carrying the added rifles. Joe waved him over.

"Billy, we're going to get this wagon loaded, but first, let's get these horses saddled and then hitched to the back of the wagon. Okay?"

"Yes, sir," Billy said as he slipped from his horse and led him to the wagon and temporarily hitched him to the right rear wheel.

Then he and Joe began saddling six of the horses using all of the remaining tack. Then they fashioned a really long trail rope for the remaining twelve horses.

"Those boys stole a lot of horseflesh, Billy," Joe said as they finished the job and attached the six saddled horses and the dozen barebacked horses to the back of the wagon.

Joe then hopped up into the driver's seat and flicked the reins after releasing the brake.

The wagon rolled quickly across the street and Joe parked it in front of the boarding house where all nine freed captives awaited with more burlap sacks full of their clothes near their feet.

"Okay, ladies, we'll load the wagon and then, anyone who wants to burn a building down will have the privilege."

Emma hadn't told any of them and there were squeals of delight from the girls and their mothers as Joe began loading the wagon. Once that was done, Joe waved Billy over again and said, "Just for your information, Billy, I went through their pockets and here's what all four of them had."

He dumped the money into Billy's palm and he quickly counted the bills and silver.

"There's only seven dollars and forty-five cents here, Joe, and that was from four of them?"

"Yup. Now, let's get this wagon and horse parade away from town before we put a match to it," then glanced at the women and said, "Ladies, we'll be right back."

"Okay, Joe!" Billy said with a grin as the wagon began to roll.

After a half a mile, Joe stopped the wagon, set the handbrake and stepped down, walked to Boomer and pulled a box of lucifers from his saddlebag. After Billy had secured his horse to the wagon wheel again, Joe and Billy began trotting back to the boarding house.

When they arrived, Joe said, "Ladies, let's go into the boarding house and find every kerosene lamp you can. Don't do anything yet, though."

With that the excited women all rushed into the house and spread out, snatching lamps and returning to the porch. It took three minutes for each of them to be armed with a potential Molotov cocktail.

"Okay, now, I'll give you each a couple of matches and then just pick out a building and dump some of the kerosene on the floor just inside the building. Then wait until I fire a pistol shot. I don't want any one building going off too quickly because they'll burn faster than you can imagine. Don't tarry, either. Once you see that kerosene catch, turn and get out of there and come here. Okay?"

There was a cacophony of 'okays', then Joe said, "Okay, ladies. Let's turn this town into hell," as he began distributing matches.

The ladies having made their building choices while they were waiting for Joe and Billy to return hustled away to their assignments while Joe and Billy watched.

"They don't seem too upset, Joe. Even Annie and Mary seemed okay," Billy said as he watched.

"That's just because they're excited about being free and getting to exercise some form of revenge. It'll catch up with them soon, Billy. I hope the three mothers are up to it when their daughters come back to earth."

"My mother is really a strong woman, Joe. I think she was stronger than my father. Not in his muscles, but you know, how she acted."

Joe nodded and replied, "That was my impression of her, Billy."

Joe pulled his right-hand pistol again when he was sure that all of the women had splattered the floors with kerosene. Most were still visible in the doorways, including Emma, who had been given the honor of burning down the hated boarding house with its four bodies.

He raised the Smith & Wesson, pointed it south and pulled the trigger, quickly holstering the weapon and scanning the doorways as the women began to race out of their buildings.

Emma was first out as she was so close, but soon all nine were jogging towards them with their skirts lifted and smoke already spiraling out of the doorways.

"Let's walk quickly but carefully to the wagons, ladies!" he shouted.

They all formed a gaggle and began walking to the wagon, but still glancing back at the rapidly growing flames. Normally, the sight of a fire strikes terror in the hearts of ranch and farm families, but not this time.

By the time they reached the wagon, and could all turn to watch, the flames were roaring into the air and smoke was clawing for the sky.

Joe and Billy then handed out the four canteens and let the women drink as they all stood mesmerized by the inferno.

There were no more individual building fires any longer as the flames had merged into one giant conflagration. Joe was in awe of the power of the mammoth blaze himself. Saying you were going to burn a town and witnessing it were two totally different things.

"We've got to get moving now, ladies. Billy will escort you back the way you came. Do any of you know how to shoot a Winchester?" Joe asked.

Emma replied, “I can.”

Jennie then said, “I’ve only fired a shotgun, but Emma can probably show me.”

“Where are you going?” asked Sarah Foster.

“I’ve got to chase down those men before they do any more damage. I know they’re planning on getting some hay and that probably means the McClellan farm. They’ve got a two-hour head start, but they’re pulling those wagons, so I might get there in time if I move fast.”

“But what if they find us?” asked Jennie Riley.

“You’ll be going in the opposite direction. I’ll be between your wagon and them.”

Then Billy asked, “Do I just follow their trail out of here, Joe?”

“Exactly. Even if they tried to follow you, they wouldn’t be sure. I’ll keep them off your trail, though. Now, when you reach that cutoff, keep going on to Mrs. Hobson’s ranch. I should be back in a couple of days. I think you’re better off there until this all settles down. Ben Hobson is there and with the firepower you’ll have, even if they swung in a big loop, you’d be able to hold them off until help arrives.”

Sarah Foster was growing concerned and asked, “What help?”

Joe simply replied, “Me.”

He then walked to his armory horse, pulled the two Winchester ‘73s and set them into the wagon with the other four repeaters and four handguns. Then he removed two of his gunbelts and set them inside along with two boxes of .44 cartridges which gave them five boxes of ammunition.

“Those cartridges will fit any of these pistols, too. Billy can give you quick instructions on the way to the Hobsons. One caution: when you stop for the night, don't build a campfire. You'll be announcing your presence to anyone within ten miles."

Then he turned to Billy and asked, "Did you get all that, Billy?"

Billy nodded.

Emma walked over and said, "We can do this, sheriff."

"Call me Joe, ma'am. You've surely earned the right to do that, too."

Emma smiled and said, "I'm Emma," then asked, "Is Billy in charge?"

Joe glanced over at Billy and said, "I don't believe so. I'm pretty sure you are."

Emma looked at her son and replied, "Maybe. You've changed him, Joe."

Joe had untied Boomer's reins from Billy's Irish and said, "He's done a lot of growing up these past few days, Emma," then walked to the ammunition horse, removed the Sharps and the ammunition saddlebags and exchanged the sawed-off shotgun for the Sharps in Boomer's second scabbard. Then he unloaded the boxes of shotgun shells from the saddlebags and laid them on the wagon bed.

After switching the lightened armory horse's reins to the trail rope, he stepped up on Boomer and said, "I'll see you ladies when I finish with those men."

Emma then said, "Joe, I heard them talking and I'm pretty sure that they're going to split up and one group is going to go and get some whiskey and beer down at the agency store."

Joe grinned and said, "Emma, now I know where Billy gets his memory for details. That's a very good piece of information. It'll make my job easier. Thank you."

Emma smiled back as Joe then set off on Boomer at a fast trot heading south.

All the women watched him ride off in a cloud of dust before Emma turned and said, “I’m going to ride one of the horses. If anyone else wants to ride a horse rather than a wagon, feel free, but we’ve got to get moving.”

Both Annie and Mary opted to ride in saddles and so did Katie Foster, the oldest of the girls, but the others all climbed into the wagon. Emma grabbed a Winchester and handed one to each of the other riding women and then she even took a gunbelt and strapped it around her waist before climbing on board the armory horse, her skirt riding up to mid-thigh. Propriety be damned, she thought. Annie and Mary each selected one of their ranch’s horses and Katie chose one of the Foster ranch’s horses, all conveniently saddled by Joe and Ben. Like Emma, the bare-legged young women didn’t care. Billy was only startled by Katie’s bare legs. His mother and sisters were, well, different.

Once everyone was situated, Sarah climbed into the driver’s seat of the wagon and the liberated convoy began rolling back west along the trail.

———

Joe guessed he was only about ten miles behind the twelve men and the two wagons. He was already trying to figure out a way to get into an advantageous position and hoped that Emma Harper was right about them splitting into two groups.

The McClellan farm was about fifteen miles southeast of the burning town, so they wouldn’t reach it for about an hour, so he might make it in time, hopefully after the first group had already split off to get their alcohol.

As he rode, he glanced behind him at the large clouds of smoke rising into the air like a giant smoke signal letting everyone know that Cooperstown didn’t exist any longer. He wondered if they’d see it and turn back.

Eleven miles ahead of a rapidly closing Sheriff Joe Brooks, the two groups had already split up as the trail to the Indian agency had already veered off to the southwest.

"It looks like Pierre was off about where that agency was," Hanger Bob said loudly to Charlie Smith over the combined noises of the wagon and the horse hooves.

"It don't matter, Bob. We're gonna get us enough booze to party for days before the next job," Charlie shouted back as they continued to separate from the crew heading for the McClellan ranch.

"Did you see the cattle ranch when we passed it by?"

"Yeah, I seen it. I hope the plan to get the cattle comes off as easy as it sounded."

"It'll be fine, Charlie. Don't worry so much!" Bob Jones shouted as he grinned.

His group was moving as fast as they could, all of them anticipating some beer at least when they reached the agency in a couple of hours.

"What do you think it is?" David McClellan asked his father, Al, as they both looked north.

"Looks like a forest fire," Al replied, "but it sure is blazing away in one spot."

"Isn't that where Cooperstown was?" David asked.

"Sure is. I wonder if those old, dried-up wood buildings finally caught fire. It wouldn't take much."

"What do you think, John?" he asked his older brother.

"I still think it's just a forest fire. Probably some prospector didn't douse his campfire well enough."

Their youngest brother, Ted, said, "I think Dave's right. I think it's that old town goin' up in flames."

"Well, either way, boys, we need to keep our eyes on it to make sure it doesn't spread to the hay. That would ruin us."

"Aw, Pa, that thing is miles away," said Ted.

"You've never seen a big forest fire, son. If it's a forest fire, it could be here in a couple of hours."

"We should get the rifles, Papa," said John, "if it's a forest fire, those antelope, deer and bears are going to be headin' this way."

"That's a good idea, John. Let's go and get the Winchesters just to be safe," Al said as they all began to walk to the house.

"I don't want to face no angry bear, Papa," Ted said as they crossed the back yard.

"Those .44s might just make him even angrier," joked David as they trotted up onto the back porch.

———

The crew assigned to take the McClellan ranch numbered eight of the twelve men, not six. The other four, including the three leaders, were all they needed to get the booze. Besides, they're the ones that had the gang's money, meaning that Hanger Bob had all of the gang's cash.

They were all jealous of Hank Anderson, who got to drive the wagon to the agency store.

"How much further, do you reckon?" asked Willie Gray.

"About another hour at this pace," shouted back Jean Martin.

None of them bothered looking behind them at the clouds of billowing smoke. Soon, though, the smell of the large fire would reach their nostrils. The only questions would be if they noticed it before they reached the McClellan farm and what would they do if they figured out that their hideout was gone.

———

"Lunch isn't for another hour, boys," Sadie McClellan said as she watched the small army of McClellan men enter her kitchen.

"I know, Sadie, but there's a big fire up north and we're picking up the Winchesters in case it heads this way and spooks a forest-full of critters into flight."

"A forest fire?" Gertie McClellan asked as she kneaded some dough.

"I think it's Cooperstown that's ablaze," said Ted said to his younger sister.

"The town is burning?" asked his mother.

"Either way," Al said, "we've got to get ready. After we get our repeaters, we'll get back to work for that hour then come back and eat you out of house and home."

Sadie laughed and said, "As you always do. I don't know how we keep any food in the larder."

Al smiled at his wife as they walked to the front of the house and began removing the Winchesters from the gun rack. They exited the house from the front door and headed back to the barn, all of their heads facing north to monitor the fire.

———

Joe had closed the gap to just three miles as he and Boomer moved at a fast trot and figured he'd be seeing the wagon soon. He knew it was only one wagon when he had spotted the second wagon's tracks peel off to the right following the trail to the Shoshone Indian store. The store was oddly placed on the reservation, as it was on a finger that jutted south, making it the most inconvenient location for the Shoshone but the best spot for the Indian agent.

They weren't supposed to sell booze at all, but everyone knew they did, even the government. Because it was on the reservation, it was out of his jurisdiction, but he wished he had the authority to shut that part of their operation down.

But today, it had to be about stopping the gang from committing another murder.

He'd passed the Larsen ranch, and had spotted their two hands out working in the pastures but didn't want to spend the time telling them of the danger because they had been bypassed and he didn't believe anyone would be returning this way. Besides, even a few minutes could make the difference.

He passed a long curve and spotted the wagon and riders in the distance, less than three miles ahead, and they were almost to the McClellan ranch, so he kicked Boomer into a canter and pulled the Sharps, checking its load as he trotted along. The Winchester had a bigger powder load, but the bullet was heavier than the Sharps round nor did it have the barrel length, so its range wasn't as far. He knew the Sharps could reach out and kill at more than six hundred yards, but his Winchester was probably only a killer at three or four hundred yards. He wanted that extra distance for at least one shot, then he'd switch to his repeater.

———

"That doesn't look like a herd of antelope comin', Pa." John said as he spotted the dust cloud of the seven riders and the wagon off to the north.

Al McClellan looked in the direction that his oldest son was looking and said, "No, it looks like a bunch of riders. I'm glad we've got these rifles, John. Let's all get into good positions while I warn your mother and sister."

"Okay, Pa," John said as he trotted to tell his brothers who were moving bales of hay.

Al trotted across the back yard and stuck his head into the kitchen, yelling, "Sadie, we've got a large group of riders comin' in. I need you and Gertie to get into the storm seller right now and take the shotgun with you. Change the birdshot shells to buckshot when you're in there. Go!"

Sadie had been through the drill before and quickly trotted to the front of the house, grabbed the family shotgun from the rack and then opened the box of buckshot shells, pulled two out and then jogged back into the kitchen where Gertie awaited.

Al was long gone to get into a defensive position while Sadie and Gertie left the house, crossed the fifty yards to the storm cellar, opened the big doors and stepped down into the darkness, closing the doors behind her. She and Gertie both sat on crude chairs in the back of the storm cellar as she swapped out the two birdshot shells for the two buckshot shells by touch.

———

Willie Gray spotted the farmhouse and barn and shouted, "There it is, boys! Another mile or so ahead!"

Lou Brown stared at the farm in the distance and shouted back, "It sure seems mighty quiet, Willie!"

"So, what? They're sodbusters. They ain't gonna be shootin' at us even if they see us. They're gonna be quakin' in their sodbuster shoes and peein' all over themselves," Willie yelled and followed it with a surprisingly high-pitched laugh.

———

Joe was close enough to be able to count the men when he momentarily pulled up and used his field glasses. Eight, including the wagon driver. That meant there were four taking the other wagon. He didn't see Hanger Bob Jones in that group ahead either. He guessed that the three leaders would nominate themselves for the booze run and leave the dangerous work to their minions.

He slipped his field glasses back into his saddlebags and resumed the canter as he held the Sharps in his left hand.

Fifteen miles northwest of Joe, the wagonload of women led by Billy and his mother was making better-than-expected progress due to the light load in the wagon.

"Billy," Emma asked, "were you and the sheriff watching the boarding house yesterday?"

Billy looked over at his mother and replied, "How did you know, Mama? We arrived the afternoon and me and Joe were watching. Joe said that he was sure that the gang would leave to go and get more supplies and we'd just watch until they left."

Emma said, "I don't know how I knew, Billy. I just felt like he was watching. I felt it deep in my bones. I was so sure of it that it gave me hope that we'd all soon be rescued, even though there were sixteen of those men."

Billy then asked, "How are you doing, Mama? Joe told me what had happened to Annie and Mary and the others. It made me really angry, but sad, too. He said that you and the other women would be okay for a little while because you were all so happy about getting free of the place, but that you'd all be really upset and sad when that feeling passed. Are you okay, Mama?"

Emma sighed and replied, "He said all that? Well, he's got the right of it. I'm a hard woman, Billy. You know that. I'd already resigned to what they'd do to me and because I was married to your father for so long, I knew I could weather it. It wasn't pleasant, I can assure you, but I'll be all right. I'll need to spend a lot of time with your sisters, just like Mrs. Foster and Mrs. Riley will have to spend with their girls. The rapes were bad enough, but now they'll all be worried about becoming pregnant with babies produced by those monsters."

“That’s what Joe said, too. Can I help, Mama?”

Emma smiled at her son and said, “You’ve already helped more than you can imagine just by living, Billy. When Joe told me that his backup man was named Billy, I thought I was ready to explode. Why did you come along?”

“I told the sheriff that I was going to follow him anyway, but I don’t think he believed it. He just seems to like me.”

“Well, I’m very happy that he did. We’ll need to think of what to do now, Billy, but we’ll talk about that later.”

Billy swallowed and asked, “Why don’t you marry Sheriff Joe, Mama?”

Emma was startled by the question and asked, “What gave you that idea, Billy? I’ve only been a widow for three days.”

“I don’t know. I really like Joe and I really like you too, Mama. You’re both so much alike, too, even more than you and papa were.”

Emma replied, “I’ll give you that. Your father always thought I was too mannish in many of my ways. I guess it’s because I’m such a hard woman.”

“Then why did papa marry you, Mama?” he asked.

Emma looked over at Billy and said, “It’s a long story, Billy. I’ll tell you about it soon. Okay?”

Billy said, “Okay,” then paused before adding, “I think you’re still pretty, Mama. Joe does, too. He said you were a very handsome woman.”

Emma laughed and said, “Maybe the sheriff needs to start wearing spectacles.”

“I don’t think so, Mama. He has really good eyes. He even spotted things before I did.”

Emma just shook her head and let the subject drop as they continued southwest.

"There are eight of 'em, including the wagon driver, Pa!" shouted John from his place behind the open barn door.

"I don't recognize any of them and they've already got those Winchesters pulled, so keep an eye on them and wait until I fire, all of you!" Al shouted back.

"Okay, Pa," came from different locations and different sons as they all waited for the riders to either pass or turn into the farm's access road.

"Did you hear some shoutin'?" asked Sorry Ferguson as he rode next to Willie Gray.

"I heard it. I don't see anybody, though, and that makes me nervous," replied Willie.

Then he turned to the riders and shouted, "Boys, those sodbusters might be waitin' for us. When we turn down the access road, spread out and be ready for gunfire. They can't shoot straight and they're probably already sittin' in their own pee, but they might get lucky, so don't ride straight at 'em, and fire at their smoke to keep their heads down."

"Okay, Willie!" shouted Black Fang, who was on the wagon, "I'm gonna leave the wagon at the end of the access road, grab my rifle and follow on foot!"

Willie waved acknowledgement as they drew within a half a mile of the access road, having never noticed Sheriff Joe just a few hundred yards back on his big gelding.

Behind them, Joe was close enough to hear their shouted conversation. He was already within range of the Sharps but wanted to get as close as he could. He was glad to hear that the McClellans were ready for the gang. It would make his job easier, so he slowed Boomer to a medium trot and took the Sharp in both hands, guiding his big gray with his legs.

———

Al didn't have to shout a warning to his sons that the riders had turned toward the farm house and were headed straight at them. He also knew that the outlaws would spot either him or one of his sons soon and probably had heard their shouts when they were a half a mile away, but it didn't matter now. He was going to protect his family and his farm.

———

Willie gave the sign to spread out and the seven riders split apart making a wide front as they all cocked their Winchesters and began to swerve left and right but still heading for the farm house, scanning for the armed farmers they knew were there.

Al waited behind the barn, his head halfway out, but motionless as he watched the men approaching. He had already cocked his repeater and wanted to let them get within range. He probably wouldn't hit any of them, but he wanted to keep them away or get them to dismount.

He suddenly popped out from behind the barn and fired at the closest rider, Barney Thomas, at one hundred and twenty yards. Then, all hell broke loose.

His boys all fired from their protected location and the seven riders all returned fire, but no one was hit in that first volley.

Black Fang had pulled the hand brake on the wagon and then stood, grabbed his Winchester and was preparing to step onto the ground when he suddenly lurched backwards and fell back to the wagon seat before a loud boom crashed across the ground announcing the massive Sharps round's arrival. The big bullet had punched into his chest and mangled his left lung and heart, killing him quickly.

Joe slammed his Sharps into the scabbard and yanked out his Winchester '76, cocking the hammer as he kicked Boomer up to a canter again.

———

The four McClellans, who were looking that way, had all seen the driver stand and suddenly fall backwards. They all also heard the very different report of a long gun and knew that they had help in the rear of the seven riders.

Most of the riders had heard the loud boom as well and several swiveled in their saddles, spotting the telltale sign of gunsmoke a quarter of a mile from the access road and then the rider racing down the road with a Winchester in his hands.

"Willie! We got company behind us!" shouted Lou Brown.

Willie then turned, spotted Joe as he turned onto the access road just a hundred and fifty yards at their backs and shouted, "You and me, Lou! The rest of you get those farmers!"

Lou wheeled his horse in a wide turn, almost colliding with Henry Pleasant before he was headed back towards Joe.

Willie went the other direction and soon both he and Lou were closing the gap between them and the oncoming lawman. They both began firing their rifles at a hundred yards.

But Joe had brought Boomer to a dust-cloud-creating stop to give himself a steady platform and took aim at Willie Gray. He squeezed off a shot even as one of their first .44s buzzed past his head.

His .50 caliber heavy round crossed the now eighty yards in a small fraction of a second catching Willie flush in the center of his chest, knocking him over the horse's rump in a back flip. He bounced twice and laid in his own dust cloud while Lou continued to fire, and Joe levered in a second round.

The distance was less than sixty yards when Joe squeezed his trigger a second time, having lost his hat to Lou's third shot. His second .50 caliber round hit Lou Brown in almost exactly the same spot that his first round had struck Willie with the same results. Over the back of his horse went Lou, and he crashed into the dirt.

Joe then nudged Boomer forward and began to fire at the other riders. He didn't do anything like shout warnings or even worry about shooting them in the back. They all knew he was there and knew he was carrying a badge. It was warning enough.

Al and his sons continued to rain .44s at the five remaining riders, and the next casualty was John McClellan, who took a .44 in his left arm that had ripped through the barn door. He dropped his rifle and then himself to the ground, grabbing at his bleeding upper arm.

The next victim wasn't as fortunate as Sorry Ferguson was drilled high in the upper right side of his back by one of Joe's .50 caliber chunks of lead, knocking him from his horse, but not killing him, until he landed awkwardly on the hard ground and snapped his neck.

That left four attackers and four defenders, and the odds had suddenly shifted dramatically against the attackers as they had a good shooter at their backs.

"Let's get outta here!" screamed Henry Pleasant to his three fellow outlaws.

"Head north to those trees!" shouted Barney Thomas.

All four riders suddenly veered northward and hunkered down over their horses' necks to avoid being hit. The trees were more than a half a mile away as they began their run to safety. It wasn't soon enough for Claude Nevers, who was hit by a .44 caliber round fired by Al McClellan as he was in the middle of his turn. Al's shot struck him on the left side of his chest and punched into his left lung after pulverizing his sixth rib. The bullet lodged inside Claude who remained hunched over his horse's mane while he began spitting blood across the horse's neck.

Joe turned Boomer and urged him forward to close the gap to the three escaping killers. He wanted them all.

He snapped off two shots at the biggest man, Henry Pleasant, who was also in the lead. If he'd been firing a Winchester '73, he would have wounded Henry, but at six feet and four inches and almost three hundred pounds, it wouldn't have come close to killing him. But the power of the .50-95 Express cartridge was not to be denied. His first slug missed high, but his second round caught Henry under his exposed left armpit and rammed into the lower half of his neck, causing massive damage that even Henry's huge size couldn't ignore. Unlike the still-riding Claude Nevers, Henry simply slipped off the right side of his horse and tumbled to the ground, rolling several times before coming to a motionless stop.

Joe didn't know that Claude had been hit and was targeting Claude for a shot when Claude mimicked Henry's slow roll from his horse and was dead when he crashed to the ground.

That left two men running for their lives from Joe's rifle.

Jean Martin and Barney Thomas were all that remained of the eight men sent to liberate the McClellan hay and women, and all they wanted now was to reach the safety of the trees just two hundred yards away.

Joe knew they intended to make the trees and that they'd be difficult to root out of there, so he did the unthinkable and aimed at their horses.

His first shot smacked into Barney's horse's rump, sending him down in a large cloud of dust, and throwing Barney from the saddle. Barney was still rolling when Joe fired his second round at Jean Martin's horse, but missed the horse entirely, catching Jean Martin low in the back, just above the saddle's cantle. The massive round smashed into his sacrum shattering the bones before it lodged in his bladder. Jean screamed and fell from his horse, bouncing several times, but still alive and wishing he wasn't because of the excruciating pain.

Joe then had to turn to see where Barney Thomas was, knowing he had only hit the man's horse.

Barney had regained his feet and was scrambling to pick up his fallen rifle to fire at the lawman.

Joe spotted him and didn't waste any lung power to shout a warning, but simply plugged him with one last round from his Winchester at forty yards. It wasn't very pretty or very nice, but Barney Thomas never got to protest as the round almost severed his head from his shoulders when it blew through his neck.

The huge cloud of gunsmoke wafted over the McClellan farm as Joe trotted Boomer over to a sobbing, moaning Jean Martin, who didn't care about Joe's approach at all. He just wanted to die.

Joe slid his Winchester back into the scabbard and walked Boomer close to Jean, dismounted and looked down at the heavily bleeding man.

"You're almost dead, mister. You one of Pierre's boys?"

Jean grimaced and replied, "I'm Jean Martin, I rode with Pierre for four years until he joined up with that bastard Hanger Bob. Now let me confess my sins so I can go to heaven. I beg you."

"I'm not a priest, Jean. You'll go where you deserve."

"But I can confess to you and you can tell a priest to give me absolution. Please!"

"I might do it if you hadn't hurt all those women, Jean. Now, I'm afraid, I'm not going to give you that chance at redemption. You don't deserve it."

Joe then pulled his Smith & Wesson, cocked the hammer and fired, putting Jean out of his misery and into eternal damnation. He then walked over to Barney Thomas's horse, apologized for shooting him and then gave him relief from his suffering with another gunshot.

He blew out his breath and slid his pistol back into the holster, flipped over the hammer loop and mounted Boomer, wheeled him back to the farm house and set him at a medium trot.

Al, David and Ted were all helping John with his wound when Joe arrived and stepped down.

"Al, sorry I was so late, but I just got here from Cooperstown. These bastards and the rest of their gangs raided three ranches west of here and killed all the men and stole all the women and took their household stuff and food. We got the women free and sent them on their way and I tracked this bunch. They were planning on stealing your hay and your wife and daughter after they killed you. Glad to see you were ready for them."

Al McClellan stood and shook Joe's hand, saying, "God bless you, Sheriff Joe. I thought we were all going to die from that crowd. We're not as good with these rifles as we should be. The only damage we received was when John took a round in his left arm, but he'll be all right. I can't thank you enough."

Joe smiled and said, "I'm glad to help, Al. I'll retrieve all those bodies and then I've got to run down the last four, which includes the three gang leaders. They're on their way to the Shoshone Indian agency store to buy some liquor. I need to stop them, too."

"We'll take care of the bodies, sheriff. You go and get the last four of those bastards."

"I'll have to return to collect the horses, weapons, and the wagon belongs to either the Fosters, the Rileys or the Harpers. The last four have the last wagon they stole."

"We'll hang onto the wagon, guns and the horses for you, but we'll burn those damned bodies."

Joe nodded then looked north and said, "We burned Cooperstown to the ground, so they wouldn't be able to go back. I let the women each burn a building in retribution for what those sons of bitches did to them."

Al replied, "It's not enough, but it's a start. I've got to go and tell Sadie and Gertie it's safe to come out now. You need to water and feed your horse before you go, Sheriff. It's another ten miles to the agency."

"I appreciate it, Al. I'll do just that."

Al waved and began trotting to the storm cellar as Joe led Boomer to the trough and let him drink. Only four left, he thought. That's almost even odds now, and they didn't know he was behind them.

While Boomer was chowing down on some hay, Al walked over with Sadie and Gertie.

"Sheriff, I told my wife and daughter what you had told me about those gangs, and they wanted to thank you for keeping them safe."

"You kept them away, Al. I just cleaned up the mess," Joe said as Sadie and Gertie both walked up to him.

The two women both kissed him on opposite sides of his face and then stepped back.

"Thank you, Sheriff Joe. Don't ever stop doing what you do for us," Sadie said.

Joe just smiled and said, "You're welcome, ma'am," then mounted Boomer and wheeled him back to the west, waved and trotted off to hunt down the last four.

The wagon was pulling into the Indian agency store as Joe was leaving the access road of the McClellan farm.

"You see all that smoke, Bob?" asked Charlie Smith.

"Can't miss it with that smell. What do you reckon? Forest fire?" Bob asked.

"Nope, I think Lawless is goin' up in smoke," replied Charlie calmly.

Hanger Bob's eyes blew open as he exclaimed, "*The town? Why would you think that?*"

"It's not spreading like a forest fire. It's all in one spot and it's the same direction as the town. I think one of those damned women started a fire in that boardinghouse kitchen and it spread like crazy through those old buildings."

"Why didn't you say anything?" Bob demanded.

Charlie shrugged and said, "It didn't matter if I did. I think the boys who were guarding them women are all dead, and I ain't sure about the eight we sent to the McClellan farm either."

That really startled Bob who almost shouted, "Why the hell would you think that?"

"Didn't you hear all the gunfire? It started with a loud report. Sounded like a Sharps or a Spencer. Then there was a lot of shooting, including some heavy loads that kept going to the end. Now, all of our boys had Winchesters, and the last shot was from a heavier rifle, so I don't think they'll be comin' back."

"How could you hear that? I didn't hear anything."

"You kept riding. Remember when I stopped for a few minutes and dropped back? It's because I was hearin' that gunfire. I think the McClellan's were ready for 'em. Probably saw that smoke and figured somethin' was comin' their way."

Bill shook his head and said, "Well, that's a fine how do you do! You're tellin' me that you think it's just the four of us now?"

Charlie just shrugged and answered, "Yup."

"Then what the hell do we do?" asked an exasperated Hanger Bob.

"For starters, we pick up supplies and our stuff and head for one of those empty ranches west of here. If I'm wrong about them all bein' dead, the others will figure it out and follow our trail."

Hanger Bob mulled it over and then said, "Let's get in there and get our stuff before we figure out what to do."

Charlie just grunted as they slowed to a stop and the three mounted men stepped down while Hank Anderson set the handbrake on the wagon and bounded out onto the ground. The four men then sauntered into the agency store.

They spotted Mort Forrest, the Indian agent behind the counter and walked his way.

"What can I do for you fellers?" he asked jovially.

"We need a few kegs of beer and a couple of cases of whiskey for starters and we'll be picking up some flour, sugar, coffee and other supplies, too."

Mort grinned and said, "I'll get the beer and whiskey from the back, but you can go and pick out what you need."

The four men then began wandering the store, picking over the stock.

"Look at this stuff," Charlie said to Bob, "no wonder the Indians hate white men. I wouldn't feed this to a hog."

"Yeah, but the tins of food are okay, Charlie. Let's pick up some of those."

So, they began loading up on beans, canned beef and potatoes and just about anything that couldn't be screwed up, but they still added two bags of flour, sugar and coffee.

When they brought their things to the front counter, Mort had rolled out the second barrel of beer and set it next to the two cases of whiskey.

"That whiskey the good stuff? I don't want any of that homebrew or watered-down stuff you sell to the Injuns," asked Bob.

"No, no, of course not. This is all bottled liquor," Mort said.

"How much do we owe you?" Bob asked as he reached in his pocket.

Mort began adding up the total and finally said, "One hundred and forty-two dollars."

Bill yanked his hand from his pocket and asked, "What did you say? This stuff shouldn't even be forty-two dollars. You can forget the hundred."

"I have costs, you know. Just shipping that stuff in here costs me and the liquor I have to pay a premium for because I'm not supposed to even have it."

"That's your problem, mister," Bob said as he tossed two twenty-dollar bills onto the counter, "that's all you're gettin' out of us."

Mort looked at the bills. He'd still be making money on the sale, but not his usual profit margin. It was a matter of principle to the unscrupulous Indian agent.

"Sorry, mister. You may as well just leave empty handed. That's not enough," Mort said as he pushed the two bills back to Bob.

Bill was about to object when Mort's face just vaporized in a cloud of blood three feet before him accompanied by a loud roar.

"Jesus!" Bob shouted as Mort fell over backwards and Charlie lowered his smoking Colt.

“I hate damned Indian agents, and this one was worse than most. Let’s get our stuff and anything else we want,” he said as he slipped his pistol back into his holster.

With the sudden option of stores available for the taking, the four men went on a shopping spree, carrying out boxes, cans and sacks to the wagon. The two cases of whiskey and the two barrels of beer were augmented by two more barrels and four more cases, emptying the store of its alcohol stock and overloading the standard ranch wagon. A freight wagon could have handled the load, but not a more lightly constructed wagon meant for use around a ranch or a farm.

“What do we do now,” asked Pierre Le Tour, as he lugged a sack of sugar to the wagon, “this will get the army and the U.S. Marshal’s office after us.”

“We’ll worry about that later. Let’s head for that ranch now.”

Twenty minutes after murdering Mort Forrest, the heavily laden wagon pulled out of the store as they headed due west using a terrible excuse for a trail.

Joe was still six miles out of the agency store and examining his bullet-holed hat. He’d buy another one back in Lander. This one was already eleven-years old anyway, but it sure was comfortable, he thought as he pulled it back on his head.

He could smell the smoke from Cooperstown in the breeze and hoped it hadn’t spread to the trees. He didn’t think it had because the smoke was still in one location and there was a good quarter of a mile of open ground around the abandoned town to the nearest group of trees, and they were on that hill.

He had already filled the magazine tube in his Winchester, so he’d have the maximum firepower available when he ran into the four men. He considered himself very fortunate to escape so far without a scratch and knew that it was as much a result of surprise as any skill on his part. The boys in the boarding house weren’t even looking for the law to make an appearance, and he was able to get really close behind the other eight at the McClellan ranch. They all just seemed so sure that no one would bother them simply because they had so many guns. Joe figured they would have been better off staying with their individual smaller gangs. At least then, they'd be more alert to possible pursuit. He just hoped that his luck held with the last four.

He also was very grateful for Billy Harper's cool thinking and notifying him of the attack on his ranch so quickly. If Billy hadn't arrived, it would have been days before anyone knew of the horrifying events at the three ranches. The gangs hadn't expected him because they thought that the law wouldn't have discovered their invasion for up to a week. Billy Harper had changed all that.

———

"Son of a bitch!" shouted Hanger Bob as he looked under the wagon at the split axle, "who doesn't carry a spare axle on these damned things?"

Charlie calmly replied, "They probably have one in the barn but don't put it on there because of the added weight for local jobs."

Bill looked up and snarled, "What are you, a teamster? What do we do with this broken piece of crap?"

Pierre said, "We'll take some of the supplies with us and leave it here. If we have time, we come back with the spare axle and fix it."

Bill stood up straight and said, "Alright. Let's grab what we can. I figure each of us can take a couple of bottles. Who wants a beer before we go?"

They all laughed and surrounded the wagon and began to yank supplies out to get to the liquor. When they reached the kegs of beer, each of them emptied their canteens of water, and after Hank Anderson smacked the end open with the butt end of his Winchester, they all dipped their canteens into the barrel and began to guzzle the surprisingly good beer. It was even moderately cold.

———

Thirty minutes later, Joe was in the agency store and looking down at the body of Mort Forrest.

He then walked to the back of the store and looked for the agency's telegraph machine. Joe didn't have a great hand at the key, but it was good enough.

He found the telegraph setup and flipped the switch to engage the batteries. Then he sat down and began to send a message to the station in Lander.

———

The Lander operator, Jim Swinton, heard the message coming across and immediately knew it wasn't a Western Union operator. He listened to the code and his eyebrows shot up as he quickly began to write down the message.

He kept writing as the key kept clacking. It wasn't the best form, but he knew who was sending it after the first sentence and thought that Sheriff Joe was doing pretty well for a lawman.

He was astounded as the message continued and Jim had to start on a second sheet. If the sheriff had to pay for this one, it would cost five dollars or more.

Joe's slow hand resulted in a five-minute-long message that would have taken a minute for a practiced hand, but it was still a very long message. Actually, it was two messages. One to his office here and the second to the army at Fort Steele. Finally, Jim heard the end of message from Joe and sent an acknowledgement, along with a sincere, GOOD LUCK.

———

Joe sat back, turned off the batteries and stepped out into the store as a group of Shoshones entered the store and noticed the dead Indian agent and the badged man leaving the back office.

"We did not do this thing!" Wild Bear shouted as Joe spotted him.

"I know. The men I'm trailing did this thing. I just notified the army that the Indian agent was murdered by the Hanger Bob gang and they had cleaned out the store of its supplies. I think you and your people should keep me from being called a liar by the government and empty this place. Would you do that for me?" Joe asked.

Wild Bear grinned and said, "We will keep your bosses happy with you, Sheriff, and do as you ask. What can we do with the body of the agency man?"

"Whatever you want. I'd bury him because he'll stink up the supplies soon, but burning isn't a bad idea either," he replied as he stepped around the counter.

"As for me, I need to grab a few things. I hadn't planned on staying out overnight," Joe said.

"I see a big fire up north. It is the dead town that was there."

"We burned it to the ground because the gang was using it as their hiding spot. Twelve of them are now dead. I'm chasing the last four now," Joe said as he grabbed a big sack and began to fill it with supplies. He added a few tin cups and plates, some tin cutlery, coffee, a slab of bacon and a few cans of beans. Why he had taken so many cups, plate, forks and spoons was beyond him, but he finally tossed in a new coffeepot, closed the bag, saluted the Shoshones as he trotted out of the agency and climbed up on Boomer.

———

The four riders, one bareback on one of the wagon pullers, had abandoned the wagon as Joe was sending his message. Free of the slow-moving vehicle, they were able to put some good distance between them and the man trying to kill them all. They may not have been aware of his presence, but the killing of the government man at the agency had them all a bit more nervous now, as did the possible loss of the rest of the gang.

"What about the other men, Bob?" asked Hank as they rode at a medium trot.

"Screw 'em!" Bob shouted back, "they're on their own, unless Charlie's right and they're all dead. If he's wrong, they'll find us. I think we might have to start worryin' about the law now. There's only four of us and that dead Indian agent is gonna be found sooner than those dead ranchers."

"I know," yelled Pierre, "I think we need to keep our eyes open and start checkin' our back trail now."

Hank Anderson didn't believe that the others were all dead. As far as he was concerned, there were still twelve more of them at their backs, one place or the other, but he didn't say anything as he rode along bareback. He was just a worker bee.

———

Back in Lander, a messenger had just dropped off a long telegram to the sheriff's office and Deputies Wheatley and Smith sat at the desk reading it.

DEPUTY SHERIFF CHARLIE WHEATLEY LANDER WYOMING

HARPER RILEY AND FOSTER RANCHES ALL ATTACKED
GANG NUMBERED SIXTEEN
ALL MALES AT RANCHES MURDERED
ALL FEMALES TAKEN HOSTAGE
FOLLOWED TO COOPERSTOWN WITH BILLY HARPER
FREED WOMEN AND KILLED FOUR GANG MEMBERS
SENT WOMEN WITH BILLY HARPER TO HOBSON RANCH
BURNED COOPERSTOWN TO PREVENT REUSE BY GANG
FOLLOWED REMAINING TWELVE TO MCCLELLAN FARM
ENGAGED EIGHT WITH HELP FROM MCCLELLANS
KILLED ALL EIGHT
FOLLOWING LAST FOUR

FOUND MURDERED INDIAN AGENT IN SHOSHONE AGENCY STORE
STORE EMPTIED BY LAST FOUR GANG MEMBERS
INCLUDING ALL THREE LEADERS
IN PURSUIT DUE WEST
WILL FINISH THIS

SHERIFF JOE BROOKS

"What do we do, Charlie?" asked Ed.

"Keep doing what we're doing, Ed. Those last four are gonna be pretty mad. We have to make sure they don't come down to the town. Let's set up at each road from that direction. I'll take the northwest and you take the north. Okay?"

"Got it. Let's go," Ed replied as they each reached for a Winchester with their left hands and their hats with their right hands.

Joe was looking at the wagon and its broken axle, noting the open keg of beer and the emptied case of whiskey.

"I hope you boys get good and drunk when I catch up with you," he said out loud.

He then untied the remaining harness horse and fashioned a trail rope, then he threw a blanket over his back and made a quick pack saddle of sorts by hanging some bags of stolen food over the animal. He wasn't too heavily loaded and wouldn't slow him down too much. He was already thinking that with the wagon no longer slowing them down, he'd never catch up with the four before darkness set in, so he'd cut diagonally and pick up the trail and bring some more food to the ladies, and then provide protection for them to the Hobson ranch.

He turned Boomer northwest and set him to a medium trot, figuring he was only about three miles from where the wagon should be.

Joe wasn't off by much in his estimation, as the wagon and riders were just two and a half miles from his position, and almost exactly six miles northeast of the four outlaws who were totally oblivious to the presence of either the sheriff or the party of mostly women.

Sarah was still driving the wagon but was getting very tired. They all were. None of them had slept well at all since their abduction, and their exhaustion added to their slide toward melancholy because of the horrors of their treatment. Even Emma wasn't immune, despite her claim to be a hard woman, but she maintained a strong presence for her daughters and the others, and even for Sarah and Jennie.

Finally, around six o'clock, Emma pulled to a stop and said, "We need to stop. I think we're all just too spent to keep going."

Then she turned to her son and said, "Billy, let's set up camp over there near that creek."

"Okay, Mama," Billy said as he guided Irish to the spot she indicated.

Sarah turned the wagon off the trail, and they bounced over the uneven ground until she pulled back on the reins and set the handbrake. Then she stood, put her hand to her back as she stretched and then stepped down. The girls all piled out of the back as Annie and Mary Harper and Clara Riley all stepped down from their saddles, rubbing their backsides after the long ride.

Emma had stepped down and engaged in a two-handed rub of her behind before stepping over to the wagon.

"Let's take the food out of the wagon and start setting up camp."

"No fire?" asked Sarah.

"Sheriff Joe said not to make a fire because we'd be seen for miles around," Emma replied.

"It's going to get cold," Jennie said as she stepped up.

“Not too bad, though,” Emma said as they began to unload the bags.

“How many bedrolls do we have?” asked Sarah.

“There are seven bedrolls, but I packed some blankets, too,” Emma said as she set down a heavy burlap sack of food.

“How about plates and spoons?” asked Jennie.

“We’ll have to manage with what we have, ladies. It’s only for a day. Tomorrow morning, we’ll reach the Hobson ranch and things should be better.”

“Why did the sheriff send us there? Why can’t we go back to our own ranches?” asked Sarah.

Billy replied, “Because they’re empty and he’s not sure they won’t swing around back to use them again. They might want some of the cattle for food.”

Sarah said, “I hadn’t thought about that,” then she shuddered and said, “the thought of that monster touching me again makes me sick.”

Emma just tightened her jaws at the thought of Hanger Bill’s stinking breath and disgusting manner and shivered herself.

Jennie then said in a low breath, “I wanted to kill that Pierre. After he hit me, I wanted to plunge a knife deep into his gut and watch him bleed to death in pain. I wanted to kill him.”

Emma and Sara looked at Jennie and knew that she had been hurt more than the other two adult women and knew that the girls still needed more of their attention, but none said anything else.

The girls were all helping to unload the food, but they were all silent, which Emma took as a bad sign. They needed to let their anger, fear and hate out. What she really wanted was a campfire, so they could all sit down and talk as a group. It would be the best way.

SHERIFF JOE

The sun was dying in the west, and the red sky spread from horizon to horizon as Joe continued to ride northwest. He soon picked up the fresh wagon tracks and turned west.

He was out of light when he heard the softer sound of women's voices mingled with sounds of meal preparation ahead and angled off the trail.

Emma was wondering about making a campfire anyway as Billy began to open the cans of beans with his pocket knife.

Suddenly, they were all startled when a loud, "Hello, the camp!" echoed across the darkened campsite.

"How are you ladies, doing?" Joe said loudly as he clanked into the camp as the tinware in the bag over the trailed horse began to rattle.

"Sheriff Joe?" asked Billy loudly.

"I thought it was just Joe now, Billy?" Joe asked as he stepped down from Boomer.

Joe's arrival had an immediate and very positive impact on the mood of everyone in the camp, including Billy.

"What happened? Are they all dead?" asked Billy hurriedly.

Joe walked into the camp leading Boomer and the trailing pack horse.

"No, there are four still alive. I think they're a few miles south. It looks like they're heading for one of your ranches."

"You got eight more?" asked an astonished Emma.

"I had help. The rode into the McClellan farm and Al McLellan and his three sons were ready for them with their Winchesters. I came up from behind and they didn't know I was there. They never checked their backtrail once. Then, it was just a matter of time. I followed the other four as they rode to the Indian agency store and found they'd killed the Indian agent and then headed west with the loaded wagon. I found the wagon about four miles west of the agency with a broken axle. They unloaded some supplies and twelve bottles of whiskey before they abandoned it. They took one of the harness team, and I have the other with me. I loaded some of the food and other supplies that you can use and then I sent a telegram from the store to my deputies and the army about the death of the agent and the twelve outlaws."

"We're all really glad to see you, Joe, but why did you come here instead of following them?" asked Emma.

"I knew I'd lose them soon in the dark and they'd still be able to ride in the night, so I thought it was better if I was here to provide protection for you brave ladies than falling into their ambush. I'll make sure you all make it to Hobson's tomorrow and then I'll go after them again."

"We were just about to have something to eat, Joe. Are you going to join us?" Emma asked.

"I will, but let's get a fire going first," Joe said.

"But I thought you said we weren't supposed to start a campfire, Joe. Did I get that wrong?" asked Billy.

"No, that's what I told you because I didn't want you to try and make one. I wasn't sure you knew how to make an invisible fire, or at least a hard-to-see fire, and I didn't know where that gang would be when you pulled over to camp. Now, I know where they are and I'm back, so I'll start making the fire right now, but first, let's unload those bags from the pack horse," he said as he turned toward Boomer.

The adult women descended on the bags and began to take out the food, tin plates, cups, cutlery and then the coffeepot, causing a lot of smiling female faces.

"Okay, I'll start building a fire pit for the campfire," Joe said as the women seemed to have the unloading well in hand.

He checked for a good location and stopped when he reached some trees covering the south that would block any light that might reach the four outlaws, then used his heavy knife to start to dig a hole for the fire pit.

Billy sat on his heels next to Joe as he dug and asked, "How bad was it, Joe?"

Joe continued to dig and said, "Not as bad as I expected. I had to shoot a horse, though, when the last of them were making a break for some trees. I hated doing that. The horse didn't do anything wrong, but I couldn't afford to let them reach the trees."

"Did you get all eight of them, Joe?" he asked quietly.

"Nope, only seven. One of the McClellans got one."

Emma had been listening to them talk and was amazed that any man would put himself in such jeopardy for other people. The McClellans were defending their home, yet Joe had ridden into a hail of bullets just to stop them. He had walked into the boarding house knowing that there were four armed men inside just to rescue her and the other women, too. *What kind of man does such things?*

When his hole was deep enough, Joe began adding kindling while Billy gathered heavier wood for the cooking fire.

Emma then took Billy's place and sat on her heels next to Joe and asked, "How are we going to cook, Joe?"

"If you look hard enough in the food bags, you'll find a big steel frypan and a grate. I found them in the kitchen. I'm guessing they were liberated from one of your ranches."

Then she asked, "Joe, why do you take such horrible risks? You have no right to even be alive after what you did today?"

Joe looked over at Emma and said, “It’s my job, Emma. You and the other ladies were being held against your will and hurt by evil men who had killed your men. Who else was going to do it?”

“No one else that I know would have even tried. You rode into the McClellan farm knowing that the odds were high that you wouldn’t ride out again, and you still rode into that mess. Why?”

Joe sighed and said, “Like I said before. It’s my job. I couldn’t let those bastards do to the McClellans what they had done to your families. It wasn’t that bad, Emma. I wasn’t even scratched.”

“Then what’s that hole doing in your hat?” she asked.

“A miss.”

Emma looked over at Joe and asked quietly, “Don’t you care about dying, Joe?”

Billy brought over some wood and dropped them to the ground before Joe could answer her question, not that he would give her an honest response anyway.

“Okay, Billy, can you find the cooking grate in the food bags and then we’ll let your mother take over.”

“Okay, Joe,” Billy said as he jogged over to the wagon where the other ladies were separating the food and non-food items onto the back of the wagon bed.

Billy found the grate and big frypan and carried them back to where his mother and Joe crouched near his newly-lit fire and wondered what they were talking about.

After Billy had gone, Emma asked, “You didn’t answer my question, Joe.”

Joe replied, “No, ma’am, I didn’t,” then struck a match to start the fire.

When the fire flared to life, Emma looked at Joe's face in the new light and saw two things that surprised her. She saw loneliness and pain, so she didn't ask any more questions.

After Billy handed Joe the grate and he placed it onto the two rocks he had moved next to the hole, then stood and turned to Emma, "The choice of menus is up to you, Emma. I'm guessing that beans will be involved."

Emma stood and smiled at Joe before she said, "That's a good guess, Joe. I'll see what else I can add to make it taste better."

Joe smiled back and said, "I'll fill the coffeepot and we can have some coffee with whatever you make."

"That sounds good, Joe," Emma said before she left to get her cans of food.

Billy followed her to open the cans while Joe carried the coffeepot to the creek and quickly filled it and then returned it to the grate and set it on top to boil. Then he walked to the trees and continued to walk until he disappeared into the small forest.

Once inside, he stopped and folded his arms across his chest. Emma had unnerved him with her questions. He knew what the honest answer to her questions were, but he didn't feel that anyone else should know. He had always taken risks once he put on the badge. It really was like he had a death wish. They weren't stupid risks. He never intentionally put himself in danger, always using the best tactics he could come up with to avoid being shot, and he'd never been hit, despite being targeted hundreds of times in his career. Some bullets had been so close that he swore he could feel the heat from the lead as it passed.

But did he really not care about dying? He hated to admit it to himself, but he didn't. Everyone in the county knew Sheriff Joe, but no one knew Joe Brooks. He wasn't even sure if he did. Even his name didn't mean anything.

When he was abandoned as a newly-weaned infant and left at the doorstep of St Patrick's church in Kansas City, there was no note saying who he was. When he had been sent to the orphanage, the registrar of the orphanage just looked down the list of children that were already there and noticed that none of the boys were named Joe. Not Joseph, just Joe. He didn't even get a middle name. His last name was given to him because the next letter to use was a 'B' and the registrar had chosen Brooks. He could have been a Booker or a Bristow or anything else, but the unnamed bureaucrat had christened him Joe Brooks.

When he had gone into the world and become a lawman, he had discovered a natural affinity for the job and had thought he's soon be a respected member of the community, and he was, but he never really felt part of the communities he lived in. Everyone else had families, but he had no one. For the first year of his independent life, he thought he'd marry and have a family of his own before he was twenty-one, but he had gone to Wyoming and found few available women and then he discovered his problem.

It was then that he became the way he was. He had no one and would never have anyone to care for. It was his own fault and he knew it. He could probably have married in the past few years, but he thought he was too old once he hit thirty. He even confessed to himself that he was just using it as an excuse. His real problem was burned deeply into his mind. He'd grown up in an orphanage and had no women in his world until he was suddenly thrust into a female-laden society and simply didn't know how to deal with the gentler sex. He could talk to them, but when it came to inviting one to share his life, he felt clumsy and oafish.

So, here he was standing in the dark, unsettled by Emma's direct question about not being afraid to die. Emma Harper had unnerved him from the first time he had seen her with those piercing blue eyes. Now, she had bared his soul and seen him as no one else had.

He blew out his breath, unfolded his arms, then turned back to go to the camp. He had to unsaddle Boomer and take care of him. He should have done that right away, and he had to clean his weapons, too.

He stepped back into the light of the campfire and was immediately put under the intense gaze of Emma Harper.

Joe looked away from her and walked to Boomer and began to strip him of his tack silently. Once that was done, he led Boomer to the creek and let him drink before hitching him in a wide patch of grass.

Billy approached and asked, “Are you okay, Joe?”

Joe smiled and put his hand on Billy’s shoulder, saying, “I’m fine, Billy. Just thinking about those last four. Let’s get the rest of the horses unsaddled. Okay?”

“Okay,” Billy said as they walked to the string of horses and began removing saddles and just setting them on the ground. They then unharnessed the wagon team and led the whole gaggle of horses to the creek and then the meadow where Boomer was already grazing.

By then, Emma had the food ready and the ladies were all lining up with their plates. Joe let them queue and walked to his saddlebags and took out his cleaning kits and slid his Winchester and Sharps from their scabbards, then sat on the ground with his saddle pressed against his back and began to clean his weapons, starting with the much-used Winchester ’76.

After the Winchester was clean, he leaned it against the saddle and cleaned the Sharps. It had only been fired once, but it left an enormous amount of residue for one shot.

He had just set aside the Sharps and unloaded his Smith & Wesson of its cartridges when Emma approached with a plate and a tin of coffee.

“Joe, you need to eat,” she said as she handed him the plate.

Joe looked up at her and said, “Has everyone else eaten, Emma?”

“Yes, they have, so you have no excuse.”

Joe accepted her plate and then set the tin cup of coffee next to him. He took a big spoonful of the bean mix and had to admit it was better than anything he could make.

"This is very good, Emma. Thank you," Joe said as he lifted another spoonful into his mouth.

"You're welcome, Joe," she replied and then said, "Joe, in a little while I want to get the women together to talk. I'm concerned that the girls are all becoming very quiet and withdrawing into their thoughts. They need to talk and get it out."

Joe put the spoon down on the plate and said, "That's a good idea, Emma. How can I help?"

"I don't want you or Billy near the fire while we're talking, but I don't want you to think we don't appreciate all you've done, either. It's just that I don't believe that most of the girls will talk with men around."

"No, I'm fine with that and I agree with you. But how are you doing, Emma?" he asked.

Emma smiled and said, "I'm doing fine, Joe. I'm a hard woman, remember?"

Joe filled his spoon again and said softly, "You're lying, Emma. Maybe even to yourself. When you and the other women are talking, I think you should start by confessing your own fears."

Emma was startled but didn't reply. She just stood and said, "We'll be starting shortly. Can the fire be any bigger?"

"Yes. It's blocked by the trees. Billy and I will stand watch on the other side of the camp."

"Thank you," Emma said as she turned to go back to the campfire.

As she walked away, Emma thought about what Joe had said and knew he was right. She had been hiding the truth from herself and decided to go first.

Joe quickly finished his supper, then put his unclean Smith & Wesson into his holster after refilling the chambers. He stood and carried his half-full coffee cup and dirty plate to where Billy was leaning against a wagon wheel looking at the girls.

Joe smiled as he neared Billy and said, "We've been asked by your mother to give the women some time alone, Billy. I've got to clean this plate and when we're far enough away, I've got to clean my pistol."

"Okay, Joe," Billy replied as he stood and followed Joe to the creek.

Five minutes later Joe and Billy were sitting on the trail as Joe cleaned his revolver.

"I noticed you looking at the young ladies, Billy. Any of them catch your eye?" Joe asked.

He could almost hear Billy's blush as he replied, "I..I wasn't looking at them that way, Joe. I..I mean, I think Cora Riley is pretty and everything, but well…"

Joe laughed lightly and said, "It's okay, Billy. Remember what I told you. Pretty soon, and I'm surprised it hasn't happened already, all you'll be able to think about is girls. I was that way when I was twelve, if not sooner."

Billy relaxed and said, "I've been thinking about girls a long time, too, Joe, but it was kind of embarrassing."

"You want to kiss Cora and hold her close, don't you?" Joe asked as he snapped the revolver closed.

"Yes. Isn't that dirty?" he asked.

"Not at all. It's just that you have to be a gentleman when you are with ladies. Girls want to be kissed, you know, but only by a boy they really like, so the hard part is finding out which girls like you. If she does, then sooner or later that will happen. Then you have to be careful."

"Careful?" Billy asked.

"You don't want to get carried away and have to marry her when you're both too young."

"Oh," Billy replied, then said, "That's why my parents had to get married, you know. Annie is almost seventeen and my mother got married when she was seventeen."

"That doesn't mean she had to, Billy. Don't underestimate your mother. She's probably the most impressive woman I've ever met."

"I know, but she told me once that she had to get married, but she never regretted it because she had such beautiful children."

Joe couldn't say much after that. He had just told Emma that she was lying to herself and here he was giving romance advice to her son as if he was an expert on the subject. He did think a lot about girls when he was young, but that's all it ever was for him because he hadn't talked to any. He'd see them, and be enamored of their female nature, but that was the total progress he made on that aspect of his life. Right now, he was thinking about Billy's mother in the same way as Emma was beginning to take control of his mind and he knew that it was wrong. *She was just widowed, for God's sake!*

"I'm kind of flying under false colors, here, Billy. I'm giving you all sorts of advice about girls, and I'll tell you a secret that may put all of what I told you sound worthless. I'm terrible with women. I never knew my mother and didn't have any sisters. I went to school with all boys and even though I liked girls, I had a hard time talking to them at all when I was your age. Then I came out west and there weren't a lot of women and I used that as an excuse not to get too close to them. You know, I'd rather face down some nasty hombre with a pair of fully-loaded Colts than talk to a woman."

"But you talk to my mother and all of the other women okay."

"I mean talking serious to a woman about love and marriage and things. I really liked this one young woman a few years back named Mary Sheehy. I know she liked me, too, but I couldn't even ask her to go to a social with me. I made up excuse after excuse until she finally married the butcher. He wasn't even a handsome man, but he was well-off. I really like your mother, and I can talk to her about anything but that. If I even think about it, I turn to jelly inside. Now, don't go telling your mother or anyone else about that. My deputies know, but you're the only other person I've ever told. I just felt like a bit of a hypocrite for giving you advice about girls."

"You sure seem to know about girls and women, though."

"I've been working with married men for years, Billy. They talk about their wives and their girlfriends a lot. I just pay attention. You're going to be a good man, Billy. I think I can trust to you keep my secret."

Billy looked at Joe, paused, and then said, "I'll do my best, Joe."

"I know you will, Billy," Joe replied.

Billy felt a bit like a cheat when he had answered the sheriff. He had wanted to avoid giving a direct answer because he might have to tell his mother, just in case.

The two banished males then sat silently as they listened to the women at the campfire sixty feet away.

———

Over by the fire, sixteen female eyes were focused on Emma as she spoke.

"A little while ago, when I told Sheriff Joe that we needed some private time to talk about what has happened to each of us because no one is talking about it, he agreed that it was a good idea, so he and Billy will stay away while we talk. After I had told him that I was worried about each of you, he asked me how I was doing, and I just laughed and said I was fine because I was a hard woman. Then he called me a liar and said I was lying to myself. I was shocked at first, but then I admitted to myself that he was right. I am trying to pretend that nothing happened, and I could just put it behind me. But I can't, and I shouldn't try. None of us should try to act as if we're the same as we were before. So, I am going to confess to each one of you how I truly feel about they did to me."

She took in a deep breath and looked at each girl or woman in turn and then began.

"When I saw Wilbur being gunned down by those three men, I was horrified. I had already sent Annie and Mary out to the pastures hoping they would be safe, but I knew what they were going to do me, and I resigned to what was about to happen, but like each of you, I was surprised when all they did was tie me up. For a little while, I thought they were just going to sell us, but then I heard them talking and I knew. When they finally took us all that first night, I thought if I just closed my eyes and pretended it wasn't happening, I'd be able to forget it later, but it doesn't work that way."

They demanded us to be active participants while we were being raped. It cost some of us much more than just physical pain. In a way, the physical pain, especially of our daughters was much easier to bear than what damage they did to our minds and souls. I'm not sure if we'll ever be able to push it completely out of our minds, but to just let it sit inside us and fester is worse. I want you all to know how I feel."

Emma took another deep breath, blew it out quickly, then her voice hardened, and her face contorted with anger and disgust.

"I hate that man who took me against my will. That Hanger Bob Jones wasn't a man. He was a stinking, dirty animal. When he climbed on top of me, I wanted to fight and knee him in his groin so hard he'd never think of touching me, but I had to let him do what he wanted because I knew what he'd do to my girls if I fought. I wanted to kill him and feed him to the vultures from the moment he touched me. *What right does he have to think that because he wants me, he can just take me? Who the hell does he think he is?"*

That bastard deserves to have his manhood cut off and watch it get thrown away before he dies. I hate him with every inch of my heart, mind and soul! Hell is too good for Hanger Bob Jones. When I think of his hand on my naked skin, I want to throw up. He didn't have the right to touch me, much less do what he did to me! No man should touch me unless I want him to. I felt dirty and ashamed even though I knew it wasn't my fault. There were times I wanted to just curl up and die, but I couldn't. I had to be strong for my daughters. I knew what they were going through was much worse because they didn't understand what to expect. I never warned them that something like this could happen, so Annie and Mary, please forgive me for not letting you know."

Annie then began to cry and said, "It's not your fault, Mama. It's those evil bastards' fault. They took me over and over until I was numb, then they just left me there like a dirty towel. I hated each one of them and wanted to rip their eyes out but knew what they'd do to me. They made me moan and wiggle around, just so they could enjoy themselves more, Mama. I felt like a whore! I was a damned whore!"

Then, the floodgates opened as each woman or girl rushed to tell of her anguish and hate for those sixteen men that had abused them. For over two hours, there was a mass catharsis of hate and anger at what they had undergone. Emma had to throw a lot of wood onto the fire to keep the campfire blazing.

It wasn't until Katie Foster spoke that the subject of pregnancy finally was mentioned.

"And what if I'm going to have their baby?" shouted Katie, "I don't want it. It would be evil and deserve to die. I'd never be able to love it. I'd hate it."

"You can put it up for adoption, Katie," Emma said, "someone will love the baby."

"But I don't care if someone else loves it!", Katie screamed, "I want no one to love it! It'll just be a sick bastard like its father! It will be a monster!"

Emma then said softly, "It will just be a baby, Katie; an innocent little baby. It won't be the baby's fault for being conceived and born."

Katie was about to argue again when Joe suddenly appeared in the flickering firelight and walked close to the fire and looked down at Katie from his six feet two inches.

In a deep, but softly compassionate voice, he said, "Mrs. Harper is right, Katie. It's not the baby's fault. How can anything as purely innocent as a newborn child be blamed for just breathing? All of you girls are worried about this, and I do understand that. You think it will rekindle your memories of how the child came to be. You think it will ruin your lives, but neither of those things will have to happen. They will only happen if you let them."

If you abandon your baby to an orphanage, your baby will never know who he is. He'll be given a name that means nothing to him or anyone else. Even if the people in the orphanage are kind, it's never the same because he'll know that they are there to watch all the children, not just him. There is nothing that can replace a mother's love. When your little boy begins to walk and hurts himself, he won't be able to run to his mama, have her pick him up and sit on her lap and get kissed and hugged and told it will get better. He'll grow up alone and empty, with a giant hole in his heart that can never be filled. Right now, it's only a possibility that you are with child, but if you do have a baby, don't discard him because of who fathered the child. Love him with all your heart and you will receive much more love in return."

Then Joe just turned and faded back into the darkness.

All the women watched him go and then turned to look at each other.

There was almost two minutes of silence after Joe had gone.

Then Emma said, "Sheriff Joe is right about any babies that are the result of this terrible time, but if any of you do become pregnant and still don't want the baby, I'll be more than happy to raise the child. I don't intend to let those evil men control the rest of my life. I intend to remarry and take care of my girls until they get married and start their own families. I am not going to give in! None of us should let them win. Sheriff Joe is bringing all of them to justice for us. He didn't rescue us just to leave us in a prison of our own making. Let's let all of our anger and hurt be replaced by gratitude for our rescue and hope for a new life that will replace the one that those poor excuse for human beings had planned for us."

She paused and then stood, looked at all of the women and said loudly, "I am going to live my own life starting right now!"

Then, Sarah Foster stood and shouted, "I am not going to let them win either. I am going to find a new husband and stay where I am on my ranch. I'll carry a gun with me and shoot any bastard who tries to touch me that I don't want to touch me!"

Jennie Riley then stood and said forcefully, "I agree with Emma and Sarah. We owe it to our girls and ourselves to make the most of the rest of our lives. I won't shun men, but I'll decide who I allow into my bed from here on!"

The girls all looked at their standing mothers and in groups of two or three began to stand and firmly profess their willingness to restart their lives and take care of each other.

Then, after Emma took a seat again, they all sat back down in a rippling descent.

Emma then smiled at the women and girls and said, "I think we're all going to be close friends for the rest of our lives."

The other women began smiling and hugs were in abundance as they resumed their private pow-wow.

Emma let the fire die as the discussion grew more positive about how they wouldn't give in and give the final victory to those evil men. Emma was even more pleased when Annie and Mary both said that they'd still go out with boys, get married and have children. The other girls all said the same thing, even Katie, so Emma felt that the campfire catharsis had been exactly what they all needed.

As the fire dwindled, Emma stood and walked out toward the trail where she could see the shadows of Billy and Joe.

She drew close and they both turned, expecting her as the voices had all dwindled away.

"All done, Emma?" asked Joe with a smile.

"We're finished and thank you both for giving us the time," she said looking into Joe's shadowy eyes.

"It's okay, Mama. Joe and I talked about a lot of things," Billy said.

"He told us a lot of things, too, Billy," she said before turning to go back to the wagon.

"What did you say, Joe? I didn't hear it so well."

"Not much. Just told them to be good to their children."

"Oh."

"Let's get back and set up the sleeping arrangements. Okay?"

"Yes, sir," Billy said as they began walking.

Hanger Bob and the others had continued to ride through the night and finally pulled over just before midnight, so they didn't overshoot their destination ranch. They didn't set up camp, just unsaddled and ground-hitched their horses.

Instead of cooking or even eating a few cans of beans, they each took a bottle of whiskey, sat with their backs against their saddles and began passing one of the bottles of whiskey around.

"This is some rotgut liquor," Charlie Smith groused after he took a long swig.

"What did you think you were gonna get, a smooth Kentucky bourbon?" asked Hanger Bob as he grabbed the bottle and upended it, letting a large flush of whiskey flow down his throat.

Hank Anderson laughed as he accepted the bottle and after the whiskey hit his tongue, he agreed with Charlie, but still took a long swallow before giving the bottle to Pierre.

'Why ain't the other guys here yet?" asked Hank.

"How are they gonna find us in the dark?" Bob snapped back.

"They ain't comin'," Charlie mumbled as he snatched the already half-empty bottle.

Joe and Billy had set up the eight bedrolls. Once they added Joe's so there were enough bedrolls for all the women and the two blankets that Emma had packed, they were able to fashion a bed for her.

After the bedrolls and blanket bed were all arranged, Joe set up a few of the burlap bags on the wagon bed for Billy to use and picked up his Winchester and left the camp to walk the perimeter.

Joe walked along and wondered what had possessed him to interrupt the women while they talked about things that only other women could share. Emma had asked him to stay away, and he hadn't. It bothered him, so he switched to a more comfortable subject – tomorrow's confrontation with the last four.

He didn't understand why they had continued west rather than return to the McClellan ranch as they had probably planned. It appeared they were heading for one of the three empty ranches to set up there. *Why? Did they somehow figure out that Cooperstown was gone and so was their gang?*

He could see how they might have realized that their new headquarters had been razed, but for the life of him, he couldn't come up with a reason for them suspecting that the rest of their outlaw band was dead. They must have been at least five miles away when the first shots were fired. *It was possible they heard the shots, but over the sound of the wagon and the horses at five miles?* Joe knew that sound was fickle. Sometimes even loud sounds weren't heard a mile away and other times, you swear you can hear a single Colt from ten miles. He didn't know the science behind it; it just was.

Joe had to assume that they knew they were alone and that they were going to a ranch house to stay. If that were true, then his job wouldn't be too hard to locate and engage them all in one place. He hoped that they all stayed together, but there was no reason for them to split up. Unless, of course, they knew they were alone and being hunted. Then, if they went separate ways, his job would be much more difficult.

He began to lay plans for them all being together until proven otherwise. He couldn't count on catching them napping again, though. He'd have to rely on the length of his Winchester '76 and the Sharps as the biggest advantage he would have.

He continued to walk, stopping every so often to listen for any possible intruders, then begin his perimeter walk again.

Joe finished his fourth loop of the perimeter and decided it was safe, so he took a seat near the trail and just listened, waiting for the late moonrise.

Joe finally just stretched out a little after midnight, knowing he'd need to be rested for tomorrow, or technically, later today. The quarter moon made its appearance just after he laid back and closed his eyes.

CHAPTER 5

Despite his jacket, Joe was freezing when his eyes popped open early in the morning just as the sun began playing off the morning dew. He hadn't removed his boots, but just stood, stretched his back and picked up his rifle, irritated with himself for not covering it and letting it get wet. He dried it as best he could on his pants and shirt before he trotted behind some bushes.

He returned and headed for the fire pit and had a fire going five minutes later. He emptied and filled the coffeepot and set it on the cooking grate before walking over to Boomer and beginning to saddle his horse. Once Boomer was saddled, he slid his '76 into its nice, snug scabbard and apologized to Mr. Winchester for mistreating his work of art.

Then he began saddling the other horses while everyone else slept.

After saddling four horses, he returned to the fire, pulled the boiling water-filled coffeepot from the grate and added the ground coffee.

Five minutes later, as Joe was sitting on his heels, he heard stirring and turned to see Billy walking his way.

"Morning, Joe," he said with a big smile.

"Good morning, Billy. Have some coffee."

Billy nodded, then crouched down and filled a tin cup with coffee.

"Getting an early start, Joe?" he asked.

"I'm planning on riding about a mile ahead of the wagon, so I can make sure the path is clear. Those four are probably going to be ahead of us and to the south slightly, and I don't want to have them bump into the wagon. I can drive them off and the gunfire will let everyone know to hunker down."

Billy sipped his steaming coffee and asked, "Do you think they know they're alone?"

"I have no idea. It's possible they heard the gunfire from the McClellan farm, and that would account for their decision to keep riding west rather than head back to the farm, but I'd be surprised if they haven't figured out that Cooperstown doesn't exist anymore. I'm assuming that they know they're being trailed now and will have their guard up. I'm just hoping that they stay together rather than split up. If they go four different directions it may take me weeks to hunt them all down."

"Why don't you have your deputies help, Joe?"

"Someone needs to stay in Lander to keep the town safe and I'm better at this kind of thing than they are. We've been lucky so far. I just hope that my luck continues and they're all in one of those empty ranch houses."

"Are all bad guys so stupid? I mean, they didn't have any lookouts and never checked their backtrail."

Joe sipped his coffee and replied, "Not stupid, Billy, arrogant. They had sixteen heavily armed men and they knew that there were only three lawmen in the entire county, and it's a big county for three men to protect. They probably hoped all of us would show up and they'd kill us and then have free reign over the whole county, but they hadn't counted on you, Billy."

If you hadn't escaped and told me just hours after they left your ranch, they would have been looking for me to show up when I finally did manage to find them. But you were smart enough to know that it was more important to get to Lander and tell me rather than do something stupid and get yourself killed. Now, twelve of their own are dead and we're still alive, all because of you."

Billy said quietly, "I never even shot at one, Joe."

"No, you didn't, and I'm glad that you didn't. You're still only a thirteen-almost-fourteen-year-old boy and killing another man is a hell of a thing to have gnawing at your insides. Even killing an evil man will sit on a good man's conscience. I've managed to live with it, but I wouldn't wish it on you."

"It bothers you because you killed them?" Billy asked with the wide-eyes of disbelief.

"No, it doesn't, and *that's* what bothers me. One of them at the McClellan farm was wounded when I hit him low in the back with a .50 caliber from my Winchester. He was on the ground dying and begged me to hear his confession, so I could pass it on to a priest and he could receive absolution for his sins and go to heaven. I refused his request and told him he deserved to burn in hell for what he did to the women. I shot him to end his suffering, but I didn't even let him talk to ease his soul's suffering. I condemned the man to eternal damnation, taking God's place in his final judgment. What kind of a man does that, Billy?"

Billy looked at Joe and said, "The best man I've ever known, Joe."

Joe couldn't understand why Billy could even think that but didn't reply. He just downed the last of his coffee, then stood and carried the cup to the creek, rinsed it out and returned it to its place near the other cups.

"I'm going to finish saddling the horses and start riding west, Billy. Let the ladies sleep as much as they need, but after all the ladies are ready, let them have breakfast and wash and whatever else they need to do. I'm going to go about two or three miles west and circle back. Get the wagon moving and I want you to ride drag to make sure they're protected from behind. If you see four riders, fire a warning shot and get the women behind protection. I'll get back here as fast as I can, which should be less than a minute. Okay?"

"I've got it, Joe," Billy replied.

Joe smiled at him and said, “I know you do,” then turned and walked back to saddle the last of the horses and then harness the wagon team.

The women began to slip out of their bedrolls when the jangling heavy harness was being hung over the team and by the time they were in harness, all of the women were up.

Joe climbed on Boomer and waved to Billy and trotted off to the west, studiously avoiding making eye contact with Emma.

After he was clear of the camp, Joe tried to keep his mind off of Emma. It just wasn’t right to think of her at all. She’d lost her husband just days earlier and Billy had said how much they loved each other, even after Billy had asked him to marry his mother. But no other woman, and, when he thought about it, no other man, had disconcerted him like Emma did. She was so strong and straightforward that she simply disturbed him, but in a good way.

He admired Emma immensely, and not just because she was still a handsome woman. It was because she was the type of woman he could talk to. There was nothing coquettish about Emma. She was an honest, strong woman that he wanted in his life, but knew he was going to have to build up the nerve while she was in mourning. He was just unsure of how long that would be. *Six months? A year? What would be long enough before he asked to see her socially, and would he ever get up the nerve?*

But he was conflicted about Emma because although he was sure that she needed time to grieve, he was still worried that if he waited too long, she’d be wooed by another man and he’d lose his chance. He’d still be alone knowing that the one woman he knew he wanted in his life was with another man.

———

After visiting the bushes, Emma strolled up to her son and asked, “Where is Joe going? He’s not leaving us, is he?”

"No, Mama. He's going to ride out a mile or so to make sure the path is clear of those four men. He said for the ladies to have breakfast and anything else you might need to do and then, when you're ready, we'll pull out and I'll ride drag to protect the back side. He said if I see them, to fire a warning shot and he'd be back in a minute. He said all the women were to seek protection until he got back."

"Okay. I'm going to start breakfast. Coffee is already made?"

"Yes, Mama. Joe made it."

"Oh."

Twenty minutes later, Billy and the women were eating a bean and bacon breakfast and Emma was pleased with how chatty all of the women were. They weren't happy chatting, but they were talking, which was a significant improvement over yesterday. She felt better for having told them all how she really felt, too.

By eight o'clock the wagon was pulling out and there was a shift in riding as all of the girls had asked to ride the six saddled horses and that meant the three matrons all sat on the driver's seat as it rocked and rolled along the trail. Emma was driving.

Billy took up his drag position as Joe had directed and thought that he saw Cora Riley looking back at him sometimes. He'd smile at her when he saw her big brown eyes looking at him and was pleased when she smiled back.

As Emma steered the wagon, Sarah Foster said, "You know, we're all widows, and I was wondering what I was going to do about it now that we're all on our way home and didn't come up with anything firm. How about you Jennie? What are you going to do?"

Jennie Riley kept her eyes focused on the right-side horse's rump as she replied, "I'm not sure yet. Losing John was bad, but losing my boys was much worse. When Sheriff Joe talked about a mother's love for her boys, it was like he had seen me holding them when they were little. It's how I remember them even though they were both already strapping big boys. Now, they're gone, and I'd sell the ranch, but not with my boys buried there. I have to stay, and that means I'll have to hire some ranch hands, which will be hard with just me and my girls. I really need to remarry if I stay. How about you, Emma?"

Emma hesitated for a few seconds, then replied, "I'm staying. I'm not going to let them win by running away. I was very fortunate that my son is not only still alive, but quickly becoming a real man, thanks to Sheriff Joe. I think Annie and Mary will be all right after a while, but I'm not sure if I'll remarry."

"You loved Wilbur a lot, didn't you, Emma. Is that why you're not going to remarry?"

Emma shook her head and replied, "No. Honestly? I didn't love Wilbur at all. He wasn't a bad husband and he loved the children, but he didn't love me. I was a confident girl even when I was young, and when I became curious about making love, I basically seduced him when I was sixteen. I was still so ignorant about the consequences though and became pregnant with Annie. We got married, and motherhood made me even more of a blunt, straightforward woman and Wilbur never adapted to the change. I believe part of it was that I took away his youth, but that was a long time ago, and now I'm such a cold woman that I don't even miss him as much as I should, Jennie."

"Then why don't you want to remarry? I know I wouldn't mind if Sheriff Joe looked my way."

Emma felt her stomach twist and said, "I just haven't thought about it that much."

Sarah chimed in, saying, "Now that Jennie's mentioned it, I know I'd set my cap for Sheriff Joe myself. If he asked, I'd stay."

Emma's stomach turned into a knot as she replied, "He is an impressive man. You both know that he was talking about himself last night, don't you?"

"When?" asked Sarah.

"When he was talking to Katie about not giving up her baby. Didn't you notice he kept referring to the lost child as 'he', and I don't believe it was for grammatical reasons. I'm almost sure that he was left at an orphanage and never adopted. He spoke about it with such passion that it had to be from personal experience. I do know how lonely he is. I could see it in his eyes."

Jennie looked over and replied, "Sheriff Joe is lonely? Everybody knows and likes him, except the bad men. How can he be lonely?"

"He has no one. I know he lives in the boarding house by himself, and he always takes the hard jobs, as if he doesn't care if he lives or dies. I asked him about that last night and he didn't answer the question. Then, when I reminded him that he hadn't answered the question, all he said was that he knew that he hadn't. Sheriff Joe is a lonely, hurt man."

Sarah said, "Well, I wouldn't mind making him feel better," then added, "there's something else we have to think about besides husbands. Our ranches have been stripped of horses, household goods and food. I don't have the money to replace any of it either."

Emma said, "Neither do I. I'll ask Sheriff Joe about that problem when we see him again. I'll bet he'll have an answer, too."

Jennie laughed and said, "You seem to think he's a miracle man, Emma. Even that day when you said he was watching the boarding house, you thought that way. Maybe you should just ask him to marry you."

Emma smiled at Jennie but didn't reply as the wagon rolled on. The reason she had said that she wasn't going to remarry was that she didn't think Joe was interested and there was no other man that could come close, as obviously both Sarah and Jennie believed.

———

The wagon had been moving to their north for more than two hours when Charlie Smith was the first of the four outlaws to stir. He rolled his tongue around his dry, cotton mouth, and blinked his eyes in the bright sunshine before sitting up, his head spinning.

Charlie sat there for another minute before he scrambled to his feet, walked fifteen feet away and relieved himself.

"Get up, boys! It's too late. We gotta get movin'!" he shouted as he walked to the creek and then flopped onto his stomach and plunged his face into the cold water.

The other three made various groans or muttered mild curses as they began to move.

Ten minutes later, they were all saddling their horses after taking another nip of the rotgut whiskey to chase away their hangovers. Each of them had a piece of jerky in his mouth as they flipped their saddles over their horses' backs.

"Ain't nobody comin' yet," Charlie groused, continuing his point from last night.

"If we ain't seen nobody by this afternoon, then I'll start worryin'," Bob said as he tightened his cinch.

They soon were all mounted and leaving their messy campsite behind, still riding west.

———

Joe had clear vision for three miles as he sat on Boomer and scanned the horizon, not seeing anyone. He then wheeled his gray gelding back toward the wagon to let them know and make sure everything was quiet. At least, that was his excuse he made for himself. He really wanted to see Emma again, despite his own firm rules about not trying to insert himself into her life. He might not be able to talk to her again, but he did want to see her.

As he approached the caravan, he noted that all of the riders were the daughters and the mothers were all lined up on the wagon's driver's seat and Emma was driving. As he was looking, Sarah Foster waved him over, so he set Boomer to a trot.

He pulled up next to the wagon and wheeled his horse around to ride next to Sarah's side and asked, "Do you need something, Mrs. Foster?"

"Call me Sarah, Sheriff," she replied with a smile, then asked, "we were talking a little while ago about what we were going to do now that we're all widows, and the subject came up about money. We don't have enough to replace what was stolen and was wondering if you had any ideas."

"I do, as a matter of fact. Now, among those twelve dead outlaws were ten wanted men with prices on their heads. It varied but seemed to average around two hundred dollars each. That's two thousand dollars or so. The other four, because it includes the three gang leaders, Hanger Bob Jones, Charlie Smith and Pierre Le Tour, are worth at least another fifteen hundred dollars. Altogether, I think the rewards for the whole gang will come to almost four thousand dollars. Divided among the three of you, that'll be about thirteen hundred dollars apiece. Now, it'll take a few days for that to happen after I get back to Lander and send out the telegrams, but I'll be able to give you each a couple of hundred dollars until the money is wired back from those that posted the rewards."

Sarah, Emma and Jennie all stared at Joe with wide eyes, but no responses, so Joe added, "If you need more at the start, I could give you five hundred apiece. That should be enough to refurnish the houses and then some."

Emma finally replied, "No…no, that's not necessary, Joe. We were all just astounded, that's all. Why would you give us that money? You are the one who earned it."

"I don't need it and you do. Those miscreants stole a lot more from each of you than just some household goods and food. They put each of you in a terrible situation and hurt each of you and your girls. The money is the least I can do."

"But what do you get out of this?" asked Jennie.

"The satisfaction of sending every one of those sons of bitches to hell, ma'am," Joe replied before tipping his hole-ridden hat and trotting away to talk to Billy.

Once he was gone, Jennie turned to Emma and said, "I can't believe this, Emma. That's more money than I've seen in my entire life. I've never even seen a hundred dollars in one place before."

Sarah then said, "He doesn't need the money? I've never heard anyone say they don't need more money."

Emma just watched the trail ahead and knew that Sheriff Joe didn't need money, but he needed someone desperately.

Joe pulled up next to Billy and said, "Just another couple of hours, Billy."

"What did my mother want, Joe?"

"It wasn't your mother who called me over, it was Mrs. Foster. They were worried about what would happen when they returned to their ranches. It'll be hard on them, Billy. You are the only man to survive those raids. There will be three ranches that need to have men to work the cattle, and that is a scary thing for women who've been through what they have. Mrs. Foster was concerned about money, and I told them that I'd divide the reward money among the three families, so they could replace what was stolen. That solves one problem, but not the others. I don't know how they'll manage without men around for protection and to do the really hard work. There are a lot of unmarried men around this part of the country, Billy. Once the word gets out that there are three widow women with ranches, they'll come in droves. Make that four widow women with ranches, I forgot about Mrs. Hobson, but at least she has two strong boys."

"That's where we're headed, right?"

"Yup. Once you're all there, I'll make a sweep of the three ranch houses and expect I'll find those four in one of them."

"Am I coming with you, Joe?" Billy asked.

"Not this time. I need you and Ben to protect all the women. Ben's not quite sixteen, and he's a good kid, so don't step on his toes. Before I go, I'll tell him that I've given you all the instructions about how to prepare in case any of those four escapes."

"When are you going to give me instructions?"

"Right now. All it involves is arming the women who can fire those Winchesters and if you see someone riding hard toward the ranch, position them in places where they can cover the entire front of the ranch, but behind some protection. Then, I want you to be visible to the rider with your Winchester on your hip, but not pointed at him. It's a way of telling him that you know he's coming. If he turns around or rides past, let him go. If he keeps coming, the second you see him pulling his rifle, hit the dirt to a prone firing position and wait until he gets in range. Make sure everyone else who has a rifle knows not to fire until you do."

Stress that. No one fires until you take the first shot. You wait until he's within range, even if he starts firing; you hold your fire until he gets within a hundred yards. Keep your sights on him as he rides in and then, when he's within range, fire. A full volley of Winchesters, even if everyone misses, will be enough to get him to change his mind. I should be along shortly after that, if not before. Got all that?"

"Yes, sir."

Joe smiled at Billy and said, "I knew you would. I'm going to get back to the point again, Billy."

Billy smiled back and nodded as Joe rode away at a fast trot.

———

"Which one is that?" asked Charlie Smith as they spotted a ranch house and barn in the distance.

"I ain't sure, but I think it's the second one," replied Hanger Bob, "the one with those three shooters that we killed before we run down their women.

Pierre said, "That one we got out of there was my wife," then laughed.

They warily approached the back of the house, and it was Hank Anderson who first noticed something was missing and asked, "Where are all the buzzards?"

Pierre looked into the sky and said, "You're right, Hank. There ain't no buzzards up there."

Now, they were all skittish as they reached the back of the house and then they spotted the two shovels lying crossed over a pile of dirt.

"Look over there! Somebody buried those three!" Charlie shouted as he pointed at the grave.

Even Hanger Bob was spooked by the thought of the bodies already being in the ground, but he recovered and said, "What did you expect? Those buzzards woulda told everyone for miles around that there were bodies here and at those other two ranches. Hell, it woulda been a damned buzzard convention."

The other three laughed at Bob's joke and they all stepped down behind the house and tied off their horses.

"Let's get something to eat," Charlie said as he pulled his saddlebags from his horse.

"There ain't any food in there, so we'll have to eat beans," Pierre said as he hung his saddlebags over his shoulder, pulled his Winchester from its scabbard and headed into the house.

Joe caught sight of the Hobson ranch house in the distance and picked up the pace to let Mrs. Hobson know what was behind him. It would put strain on her home, but only for a day, Joe figured. With the bedrolls, they could even arrange sleeping in the barn loft if need be, but first, he needed to let her know that she was about to have ten guests.

He turned into the access road five minutes later and spotted Mrs. Hobson and her daughter, Margie, outside hanging laundry. He waved when they looked his way and they both waved back. Abby Hobson began straightening her hair as she stepped away from the clothesline. Margie noticed and giggled at the sight. Since his visit, all her mother had talked about was Sheriff Joe.

Abby couldn't believe that the sheriff was back so soon, thinking that he must not have found the women or the bad men. She was wearing a big smile when he drew within normal talking range.

"Hello, Sheriff. Didn't you find the bad men?" she asked.

"I found them, ma'am. They're all dead except for four of them. I'm getting ready to go after them right now, but I have an enormous favor to ask of you."

"Anything you need, Sheriff," Abby said as she looked up at Joe, shielding her eyes in the bright sun with her right hand.

"I have a wagon and some riders coming behind me about a mile away. Mrs. Harper, Riley and Foster along with their six daughters are heading this way. I don't want them to return to their homes yet because I believe those last four outlaws are using one of them as a hideout. I'd really appreciate it if they could stay with you for a day or so until I can take care of the problem. They have some food with them, and I'll give you some cash to help with expenses. Would you be able to help?"

Abby was stunned for a few seconds, and asked, "How many did you have to kill?"

"Twelve, but Al McClellan or one of his boys got one of them. They were trying to get his hay and his wife and daughter when I got behind them. Mrs. Hobson, just to let you know, these women and girls were all abused by those men. They're doing better than I had hoped, but I think it's still going to be very hard on them. Those men all deserved to die, as do those last four."

Abby slowly nodded and replied, "Yes, they do, Sheriff. I was just astonished by the number, that's all. Of course, they can stay here, and I don't need a dime. We have plenty of food on hand and I'm sure that Ben wouldn't mind having six young women in the house."

"I appreciate it, ma'am. How is Ben doing?"

"He's never been more helpful, and I can never thank you enough for what you did for him."

Then she looked to her left and said, "Is that the women?"

Joe turned to check, then turned back and said, "Yes, ma'am. I've explained to Billy, that's Emma Harper's son, what to do while I'm gone. Tell Ben that it's no slight on him, it's just that I had time to tell Billy what to do in case one of them escapes and swings around to your ranch. It's not likely, but I think you should be prepared."

"Here comes Ben, now. Do you have time to tell him? I think he'd be happier if you did rather than me."

"Yes, ma'am. I'll talk to him."

"Sheriff, could you call me Abby, please? I'm not that old, you know."

Joe smiled at her and said, "I know, Abby. It's just a matter of respect."

Abby smiled as Ben strolled up and said, "Howdy, Sheriff. What happened with the gang?"

"I just told your mother, and you can get all the details from the women and Billy Harper. They'll be here shortly. But the basics are that the women and girls were all taken to Cooperstown and now they're free and will be coming down your access road in a few minutes to stay here a day or so until I go and kill the last four. I've already told Billy Harper what needs to be done to protect everyone here in case one of them escapes. He'll tell you, but I need you both to work together. And please be careful around the girls. They've all been hurt badly by those men and need to be around kind and gentle men for a while. I know that you're a good young man, Ben, and you'll do the right thing."

"I will, Sheriff. I'll work with Billy and make sure everyone stays safe. Good luck with those four."

Joe smiled and nodded at Ben then turned to Abby and said, "I've got to get going, Abby. Hopefully, I'll be back in a few hours and this will all be over."

"Take care, Sheriff," Abby said.

"Call me Joe, Abby," he said as he tipped his hat and then wheeled Boomer around and trotted away to meet the oncoming wagon.

Ben and his mother watched him ride away and Abby sighed as Margie walked close and put her arm around her mother, saying, "I hope Sheriff Joe can get those last four and not get hurt."

Abby put her arm over Margie's shoulder, gave it a squeeze, and said, "I think that's what every woman on that wagon and riding those horses wants to happen, Margie, and that includes me."

Joe stopped Boomer when the riders and the wagon were just a few hundred yards from the access road and waited for them to reach him. He spotted Billy riding up quickly from the back and wasn't surprised one bit to see Cora Riley riding alongside as they trotted past the wagon.

When the two riders were close, Joe grinned at a red-faced Billy and said, "Mrs. Hobson said that you're all welcome and Ben Hobson said he'd help to keep the ranch safe, so I'll press on to the ranches and see if I can find those four men. You can handle it from here, okay?"

"Yes, sir."

Then Joe said, "Wait a minute, Billy. I just thought of something. I told the ladies they could have the reward money, but I should really put it in writing, so hold on."

He turned and reached into his saddlebags, pulled out one of the wanted posters and a stubby pencil and flipped the poster to the blank side and began to write. After just a few minutes, he folded the poster, slipped the pencil into his shirt pocket and handed the paper to Billy.

"That's just in case, Billy. It'll make sure that the reward money goes to the three mothers."

"Okay, I'll hold onto it, Joe, but you'll be all right. Is this poster one of the twelve dead ones?"

"Yes, sir. It's the one on Henry Pleasant, and he was anything but that. I'll be back soon, Billy."

Then he set Boomer off at a trot and waved at the ladies in the wagon as he passed, but his eyes locked on Emma's for just a second as they moved in different directions.

Billy opened the wanted poster and read about Henry Pleasant. There was a three-hundred-dollar reward for the man for murder and robbery. He'd killed three men and been accused of robbing four stages. Then he flipped it over and read Joe's hastily scrawled instructions. It just said that all rewards for the deaths of the Hanger Bob Jones, Charlie Smith and Pierre Le Tour gangs was to go to Emma Harper, Mrs. Riley and Mrs. Foster. Billy noticed Joe had only his mother's name included her Christian name. Then, he read further and felt sick when he read that Joe had written a short will, leaving everything he owned to his mother. It was like he expected to die.

Cora asked, "What does it say, Billy?"

Billy looked her way and replied, "It says to give all of the reward money to our mothers and Mrs. Foster."

"The sheriff is a really good man, isn't he, Billy?"

"The best, Cora. I think he's the bravest man I've ever met."

"I do, too, but you're brave, too, Billy."

Billy smiled at Cora, who smiled back as the wagon stopped nearby.

Emma asked loudly, "What did Joe give you, Billy?"

"I'll show you when we get to the ranch, Mama. Joe said Mrs. Hobson is glad to have us as guests."

"Okay," Emma replied as she snapped the reins, getting the team moving again.

———

"I'm kinda getting antsy, Bob," Charlie said as they sat at the kitchen table, a half-full bottle of whiskey sitting in the middle.

"I don't like this at all. I don't like not knowin' what's goin' on. Where are all the men and why was them bodies buried?" he continued.

Pierre then said, "I don't like bein' cooped up in this house like this with no lookouts. We shoulda had lookouts back at Lawless."

Bob replied, "Well, that's all behind us now, so there's no use worryin'. To tell the truth, I was kinda thinkin' we had too many men anyway. Tryin' to feed sixteen mouths and have that many horses meant we woulda had to keep raiding just to keep eatin'. Now, even if they show up, I think we just break up the big gang and go our own ways. Heck, we knocked off that Indian agency store easy and shoulda looked for where he kept the money. I'll bet just the four of us could make some serious money in these small towns around here. No law and a bunch of ranchers and sodbusters. Who could stop us?"

"That damned sheriff that nobody seems to want to talk about. We shoulda just rode into Lander with the entire bunch and killed him and those two damned deputies instead of waiting for him to come after us, Bob. He's probably still sittin' in Lander ignorant of what's been goin' on right under his nose," replied Pierre.

Hank then stood and said, "I'm gonna go out front and sit on the porch to keep an eye out in case he shows up here. I don't like havin' those graves dug in back."

Bob looked over at him and said, "That's a good idea, Hank. Grab your Winchester before you go."

"Yeah, yeah. I got it," he snapped as he grabbed his carbine and walked down the hallway to the front room.

———

Joe turned south when he reached the road to the three ranches. He'd keep Boomer to a slow trot to keep the dust down and had already taken out the field glasses.

The first ranch he'd reach would be the Foster ranch, then would come the Rileys and finally Emma's. Joe knew that if he was wrong, he'd have to find their trail even if it meant going to the spot where he had made the decision to rejoin the wagon, but they had been riding due west for too long to turn back or suddenly veer south toward Lander. Besides, he knew that his deputies should have the roads covered. No, they had to be at one of the ranches. He hoped it was the Foster ranch because there was good cover just north of the ranch house.

The Riley ranch would be the worst of the three because it was so open. There was over a mile of clear ground surrounding the ranch house and he couldn't sneak up on anyone in that house, unless they were still so arrogant not to post a lookout even with their diminished number. Joe didn't think that was likely either.

He finally spotted the Foster ranch access road in the distance and slowed Boomer down to a walk. He left his Winchester and the Sharps in their scabbards as he stared at the ranch, waiting for the ranch house to appear in view.

He caught the edge of the barn after two more minutes and turned Boomer off the road into the rough ground. He entered the trees and kept Boomer walking until he knew he'd be able to see the house, which should be about another half a mile away. He turned Boomer south again and walked him until he could see the trees thinning and then pulled him to a stop.

He stepped down and just took the field glasses with him and walked to the edge of the trees but stayed back enough so there was no sun that could glint off the lenses. Joe looked first with his naked eyes, didn't see anything, then pulled the field glasses into position and could see the front of the Foster ranch house clearly.

There was no motion inside and no smoke coming from the cookstove pipe or the fireplace. Even if they had used the cookstove two hours ago, there would be some smoke from the pipe, but there wasn't a wisp. He was certain that there was no one there, so he turned back to Boomer, mounted him and then rode out of the forest and trotted toward the house. If there was someone there, he'd find out soon enough.

But there was no morning-shattering gunfire as he reached the house and quickly stepped down. He pulled his right-hand Smith & Wesson, reminding himself to switch the pistols to keep the wear even, then walked onto the porch and swung the door open.

After the loud screech had ended, Joe stepped inside and walked quickly through the house to be sure it was empty, then trotted back out of the house and mounted Boomer, walked him to the trough and let him drink while he thought about the Riley house, which was next on the list.

Maybe, if he approached from the south and got in behind the barn, they wouldn't spot him. It was the best he could do, but it meant going cross country rather than using the road.

He had already increased his odds of finding the outlaws to fifty percent, assuming they were in one of the ranches, so he figured cutting a wide southeastern loop around the Riley house would be a wise choice.

So, after Boomer was finished drinking, Joe headed due east out into the pastures of the Riley ranch where their hundred and twenty head of cattle grazed peacefully, oblivious to the turmoil that had come to their home. He kept riding east for another five minutes before turning south. He knew that the three ranches were each on a single section of land, which was small for this part of the world. There were some ranches in the county that were sixty-four sections, but right now, that one section of open land was going to present a problem if those four men were holding out at the Riley ranch.

As he rode south, he kept his attention to the west, but still would scan the ground for tracks, knowing they had to cross this ground to reach the ranch house. After three more minutes, he found four sets of tracks heading west and knew he had found his targets.

He quickly stopped Boomer and looked right, spotting the ranch house and barn in the distance about two miles west. He pulled his field glasses to his eyes, spotted the smoke from the cookstove and blew out his breath.

He swiveled in his saddle, replaced the field glasses in his saddlebags and then took out a box of .45-90 Express cartridges for his '76 and dropped another dozen rounds into his right jacket pocket. He replaced the remaining cartridges in his saddlebags, then took out the Sharps ammunition, dropped another eight rounds of the Sharps cartridges in his left pocket before slipping the half-empty box back into the saddlebags. He was ready.

He set Boomer off to a medium trot, no longer worried about dust as he rode south to get far enough away to swing around behind the barn.

"What's that?" Charlie Smith said as he looked out the kitchen window.

He held the coffeepot in his hand as he stared through the dirty window, wondering if his eyes were playing with him.

"What are you lookin' at, Charlie?" asked Pierre.

"I ain't sure. It looks like a dust cloud, but it could just be a dust devil. I thought I mighta seen a flash of somethin', but now I'm not so sure," he replied as he kept staring.

"Want Hank to go and take a look?" asked Bob.

"Nah. I'm gonna head out to the back porch myself. I need to get outta this house for a while anyway." Charlie said as he grabbed his Winchester and yanked open the back door.

"Maybe it's the guys following our trail, Bob," suggested Pierre.

"Maybe, but they'd be makin' a helluva bigger dust cloud than a dust devil," Hanger Bob replied.

Charlie walked out to the porch and screened his eyes from the sun as he peered east. The dust cloud was to the southeast now, but he couldn't see what was making it at this distance because of the tall bushes and trees scattered around the edge of the property.

He turned and walked back inside, still uneasy about the sighting.

"Say, Bob, I didn't see what was makin' that dust cloud, so I'm gonna go and check it out. I'll be back in a little while, tell Hank not to shoot me if he sees me comin' in."

Bob laughed and said, "Maybe I will and maybe I won't, Charlie."

Charlie snorted, then grabbed his hat and walked down the hallway, crossed the main room and onto the front porch where Hank

Anderson sat with his Winchester leaned against his leg. He looked up at Charlie when he crossed through the doorway.

"Hank, I'm gonna saddle my horse and ride east to check out a dust cloud that I saw. Keep your eyes peeled and don't go shootin' me when I get back."

Hank grinned and replied, "I wouldn't shoot you, Charlie. I might shoot Hanger Bob, though."

Charlie stepped off the porch saying, "Good luck with that, Hank," then turned and headed for the barn.

———

Joe had spotted some movement at the ranch house and cursed himself for creating the dust cloud. Now, he had a problem. They had seen him, but he wasn't sure if they knew he was the law. He might just be a hunter or a ranch hand from a neighboring ranch, but he couldn't take a chance that he wasn't going to ride into a trap, so he slowed down again, reduced his dust signature, and kept moving south.

He finally turned west again when the trees allowed him some cover and he disappeared from view, but he was a good mile and a half from the ranch house now. He'd have to stop periodically and check to see if any of the four exited the house to hunt him down. If they did, he'd prefer that all four of them come out. He'd be able to wait until they trailed him close and then take them all out with his Winchester. No more Mr. Nice Guy, not with the odds four to one against him. At least, he'd shoot them in the front, and they'd get about a half a second warning from his Winchester's muzzle. That was a better chance than they gave their victims.

———

Charlie had his horse saddled and was climbing aboard while Joe was holding Boomer still and watching the ranch house a mile and a half to the southeast. Joe spotted him as soon as he cleared the barn and began to ride more easterly than southerly, but he was still heading for Joe.

Joe thought about using the Sharps, but he wanted a second or even a third shot if needed, and that meant the Winchester. He stepped down, pulled his '76 and walked to the edge of the trees, keeping an eye on the rider who was now less than a mile away. Joe wasn't sure at this range, but he looked like Charlie Smith, the leader of the half-breed gang. Charlie was the shortest of the three gang leaders and wore his jet-black hair long.

———

Charlie was riding at a medium trot as he scanned the landscape. The dust cloud was gone, and he hadn't seen any more dust devils, so he assumed there was a rider nearby, and decided to shift more easterly to check for tracks at the edge of the property.

He also pulled his Winchester and cocked the hammer. Charlie Smith was not about to be surprised by anyone.

———

Joe noticed the change in direction and began running quick calculations in his head. The alteration in his path would keep him around two hundred and fifty yards away and more importantly, moving across his line of vision, which meant he'd have to lead him at an extreme range. It would be a difficult shot at best. Joe then looked back at the house. No one else was coming, so he'd have a chance to get Charlie Smith, but a gunshot would alert the ones in the house. Still, cutting the odds to three to one sounded appealing to Joe.

He then turned quickly and jogged back to Boomer, unhitched him from the branch, and stepped up. He walked Boomer to the last tree in line and watched as Charlie Smith passed him and kept riding east, oblivious to the lawman just a couple of hundred yards away.

Joe then walked Boomer out of the trees and began following Charlie, but the intercepting angle began decreasing the gap between the two antagonists even though Charlie Smith was trotting at a slightly faster pace.

After another minute or so, Joe had cut the distance to a hundred and fifty yards and brought his rifle to bear on Charlie Smith's back.

"Charlie!" Joe shouted then waited for his reaction.

Charlie was startled by the shout and quickly brought his rifle to his shoulder and whipped it around toward Joe.

Joe let him take his shot, knowing he was risking being hit, but the odds were that he wouldn't take a bullet.

Charlie fired, but never had a chance to find out if he'd hit his target when Joe's .50 caliber missile slammed into his right shoulder, exploding the bone and ripping arteries apart as the lead and bone fragments all scattered. He screamed, dropped his rifle and was reaching for his pistol with his left hand when Joe's second shot arrived, putting that small chance for survival to rest. The second large bullet plowed into Charlie's chest, almost dead center, ending his screaming and knocking him from his horse.

Joe didn't take a second to evaluate Charlie's condition, but whipped Boomer around and charged him toward the house, a mile and a half away.

———

In the house, Pierre jumped up from his chair, shouted, "Son of a bitch!" and grabbed his Winchester while Bob did the same. Both rushed to the back porch and spotted Joe flying down from the pastures, his badge flashing in the morning sun.

"It's that damned sheriff!" shouted Bob as Hank Anderson came racing from around the side of the house.

"How do you want to handle this, Bob?" asked Pierre loudly.

Hanger Bob Jones, feared outlaw and killer of seven men, said, "Let's get our horses and split up. He can't follow us all."

Pierre was disgusted and snarled, "If you wanna run, Bob, you go ahead. I'm gonna shoot it out with that bastard!"

Bob didn't care what Pierre thought. He raced across the yard, leapt on his horse bareback and set him to a trot until he cleared the barn and then raced off to the west, leaving Pierre and Hank to face the onrushing lawman.

"Hank, get over near the barn, behind that open door. I'm gonna get behind that trough. When he gets in range, we'll both let him have it."

"Okay, Pierre!" Hank shouted as he sprinted toward the barn.

Pierre ran the thirty feet to the trough and ducked behind the heavy wood for protection. He would have had a lot more protection if it had been filled with water, but it wasn't even half full as he crouched behind his cover, waiting for Joe to come within range.

Hank was half-hidden behind the barn door doing the same.

Neither man had distinguished the marked sound difference between the .44 caliber Henry cartridges that their Winchester '73s fired and the much more potent .50 caliber Express cartridge. They only saw the sheriff riding toward them with a Winchester in his hand. It was a costly lack of knowledge.

———

Joe had seen Hanger Bob make his break, and knew where the last two were, and had no intention of getting closer than two hundred yards. He had an advantage in firepower and he intended to make full use of it.

Pierre and Hank watched as Joe slowed his horse to a trot and then to a walk and were both confused by his actions. He was still in the open, and in another few seconds, he'd still be within range of their rifles, so what was he doing?

Pierre and Hank both ducked behind their cover to give the lawman another few seconds to draw within range.

Joe kept walking Boomer until he was about a hundred and sixty yards out. He then pulled his big gray to a halt and aimed at Pierre Le Tour. He could see the man's hat sticking above the trough, making him an easy target. He dropped his sights onto the trough, just four inches below the top of the back side and squeezed his trigger.

Pierre had decided to take a peek and almost giggled when he saw the smoke bloom out of Joe's Winchester at that range and with him hiding behind an inch and a half of water-soaked pine.

He was then shocked when that inch and a half of water-soaked pine exploded, and a fifty-caliber slug of lead blasted through the wood and punched into his chin while splinters flew into his face and arms.

He screamed, dropped his rifle and stood, his hands automatically grabbing for his face with its non-existent lower jaw. As soon as he stood, Joe's second shot ended his misery when it ripped into his chest.

Hank had watched Pierre take the hit and knew he was a dead man, barn door or no barn door, so he quickly threw down his rifle and stepped out from behind the barn door with his hands raised.

Joe wanted to shoot him so badly for what he had done, but he couldn't. He trotted Boomer up to Hank Anderson and shouted, "Get on the ground on your belly and keep those hands on the ground above your head!"

Hank dropped to the hard dirt and closed his eyes tightly while his heart pounded against his chest, still horrified at the sight of Pierre's half-face. He was doing everything he could to keep from crying.

Joe reached Hank Anderson, slipped down from his horse and pulled out his one set of handcuffs. He walked behind Hank and said, "Put your hands behind your back."

Hank quickly complied and felt the strangely reassuring sensation of handcuffs being tightened around his wrists. He wasn't going to die today.

Joe pulled Hank's Colt from his holster, then stood up and pulled Hank to his feet.

"What's your name?" Joe asked.

"Hank. Hank Anderson," Hank replied quickly.

"You're under arrest for murder, rape and kidnapping, Mr. Anderson, and I will be there to watch you hang."

Then he led Hank into the barn, sat him down and tied his ankles with pigging strings.

"I'm going to chase down your boss, Hank. I'll be back in a little while and don't think about whining for water. You just sit there."

Hank wasn't going to whine about anything as he watched the sheriff leave, climb on his horse and ride off.

Hanger Bob had raced his horse north out of the ranch and had passed the Foster place. He needed to get away first, then he needed a saddle. He still had his Winchester and his Colt, though, so he should be able to relieve someone of his saddle; maybe some money, too. All of the gang's cash was in his saddlebags back at that ranch.

Bob didn't feel ashamed one bit for running. This wasn't a matter of being a coward, it was just a smart move. That damned lawman had killed Charlie and he knew how good Charlie was with his rifle. Charlie was a lot better than he was with his one eye, and if Charlie couldn't get him, what were his odds?

He'd heard the gunfire in the distance, even over the rumbling sound of his horse's hooves. He then spotted wagon tracks and followed them west, knowing they'd lead to a ranch.

———

Emma was talking to Billy as they sat on the front porch. She had the wanted poster in her hand and was still coming to grip with what it said.

"Why would Joe write this, Billy? This doesn't make any sense at all. He doesn't even talk to me that much."

"Yes, it does, Mama. I think Joe really likes you. He said you were the most impressive woman he'd ever met."

Emma felt a rush but asked, "Did he really say that, Billy, or are you making it up?"

"No, Mama, I'm not. Joe told me to never underestimate you because you were the most impressive woman he'd ever met."

Emma looked at the words on the poster:

Everything I own goes to Emma Harper. All of it.

Emma folded the sheet and handed it back to Billy, then she squinted as she looked eastward and said quickly, "Billy, someone's coming and it's not Joe!"

Billy stood quickly and spotted the bareback rider ripping up the trail leaving a large dust cloud behind him.

"It's that Hanger Bob Jones!" Billy shouted as he reached for his Winchester.

Emma grabbed her repeater and they trotted out to the yard.

Billy shouted, "Trouble comin', Ben!"

Ben yelled from behind him, “I see him, Billy, let’s get ready.”

Billy just began walking toward the access road with his Winchester. He cocked the hammer and stopped, put the butt on his hip and stood watching the rider.

He felt movement beside him and smiled when he saw his mother doing exactly the same thing with her rifle.

———

Hanger Bob spotted the movement when he was a half a mile from the ranch and then had to stare with his one good eye when a boy and a woman both walked away from the house with Winchesters and stood side-by-side, letting him know they were waiting for him. He then saw other women and another boy with Winchesters. *My God! It was an army of women and children with guns!*

He finally recognized his ‘wife’ and knew that the women had been freed and that meant that Charlie had been right, and he was probably alone now. He also knew it would be suicide to keep riding into that ranch, so he just thundered past the access road and kept going, looking over his shoulder as he did to make sure no one was following.

They all watched him ride west and then disappear into his own dust cloud.

“Do we go after him?” Emma asked, “I know I’d like to personally shoot that bastard!”

Billy replied, “No, Mama. Joe will be along shortly and then he’ll tell us what to do.”

“You don’t think Joe was shot, do you?” she asked.

“No, Mama. I’m sure that he wasn’t. That outlaw was running from him and I’m sure he’s all alone now.”

Emma then said, "I'll go and tell the others," then trotted back to the house.

Joe had Boomer at a fast trot as he made the turn toward the Hobson ranch. He could trail Hanger Bill's horse easily until it was mixed with the large herd of horses and the wagon tracks that he had led to the ranch just hours earlier.

He hadn't heard any gunfire and that meant that Bob Jones either kept going past the ranch after seeing the display of firepower that was waiting for him, or he had left the trail before he got there.

Hanger Bob's tracks lost, Joe stopped looking at the trail itself and began to scan the ground on either side to see if the outlaw had left the trail and gone cross-country.

He reached the access road to the Hobson ranch and kept going, soon picking up Bob's trail again. He picked up the pace and had Boomer moving at a medium trot following the easily spotted hoofprints.

"Where is Joe going?" asked Sarah Foster as they all stood on the front porch watching him ride past.

"He's going after the last one," replied Emma.

Sarah sighed and said, "I hope he doesn't get hurt."

Jennie then added, "I hope he stays safe, too."

Neither Emma nor Abby Hobson commented.

Joe followed the trail until it disappeared six miles away. The trail itself had been long gone, but now, the ground became too difficult to track and Joe didn't want to walk into an ambush. He finally stopped Boomer and cupped his hands over his mouth.

"I've killed all of your men except for Hank Anderson, who will hang in a few days! I've burned Cooperstown and you are alone Hanger Bob! I will get you, but I need to clean up the mess you left first. You are nothing now and never were!"

Then he wheeled Boomer around even as his shouted warning echoed through the mountains west of the ranch.

Four miles northwest of Joe, Bob Jones heard the threat and seethed. He knew the lawman wasn't lying, but that didn't help him now. He wasn't very good outdoors, so he needed to get some food and supplies, then he'd get that damned sheriff.

———

Joe had to go and bring Hank Anderson into Lander, and it was getting late in the afternoon. He also needed to eat and take care of Boomer. With Hanger Bob still on the loose, the women couldn't return to their homes yet, and then there was the wagon and horses at the McClellan ranch, the axle-broken wagon west of the Shoshone Indian agency store and all that paperwork he still had to do.

He turned into the access road and wasn't surprised to see everyone waiting for him as he walked Boomer down the road. His eyes naturally searched out Emma and found her right out front with Billy.

He halted Boomer before the crowd and stepped down.

"Did you get him, Joe?" asked Billy.

"Nope. He rode up into those foothills. I warned him before I left, but I have Hank Anderson tied up in the Riley barn and two dead outlaws I have to deal with, too, so I'll be heading out shortly. I won't be back until the morning, if then. I'm going to have to trail Hanger Bob, and that might take a few days, but I have to do it."

Emma asked, "Would you like to get something to eat before you leave, Joe?"

Joe smiled at her and replied, "I'd like to, but I really need to get going. I don't like trailing prisoners when it gets dark, even if they're trussed up. I need to get him into the jail today. I'm just going to get water into Boomer and head back to the Riley ranch, load up the two bodies and Hank Anderson and then go to Lander, brief my deputies and write my report."

Emma just nodded before Joe returned to Boomer and led him to the trough. Billy and Ben followed, and as Boomer drank, Joe told them to keep an eye out for Hanger Bob, but he didn't believe he'd come back to the Hobson ranch.

"How bad was this gunfight, Joe?" Billy asked.

"Odd; as they all are. One of them rode out of the house looking for me and I snuck up behind him and called his name. He turned and fired and then I did. The second one was hiding behind a half empty trough. I have no idea why he thought he was safe. The third one gave up after seeing the guy behind the trough get hit.

"I've got to go, men," Joe said as he stepped up into his saddle again.

He gave a short wave to Ben and Billy and then another to the assembled ladies on the porch as he trotted past and down the access road.

———

Hanger Bob figured he'd waited long enough, so he walked the horse down from the foothills and reached level ground. He didn't want to ride past that ranch again, so he started out cross country heading south.

His stomach was grousing, and he wasn't happy with riding bareback. He was even getting tired of having to hold onto his rifle for so long. He was getting ornery and wanted to kill someone.

Boomer made short work of the ride to the Riley ranch, arriving less than an hour after leaving the Hobsons. He then rode Boomer to the barn, stepped down, then pulled the canteen from his saddle and walked inside.

Hank Anderson raised his head and Joe saw his swollen, red eyes and thought he had been crying.

"Alright, Hank, I'm going to give you some water and then I've got to load those two bodies onto their horses."

Before he drank the water, Hank asked, "Did you get Hanger Bob?"

"Nope. He ran into the hills and I needed to get back here. I'll find him. He didn't do right by you, did he, Hank? The man lit out when you could have used his rifle."

"Yeah, I know. The damned coward hung us out to dry. I'll shoot him if I see him again."

Joe didn't comment on that remote possibility but upended the canteen and let him drink. Then, he stood and said, "I'll be back in a half an hour, then I'll get you mounted for the two-hour ride into Lander."

Hank didn't reply, so Joe just walked back out of the barn, hung the canteen back on Boomer and then returned to the barn and began to saddle the two unsaddled horses in the barn. Charlie's horse should still be saddled in the pasture somewhere.

After saddling the two horses, he led one of them to the trough, stepped down and could already see the gruesome damaged done to Pierre Le Tour by the heavy rounds from his Winchester. He decided a tarp would be necessary to cover the damage from the eyes of any of the citizens of Lander, so he returned to the barn and found a poor example, but it would do as he carried it back to the trough.

He stretched out the tarp, then walked to Pierre's carcass, picked it up the back collar and the waist of the pants, lifted it from the ground, carted it to the tarp and lowered it to the canvas face down. He then rolled the tarp over the body and lifted it onto the saddle and tied it down.

He then hitched the corpse-carrying horse to the back rail and climbed back on Boomer to go and get Charlie Smith's remains.

Joe spotted Charlie's horse still grazing nearby, so he pulled up next to the animal, reached over and took its reins, led it to Charlie's body and stepped down. After making a trail rope and connecting the horse to Boomer, he loaded the second body onto the saddle.

After tying it down securely, he turned the two horses around and headed for the house. As the rode along on the way back, Joe thought about Hanger Bob riding bareback and suddenly realized that he hadn't checked the saddlebags of the three gang leaders. He figured if anyone had anything valuable, like cash, it would be one or all of the gang leaders.

Joe walked the trail horse back to the house then hopped down and stepped over to the horse with Pierre's body. He checked the saddlebags and found some nasty clothes, two boxes of .44s and one bottle of whiskey. He tossed the clothes and the whiskey, left the cartridges inside and then grabbed Charlie's saddlebags and found some very dirty clothes, one box of cartridges and two bottles of whiskey. He emptied both bottles and tossed them aside then dropped the filthy clothes on top of the bottles, leaving only the cartridges inside. Before checking the last set, which must have belonged to Hanger Bob, he cleaned up the bottles and clothes and dumped them into the trash bin near the back door.

Then, he walked over to the only saddlebags he hadn't checked, opened the set and found one bottle of whiskey, some not-so-filthy clothes, two boxes of cartridges and a thick leather pouch.

Joe pulled the pouch from the saddlebags, flipped open the flap, exposing the contents to the sunlight and saw currency – lots of currency. He did a quick count and came up with just under four thousand dollars.

"I stand corrected, Billy," Joe said out loud as he closed the pouch and slid it into his own saddle bag.

He then returned to the barn and pulled his knife, cut Hank's ankle bonds, stood him up and led him in a stumbling gait to his horse and got him in the saddle then tied his ankles to the stirrups with fresh pigging strings.

"Stay there, Hank, we'll be leaving in a minute," Joe said straight-faced before he jogged to the back of the house and walked Pierre's body-draped horse back to Boomer and added it to the trail rope before adding Hank's.

Ten minutes later, Joe had them all moving at a decent speed toward Lander as the sun dropped lower in the west.

Bob Jones had been riding south across some rugged country for four hours now and guessed he was near that ranch where he had left his saddle and the all-important saddlebags. He hoped that the sheriff hadn't looked inside, but if he had, that would put him in bad shape. At least he'd have a saddle again, and he wouldn't have to carry the damned rifle.

It had been almost fifteen years since Hanger Jones had worked alone and that was when he had two good eyes and was just a kid of twenty-two. Now, he was older, didn't see half the world, and the half he did see wasn't as good as it used to be. He couldn't afford to get into a shooting match with the sheriff or anyone else for that matter. He was angry with himself for growing old as he turned northward again to return to the Riley ranch and get his saddle and, hopefully, his money.

It was after six o'clock when Joe walked Boomer trailing the three horses into Lander. Most of the businesses were already closed down for the day and the folks were eating supper, so it was quiet when he stopped the parade in front of his office, noticing that a lamp was lit inside.

He slowly stepped down, threw Boomer's reins over the hitching rail and swung open the door, surprised to see both of his deputies still in the office. He thought one would be there, but not both of them.

They both hopped up from their chairs and shouted, "Joe!" at the same time, before they stepped over and began to shake his hand and pound him on the back.

"Calm down, boys. We have work to do," he finally managed to say.

"We were gonna wait another half an hour, Joe. We figured you'd be making it back today, sooner or later."

"Well, I'm back and I have a lot to tell you both, but first, I'd appreciate it if you both could step outside and help me with one live prisoner and two dead outlaws."

"Let's go, Ed," Charlie Wheatley said as they both stood and followed Joe outside.

"Ed, after I unhitch the two carcass-carrying horses, I need you to take them down to Peabody's and just have him and his assistant unload the two bodies. If you want to try and identify them, you can, but I know you don't have the strongest stomach and one of them, Pierre Le Tour, took a fifty caliber into his lower jaw and he doesn't have one anymore. The other body belongs to Charlie Smith, the leader of the half-breed gang. Up there on the horse is Hank Anderson, who was a member of Hanger Bob Jones' little band of merry men. Hanger Bob is the only one unaccounted for and I know where he probably is going to be in a little while. I'll need to get Hank locked up and the three extra horses taken to the livery, Charlie. I'm going to go into the café to get something to eat and bring something back for Hank and then write my report."

"We'll take care of it, boss," Charlie replied as he walked over to Hank's horse, pulled his knife and cut the pigging strings on one side before walking to the other side and slicing the bindings loose, then helping Hank down from the saddle.

Joe then walked to Boomer, opened the saddlebag and removed the pouch before helping to guide Hank into the jail.

Ed then led the three horses to a trough to drink before walking them down the street to the undertakers.

Charlie and Joe marched Hank inside then Charlie loped ahead, unlocked one of the two cells and Joe removed Hanks handcuffs and let him walk into his new home. Charlie clanged the door shut then he and Joe returned to the desk.

"I've got to put this in my office safe before I go and get something to eat. I found it in Hanger Bob's saddlebags. It has almost four thousand dollars inside, and I plan on giving it to the three families that his gang attacked along with the reward money from the dead outlaws."

Charlie stared at the pouch for a few seconds and then looked up at Joe and asked, "Can we do that, Joe? I mean the reward money is yours to do with what you wish, but can we just give away recovered loot like that?"

"I'll go and have a chat with Judge Moore about it when I get back. I'm sure he won't mind. We have no idea where they got the money and it'd be hell to try and find out. Then, people would exaggerate how much they lost and people who had never lost a dime would come out demanding some, so it's a lot better to just make it disappear. Legally, of course."

Charlie grinned before saying, "Sounds good to me, Joe."

After he had locked the pouch in the safe, he passed Hank, who had heard him say that Hanger Bob had four thousand dollars in the pouch and was more than just a little miffed. Joe told Hank he'd bring him some food in a little while, then left the office and walked north on the boardwalk to Minnie's Café.

He found a seat and an older waitress approached their table.

"Good evening, Joe. Not eating in the boarding house tonight?"

"No, Lizzie. Just got back from hunting down a gang of criminals and need to make my report."

"Good for you. What can I get you?"

"The chicken sounds good. I'm going to need a tray to take back to a prisoner, too."

"I'll be right back with some coffee, and I'll have your food shortly."

"Thank you, Lizzie."

Joe practically inhaled his baked chicken, mashed potatoes and gravy, and after he finished his coffee, he dropped a silver dollar on the table and left the café with Hank's tray.

They returned to the office, found both deputies still there, with Charlie in the chair and Ed half sitting on the desktop. Ed slid off and relieved Joe of the tray and took it to Hank.

Joe then stepped up to the desk and said, "Charlie, I'm going into my office and write my report. While I'm writing, I'll tell you and Ed the details of what happened. I'll certify the deaths of all fourteen of the gang members. You can get their names from Hank, although we have most of them with the wanted posters anyway. In the morning, send out telegrams to those offering the rewards and have them sent to me. I'll handle the distribution to the ladies. After I finished, I'm going to head back to the Riley ranch because I think Hanger Bob will go back there for his money."

"You ever gonna sleep again, Joe?" asked Charlie.

"I'll be okay, Charlie. Let's head to my office."

For the next forty minutes, Joe wrote and talked to his deputies to bring them up to speed on what had happened since he left Lander.

When he finished, he handed the six pages to Charlie and said, "I'm going to get going again, Charlie. If you see Judge Moore, let him read the report and tell him what I plan to do with the money."

"I'll do that, Joe."

"The town is in your hands, Charlie," Joe said as he rose from behind his desk.

Charlie asked, "Are you still gonna quit, Joe?"

"Maybe not, Charlie."

"Good. Don't even think about it because we need you," Charlie replied.

Joe smiled, grabbed his hat and said, "I'm not so sure about that, Charlie," then walked from his office, stepped outside, mounted Boomer and trotted north out of town.

———

"Damn it!" Hanger Bob shouted when he saw his missing saddlebags.

He was almost as irritated by not finding any of their other horses in the barn, either. He finally just saddled his horse, then led him to the back of the house, and walked into the house after tying off his animal.

He entered the cold room and found a jar of pickles, another of strawberry jam, and some butter. He took them all out to the kitchen and opened the pantry finding just one can of beans. He angrily snatched the beans from the shelf and slammed it on the cookstove, but soon realized that was a bad idea when the can bounced from his hand and almost hit him in the forehead.

It did nothing to improve his mood.

He didn't bother with plates because there weren't any. He opened the can of beans with his knife and then opened the jar of pickles. He ate a pickle as he hunted for something to use to pour the beans into, but didn't find anything remotely suitable, so he just pushed back the sharp top and upended the can into his mouth. Once his mouth was full, he chewed the cold beans and then did it twice more until the can was empty. He belched and then wiped his mouth with the back of his sleeve before taking out another pickle and finishing it in four big bites.

When he finished with the second pickle, he worked the kitchen pump until water flowed and then stuck his mouth into the flow and began to slurp at the running water.

The man who had demanded respect from fifteen men and was feared wherever he and his gang had roamed, disgustedly plopped down into the chair and recognized the depths to which he had fallen. He was worth seven hundred and fifty dollars to someone, because that was the current price on his head.

"I wonder if I'd get the reward if I turned myself in," he said out loud before cackling at his joke.

He belched again, then opened the jar of strawberry jam and just stuck his hand into the jar and scooped out a large glob of the gooey, sweet red condiment. He lifted it above his head and let it flow slowly into his mouth. Then he licked his hand and repeated it twice more before he returned to the pump and washed his hands.

After drying his hands on his pants, he began to wonder if he should stay in the ranch house or leave in case that sheriff came back. The question was answered for him when his stomach suddenly protested the sudden mixture of pickles and strawberry jam and Hanger Bob heaved, his odd dinner splattering all over the kitchen floor.

He swore again, walked to the pump one more time and rinsed out his mouth before leaving the kitchen and its stinking mess and mounting his horse. He needed food and none of the three ranches had any. He did know of one other place that was due east where he knew there was some food. There was a whole wagon full of supplies sitting four miles west of that Indian agency store.

He turned due east and started following his own tracks at a medium trot. He wanted to make use of the existing light as much as he could.

He was six miles east of the ranch as sunset arrived, but he kept riding.

———

Joe had Boomer moving at a good clip through the fading light, and passed the Harper ranch, where this all started. Joe knew he was close to the Riley ranch after he had left it behind.

Twenty minutes later, he slowed before reaching the Riley ranch. The moon wasn't up yet, so he approached slowly, walking his horses toward the house, his Winchester pulled and cocked.

Joe pointed Boomer toward the barn to see if Bob Jones had been there, and as he neared the barn door, he stopped short to listen for the sound of a hammer being drawn back. After thirty seconds of complete silence except for Boomer's breathing, he then dismounted, leaving Boomer just standing there as he entered the barn. It didn't take long to notice the missing saddle, even in the low light. He lowered his Winchester and turned back to the barn doors and stepped outside.

Joe then trotted toward the back of the house, and before he reached the porch, he knew that Hanger Bob had been inside. His eyes were watering as he swung the door open and spied the mess on the floor, grateful there wasn't much light.

But he had to make sure that Bob wasn't still in the house, as unlikely as that may have been, so he entered the kitchen, holding his breath as he noisily walked through the house, hoping to stir the outlaw into action, but not expecting to find him there. No one, not even a low-life like Hanger Bob would stay in a house with that smell.

But the house was still Jennie Riley's, so he decided to clean it up as best he could. He went back into one of the bedrooms and found some worn men's shirts and returned to the nauseating kitchen. Joe soaked the shirts in the sink and wasn't surprised to find a bar of soap, so he lathered the shirts and then did a quick job cleaning up the stinking mess and running the shirts to the porch and hurling them away from the house. He bent at the waist and began taking deep breaths as he braced himself with his hands on his knees.

He then returned to the still foul-smelling kitchen, opened a window, hunted for any sort of container, found a dented small pot in the back of the cold room. He shaved off some soap and pumped the pot full, swished both of his hands through the water building up some suds before drying his hands on his pants and dumping the sudsy water over the cleaned vomitus area.

It would be okay in the morning, he thought, but he wasn't about to stay in the house overnight. He'd stay in the sweet-smelling barn, probably the first time that adjective had been applied to the building since horses had first taken up residence.

Twenty minutes later, Joe was lying atop his bedroll in the barn while Boomer was still eating some oats from the feed bin, unsaddled and content.

Joe was far from content. Tomorrow morning, as soon as there was light, he'd have to find where Hanger Bob had left the ranch. If he took the road, it would be a hard trail to follow, but Joe hoped that Bob was still too twitchy after the gunfight and would avoid the roads. He stared at the barn's beams and tried to think of another place nearby that might entice Bob. It would have to be an easy target because he was alone. He also had that eye patch, which meant he lost a lot of his peripheral vision. Joe then wondered how that affected his aim. *Was that why Bob had run from the earlier confrontation at the Riley ranch?*

As he began drifting to sleep, he spent most of his time wondering where Bob might go, but it was interspersed with too much thought of Emma, which still was a dilemma for Joe.

———

While Joe was trying to think of where he might be going, Hanger Bob was laid out on the ground in his bedroll looking up at the moonless, starry sky, only he wasn't impressed with the powerful beauty of the Milky Way. His stomach was still empty, and he had no money, but he knew where he could get some. Four miles past that broken wagon and its food, was the empty Indian agency store and its cash drawer was probably still full.

He'd get up early and go and visit that store, get something to eat and with the money, he'd be able to head for one of those small towns and buy what he needed.

Then Bob smiled and thought, why buy anything? He had depended on Charlie Smith for information about who ranched or farmed, but how hard could it be to find a small farm or a ranch and just take what he wanted?

He'd still go to the agency store first, though.

CHAPTER 6

Hanger Bob was up first the next morning when he was greeted by a light rain that began shortly before sunrise.

"Damn it!" he shouted as he spluttered and wiped the moisture from his face. He quickly slid out from his bedroll and realized he didn't have a rain slicker. He rolled the bedroll back into its traveling shape and pulled on his hat, then saddled his horse, put the bedroll over the back of the saddle and began riding east, hoping to get some breakfast from the wagon.

———

Joe's reaction to the rain wasn't much nicer than his prey's. If the rain got any harder, he'd lose the trail altogether, and it was already looking as if it would soon get much harder.

He quickly pulled on his boots, and after emptying his bladder, he quickly saddled Boomer, threw his slicker over his head, reached into his left-hand saddlebag and pulled out a small tarp. After he mounted Boomer, he laid the tarp across his saddle horn and tucked the ends in the rifle scabbards to keep them dry.

Now, as he prepared to leave the barn, he had to try and guess which direction Bob would have gone. He sat on Boomer at the open barn doors and looked in both directions, made up his mind, rode the gelding into the rain and turned east.

He was gambling that Bob might seek his old gang and head back towards the Cooperstown location. He hadn't thought about the broken supply wagon or the Indian agency store, but his missed guess didn't hurt the outcome. He had made the right decision for the wrong reason.

Joe rode across the pasture, seeing hoofprints everywhere. He spotted Charlie's and then the four sets coming into the ranch and then, he spotted a set of prints riding east that were made by a single rider and were recent.

As he rode east into the increasingly heavy rain, he hoped those prints were not only Bob's but wouldn't wash away.

———

Twelve miles ahead, a miserable Hanger Bob plodded along, his head down and water racing from his hat's brim in heavy sheets. He was so angry, he didn't even cuss. He just kept his jaws tight as he continued to walk his horse, looking up every few seconds hoping to see that elusive wagon.

He had been following the trail he had made with his three partners just yesterday morning. He was surprised that he actually missed Charlie Smith. For some reason, he and the half-breed had gotten along. Pierre Le Tour had just latched his gang onto theirs thinking he'd get more loot and notoriety, but Bob and Charlie had gotten along. It helped that Charlie knew the area better than anyone else in the group. It had been Charlie's idea to take over that abandoned town and it was a great idea except for that damned sheriff. *How the hell did he get onto them so fast?*

He was beginning to wonder if someone had come along, found the wagon, fixed it and driven it off when he finally spotted the still loaded wagon a couple of hundred yards right in front of him.

He almost giggled as he kicked his horse into a trot. There might not be a slicker in that stack, but there were still three cases of whiskey to warm him up, some food to fill his belly, and an Indian agency store less than five miles straight ahead.

———

While Bob was finding his much-needed supply wagon, Joe was still on his trail. The rain was making tracking difficult in the mud, but he had noticed that the new hoofprints were following the same trail of the four sets of hoofprints heading toward the Riley ranch.

Hanger Bob was heading back the way he came as he had suspected, then Joe wondered if it wasn't the food on the damaged supply wagon that was luring Bob in that direction. The reason didn't really matter, at least he was sure that Bob was going toward the wagon.

———

Bob was like a little boy in a candy store with no adults anywhere. He had found the whiskey, pulled a bottle free of its case and taken two long draws before setting it aside and finding a can of peaches. He opened the peaches and scooped them out with his fingers before guzzling the sticky, sweet syrup.

But he needed a bag, so he sliced open a burlap bag of flour and dumped its already caked contents onto the ground and began filling the bag with food.

Then, he repeated it with a second bag and tied both together making an ad hoc set of saddlebags. He hung them over the back of his saddle, took the bottle of whiskey with him and remounted his horse. He was still wet, but in much better spirits as he trotted east toward the agency store.

Forty-five minutes later, the store came into view and Bob scanned the area for movement, but didn't see anyone, which wasn't surprising in the rain. He reached the store and thought it was empty because there were no horses out front.

He stepped down, tied off his horse and walked through the still-open door, then smacked into a small Shoshone woman carrying out an armful of blankets. She fell to the floor onto her back and the blankets scattered around her.

Bob looked down at the woman and then quickly glanced around for her husband or brother but didn't see anyone.

He closed the door behind him and said, "Well, well, well. Isn't this a pleasant surprise?"

The woman obviously didn't speak English but didn't need a translator as she looked at the evil man. She scrambled backwards on her hands and feet as he slowly walked her way.

Then, she reached to her waist and pulled a small knife from its sheath showing him the blade to ward him off.

Bob lost his grin and snarled, "You wanna play rough, do you?"

He then pulled his Colt out and cocked the hammer, pointing it straight at her frightened eyes.

Then, Bob quickly tired of the whole woman thing. Women seemed to cause him more trouble than they were worth. He simply pulled the trigger, sending the .44 through her thin neck. The blood pulsed from a ruptured carotid for a few seconds before it just stopped. Without another glance at his victim, Bob holstered his pistol and walked quickly to the cash drawer. He slid it open and was rewarded by seeing currency sitting in three compartments and silver in a fourth. It wasn't as much as he expected to find, but the eighty dollars or so would go a long way to getting him out of trouble.

He scooped out the cash and then returned to the amazingly depleted shelves but found a rain slicker and some saddlebags. He donned the slicker and then began filling the saddlebags with things he would need from the diminished stock.

His shopping complete, Bob stepped over the dead Shoshone woman and opened the door to find three Shoshone standing in the rain staring at him. He quickly pulled his Colt and backed them all away as he tossed the saddlebags over the horse and stepped up, keeping the Indians under his pistol before he turned and rode away.

The three Shoshone ran inside, and Young Buffalo wailed when he spotted his wife sprawled out on the floor. There was nothing that any of them could do because if they chased after the one-eyed white man and killed him, there would be severe repercussions against their tribe.

His friends tried to console him, but Young Buffalo was mired in a conflict of anger and grief as he looked at the peaceful face of his wife of eight months.

Joe arrived at the wagon thirty minutes after Hanger Bob had left the agency store and took note of the open whiskey case and the mounds of flour on the mud. He knew he had gained on Bob because he had spent so time to take things from the wagon.

He set Boomer east toward the agency store at a medium trot, hoping Bob had decided to stay indoors and get warm.

He saw the outline of the agency store through the rain and slowed to see if Bob's horse was out front. When he hadn't spotted the horse, he decided to make sure that the outlaw wasn't inside anyway and walked Boomer to the hitching rail and stepped down. He tossed his reins over the rail and stepped up onto the low porch.

Inside, Young Buffalo's anger had surpassed his grief and he wished he had thrown his knife at the white man even if it had meant his death.

Then they all turned when they heard bootsteps on the wood outside, and Young Buffalo slipped his blade from it sheath and prepared to pounce as the door swung open.

Young Buffalo saw the rain slicker and lunged at the white man with his blade, plunging it into the man as he screamed.

Joe was stunned by the sudden attack and had instinctively jerked his hands in front of his face, as Young Buffalo's blade sliced into his left forearm accompanied by his blood-chilling screech.

No sooner had Joe fallen to the floor with blood pouring from his arm than Young Buffalo realized his mistake as did his two friends. This white man was not wearing the eye patch.

Then, to make things even worse, one of his friends identified him as Sheriff Joe and Young Buffalo thought about ramming his knife into his own belly. He had not only shamed himself and his tribe, he had attacked and wounded a white lawman. There would be hell to pay for what he had done.

Joe knew he was losing a lot of blood, so he managed to get to his feet and, holding his arm as tightly as he could, looked around for something to stop the bleeding, saw the dead young Shoshone woman on the floor and understood the reason for the attack.

But his priority now was to staunch the flow of blood and get the deep gash sewn closed.

"I am sorry for your loss. The man who did this has killed many others and I must find him to kill him. I need to stop the blood and stitch the wound. Can you help me?" Joe asked.

"I will help you. Blue Sparrow was my wife and I was so angry I attacked without looking. I am ashamed," Young Buffalo said.

"I understand. This is not your fault. This is the fault of the evil one that I follow. I promise you that I will kill him myself, but I need to be able to travel soon and run him down."

Young Buffalo and his friends then moved to Joe and helped him into the back office with the telegraph set, where he laid down on the bed used by the Indian agent.

One warrior held Joe's arm while Young Buffalo walked back out to the store and found a sewing kit, the only one still on the shelves. He returned and then sat on the floor while his two friends held Joe's upper arm and wrist.

Young Buffalo then began to stitch the wound closed. Joe didn't watch as he clenched his jaw and felt the needle piercing the skin and the creepy feeling of thread being drawn through the muscle. It took thirty stitches to close the wound, and Young Buffalo's hands were coated with Joe's blood by the time he finished the job.

Joe was barely conscious when he said, "Whiskey. Pour whiskey on the wound. It stops infection."

There was a quarter-full bottle near the dry sink, so one of Young Buffalo's friends stood and grabbed the bottle, yanked out the cork and doused the newly closed wound with the contents of the bottle, making Joe jump in reaction to the sudden burst of pain.

"Thank you," Joe whispered, "I must go now. I have to…"

Then he passed out.

As Bob Jones rode east, retracing his route to the cutoff, he debated about which direction he would be going when he arrived at the cutoff. He recalled the original plan to get the hay from the McClellan ranch, and Charlie had said something about getting some cattle from a small ranch just north of the farm. He said the woman in the house was too old, but they had a couple of ranch hands. At first, he thought that might be a problem, but then he thought the rain might be a real break in this case. They'd probably be in the barn or the bunkhouse. If he rode in with the rain as cover, he could shoot both of the hands before getting to the house and then he'd just have an old man and an old woman to worry about. Then, he'd have a house to himself and could relax for a while and stay dry.

If he had known about Sheriff Joe's injury, he would have turned right around and gone back to finish the job, but he didn't, so he headed north to that cattle ranch.

Joe stayed unconscious for another four hours. While he lay there, Young Buffalo and his friends took Blue Sparrow's body back to her parents and explained what had happened to their chief. Like Joe, he understood why Young Buffalo had acted, but he was much more severe in his admonishment of the young warrior and told him that he was very fortunate that it had been Sheriff Joe and not some other white lawman that he had cut.

Young Buffalo accepted the rebuke and said he would ask his sister to stay with the sheriff until he was able to travel again, and the chief agreed.

So, when Joe's eyes finally did open, he saw the very different face of Shining Rain sitting four feet away. His left arm throbbed something fierce and he noticed that it was covered with a green poultice that was held in place with leather strips.

Joe smiled and croaked, "Hello."

Shining Rain didn't speak English at all, so she just smiled back.

Joe then asked in Shoshone, "Water?"

Shining Rain was surprised that he spoke her language but stood, walked to the pump, filled a glass with water and brought it to him. She put her hand behind his head as he tried to sit up, and after two attempts, finally managed to stay up at a sufficient angle to allow him to drink before settling back down.

She asked if he could speak Shoshone and he just said, "Small."

Shining Rain understood and asked if he was hungry, but Joe shook his head. He just wanted to sleep.

So, he closed his eyes and drifted off again.

The rain was slowing down, and Olaf Knutson stuck his hand out of the small bunkhouse and turned to his brother.

"Lute, I think it's stopping. We might be able to get that corral gate fixed soon."

Lute tilted his head back as he lay on his bunk, seeing his brother upside down as he replied, “Olaf, sometimes you go too far. Mr. Larsen said we should stay in the bunkhouse until it stops. So, we wait until it stops, not until it almost stops.”

Olaf returned to the bunkhouse and flopped on his own bunk.

“Sometimes, Lute, I think you aren’t Swede at all. I think you might be Fin or even a Russian.”

Lute laughed and said, “I think you must be a German; you love to work so much.”

Olaf laughed at his brother’s kidding. They’d been together since they’d been born eleven minutes apart twenty years ago and had worked for the Larsens for three years now.

He was preparing to tell Lute that he must have been an Italian, when a shadow blocked the weak light from the door. They both glanced up, expecting to see Mr. Larsen. Olaf stayed alive long enough to see a man in a slicker with a patch over his eye and a pistol in his hand. Lute never lived that long as the Colt boomed in the small bunkhouse and was immediately turned on Olaf and fired again.

They died eleven seconds apart.

Bob quickly turned back to the house and walked quickly to the back side of the house where he could see smoke coming from the cookstove pipe.

In the kitchen, Roger and Bertha Larsen were having a cup of coffee. Both were in their early sixties and had never had any children but regarded the Knutson twins as their boys. Roger had heard a boom in the distance but put it off as thunder.

They were discussing how many of the cattle to send to market when the door burst open and Bob walked in. He didn’t wait for protests or screams but shot Bertha first because women were beginning to annoy him, and then quickly shot Roger.

Just five minutes after his arrival, Hanger Bob Jones was the only living human on the ranch.

———

Joe had awakened twice in the last six hours and had just drifted right back to sleep. Shining Rain had remained at her station. She was repaying the family debt that had been created by Young Buffalo's attack, but as she looked at the white lawman, she knew of Sheriff Joe's exploits around the reservation, even though he didn't have any authority on Shoshone land. But he was allowed to chase lawbreakers who had tried to find refuge on the protected land and heard of his recent rescue of all of the women and his ferocious gun battles with the outlaws. She tried to match the face of the fearsome warrior with the kindly face she saw sleeping peacefully and found it difficult. She had always thought of warriors as fierce, frightening men with scowls and anger in their eyes. Maybe when he awakened again, she would look at his gray eyes more closely.

———

Bob was feasting on bacon and eggs and had taken off his wet clothes and had them hanging over chairs to dry, but before he changed, he had dragged the two bodies out into the drizzle and dumped them onto the back yard for the coyotes because the buzzards weren't flying today.

He had rummaged through the house and found a stash of almost a hundred dollars. This was turning out to be a very good idea, he thought as he threw a large forkful of scrambled eggs into his mouth.

———

It was getting late and the two deputies were sitting in chairs in the front office listening to the wall clock tick.

Charlie said, "I don't think he's coming back today, Ed."

"What happened, Charlie? You don't think Hanger Bob got him, do you?"

"Nope. I just figure he's out chasin' the man. In the rain, that would be a lot harder."

"Yeah, that's probably it. What did Judge Moore say?"

"He agreed with Joe, of course. The problem now is the trial for Hank back there. Mr. Masters wants to go ahead with the trial the day after tomorrow, so if Joe doesn't come back, one of us is going to have to ride out to the Hobson place and tell the ladies they're going to have to testify."

"I'll do it, Charlie," Ed said.

"Okay, you're nominated if Joe doesn't show up. Let's go home."

"What about our prisoner?" Ed asked.

"He's not goin' anywhere and he has a chamber pot and water. He'll be here when we get back in the mornin'."

"Okay," Ed replied as the two deputies stood and headed for the door after turning out the lamp.

The rain was gone early the next morning and bright sunshine returned, flooding the back room as Joe opened his eyes and took a deep breath before yawning. He slowly sat up, didn't feel too bad, and swung his legs to the floor.

He saw Shining Rain sleeping in a chair nearby and tried to be as quiet as possible as he tiptoed away from the backroom and into the store. He opened the door, walked outside and felt immense relief as he emptied his bladder into a nearby puddle. After buttoning his trousers, he examined his wound and although there was no doubt that it was there, it didn't feel nearly as bad as he expected. But when he looked for Boomer, he couldn't see him anywhere. He returned to the store and spotted his tack and rifles sitting on the floor in the first aisle.

When he turned to the back room again, he saw the smiling face of Shining Rain and asked, "Horse?"

She just pointed to the back of the store and said, "Fence," so Joe assumed she meant corral.

He then said, "I must go."

Shining Rain shook her head and said, "Eat first."

Joe nodded and walked to his saddlebags took out some jerky and took a bite of a large stick and walked to the back room, passed Shining Rain and sat at the telegraph set. He flipped the battery power on again and began tapping the key, waiting for Jim Swinton in Lander to acknowledge. Once he received Jim's initials, he began to send his message. This one wasn't as long, and as soon as he finished, he received the acknowledgement signal from Jim and shut the system down again.

He stood and, still chewing his jerky, he passed Shining Rain, smiled at her and said, "Thank you."

She just looked up at the tall man's gray eyes and smiled back.

Joe found his hat, slapped it on his head and left the store to go and find Boomer.

———

Hanger Bob luxuriated in sleeping in a nice bed for a change and even shaved that morning. He left the house, walked out to the corral and selected a nice horse, walked him into the barn and put on a nicer saddle than his horse was wearing. Once the new horse was saddled, he found an extra set of saddlebags and returned to the house, ignoring the dead bodies lying awkwardly on the ground nearby.

He carried the saddlebags inside and began filling them with food, then he picked up the two boxes of .44 cartridges he'd found the night before and a spare Winchester. He felt as if he'd struck gold when he finally left the house with the two heavy sets of saddlebags and put them both across his old horse's saddle and tied them down. Then he stepped up onto the new horse, looked briefly at the bright sun and rode out of the ranch heading south.

He passed the cutoff forty minutes later and kept riding at a decent speed.

———

Joe had Boomer saddled, his Sharps and Winchester in their scabbards and waved to Shining Rain as he trotted away. Getting the saddle over Boomer's back had been difficult, but he was glad it was his left arm that had taken the damage as he rode east at a fast trot. If his right had taken that blade, he wouldn't be nearly as effective with his pistols.

———

Ed was already on the road to the Hobson's ranch when the telegram from Joe arrived at the office.

Charlie quickly opened the telegram and read that Joe was in pursuit of Hanger Bob and that he had been slowed by an accidental stab wound to his left arm. He then mentioned the death of a Shoshone woman at the hands of Hanger Bob.

Charlie knew that for Joe to mention it in a telegram, it must have been a nasty stab wound, but it also meant that Joe wouldn't be there for the trial.

———

Hanger Bob had slowed as he passed the McClellan farm and noted the large number of men working outside. No wonder he had lost his gang, he thought, as he then picked up the pace and soon left the farm behind.

———

Joe arrived at the turnoff and decided to head north. He saw two sets of hoofprints and either they belonged to someone else, or Bob had stolen a horse from someone and the only other ranch or farm in the area was the Larsen spread just north of the turnoff.

He turned north and after a couple of miles, his stomach flipped when he saw a large number of buzzards overhead. He accelerated Boomer and twenty minutes later, turned into the access road of the Larsen ranch. He didn't care if Hanger Bob was still there as he raced toward the house and didn't even bother pulling his rifle as Boomer thundered across the turf.

Joe spotted some of the vultures walking on the ground at the back of the house and veered Boomer in that direction. The big birds began to spread their enormous wings and quickly took to the sky as he roared toward them.

He brought Boomer to a dusty halt as he leapt from the saddle when he spotted the two bodies lying on the ground. He had seen so much death and dying by now, he thought he had grown used to it, but seeing the tortured, grotesque bodies of the two innocent elderly people threw him into a rage that he had never felt before. He'd met the Larsens several times and two nicer people had never walked the face of the earth. And now, they were both dead because of that bastard!

He stormed into the house, leaving his revolvers in their holsters, as he walked into a bedroom, found an unmade bed and knew that that heartless one-eyed monster had slept in it last night. He yanked off the blanket and returned to where the Larsens lay in permanent rest. He gently lowered the blanket over the bodies and picked up some rocks and placed them on the corners to keep the buzzards at bay for a little while.

He then mounted Boomer and trotted over to the bunkhouse and didn't dismount as he peered inside and saw the Knutson twins lying on their bunks, blood splattered everywhere.

If it wasn't for the knife wound, he would have taken the time to bury them, but he couldn't do it even if he tried.

But the rage that was in him for the senseless deaths of the Shoshone woman, and now the Larsens and the Knutson boys was reaching epic proportions. He had to stop that murderer and he had to do it soon.

———

"You don't know where he is?" asked Emma as she stood with the others facing Deputy Ed Smith.

"No, ma'am. He left the night before last and we haven't heard from him since, but that's understandable with the rain and all. I'm sure he's okay."

"Do we all have to be there for the trial?" asked Sarah.

"Just the nine ladies and Billy over there, ma'am. It's scheduled for ten o'clock tomorrow mornin'."

Emma was more than just a little uneasy after hearing that Joe hadn't been heard from in almost two days, but there was nothing she could do about it and that bothered her, too.

"Well, folks, I've got to get back," Deputy Smith said as he tipped his hat, then turned and climbed aboard his horse and waved before riding off.

Billy looked at his mother's worried face and said, "I'm sure he's okay, Mama."

Emma just nodded, still unsure.

———

Joe was still furious when he turned into the McClellan farm, and was immediately spotted by John McClellan as they were all still on alert after the shootout. He waved at Joe who waved back in acknowledgement.

John shouted, "Sheriff Joe is coming!"

His father and brothers trotted out of the barn and thought initially that he was coming to take the wagon, horses and guns with him, but he was riding too fast for a routine reason.

He pulled Boomer to a stop and didn't even bother getting down from the saddle as he said, "Al, I've been following the last member of that big gang; their leader, Hanger Bob Jones. He murdered a Shoshone woman at the Indian agency store, then rode north of here and murdered the Larsens and the Knutson boys. I was stabbed yesterday and couldn't bury the bodies. All I could do was to cover the Larsens' bodies with a blanket to keep the vultures away. The Knutson boys are dead in the bunkhouse. I really hate to ask this of you, but could you and your boys drive down there and bury them?"

Al was shocked at the loss of his neighbors but replied, "We'll take care of them, Joe. Are you going after that murderous bastard?"

"I aim to put every bullet I have through his carcass, Al. I'll come back here and let you know when it's over, so you don't have to worry."

"Don't worry about us, Joe. I'll just send two of the boys to the Larsens. They were good folks, Joe."

"I know. I'm just fed up with all of the good people suffering because of one soulless son of a bitch. Send your boys with the strongest stomachs, Al," Joe said as he gave a quick wave, then wheeled Boomer around and trotted him down the access road and quickly turned onto the road at a fast trot.

Al turned to John and asked, "John, which two can do this job?"

"I'll do it, Papa," he replied.

Then David said, "Me, too, Papa. We'll go and get the shovels and a pickaxe."

Al touched both his sons on their shoulders and said, "Say a few words over the graves when you're finished, boys. They deserve that."

"We will, Papa," John said before he and David turned and walked to the barn to retrieve the tools.

———

Hanger Bob was riding along at a medium trot, content in his improved status. He had a full stomach, the sun was shining, he had money in his pocket and two Winchesters and plenty of ammunition, and the ease with which he had obtained everything had given him a new path to more money. The small outfits were so focused on work that they didn't even go around with guns anymore. It was like taking a sucker from a four-year-old.

Yes, sir, he thought, life is going pretty good today after yesterday's debacle.

———

Joe was following the two sets of hoofprints which was made easier by the recent rain that had washed away much of the older prints. He guessed he was two or three hours behind Hanger Bob.

He'd killed thirteen men in the past few days; thirteen evil, heartless men, and he wanted desperately to make it fourteen. Then, he'd just walk away. He just didn't think he could do this anymore. He'd witnessed so much bad over the years, but it had been so concentrated over the last week since Billy had told him about the attack on his ranch. All of those husbands and sons had died at the hands of that gang and their wives and daughters kidnapped and raped. Even with only one on the loose, five more had died and he didn't doubt that more would die unless he put a .50 caliber round through that man's brain. He wouldn't aim at his heart because he didn't have one. He'd put that big round right between his eyes, or in Hanger Bob's case, his eye and his patch.

Joe knew he was becoming almost heartless himself as he rode to kill Hanger Bob. He wouldn't hesitate to pull the trigger and he was resigned to his own ultimate fate for killing so many men, especially Jean Martin who had asked him to hear his confession. That decision still gnawed at him.

The longer he rode, the more he brooded, and he didn't even notice the landscape as it passed anymore. He was just focused on the road ahead as it wound its way past obstacles and crossed creeks and streams. He had to stop twice to let Boomer drink and rest, but the big gelding was game as he maintained the fast trot to hunt down that bastard.

It was past noon and Hanger Bob was pulling some food out of his saddlebags to eat as the horse trotted along, and when he turned his head, thought he might have heard hoofbeats behind him. He had just passed a curve that went around a large rock outcrop, so he couldn't see anything, but he was sure he heard hooves, so he pulled off to the side of the road, turned his horse and removed his Winchester from its scabbard. He levered in a new round to be sure, spitting a perfectly good .44 out of the rifle as he aimed at the road behind him.

Joe was still focused on the road ahead and deep in thought as he rounded the curve and suddenly saw the two horses and Hanger Bob standing off to the side of the road sixty yards away with a Winchester in his hands. Instinct more than anything else made Joe drop to Boomer's neck as Bob fired.

The slug slammed into Boomer's neck between Joe's head and his right wrist, splattering blood in his face and eyes. The big gelding screamed and went down hard on his left side, plowing into the dirt. Joe didn't have time to kick free from his dying mount but had to ride down with the horse.

Hanger Bob was already levering in a new round as Boomer fell, and he exulted that he had killed the sheriff, but was immediately worried that one of his deputies might be near, so he swung the Winchester toward the road and waited for a second lawman.

Joe was stunned when he smashed into the ground but didn't lose consciousness as his hat softened the blow. But Boomer was on his leg and he was trapped; trapped, but not defenseless. He quickly wiped away Boomer's blood from his eyes and slid his '76 from its scabbard.

Bob caught the sudden movement, realized that the sheriff was still alive and fired a second round, but the sheriff was off to his left and Bob had a hard time aiming and focusing before the shot and knew he had missed.

The sheriff may be trapped under his dead horse, but the sight of that Winchester being pulled from its scabbard spooked Bob and he spurred his new horse away from the gunfight and raced away, trailing his second startled animal behind him.

Joe took a quick shot at the receding outlaw, but his still slightly blurry vision caused him to miss. Once Bob was gone, Joe cursed himself for woolgathering. It had cost his trusted horse his life. He flopped back to the ground and began squirming to get his leg free from under Boomer, hoping it hadn't been injured. It didn't feel broken or anything, but he could still mess it up trying to get it out from under the big animal.

His freshly repaired left arm was bleeding by the time his left boot popped free of Boomer's body. Joe didn't have time to mourn his equine friend as he pulled his saddlebags free, then managed to get his Sharps out from under Boomer. He hung his canteen over his left shoulder and his saddlebags over his right, then took a rifle in each hand and began to walk south. His left leg was sore, but nothing was bad enough to slow him down. He was driven by a blinding hatred for Hanger Bob Jones.

———

Hanger Bob had slowed his horses to a medium trot and kept looking over his shoulder, knowing that the sheriff, even if he got free of the horse, was stranded. If he walked the eight or nine miles back to the McClellan farm, it would take him three or four hours, unless he broke a leg or something, and even if he didn't, he'd have to get a horse and chase after him again, and by then, it would be close to sunset and he'd never make it.

Finally convinced he was safe, Bob slowed the horses to a slow trot, stopped at the first stream he spotted and let the two animals drink and then graze in a nearby small field.

He took the time to drink some water and fill his canteen. He may have hit the sheriff's horse, but he had been aiming at the man's silver star-emblazoned chest. He had missed by almost two feet. He had to store that piece of information away, so tonight, when he stopped to camp, he'd do some target practice shooting to try and improve his aim.

Two hours later, he had totally dismissed Sheriff Joe.

———

"Joe was stabbed?" asked Ed after he had walked into the office.

"That's what he said. Accidentally stabbed. But he said he was still going after Hanger Bob. Are the witnesses coming to the trial tomorrow?"

"Yup. All of 'em, even the kid. They were kinda worried about Joe. You ain't worried, are you, Charlie?"

Charlie didn't answer right away because he was worried. For Joe to even mention that he had been stabbed meant it was probably serious and he'd been after that bastard for days now.

But he said, "Nah. I'm sure he's fine."

———

Joe hadn't walked this far in years after he had walked for four hours, or at least ten miles, maybe twelve. He'd stopped twice to refill his canteen and catch his breath and also fashioned a harness to allow him to carry the Sharps over his shoulder using the saddlebags as a cushion. He guessed he was carrying twenty pounds of guns, another twenty of ammunition and supplies, and his left arm was throbbing again, which was what had necessitated the sling for the Sharps. Why he had even bothered with the long-range carbine was a mystery to him. His Winchester could reach almost as far and had more punch at closer ranges. The truth was, he finally admitted, he didn't want anyone else to get his hands on the weapon.

He was plodding along and after another hour, he finally decided he'd have to leave the Sharps. He began scouting for a decent hiding place and it didn't take long to find one. He left the roadway and walked to a rock formation that looked as if a giant bear had clawed the face of the rock, leaving deep, vertical grooves on its face. He found the deepest one and stood the Sharps inside, then set down his saddlebags, removed the cartridges for the weapon and set them deep in the bordering groove. He then stepped back, couldn't see them, then rebalanced the saddlebags' loads and hung it over his shoulder before starting to walk again.

Once he was underway, he chastised himself for bringing the heavy gun with him in the first place. As he walked, he thought about poor Boomer lying in the roadway and knew what would happen to the carcass. The road wasn't well traveled at all and a dead horse attracts a lot of scavengers.

He hoped that the McClellans were able to bury the Larsens and the Knutson boys before the four-footed creatures arrived.

He found himself sinking deeper into a morbid mood and shifted to thinking about Emma. He thought that would help, but it just made him feel worse. He believed he couldn't do the job anymore and told himself that most people just smiled at him and wished him well because he wore the badge. Take off the badge, and he was just Joe Brooks, a man with no real name and nothing to mark him as different. He had nothing to offer Emma, so he was in a total sulk when he told himself that Emma would be better off with another man when she finished grieving for her husband, but he kept walking.

Hanger Bob had set up camp fourteen miles ahead of Joe and even had a nice fire going as he made himself some coffee and fried up some bacon. When he had finished eating his bean and bacon supper with two cups of coffee, he took the newly-acquired Winchester, checked its load and walked away from the camp fifty feet and searched for a target. He found a fallen pine log about eighty yards away with a few stubby branches still sticking from the trunk.

He settled into a shooting stance, cocked the hammer, took careful aim and squeezed the trigger. The rifle kicked against his shoulder, but he didn't see any impact on the target. He lowered his aim to the trunk itself, levered in a new cartridge and fired again. The bark flew from the log about three feet right of where he had been aiming. Three feet!

He swore and fired six more shots in frustration at the same point of the log. The closest he got was a foot and a half, and this was at eighty yards! He thought it was the gun, so he switched to his other Winchester and did better, but only marginally so. He realized that it had been three years or longer since he'd fired a rifle at a target. He'd shot a lot of times to scare people or just to shoot the Winchester, but he'd never paid attention to his loss of accuracy. He had no idea why it was this bad, but he had to keep that in mind. He then walked closer to the log and pulled his Colt.

His target shots with his revolver were much better, but still not as good as they should have been. He'd used the Colt a lot more than the Winchester over the past few years, but again, he'd never paid attention to his accuracy. At least, now he knew that getting into gunfights wasn't a good idea, especially one with that damned sheriff.

Without the sound of horses' hooves to block the sound, even at that distance, Joe heard the distant sound of gunfire echoing off the nearby mountain face. He had no idea how far ahead Hanger Bob was or why he was shooting, but the sound gave him renewed belief that he would catch up with the man, but only if he kept walking.

The sun was down, and Joe was still plodding along, his Winchester hanging loosely over his right shoulder using the homemade sling he had scavenged from the Sharps.

He had recovered from his sulky mood but hadn't changed his mind about quitting or about Emma, and began to believe both were perfectly rational decisions, not assigning any blame to his exhausted state.

He'd checked his left arm wound twice and was pleased that it had stopped bleeding after Boomer had gone down. He looked at the poultice and wondered how long he was supposed to leave it in place. He had never asked and added it to his list of mistakes he had made that day. If he had turned right at the turnoff, he probably would have run Hanger Bob down in a couple of hours. If he hadn't been off in some dream world, Boomer would still be alive, and he'd probably have killed the bastard by now. He was just getting too old to do this job anymore.

Joe now had to fight off the growing fatigue as he kept shuffling southward, one footfall after another. His feet were numb, and he was beginning to feel too much of the road in his right foot, which mean the boot sole leather was getting too thin. He hoped it would hold out long enough to reach Bob.

He was sure of one thing, though. If he didn't get to him tonight, and Bob mounted his horse tomorrow, he'd never be able to catch up. Each day would be the same; he'd get close, Bob would ride off and he'd get close again. Maybe that would be the story of the rest of his life. Just like a perpetual nightmare where he followed Hanger Bob all the way down to Central America, maybe the tip of South America.

The thought made him laugh lightly.

Sheriff Joe Brooks thought he was losing his mind, not realizing that his body had never fully replenished his lost blood from the stab wound. He needed sleep desperately and was denying himself the rest his body demanded. Instead, he was growing sulky, punchy and morose.

Finally, just a little after midnight, Joe simply couldn't go on any longer and walked two feet off the road, set his Winchester and saddlebags down and didn't even take off his guns as he dropped into some grass, laid flat on his back and closed his eyes.

CHAPTER 7

Four hours. That's how long Joe slept, and what awakened him wasn't a pleasant dream or even a nightmare. It was a sound that would have awakened the dead.

The predawn was still forty minutes away when a pack of coyotes approached the sleeping lawman. He was breathing deeply, which made the animals wary. The smell of gunpowder made them more cautious as they stealthily approached Joe from all sides.

But they hadn't picked up the scent of the cougar that was also interested in the sleeping man. She was just a hundred feet behind the pack leader when she suddenly snarled to scare away the coyotes.

That sound blasted Joe awake and he automatically grabbed his nearby Winchester and cocked the hammer, his night vision available immediately in the moonlight. By the time he reacted, the coyotes had all scattered from the cougar's claim and that left him with the big cat just fifty feet away. He didn't want to fire and alert Hanger Bob to his presence, so he just aimed the Winchester at the big cat and stood. He then walked toward the puma; his eyes locked on the mountain lion.

She wasn't happy with this sudden change and hadn't been able to see the man well past the coyotes, yet there he was walking towards her unafraid with a weapon in his hands. She had encountered men with rifles before and had narrowly escaped twice. She wasn't about to risk it again, and bolted away, running in a fast zig-zag to avoid being shot.

Joe blew out his breath and wiped his forehead. He still had to worry about that pack of coyotes though, but hoped he was big enough to keep their interest away. Everything depended on how hungry they were.

He picked up his saddlebags, hung them over his shoulder and regained the road. He should have felt better but he wasn't sure how much better he was as he set out south again, chewing on some jerky as he stepped along.

———

Four miles away, Hanger Bob was still in deep sleep in his bedroll. He had no concerns, and he trusted his natural defensive instincts to wake him if there was any danger.

Before he had fallen asleep, he had come up with a basic plan for action. He'd work his way south toward Colorado, which would get him out of the jurisdiction of that sheriff once Bob left his county. Then, he'd bump into the Union Pacific somewhere on the trip and ride east until he found a station. Then, he'd be home free.

———

Joe was already tired as sunrise bloomed across the sky. Normally, Joe would have taken the time to watch nature's daily display, but not today. He kept walking, hoping that Bob hadn't gone yet.

———

Bob was stirring as Joe was two miles north of him. He looked around, was pleased with the absence of anyone or any creature that could cause him trouble and slid out of his bedroll.

Ten minutes later, he had his fire going and had tossed some bacon onto the frypan as the coffeepot's water began to heat. As each slice was dropped into the skillet, it quickly sizzled and began to shrivel and Bob' mouth began to water.

He unloaded another can of beans and vowed to get some eggs at the next stop as he began to open the can.

Joe was a half a mile from Bob's camp around another curve when he picked up the unmistakable scent of frying bacon. His stomach gurgled in readiness to digest the tasty morsel that it expected shortly.

Joe then slid his Winchester from his shoulder and kept walking as he cocked the hammer. It might not be Bob, he kept telling himself; it might just be a hunter or some other wayfaring soul, but he knew that it was Bob. He knew Hanger Bob's moment of reckoning was imminent.

Bob flipped his bacon and watched it expectantly as it continued to sizzle and pop, turning that wonderful shade of brown that only bacon seemed to possess. The open can of beans sat nearby, waiting its turn in the skillet, and he had a tin plate and a fork sitting next to a tin cup for the almost ready coffee, too.

Joe passed some rocks on his right and saw Hanger Bob crouched over a cooking fire two hundred yards away. His fatigue a thing of the past, Joe continued to walk, his Winchester aimed at Bob's back. He could have legally shot him already, but he wanted to get close and he wanted Bob to know he was about to die.

Bob flipped the bacon onto his plate and then dumped in the beans, which would pick up the added flavor of the bacon grease. He sprinkled on some salt, stirred the beans, then pulled his coffeepot from the fire and dumped in the coffee grounds, letting that explosive smell of coffee fill the air.

"That smells really good, Bob!" Joe said loudly.

Hanger Bob was startled beyond imagination and began to reach for his Winchester, then quickly drew his hand back and put both of them into the air.

Joe continued to walk the last hundred feet to Bob with his Winchester pointed at his back, hoping Bob would go for his pistol. He knew he could shoot the outlaw, and no one would care which side of Bob had the entrance wound. He was wanted dead or alive and he didn't know of any bounty hunters who wouldn't have taken the shot, but he didn't. He needed Bob to make a hostile move.

But Hanger Bob wasn't stupid. Once the sheriff had called out to him, after his instinctive reach for his rifle, he knew that he wasn't going to be shot in the back. His only chance for survival was in delay.

Joe walked right up to Bob and rammed his Winchester's muzzle against the outlaw's back.

He then leaned forward, ripped Bob's Colt out of his holster without bothering with the hammer loop and tossed it aside.

"Get on your stomach and put your hands behind your back."

Bob flopped down and put both wrists against his back while Joe pulled his handcuffs and locked them over his wrists, then pulled some pigging strings from his jacket pocket and painfully trussed his ankles together.

Joe then rolled him onto his back and pulled him into a sitting position, slid him ten feet away from the fire and left him there without saying another word.

Joe finally just walked to the fire, poured himself a cup of Bob's coffee, scooped the beans onto the plate with his bacon, took a seat and began to eat real food.

Bob just stared at the sheriff wondering what he was going to do. He expected some sort of threatening chit-chat about how he was going to hang for what he did or how he was going to shoot him if he so much as blinked, but the sheriff just sat there and ate his breakfast as if Bob had cooked it for him.

Once he was finished, Joe just walked over to the bedroll, took off his hat, stretched out and fell asleep leaving a totally confused and hungry outlaw sitting on the ground.

Joe slept until almost ten o'clock, recovering some of the sleep he'd missed, and his much-improved frame of mind. When he awakened the second time, he just walked to the coffee pot, felt the temperature and poured himself a lukewarm cup of coffee without so much as looking at his prisoner.

In Lander, Judge Moore entered his courtroom and took a seat, allowing everyone else to sit down.

The trial of Hank Anderson was underway, and the prosecutor had already told him that Sheriff Joe was still out hunting the gang leader, but he had the sheriff's report, which the judge had already read.

With ten witnesses, everything was a foregone conclusion, and by eleven-fifteen, the jury was already returning with their guilty verdict. The judge sentenced Hank to be hanged the following morning at ten o'clock, and a resigned Hank Anderson was escorted from courtroom by Deputy Ed Smith.

Before the witnesses left, Deputy Charlie Wheatley approached the three adult women and said, "Ladies, I need you to stop by the office before you leave and pick up your money."

Emma replied, "Isn't that kind of fast, deputy? Joe said it would take a few days for the reward money to come in."

"Yes, ma'am, he was right about that, but this was the money he recovered from Hanger Bob's saddlebag. He cleared it with the judge to award it to each of you."

Sarah asked, "How much is it?"

Charlie replied, "After we counted it out, each of you will get $1324."

Jennie's eyes bulged, and she asked, "How much?"

Charlie smiled and repeated, "One thousand, three hundred and twenty-four dollars."

Jennie grinned and said, "Let's go, ladies!"

She took Charlie's arm and they all left to go to the sheriff's office.

Emma had already asked where Sheriff Joe was, and she was told that they still had no idea. The money was secondary to Emma.

Joe had turned south with Hanger Bob firmly bound to his own horse, while Joe rode the horse that Bob had stolen from the Larsens. He expected that they would arrive in Lander around noon tomorrow.

He had still not said a word to Hanger Bob and knew it was driving him crazy because Bob kept screaming at him to say something as Joe was getting him onto the horse.

Before he had arrived in Bob's camp, he was planning on doing exactly what Bob had expected once Bob threw up his hands. He wanted to explain to him in detail how he would die, but then he thought that in Bob's sick mind, he actually may take some perverse pleasure in the threat, so he had decided not to say a word to the bastard for the entire trip to Lander and was glad to see that it bothered the outlaw so much.

Charlie Wheatley counted out each new widow's money and gave them each a thick envelope to keep it together. Things like this had never happened before, so Charlie didn't even get a receipt for the cash.

"The reward money is beginning to arrive already, but I think it's better if it was all in and we'd get a real read on the total. Lots of times, the wanted posters we have are old, and this group usually operated around Laramie and Cheyenne, so the amounts might be higher than we have on the posters. Then, there's still the reward for Hanger Bob Jones," Charlie explained.

"There's still no word from Sheriff Joe?" asked Emma.

"No, ma'am, but I'm sure he's all right. He's been gone longer than a week before chasing down outlaws. It's a big county."

Billy then asked, “How come there haven’t been any more telegrams?”

“The only telegraph in that whole area is in the Shoshone Indian agency store, so the sheriff can only let us know what’s going on if he’s in that area. He’s probably chasing Hanger Bob all over creation.”

Billy nodded, but like his mother and sisters, was getting very worried about Joe.

“Can we go to our homes now, Deputy Wheatley?” asked Sarah.

“I think it would be okay, ma’am. The sheriff was after that outlaw on the eastern side of the county.”

“Thank you,” Sarah said as they all turned and left the office.

Once they were outside, the three mothers huddled and talked about returning to their homes.

“We’d have to stay in town and do some shopping for dishes, and food and things if we moved back into the houses,” said Jennie.

“Why don’t we refill each house one at a time,” suggested Emma, “we buy mattresses, dishes, pots and pans for one house, we all stay there and set it up, then we come back tomorrow and do it again to the second and then the third. In three days, we’d have all of the ranches restored to the way they were.”

“Except we won’t have husbands,” Sarah said quietly.

“No, we won’t have husbands,” said Emma, “but Ben Hobson and Billy will help.”

“I meant the other part of having a husband, Emma. I don’t want to sleep alone. I haven’t slept by myself for almost twenty years and I’m not sure I can deal with it now.”

“We’ll all still be together for the next few days and we still have our girls,” Emma replied.

"It's not the same, Emma. You know that," Sarah said.

Jennie then said, "I think we're going to be besieged by lonely men looking for wives after the word gets out about three widows with ranches, I mean, four widows with ranches all in one area."

Sarah looked at Jennie and said, "I know, but I was kind of hoping that Sheriff Joe would come back."

Jennie smiled at Sarah, patted her on the shoulder then replied, "I don't believe you're alone in that hope, Sarah."

Emma just smiled. That wanted poster last will that Joe had written had seemed so final to her, so she began to believe that Joe wouldn't be returning from this mission, and her stomach plummeted.

But they agreed with Emma's solution, and with a lot of money to make it happen, they drove the wagon to Johnson's General Store and the entire group entered and explained to Henry Johnson what they needed, and he was only too happy to oblige. He'd be able to sell them the lamps, mattresses, bedding, kitchenware, towels and food for the three houses from his stock, but he'd have to order most of the furniture they'd need.

So, for an hour, the women rummaged and bought what they needed to fill the Harper house as it had been the first one attacked. They also added some clothes for all of them, including riding outfits so they wouldn't have to show so much of their legs as they had to do on the ride back from Cooperstown.

So, with a heavily loaded Riley wagon and Abby Hobson's wagon for the girls to use, they left Lander and headed for the Harper ranch. Abby Hobson drove her wagon and Jennie piloted her wagon with Ben Hobson and Billy Harper riding along. In addition to the Winchesters in their horses' scabbards, each teenager was armed with a Colt around his waist and there were two more Winchesters in the foot well of each wagon.

By the time they returned to the Harper ranch, it was almost five o'clock and it was like a swarm of ants as they began unloading the wagon's cargo into the house. Emma and Abby began cooking dinner for everyone while the others began setting up the house, and by the time sunset arrived, the Harper ranch house had returned to full functionality.

While everyone else sat around having coffee, Emma left the house and walked to where Joe had buried her husband. She stood over the grave and didn't know what to say at first.

But as the sunset was dying, Emma said, "Wilbur, we never really should have done what we did when we were young, but I don't blame you. It was my fault. I know that you didn't love me, and I think that sometimes you resented being forced to marry me when you were so young. But you did love our children and I thank you for that. Many men would have treated the children badly, but you didn't."

I suppose I should have been a more submissive, gentle woman, but it wouldn't be who I am. I feel bad that I don't mourn for you as I should, but I think you understand. But now, I have a new chance to find the love that I dreamed about when I was that foolish young girl that willingly gave herself to you. The man that saved me and our girls has already taken my heart, and not because he's a brave, handsome man, but because he's so thoughtful and filled with compassion. But he's also so lonely and hurt that I want to hold him like the lost little boy that he had been when he was in the orphanage. I know I can help him just like he can help me. The others think that men will descend on our ranches like locusts trying to woo the widows, but I won't care. I'm going to wait for Joe. No other man will enter this house or sleep in my bed. I just wanted to let you know."

Emma exhaled, turned and walked back to the house to join the others.

———

Joe and Bob pulled over to set up camp after sunset, still fifteen miles from Lander. He hadn't so much as looked at Hanger Bob the long, boring ride, despite Bob periodically launching into all sorts of vitriolic diatribes. He'd yell how he'd had that Emma woman and graphically described what he had done to her. He'd shout how the youngest girl, fourteen-year-old Cora Riley had been subjected to multiple assaults by his men. Then, he attacked Joe's masculinity and called him every conceivable insulting name he could think of.

When he had talked about Emma, Joe had been so very close to turning with his Smith & Wesson and blowing his mouth off, just like the wound that Pierre had suffered, but he had remained silent. He had a similar reaction when he bragged about Cora and the other girls, but when Bob shifted to personal attacks on him, it became ridiculous and Joe found himself enjoying the variety of insults.

But his absence of any kind of communication was driving Hanger Bob into fits of frustration.

When he pulled over, he continued his silence as he untied Bob from the saddle and pulled him to the ground. After letting him take care of his private needs, Joe tied his ankles again and unsaddled the horses. The bags of food that Bob had stolen did come in useful as Joe cooked a decent supper. They had ridden through lunch because Joe wasn't hungry and it had added to Bob's verbal assaults, which made missing his own lunch worthwhile.

He finally set a plate of food on Bob's lap and left a cup of coffee next to him as he leaned against a pine tree. Bob devoured the food and was drinking the coffee and glaring at Joe.

"You think keepin' quiet bothers me, but it don't. You're just a big sissy who's scared of me. I don't think you'd even face me with a pistol in my hand. You snuck up behind me like the back shooter you are."

Joe finished his coffee, took Bob's plate and cup, carried them to the nearby creek, washed them and set them on the ground near the campfire. He walked over to Bob, slid him from the tree and just let him lie flat on the ground while he slid into his bedroll and closed his eyes.

———

Joe had Bob in the saddle just an hour after sunrise after he had shared a normal breakfast with his prisoner, expecting to reach Lander before ten if he kept up a decent pace. What he did when he arrived was the question.

The image of the Larsens lying in their contorted death positions still hung in his mind and made keeping silent easier as he spent so much time ruminating on the almost seemingly pointless nature of his job. He'd worked so hard, yet over the past week, eleven innocent people had died, and he hadn't been able to stop it. He knew that it was a big county and bad men would take advantage of the innocent everywhere, but it didn't make it any easier when you find nine women, some of them barely teenage girls, being held in a filthy, broken-down town for a bunch of outlaws for their sexual satisfaction; women who had their husbands and sons taken from them; an innocent young Shoshone woman murdered; a kind, elderly couple killed and tossed out into the rain like garbage and twin brothers assassinated before they could even begin their lives in earnest. *What was the point of even having laws when it was always punishing the miscreants after they'd done their evil?*

That was Sheriff Joe's frame of mind when he and Hanger Bob arrived in Lander in mid-morning. When they entered the town, Joe steered the horse to his office and as he drew close, he saw his two deputies escorting Hank Anderson out of the jail.

They both spotted Joe, and Charlie told Ed to hold onto Hank while he talked to the boss, then he trotted over to Joe as he dismounted.

"Joe! You're back! You had us all worried to death!" Charlie shouted as Joe walked up to him.

"I'm fine, Charlie. What's with Hank?"

"We're takin' him out back," Charlie said.

"Okay, I'll lead Hanger Bob's horse back there, so he can see what's waiting for him in a few days."

"Where did you get cut, Joe?"

"Left forearm. It'll be okay. You go and get your prisoner ready for execution."

"We'll talk to you later, Joe," Charlie said before jogging back to Hank.

Joe just unhitched Bob's horse from his and left him in the saddle as he led the horse and Hanger Bob behind Hank Anderson and the deputies to the gallows behind the courthouse.

There was already a crowd assembled in back as Hank was led up the gallows steps. Many of them began pointing and chatting when they recognized Joe and the black-patched outlaw chief.

Joe didn't say a word as he led the horse with a glaring Hanger Bob sitting in the saddle. Bob knew why the sheriff was doing this and began his loud insults again, but Joe didn't care as he led the horse across the alley and turned it around, so Bob would have a good view with his one good eye.

Hanger Bob continued his loud rants until the hangman lowered and tightened the noose around Hank Anderson's black shrouded head, when Bob suddenly lapsed into silence. A preacher was standing next to Hank as the hangman took two steps back then one side step. He put his hand on a lever, pulled his pocket watch and flipped it open. He stared at the pocket watch while everyone else stared at Hank. For almost two minutes the scene was deathly silent, then, just when everyone had become accustomed to the silence, he yanked the lever opening the trap door beneath Hank Anderson's feet, letting gravity do its work. Hank bounced once when he reached the end of the rope and there was a collective gasp among the crowd. Joe then simply led Hanger Bob's horse away from the alley and back through the side alley to the front of the jail.

Without saying a word to Bob, he sliced the pigging strings holding him in the saddle and helped him to the ground, marched him into the jail, and then undid the handcuffs before pushing him into the cell and slamming the door closed.

Before his deputies returned, Joe walked into his office, took a seat and began to write his report. He had finished two pages when Charlie and Ed entered his small office and took seats in the two chairs opposite Joe.

Joe kept writing and began by saying, “He murdered a young Shoshone woman at the Indian agency store, then he murdered the Larsens and the Knutson brothers. He even killed Boomer. I had the McClellans bury the Larsens and the Knutson boys, and the Shoshone took care of their loss.”

“You caught Bob after he shot Boomer?” asked Ed.

“He killed Boomer and my left leg was trapped under him. He was about sixty yards away with his Winchester, but I was able to pull mine while I was trapped, and he took off south. It took me a while to get out from under Boomer’s body, and then I just followed his trail on foot.”

“You caught up with him on foot?” asked Charlie with wide eyes.

“He stopped to make camp about twenty miles south and I guess he didn’t think I’d follow.”

“How is your arm, boss?” Charlie asked.

Joe looked at the poultice-covered wound and said, “It feels okay. I’ve got to see Doc Riddle when I finish writing this. Did Judge Moore give the women the money?”

“Yes, sir. We distributed it yesterday and they went to Johnson’s and filled up a wagon with stuff. Henry said that they were coming back to pick up another wagon load today and then another one tomorrow. They’re movin’ into their own ranch houses.”

Then Ed said, “We figure every single feller within two hundred miles will descend on those widows.”

Joe paused writing for a few seconds, then replied, “You’re probably right,” before he resumed writing his report.

As he continued, he told them the details of the chase and mentioned that he hadn't said a word to Hanger Bob after getting him on the ground just to infuriate him.

When he finished the report, he set aside the pen and said, "I'm going to have to go and see the doc. Ed, can you run this over to the prosecutor's office? After the trial, I'm going to have to ride back to the McClellan farm to let them know that the gang is all gone and pick up a wagon, a bunch of horses and guns that were left there by the eight men who attacked the farm. I need to pick up my Sharps on the way, too. I had to hide it in some rocks because it was just too heavy to carry."

After the ink dried, Joe put the pages together and handed the report to Ed.

"This shouldn't take long. I just hope the doc doesn't have to swap out those stitches."

"How many are in there, Joe?" asked Charlie.

"Beats me. I wasn't watching. I'll be back in a little while," Joe said as he stood.

His deputies rose, and Joe followed them out of his office, then picked up his hat and pulled it on over his head. When he stepped out onto the boardwalk, Joe realized he didn't take care of the two horses and exhaled sharply. He was getting forgetful.

He untied the two animals and led them down the street to Mason's Livery.

After leaving them there, he walked another two blocks and turned on a side street to go to Doc Riddle.

Ten minutes later, white-haired, but still only forty-two-year-old Doctor Thomas J. Riddle was examining Joe's wound.

"That's one hell of a slice, Joe. The good news is that the Shoshone that sewed it up did a real good job and I'd like to know what was in that poultice they put on there because it's not swollen as much as it should be. I'll put a bandage on it and come back in ten days and I'll remove the sutures. If you start feeling like it's getting hot or it starts oozing pus, let me know."

Joe replied, "And you'll cut off my left arm, won't you, Doc? Well, if it does those things, I'll just walk off into the forest like an old bear and find a cave."

Doctor Riddle laughed thinking Joe was only joking.

"Just come back in ten days, Joe," he said as he finished wrapping a bandage around the wound.

"I will, Doc. I appreciate it," Joe replied as he rolled his blood-encrusted sleeve over the bandaged arm.

"And put on a clean shirt, for God's sake. You'll scare every woman in town and half the men."

Joe nodded, stood and left the doctor's office. He stopped at his room at the boarding house on the way back and changed his shirt, knowing he was in dire need of a bath, a shave and a haircut. So, he walked to the barber shop and spent the next half an hour taking care of each of those problems.

A refreshed Sheriff Joe Brooks then returned to his office.

———

"*The sheriff's back*?" asked a startled Emma.

"Yes, ma'am," replied Henry Johnson as he was totaling up the large order, "brought that Hanger Bob Jones right to the hangin' of his partner. That one-eyed son-of-a..., oh, excuse me, ma'am. That outlaw boss was cussing and throwin' every insult you can think of at Sheriff Joe and he never even looked at the bas..., sorry, ma'am. He never even looked at the noisy man. Then, when Hank was gettin' ready to drop, Hanger Bob just shut up. After it was over, the sheriff took him to jail."

"Is he there now?" she asked as Billy listened carefully.

"I think he had to go to the doc to get his cut fixed. Ed Smith stopped by and said that the sheriff tracked Hanger Bob almost thirty miles on foot to catch up with him after that…outlaw…shot Joe's horse right out from under him. I've gotta tell you, Mrs. Harper, we have one heck of a lawman in our sheriff."

"We have one hell of a man in our sheriff, Mr. Johnson," Emma replied as Henry Johnson smiled.

The other two widows had heard the news and were standing by listening to the conversation between Emma and Mr. Johnson.

After they paid for their second extensive order and had it all loaded into the wagon for Mrs. Riley's ranch, Emma and Billy mounted their horses while Sarah and Jennie climbed aboard the Riley wagon.

"Are we going to stop at the sheriff's office, Emma?" Jennie asked as she took up the reins.

"Of course, we are. We have to find out what happened," she replied loudly from her horse.

After responding to the question, Emma and Billy set off quickly to ride the three blocks to the sheriff's office.

———

"The trial is set for tomorrow morning at ten, Joe," Ed Smith said as Joe nodded.

"Someone will have to ride out to notify the ladies that their presence will be required at the trial," Joe said quietly.

"I'll take care of it, Joe," Ed replied with a grin.

Joe looked up and said, "I thought you were calling on Charlotte Peterson."

"I am, but that doesn't mean I can't appreciate seein' a whole lot of pretty ladies."

"Okay, Ed, you can let them know, but please behave yourself around them. They've had a bad time."

"I know, boss. I was just kinda kiddin' around."

Joe nodded as the door opened and three of the aforementioned pretty ladies entered along with a grinning Billy Harper.

Joe stood as he and Emma shared a glance for a second and Joe forced himself to look away.

"We just found out you returned, Joe, and the whole town is buzzing about how you caught Hanger Bob," gushed Sarah.

Joe just shrugged and said, "It's my job, Sarah. His trial is set for tomorrow morning at ten o'clock and you and your daughters and Billy will have to be there as witnesses. I doubt if you'll all be called, but Mr. Charles, the prosecutor, will want you all there anyway."

"We were going to come into town anyway, Joe. We have the load of things for my house in the wagon and tomorrow we've got to come back to buy Sarah's things," said Jennie.

"That's fine. Speaking of wagons, I'm going to ask to borrow Billy for a couple of days right after the trial tomorrow, Emma. Is that okay?"

Emma smiled and replied, "Anything you ask is yours, Joe."

Joe couldn't help but smile in return. Then he said, "I've got to run up to the McClellan ranch and retrieve your wagon, a bunch of horses and weapons, and then swing west and pick up Sarah's wagon, repair the broken axle and bring it back, too."

"Okay. Then, you'll be stopping by the ranch when you get the wagon?" Emma asked.

"Yes, ma'am."

She really wanted to spend some time to talk to Joe, but with Sarah, Jennie and Billy there and the two deputies as well, she knew that wasn't possible.

"Well, we have to go," she said.

"I'll be ready to ride tomorrow, Joe," Billy said as he waved.

Joe just waved back; the four left the office and silence descended in the room as the three lawmen watched two women board the heavily-loaded wagon and Emma and Billy mount their horses. Joe had noticed Emma's new riding skirt and blouse and had to admit that he was more than impressed, but it didn't matter. She was in mourning and that was the end of it, again using an excuse to cover his real problem.

He said to Charlie Wheatley, "I need to get another horse. I'll use the one that Bob stole from the Larsens, so I can return it to their ranch and ride one of the eight outlaw horses that I'll pick up at the McClellan farm to come back, but I need to find a good horse to replace Boomer."

"Did you check out Pete Mason's corral?" Charlie asked.

"I was just there dropping off those two horses. None of the ones he had impressed me too much."

"You'll find one, boss."

"Anything going on while I was gone?" Joe asked.

"Not much. We got a reply from the army. They said that they'll be sending a new Indian agent from Laramie in a day or two but didn't have a name yet. Your rewards are comin' in and so far, the total is over thirty-two hundred dollars. We're just dropping the vouchers in your box as they arrive."

“Okay. I’ll go over and send out the telegram to the ones offering the reward on Hanger Bob. His was the biggest of the bunch. Once we have the money, I’ll break it down into four piles and you can run it out to the ladies, Ed.”

“Don’t you want to give it to them, Joe?” he asked.

“No, I don’t think so. I’d remind them too much of the ordeal they went through. They need to get that behind them.”

“They seemed mighty happy to see you a few minutes ago, Joe,” Charlie said.

“They had to be polite, Charlie. I’m going to go and talk to Mike Charles about Hanger Bob out there. I don’t think this is going to be a long trial.”

“Mr. Armbruster won’t like defendin’ him, that’s for sure,” Ed said with a grin.

Joe just smiled, grabbed his hat and left the office to talk to the prosecutor next door.

After he’d gone, Charlie looked at Ed and said, “There’s somethin’ different about Joe. It’s like he’s mad at himself.”

Ed replied, “Well, he did just kill a dozen men in the past few days, Charlie. Even with them all needin’ killin’, it’s still gotta wear on him.”

“I don’t know if he’s gonna stay now, Ed. He was only talkin’ about quittin’ before, but I think he’s gonna leave now.”

“What could he do? Where could he go? I mean, he’s got no family or anybody else. We’re all he’s got.”

Charlie stared at the closed front door and said, “That’s really sad, Ed.”

Sheriff Joe and Fremont County prosecutor Mike Charles talked for twenty minutes about the case. Mike really just wanted to flesh out Joe's report that he had on his desk.

"You didn't mention your wound in the report, Joe. Why's that?"

"I didn't want to create any trouble for the Shoshone. You know how the government goes crazy if they attack a white man, even accidentally. It doesn't have any bearing on the case anyway."

"I know. I was just curious," then he leaned back and locked his fingers behind his neck and asked, "Are you okay, Joe? You've had one hell of a week."

"I'm fine. I just need to get this trial out of the way and clean up the messes that they left behind up north. Then, I might take some time off."

"Your deputies seem to think you might be quitting."

"I've been thinking about it, Mike. Do you ever feel how pointless our jobs are? We're trash men. All we do is clean up after men without any conscience sow havoc across our county. They murder, steal, rape and we hang them, but those victims are still dead, and the women have to live with what happened to them for the rest of their lives. Hanging doesn't undo the pain they leave behind."

Mike straightened out and then leaned forward before saying, "I know how you feel, Joe. But when we take those bad men out of society, we're stopping them from doing it to other innocent folks. We can't arrest them and hang them because they're thinking about doing something bad. The best we can do is make sure we catch them as soon as possible and make sure they don't do it again."

Joe nodded but didn't say anything for almost a minute.

Then, just as Mike was going to say something, Joe said, "I've got to get back to the office, Mike. I appreciate what you said."

Mike stood and shook Joe's hand and said, "Don't quit, Joe. This county needs you."

Joe just nodded again, made a grim attempt at a smile and picked up his hat. Mike had seen the bullet hole in the top of the hat but hadn't commented.

Once Joe left the office and stepped out into the sun again, he just stood on the boardwalk for thirty seconds and looked at the town. For a county seat, Lander wasn't a very big town, with only about four hundred residents, but it was the biggest town in the giant county. There were only seven other towns, but there were a lot of ranches and farms. Altogether, he guessed the current population of Fremont County was around two thousand. He wondered how many were bad men that were even now planning on taking advantage of the inability of the three lawmen to cover the vast area.

He shook his head, pulled on his hat and turned to go back to the office. As he walked along the boardwalk, he greeted several citizens who smiled and said, "Good afternoon, Sheriff Joe." He smiled and returned their greetings.

Sheriff Joe. Everyone called him that. No one ever called him Sheriff Brooks unless they were from out of the county. He'd never really paid that much attention to it before. It was as if they all knew he really wasn't a Brooks at all, but he was the sheriff, so everyone called him Sheriff Joe.

He turned into his office and closed the door behind him. The only one in the office was Hanger Bob, who was laying on the cot in his cell staring at the ceiling. He hadn't spoken since Hank Anderson's hanging and after tossing his hat onto a peg, he was walking past the cell to go to his office when he stopped and turned to look at Hanger Bob.

"Why did you kill that Shoshone woman, the Larsens and the Knutson boys?" he asked in a normal voice.

Bob didn't even look his way, he just said, "I felt like it."

Joe closed his eyes for a moment, then turned and walked into his office, closed the door and sat behind his desk.

It was close to supper time by the time the Riley house was returned to normal. All of the girls, as well as Abby, Ben, Margie and Harry Hobson all pitched in to get it done quickly.

Emma and Jennie made a large dinner for everyone that had to be eaten in scattered locations throughout the house and even out onto the porches. The three mothers were having coffee in the kitchen and enjoyed sugar and cream in their coffee for a change.

"How do you think this trial is going to be," Jennie asked Emma.

"The same as the other one, only faster," she replied.

Sarah said, "At least the sheriff is going to be there. I can't believe he walked that far without stopping to catch that monster."

Jennie then added, "I don't understand how any one man could have done all that he did in the past week. We're all sitting here eating and talking because he rescued us so quickly and then chased down the other twelve. How is that even possible? He wasn't even shot with dozens of bullets aimed at him. It's as if he has a giant guardian angel."

Emma said quietly, "He *is* a guardian angel. He's our guardian angel. He's the entire county's guardian angel."

"Ed Smith told me that he's thinking of quitting," Jennie said.

Emma replied, "Who can blame him? He risks his life almost every day and I don't think he's even taken a day off in years. Everyone expects him to be on the job all the time and he is. No man should be expected to live like that."

"Emma, wives and mothers never get a day off, either," Jennie said with smile.

"But we aren't alone," Emma replied.

Joe was alone in his cot in the back room of the jail rather than go to his room at Underwood's Boarding House. He needed to stay with the prisoner and had sent his deputies home after having Ed deliver a tray of food to Hanger Bob. He had skipped eating himself as he lay on the cot debating about what to do after he'd returned the wagons. He didn't want to turn the horses and saddles or guns over to the county, because they really didn't have the facilities to deal with them.

He'd have a lot of horseflesh to distribute and he knew that the three widows' ranches were already populated with the horses that had been stolen by the gang, but he figured if he gave them to the ladies, it would only be three more horses apiece, and that would help. So, he'd pick up the wagon tomorrow, head for the broken wagon, replace the axle and then he and Billy could each drive a wagon to their respective ranches.

What happened after that he still had no idea.

He had to ignore Hanger Bob's loud snoring in order to fall asleep, but he was still so tired that he drifted off faster than he expected.

CHAPTER 8

By seven o'clock, Joe had already had breakfast at the café, carried a tray back to Bob's cell and reviewed his report, not that it really mattered.

Charlie Wheatley arrived at seven-thirty and Ed showed up two minutes later.

"You're leavin' right after the trial, Joe?" Charlie asked as he hung his hat.

"Yup, that's the plan."

"Are you gonna stay on the job after that?" Ed asked as Charlie shot him a nasty glance.

"I'm not sure, Ed. I may take some time off to think about it."

"Take as long as you need, boss," Charlie said, "things are quiet, and you haven't taken any time off in five or six years."

"Maybe I'll do some fishing," Joe said as he sipped some office coffee.

"That's the ticket," said Ed enthusiastically, trying to recover from his poorly chosen question.

———

Jennie Riley was driving her empty wagon as it rolled into Lander. All of the daughters, as well as Abby, Emma and Sarah were in saddles now that they all had proper riding clothes. Billy was riding beside Cora, which was expected now, but the surprise was when Ben Hobson started riding with Annie Harper.

As they passed the sheriff's office, several heads turned to the closed door, including Emma's, but no one could see any sign of Sheriff Joe.

Inside the office, Charlie and Ed were shackling Hanger Bob's ankles for the walk next door to the county courthouse.

At 9:45, the deputies escorted the outlaw chief out of the office as Joe walked behind, then closed and locked the office door as Bob clanked along down the boardwalk.

When they noisily entered the full-to-overflowing courtroom, everyone's face turned to the prisoner as he was led to the front of the courtroom and took a seat at the defendant's table. His defense attorney, Jack Armbruster, didn't talk to him, but was reviewing papers spread on the table.

Joe walked over to the prosecutor's side and took a seat next to Mike Charles, who glanced over at Joe and smiled. Joe just nodded as they awaited the arrival of the judge.

Joe hadn't looked at the other prosecution witnesses in the first row because he didn't want to be distracted by Emma. At least that was the excuse he gave himself.

Judge Moore entered the courtroom as everyone rose from their seats.

After the two attorneys' opening remarks, Joe was called to the stand. He kept his eyes focused on the prosecutor as he asked his fairly simple questions which essentially asked him to verbally repeat his report for the jury.

The defense attorney asked some pointless questions just for appearance, but this whole trial was a foregone conclusion, and everyone knew it. The mere presence of the three women and their six teenaged daughters were more than enough to ensure that Hanger Bob would walk those scaffold steps tomorrow.

Mike Charles had decided not to call any of the women, knowing how difficult the testimony of the three mothers had been in Hank Anderson's trial. He hadn't called any of the girls in that trial in deference to their innocence, knowing that it didn't matter to the jury. They all knew what had happened.

So, after Joe left the stand, the prosecution rested, and so did he defense, not daring to put Hanger Bob Jones on the stand.

The jury was out for nine minutes before returning with their guilty verdicts on multiple counts of murder. Judge Moore sentenced him to hang the next morning at ten o'clock.

Joe followed his deputies as they almost had to drag Bob back to the jail. He wasn't squirming or kicking, he just went limp. They felt as if they were carrying a dead body back to the office, and maybe they were.

After he was put into his cell, Joe said, "Charlie, are you okay with the hanging tomorrow?"

"Not a problem, boss. If he had any of his gang members out there, I'd be worried about it, but Bob's alone now. There won't be anyone doing any shooting."

"Okay. Then I'll go and saddle a horse and get heading northeast to the McClellan farm."

"We'll see you when you get back, Joe," Ed said as the sheriff picked up his heavily packed saddlebags, draped them over his shoulder, gave them a short wave and turned to leave.

He almost ran into Billy Harper when he opened the door.

"Oh! Sorry, Joe. Are we leavin' now?"

"That's the idea. Did you have to help load the wagon or something?"

"No, sir. Ben is there, and Mr. Johnson was really happy to help."

Joe smiled and said, “I bet he is. I’ve got to saddle a horse, but I’m all packed. We’re going to ride fast and should make the McClellan farm by late this afternoon if we do. Okay?”

“Yes, sir. I’m ready.”

Joe put his hand on Billy’s shoulder, said, “Good man,” then they left the office.

Billy led Irish down the street as he walked beside Sheriff Joe, who was using the street rather than the boardwalk because Billy had a horse to lead.

“Remind me to get my boots resoled, Billy. I swear my right boot is down to paper thin. I can feel every pebble right through to the top of my foot.”

“Why don’t you just buy some new boots right now and break ‘em in?”

“I could, but they don’t usually have them in my size. I have big feet – size twelves. I’d have to special order them and I haven’t gotten around to it. I’ll order some and get these resoled over at Brewster’s when I return.”

“How are your mother and sisters, Billy?” Joe asked as they passed Johnson’s General Store with the wagon and string of horses out front.

“Annie is interested in Ben Hobson and Mary is doing okay. My mother is worried about you, Joe. You oughta go and see her.”

“She has a lot of things to do, Billy,” Joe said as they reached the livery.

“Our house is almost back to the way it was, Joe. After she helps with the Foster house, she’ll be done.”

“She’ll still have a lot of work, Billy. Women’s work never ends.”

"Mrs. Riley said that when my mother said you hadn't taken a day off in years."

"She's right about that, too, but once a woman marries, she's on the job non-stop until she dies. Men can at least screw off on the job. I may not have taken a day off in five years, but a lot of those days were just boring, sit around the office and count the number of knots on the wall kind of days."

Joe began saddling the horse that Bob had stolen from the Larsen ranch as Billy watched.

"Is that one of the outlaw's horses?"

"No, this one was stolen from the Larsen ranch by Bob Jones after he murdered the Larsens and their two ranch hands, the Knutson brothers. I'm going to leave it there and drive your wagon to the broken wagon near the Indian agency store. We'll swap out that axle and return them to their rightful place. I've decided to divide the outlaw horses at the ranches, too. If anyone wants any more weapons, there are a slew of rifles and pistols available."

"I think we have plenty, Joe, but some of the girls may want their own now after seeing my mother and the other ladies with them."

"We'll ask when we get back, Billy," Joe said as he pulled the cinch tight and checked the saddle. The stirrups were a little short and he wondered if he should pick up his old saddle. They'd have to pass Boomer's remains on the way back, so he might just have to toss it into a nearby gully. He'd decide when he saw its condition, and he had to remember to pick up the Sharps, too.

"Let's ride, Billy," Joe said as he mounted the horse.

Billy stepped up on Irish and they rode north out of Lander, then turned on the northeast fork just outside of town.

Emma had watched through the window as Joe and Billy passed by the store as they were buying all of Sarah's things. She had wanted to go to the office and talk to Joe before he left, but she hadn't for the strangest of reasons. She felt like she would be cheating on her dead husband. A husband she had never loved but had treated her acceptably for seventeen years. Half of her life was spent with Wilbur Harper, and as much as she wanted to be with Joe, she felt as if she was preparing to have an affair like she had thought about having twice before.

She knew that this was much different, beyond her widowhood. She knew when she thought about entering the affairs that they would be nothing more than that, but she knew without a doubt that she loved Joe Brooks and wanted to spend the rest of her life with him. Yet, there was that nagging sense of guilt that was in the way. She would wait, but then worried that one of the other women wouldn't.

"How does that gelding ride, Joe?" Billy shouted as they finished their first hour of travel.

"He's got a bit of a jolt that would make me crazy if I had to ride him a long time," Joe yelled back.

"Isn't this a long ride, Joe? I mean it's almost thirty miles."

"Nope. Long rides have to be over a hundred."

"What's the longest you've ridden in one day, Joe?"

"Oh, I'd say about a hundred and fifty miles."

Billy thought he hadn't heard right and asked loudly, "Did you say a hundred and fifty miles?"

"Yup. I had to try and stop a stagecoach robbery. I found out about their plan in Lander in the afternoon but had to stop overnight to get a little sleep. I got up before predawn but got there too late when the three outlaws hit it at three in the afternoon, so I kept trailing them and caught up with them when I saw their campfire. Just like those sixteen outlaws, they were arrogant enough to believe that they were safe. I brought them all in and everyone got their property back."

"Did they all hang?"

"Nope, they didn't shoot anybody, so they're all in the territorial prison in Laramie for another three years."

"Are they going to come back and try to shoot you for sending them to prison?"

"Nope. They were grateful I didn't just hang them out there on the open range."

Billy looked at Joe and wondered how many other stories he had.

They stopped twice to give the horses a drink and a rest, and Joe and Billy filled their stomachs with jerky and crackers, but at three-thirty, they reached the rock with the hidden Sharps, and Joe took a few minutes to pick up the carbine and ammunition before they restarted.

An hour later, they reached what was left of Boomer and the saddle. It was a disaster, so Joe just motioned to Billy to keep riding.

Billy was glad he had only eaten jerky and crackers after seeing what the coyotes, buzzards and whatever else had visited the carcass.

It was after five o'clock when they arrived at the McClellan farm and they wheeled their tired animals onto the access road. Joe waved at David McClellan who was walking from the barn to the house, and shouted to the house that the sheriff was coming in.

Joe and Billy slowly approached the farm house as the rest of the McClellans arrived.

"Welcome back, Sheriff Joe. Did you get that last one?" Al McClellan asked.

"He's in jail in Lander and will be hanged tomorrow morning. I caught up with him about thirty miles south and could have shot him, but he was facing away and put up his hands."

"You're just doing what's right, Joe. Come to pick up the wagon, horses and guns?"

"Yes, sir, but we'll probably do that in the morning. I have to return this horse to the Larsen ranch, so I'll just take one of those outlaw horses along."

"There's no need, sheriff. We brought all of their remaining horses here. We have too many in our corral now and I'd appreciate it if you could take them off our hands. We don't need as many horses as cattle ranches. The Larsen ranch may just go into neglect now. They didn't have any children and with the Knutson brothers dead too, there's no one to take care of the place. We moved the horses, so they wouldn't die, but those cattle are going to turn into mavericks."

"How many are over there, Al? Do you know?"

"Oh, not many. Maybe a hundred or so."

Joe shook his head. When would the misery end?

"Okay, Al. I'm not going to impose, so Billy and I will ride over to the Larsen place and stay there overnight, and we'll be back tomorrow morning to pick up the horses, wagon and weapons. Was there a spare axle under that wagon, Al?"

Al turned to his sons and asked, "Did anyone see an axle?"

Ted answered, "Yes, sir. And there's a jack and a can of axle grease, too."

Al then turned back to Joe and said, "I guess you're all set then, Joe. You sure you don't want to join us for supper? I'm sure Sadie wouldn't mind."

"No, I appreciate the offer, Al, but we'll head to the Larsen's and see you early tomorrow."

"We'll see you then, Joe," Al said.

Joe and Billy waved, wheeled their horses and trotted out back down the access road and turned north on the trail.

"That's going to be quite a string of horses we'll be trailing, Billy. I'm guessing fourteen or fifteen."

"Why are we going to the Larsen ranch, Joe?" Billy asked.

"I didn't want to disrupt the McClellans, Billy. Besides, I wanted to look at the ranch."

"Your deputies said you're thinking of quitting, Joe. Is that why you're looking at the ranch?"

"Maybe. I'm still not sure, but I'm just tired, Billy."

Billy didn't say anything more as they rode the short distance to the Larsen ranch.

They pulled in at quarter past six and headed for the barn to give their animals a much-deserved rest, some food and water.

After they had unsaddled the horses, brushed them down and set them in stalls with almost full feed bins and troughs, they took their Winchesters and saddlebags with them to the house. Joe left the Sharps in its scabbard in the barn.

As they neared the house, Joe spotted a large mound of dirt about two hundred feet northeast of the house where the McClellan boys had buried the four bodies. There was the sound of lowing cattle in the pastures as they stepped up onto the back porch and swung the back door open, entered the kitchen and set down their rifles and saddlebags.

The kitchen was remarkably clean and still stocked with food.

"It looks like nothing has been touched at all," remarked Billy as he scanned the room.

"Hanger Bob only spent one day here, and all I found was some dirty dishes and a messed-up bed in the first bedroom. I guess the McClellans cleaned it up when they came to bury the bodies."

"Are we going to sleep in the house?" Billy asked.

"Why not? It's a really nice house. Let's get this cookstove going and we'll have some supper."

The last of the widows' ranch houses, Sarah Foster's, was now complete, and the women and Ben Hobson were having their last supper together as a group.

After they'd eaten, the four ranch-owning women all sat at the kitchen table having coffee.

"Joe is going to bring your wagon back tomorrow, Sarah," Emma said, "He'll be bringing a bunch of horses, too."

Sarah smiled and said, "Maybe I'll convince him to stay."

Emma asked, "Sarah, I need to ask you and Jennie something. We've only been widows for a little over a week now. How long do you think we should wait to remarry? Abby, you've been a widow now for three years. Why haven't your remarried and how hard has it been?"

Abby said, "I haven't remarried because no one has asked me. We're kind of hidden up in this corner and until Sheriff Joe arrived, the only men I've seen have been Henry Johnson and Lou Taylor at the feed and grain. I suppose if I had made an effort, I could have met more, but I'm just so busy all the time. And yes, to your second question, it's been very hard. The hardest part is being alone. For the first few months after Tom died, I felt so empty sleeping in that bed my myself, but I had my four boys and Margie, so I had a lot to do to keep me from dwelling on it."

Then, when the boys went off to go into a life of crime, I was devastated, and not just because of the increased work it meant for me. When Sheriff Joe returned Ben to me, I can't tell you how grateful I was. I believe my older two boys were going to go that way anyway, but Ben had just followed them. Sheriff Joe could have brought him back to Lander to be hanged, but he didn't. He just brought him home and told Ben to listen to me. Ben's return was a godsend. It helped me with my work and with my spirit. Now, with all this publicity of the four widowed ranchers, I think I won't be alone much longer."

Sarah then added, "I'm going to confess to all of you that I didn't have as happy a marriage as I should have. Mike was a difficult man and he and our son, Abe, could be vicious at times. He doted on Abe and ignored our girls. I was horrified when he died, but I'll admit to a measure of relief, too. I feel like a heartless bitch for feeling that way, but I'm glad I finally admitted to it, too."

Jennie sighed and said, "Mine wasn't a bad marriage, it was just a marriage. We had good times and bad ones. John and the boys spent most of their time doing men things and I spent time with Clara and Cora showing them how to run a household. There wasn't a lot of romance or things we all used to dream about when we were girls, but that's the way it is."

I miss John and the boys, and I still have nightmares when I think of that day and the days that followed, but like you said before on that night around the campfire, Emma, I'm not going to let them ruin my life. I'm going to remarry and not look back. I'm going to choose better this time and maybe I'll get some of those romantic dreams fulfilled after all. I'm not going to live my life as a grieving widow."

Emma said, "That's what I was concerned about. My marriage was sort of like yours, Jennie, only I married Wilbur because I had to. I got pregnant when I was sixteen and it was mostly my own fault. I took one step past those same dreams about romance and love with a boy that was just a boy. I never loved Wilbur and I'm sure he never loved me. He probably blamed me for taking away his youth, but I don't know. He did love our children, though, so there was that, but now, I feel suddenly feel guilty about wanting to get married again."

Abby smiled at Emma and asked, "It's Joe, isn't it, Emma?"

Emma smiled back and said, "Yes, it is. I've never met another man like him. I want him so badly and I know he likes me. When he rode off to get those last four, he left a wanted poster with Billy that said to divide all of the reward money between us. Then, underneath it, he had added a very short last will and testament leaving everything he had to me."

The other women all looked at her with wide eyes and raised eyebrows.

Sarah asked, "He did? Why didn't you say anything? I know I was making my own plans on the Joe front, and I'll bet I wasn't alone, either."

"I didn't want to say anything, because I was concerned about why he wrote it. He expected to die, and then he had to chase down the last one and I thought he wasn't going to come back."

"So, now what are you going to do, Emma?" asked Abby.

"I'm not sure, yet. I need to get settled before I can even think about it. He'll be coming by tomorrow with our wagon, so maybe I'll see him then."

"Well, in light of the will, we'll all bow out of the Sheriff Joe race," said Sarah with a big grin.

The others all laughed, including Emma, who felt relieved and was glad she asked the question.

Joe and Billy finished their late supper and were having coffee in the kitchen.

"This is a big house, Joe. How come it's so big and there were only two of them?"

"My guess is when they built it, they were hoping on having a big family, but that didn't happen. The house had had new rooms added to it over the years, as if they thought by adding a new bedroom, they'd be turning it into a nursery soon. They were wonderful people, Billy. They had both hit sixty years old the same month last year and told me that they were still hoping to have that baby."

Bertha Larsen reminded me a lot of your mother. She was a witty, but strong woman. She wore britches a lot of the time and she'd have a rifle or a shotgun with her, too. I bet that Hanger Bob just caught them by surprise in that rain. If Bertha had seen him riding down the access road, they would have had to bury Bob in the back yard. Roger was a good man and matched Bertha with his quick tongue. Watching them together was like enjoying a circus. They really loved each other and if you saw one you saw the other. Why God chose not to bless them with children, I'll never understand. Growing up in a home with that much love would be the greatest blessing any child could have."

"What were your parents like, Joe?"

Joe smiled and replied, "I have no idea, Billy. I was abandoned by my mother when I was a baby and I never knew her name or my father's name. If it was biologically possible, I could have just popped up in a cabbage patch."

"How did you get your name, then?"

"The registrar at the orphanage didn't have a Joe and the letter 'B' was next up on the list for abandoned babies. He didn't waste time with a middle name, though. It must have been nice having parents that loved you."

"It was. My father showed me all sorts of things, but he didn't tell me about boys and girls. My mother would have if I'd asked, but I was too embarrassed. I know I told you that my mother and father had to get married when they were only a little older than I am, but I don't think they loved each other. They talked to each other like they had to live in the same house together, but it was like there was a wall between them. My sisters noticed it too. That's why I asked if you'd marry her. I know she really likes you, Joe, and I know you really like her, too, or you wouldn't have written what you did on the wanted poster."

Joe grimaced as he asked, "You didn't show it to her, did you, Billy?"

Billy replied, "Yes. You didn't tell me not to, Joe. I wasn't supposed to let her know?"

Joe sighed and said, "No, it's my fault. I should have just left it in my saddlebags. Someone would have found it, but if I was killed, then the only ones who would have found it would have been the bad guys. Maybe I shouldn't have written it in the first place. At least that second part."

"Why not? Don't you like my mother?"

"How I feel about your mother isn't important, Billy. I don't even know if I'll keep doing this job after I get back."

Billy started to add something, when Joe held up his hand.

"Let's talk about something else not so stressful. Have you ever changed a wagon axle before?"

"No, sir. But I saw my father do it once."

"Good. I've done two before, so I'll show you how to do it and you can help."

"Okay."

"Now, let's talk about something exciting, like fishing," Joe said with a smile.

Hanger Bob lay on his cot trying to think of a way to escape his fate again. He'd almost been hanged once, and he didn't want to feel that rope around his neck again. If he made an escape attempt, it had to be early in the morning because the deputies were already gone for the night.

But if only one brought him breakfast in the morning, he'd have a chance. Now, all he had to figure out would be where to go if he did break out of jail.

———

Just after an early breakfast, Joe and Billy had mounted their horses and Joe told him that he wanted to ride the pastures to see the herd and the land, so they turned east after leaving the barn.

They trotted through the heavily grassed fields and soon reached the herd. It wasn't the biggest of herds, about a hundred and ten animals, but they were all well-fed and watered because of a split creek that began on the northeastern corner, then just a hundred yards later, split into two streams, once cutting through the pastures north to south, and the second flowing west.

"Let's follow that western stream, Billy," Joe shouted as he pointed at the eight-foot wide creek.

Billy just followed Joe's direction change and they rode to the stream and followed the bouncing, rushing water as it cascaded over rocks and formed pools as it boiled westward.

"Do you see what I see, Billy?" Joe shouted.

"Fish!" Billy yelled back.

"Cutthroat trout, Billy!" Joe replied as he smiled.

They continued west until they reached the roadway and the stream pooled into a decent sized pond before crossing the road.

"I wonder how the trout deal with the road?" asked Billy.

"There's not much traffic up here, so they probably don't even notice it. Let's head to the McClellans."

They turned south on the road and set off at a medium trot.

———

In his cell, Hanger Bob was waiting for the deputy to arrive with his food, his plan already set in his head. Now, he just hoped it was only going to be one deputy and not two and really hoped it was going to be that young one.

Ed Smith was carrying Hanger Bob's last meal of steak and eggs under the tin covers on the tray. He knew there would be a large crowd at the hanging in two and a half hours and he could understand why.

He had to balance the tray as he unlocked the door to the office, then stepped inside, closing the door behind him.

"Last meal time!" shouted Ed before he giggled.

Bob just sat up on his cot and slowly stood back against the wall opposite the bars as he had been told to do. Ed took the keys from the desk drawer, carried the tray to the cell and set it on the small table across from the cell door, unlocked the door and swung it wide.

He approached Bob with the tray in his hands and as he started to hand it to the prisoner, Bob yawned and then slid his fingers to his eye patch as if he needed to scratch his eyebrow and quickly flipped the patch onto his forehead exposing his hideous dry eye socket.

Ed cringed and looked away at the gruesome sight and Bob took advantage of the expected loss of eye contact and slammed the tray of food up into Ed's face. The tin covers and then the china plates smacked into the deputy's face and he was knocked backward.

Bob knew he had the advantage now and kicked Ed hard in the knee, Ed screamed as the pain shot through his thigh and rocketed up his spine. He fell to the floor in agony as Bob reached down to grab Ed's pistol.

Charlie Wheatley was thirty feet away from the jail when he heard Ed's scream, knew there was a serious problem, and quickly loosed his pistol's hammer loop, yanked the Colt from the holster and cocked the hammer as he quickly crossed the remaining ten yards. He yanked the door open and spotted the prisoner trying to yank Ed's pistol from his holster, but because of the awkward angle was unsuccessful.

"Stop or I'll fire!" shouted Charlie as he walked into the office, his revolver pointed at Hanger Bob's face.

Charlie ignored the eye socket as Bob turned, saw the Colt's muzzle looking like a cannon pointed at his head and stepped away from Ed with his hands in the air.

Charlie then walked over to the cell and shouted, "Get on the floor, you bastard and be grateful I didn't send a .44 through that other eye of yours."

Bob laid on his belly with arms over his head but keeping his one good eye on the second deputy hoping he'd get a chance.

But Charlie just got close to Ed, looked down and said, "Can you get out of there by yourself, Ed?"

Ed flexed his knee slightly and said, "I think so, Charlie. I really screwed up."

"Just slide out of there and we'll clean up his breakfast before we hang the son of a bitch."

Ed sat up and slowly stood, using the cell bars as support as he put all of his weight on his good leg. He then just swung himself out of the cell and limped to the opposite wall. Charlie had never given Bob the chance to make another attempt, but he had hoped to cheat the hangmen if Bob had tried.

Once Ed was clear, Charlie swung the door closed, made sure it was locked and turned to Ed.

"What happened, Ed?" Charlie asked as he holstered his pistol.

"I was givin' him his food and he flipped that patch off. I looked away and he attacked me. I really screwed up, Charlie."

"As Joe always told me, Ed. Lesson learned. Let's clean this up. How bad is your leg?"

Ed flexed his knee a couple of times and replied, "It's not so bad now. When he kicked it, I thought it snapped in two."

"Well, go and sit down and I'll clean up the mess."

Ed nodded and then hobbled to the desk and slowly lowered himself into the seat, still embarrassed by his almost deadly mistake.

Joe and Billy didn't have to saddle the horses when they arrived at the McClellan farm. All eight of the outlaw horses and three of the McClellan horses were saddled leaving three unsaddled. Two of the three that were unsaddled, Al McClellan identified as draft horses, which would prove useful.

The weapons were all loaded into the back of the wagon and Joe pointed out the two Henry rifles among the Winchester '73s to Billy, and when they looked at the eight pistols, he was surprised to find a Colt New Army percussion pistol, along with two Remingtons and one Smith & Wesson, along with the five Colt Peacemakers, although those particular guns had hardly earned the moniker.

Billy and Joe set up two long trail ropes, added Irish and the last of the Larsen horses that Joe had ridden in on, and then shook hands all around, waved to Sadie and Gertie McClellan who were standing on the porch, climbed aboard the wagon and set off west to the Shoshone Indian agency store.

Ed had recovered enough and had enough time to return to his room at the boarding house and change his food-covered clothes to be present and assist Charlie in escorting Hanger Bob to the gallows.

As he had done at the trial, Bob went limp, making the two lawmen have to drag him to the gallows steps. The crowd for today's hanging was almost double what it was for Hank Anderson's just two days earlier.

When they reached the bottom of the steps and Bob was still uncooperative, Charlie said, "Bob, if you don't walk up those steps, I'll have the hangman throw that noose around your neck where you stand and drag you up the steps like a piece of meat."

Bob glared at Charlie but began to walk again as the two deputies accompanied him up the steps.

Once there they stepped aside and let the hangman do his job.

As Hanger Bob stood on the trap door, he anxiously scanned the large crowd for one of his men. He was hoping that the damned sheriff had lied to him about killing all of them. Nobody could kill all of them by himself. Nobody! He tried to convince himself that his men would burst out of the crowd with their Colts pouring lead into the hangman and the deputies just as they had done before. This time, he thought, I'll lower my head, so I don't get a splinter in my other eye.

He was still swiveling his head back and forth looking for his non-existent outlaw brothers when the hangman lowered the hood over his head. Then, when all he saw was black, he finally knew that they weren't coming, and the ferocious murder and gang leader began to cry underneath the hood.

He continued to sob and shake as the hangman lowered the noose over his neck and Bob felt the rope tighten.

He began to sob, "No. No. No," as the hangman stepped back and opened his pocket watch. Then, Hanger Bob peed all over himself as he kept waiting for the drop.

The hangman ignored the smell as he watched the watch's hand approach the minute mark. He was a precise man. When it hit twelve, he yanked back the lever and Hanger Bob lived up to his nickname as he plunged below the wooden floor and the noose snapped his spine.

Ed and Charlie then walked down the steps and returned to the sheriff's office, leaving the hangman and the morticians to do their job.

Joe and Billy hadn't stopped at the agency store because there was no reason but continued on to the damaged wagon.

An hour after passing the store, they arrived, finding the wagon and its contents surprisingly intact.

"Now, that's a surprise," said Joe, "I expected to find it stripped of its cargo. Now, we've got to move anything worth salvaging to your wagon, Billy."

"Okay. Let's get to work then." Billy said with a grin as he hopped out of the wagon.

He knew it was their wagon because aside from normal differences, he had carved his initials in the seat.

"What's that?" he asked when seeing the white mounds.

"Bob dumped two bags of flour to use the bags and it was raining at the time, so they're kind of lumps. They'll be gone eventually."

Joe lifted the cases of whiskey from the wagon, opened the top and began taking each bottle and hurling it against a nearby tree until the remaining bottles of whiskey were nothing more than a wet collection of glass. When he found the beer, he smashed open the top and dumped it onto the ground but kept the kegs.

It took them another fifteen minutes to transfer the food and other worthwhile supplies to the Harper wagon. Now came the real work.

It took forty-five more minutes to replace the axle, but when they were done, the Foster wagon was repaired and ready to roll. Joe and Billy harnessed the two draft horses from the Larsen ranch and then they shortened the trail ropes, so each wagon pulled the same number of horses.

"Okay, Billy, let's head back to that trail. It'll take us to the Foster ranch and then we'll work our way south to your place. Okay?"

"Okay, Joe. I'm ready."

With that, the two wagons began rolling and then follwed the same path that Joe had used to catch up to the caravan leaving Cooperstown.

It was a lot slower going with wagons as opposed to just riding, but they had the luxury of being able to eat and almost lounge as the teams rolled the wagons westward after linking up with the trail. They stopped every couple of hours to let the animals drink, but by four-thirty, they were pulling into the Foster ranch.

Joe had already divided the horses and planned on leaving a couple for Abby Hobson with Sarah Foster to hold until Abby could pick them up.

Sarah was in the kitchen preparing to cook supper when Rachel shouted, "Mama, Sheriff Joe is coming down the road with wagons and lots of horses!"

Sarah quickly dried her hands on her apron and trotted to the front of the house, then out the front door onto the porch. She waved at Joe and Billy and they both waved back.

When they reached the ranch house, they pulled the wagons to a stop and Joe and Billy both stepped to the ground.

"Sarah, this is your wagon, and I left a couple of Winchesters in back if you want to arm Rachel and Katie. It's trailing some horses you can have and if you don't mind, could you give a couple to Abby Hobson?"

Sarah smiled at Joe and replied, "Of course, I will, Joe. Won't you and Billy come in?"

"I'd like to Sarah, but we have to get the other horses and the Harper wagon delivered today, too."

Sarah grinned and was short of winking at Joe, thinking Joe wanted to visit Emma at the end of the trip, so she said, "I understand, Joe, and good luck."

Joe didn't understand why he was being wished good luck, but said, "Thanks, Sarah."

Then he waved to Rachel and Katie, stepped up onto the driver's seat of the Harper wagon and let Billy take the reins as he turned it around and they departed the Foster ranch.

"We've still got a lot of horses, Joe," Bill said.

"We'll drop four of those in back at the Riley ranch and then we'll head to your place."

"Have you picked out one for yourself, Joe?"

"I'll use that pinto until I get my own. I like his gait and he's a handsome boy. Pintos just aren't a smart thing for lawmen to own because of the sharp black and white contrast."

"Oh."

Less than an hour later, they turned into the Riley ranch, and Joe asked Jennie if she wanted some Winchesters for her daughters, but Jennie declined. While he was talking to Jennie, Billy was spending as much time as he could with Cora.

Jennie invited them to stay for supper, but again, Joe declined saying he had to drop off the remaining horses and the wagon to the Harpers. This time, when Jennie wished him good luck, she did wink. Joe smiled at her, as Cora and Clara led away the horses.

Joe then moved his saddlebags and rifles from the Larsen horse with that annoying gait, and spent a few minutes adjusting the stirrups for his height which also gave Billy a couple of more minutes with Cora.

Then, Joe mounted the pinto and when Billy walked out, said, “I’ve got to get back to Lander and make sure that hanging went okay. I just don’t trust Hanger Bob.”

Billy looked up and said, “You should come over and have supper with us, Joe.”

“I really do need to get back, Billy. It’s a short drive. Tell your mother and sisters I said hello.”

“Okay,” replied a frustrated Billy Harper, who knew his mother was looking forward to seeing Joe.

Joe gave a short salute to Billy, turned the pinto and trotted off, turned left and headed south.

Billy smiled at Cora then stepped up into the driver’s seat, released the handbrake and started the wagon for the trip home.

———

Joe was happy with the pinto’s ride and was thinking about keeping the horse as his permanent ride as he passed by the Harper ranch. He could see smoke rising from the cookstove pipe and knew that Emma was making supper. He tried to rationalize that he had to get back to Lander for one official reason or the other, but he knew the real reason. It was the same flaw in his character that had driven him to wait too long for Mary Sheehy and lost her to the butcher. He was simply afraid of asking her about anything as serious as marriage, and the more he thought about it, the more he couldn’t do it.

Sheriff Joe Brooks was simply running away.

———

"Mama, I think that was Sheriff Joe that just rode past," Annie said as she walked into the kitchen from the main room.

"He rode past? Where is Billy and the wagon?" she asked.

"I don't know, Mama. I might be wrong, though. He was riding a pinto."

Emma stopped working and said, "He lost his horse when Bob Jones shot it, so he might be riding a pinto."

"I thought you said he was coming to visit," said Mary.

"That's what I thought Billy said. He'd be dropping off the horses and the wagon."

"Are you going to marry him, Mama?" asked Mary.

"Not if he doesn't want to marry me, Mary. It's not up to me."

"Why not, Mama? You always seemed to be the boss around the house. Papa used to complain that you wore the pants in the house because you acted like a man a lot of times."

Emma smiled and said, "Yes, I did, didn't I?"

Annie then said, "Then if you want to marry him, Mama, you should go and ask him to marry you."

Emma was going to object again, but instead asked, "Would you mind if I married Sheriff Joe?"

Annie and Mary both giggled and Annie replied, "Of course not, Mama. We both really like him, and we know he likes you a lot."

Emma sighed and said, "I know he does, and that's what surprises me. Now that this is all over, I thought he'd be paying me more attention, but instead it's like he's trying to avoid me."

"Then just ride into Lander and ask him to marry you, Mama," Mary said with a big grin.

"We'll see," Emma said as she returned to cooking.

Twenty minutes later, Billy turned the wagon into the ranch and waved at his sisters who were sitting on the porch steps.

Annie and Mary bounced up and Mary trotted back to the door and shouted, "Mama, Billy's here!"

Emma set aside her butcher's knife and walked out to the front of the house and was surprised to see a fully laden wagon leading six horses, all but one saddled.

She stepped down from the porch and waited with her girls for Billy to bring the wagon to a stop.

When he did, he hopped down and jogged over to his mother and gave her a hug and a kiss on the cheek.

"What do you have there, Billy?" she asked.

"Well, for starters, it's our wagon. Then we stopped and unloaded all of the supplies from the broken wagon except for the whiskey and beer. Joe smashed all the whiskey and dumped the beer on the ground but kept the wooden cases and the barrels because he said they were still useful. Then there's the food and a bunch of rifles and pistols in there too with boxes of ammunition. The horses are ours, too."

"What about Joe? Why did he ride past the house without even stopping?" Emma asked.

"He said he had to go and make sure the hanging didn't have any problems."

Emma wasn't buying the excuse, but just nodded and said, "I'm cooking dinner. Why don't you and your sisters bring the wagon into the barn and take care of all the horses? We'll worry about unloading the wagon tomorrow."

"Okay, Mama," Billy said as he hopped back into the wagon and headed for the barn.

———

"I really messed up, Joe. If Charlie hadn't come in when he did, I would have been dead, and you'd have to chase that bastard all over hell again."

"Ed, that's how we learn. You'll be okay. How's the knee?"

"It's okay, but I don't think I should be a deputy anymore, Joe. I really, really screwed up."

"I'm not going to deny that, Ed, but let me tell you a story. When I was twenty, a little younger than you are now, I was bringing a prisoner named Burnt Powder, in from out in the wild country."

Ed interrupted, asking, "Burnt Powder? How'd he get that name?"

"His real name was Bernard Powder, but he didn't want to be called Bernie, either. So, he began calling himself Burnt Powder as if he'd just fired a gun to make himself sound tougher than he was. Personally, I thought he was more of a Bernie. Anyway, Bernie was on the run for shooting another poker player that he had accused of cheating. Now, that happens all the time, but the kid's father was also the town's mayor, so he lit out and I was assigned the job of bringing him back because Bernie wasn't considered a real threat."

So, I found him three days later in a box canyon and just waited him out. He didn't have any water where he was, and he finally gave up and walked out with his hands up. He looked like a lost puppy, so I just took his guns and we headed back. It was the second day on that return trip when we were coming down this incline and suddenly, Bernie launches himself across from his horse and knocks me off of mine. We both go rolling down this hill and Bernie thinks he's made his escape, but I didn't lose my pistol, and I put him under my Colt and he meekly got back on his horse and I tied him down this time. When we got back, I felt like you did. I tried to turn in my badge to old Sheriff Randolph, but he told me to learn from my mistakes, and here I am, still wearing a badge fourteen years later."

Ed smiled and said, "Really? Wow, I never would have guessed, Joe. I guess I'll just do better."

"I know you will, Ed. Bob's hanged and that's all that matters."

"Well, I'm gonna go and get something to eat. You comin', Joe?"

"Not this time, Ed. I've got to write up that paperwork."

"Oh, by the way the voucher for Hanger Bob came in. It was a thousand dollars by its lonesome."

"I feel kind of bad about that. Only two of that crowd didn't have bounties on their heads, and one of them, Claude Nevers, was killed by a round fired by Al McClellan."

"I don't think he'll care, Joe," Ed said as he stood and then left the office closing the door behind him.

"I suppose Ed's right. Anyway, I'll swing by the bank tomorrow and get the money broken up for the women. Let's lock this place up and go home, Charlie."

Charlie then looked at Joe, smiled and said, "When you told me that story two years ago, the prisoner's name was Bent Barrel, you called him Bennie, and he was guilty of being a peeping Tom."

Joe laughed and stood, saying, "And you're still here, Charlie. Let's get out of here."

CHAPTER 9

At nine o'clock the next morning, Joe took the $4450 in vouchers to the bank and with only a minor grimace from the cashier, had them converted to cash, which took some amount of searching in the bank. The bank president was soothed when Joe told him he'd recommend that all of the women start new bank accounts and deposit their other cash there as well.

Joe left the bank and walked back to his own office with the large envelope of cash.

When he entered his office, Ed asked, "All taken care of, Joe?"

"All taken care of, Ed," Joe replied as he walked back to his office.

He took a seat behind his desk, took out the cash and began counting out the money. He wound up with four piles of thirteen hundred apiece for the three new widows, and one of five hundred for Abby Hobson and pocketed fifty dollars for some supplies.

He stuffed the cash into four envelopes and labeled each of them, then he wrote a short note below each of the names saying that it would be wise idea to create bank accounts and deposit all of their cash into the bank rather than leaving it around the house.

He took the four envelopes out to Ed and handed them to him.

"Can you deliver these to the ladies, Ed? I'm going to head out in a little while to take some time off to do some serious thinking."

Ed nodded but was concerned about what kind of serious thinking Joe was going to do. *He couldn't quit!*

"When Charlie comes back tell him I'll see you both in a few days."

"Okay, boss," Ed replied.

Joe grabbed his hat, stuck his finger through the hole and recalled his boot problem, but it was too late to do anything about them now.

He pulled on his hat and walked back out to the street, stopped on the boardwalk, took a deep breath and mounted the pinto and turned him north to Johnson's General Store.

———

"He's just going away, and nobody knows where he's going?" asked Emma.

"My impression was that he didn't want anyone to know, ma'am," Ed said as the envelope of cash sat on the kitchen table between them.

Ed was very uncomfortable as Emma tapped her fingers on the table, her mind churning with all sorts of conflicting thoughts.

"I've got to deliver these other envelopes, Mrs. Harper. Do you have anything else you need to know?"

Emma had to shake her cobwebs from her mind before she replied, "No, I'm sorry, Deputy. You can press on."

"Thank you, ma'am," Ed said as he snatched up his hat and quickly left the kitchen.

After he'd gone, Emma stared at the envelope of bills and just couldn't make any sense of Sheriff Joe Brooks. She was sure that he had feelings for her, and knew that she loved him, but why was he running away and hiding? It surely wasn't because of some sinister gang.

She picked up the envelope and walked to the pantry and took out the other envelope. She spread the cash out from both envelopes and counted it out. Altogether, she still had over twenty-four hundred dollars even after setting up the house, and she still had the ranch account at the bank, although the balance rarely exceeded two hundred dollars.

So, Joe had given the widows over eight thousand dollars as if it was just pretend money, was prepared to give her all of his money, then goes off and hides. She was getting frustrated as she began to slide the cash back into the envelope.

She still held it in her hands when he heard giggling out in the front room, so she stood, walked down the hallway and saw a red-faced Billy sitting with Cora on the couch. Both turned to see her, and Cora also flushed.

"Cora, how did you get here?" Emma asked.

"On my horse, Mrs. Harper. The one that Sheriff Joe gave me. At least my mother said he did. I have a rifle, too, so it's okay."

"No, that's okay. I was just curious."

Cora smiled at Billy then looked at Emma and said, "Well, I should be riding back."

Then she looked back at Billy and said, "I'll see you later, Billy."

Billy was still red as he looked at Cora, smiled back and said, "I'll see you then, Cora."

Emma wanted to giggle herself at the young couple as Cora gave a coy little wave to Billy and left the room, crossed the porch and with Billy's eyes locked onto her, mounted her horse and waved again before turning and riding off.

Billy then turned to his mother and said, "I'm sorry, Mama, I don't know how it happened. Really!"

Emma said, "Let's go out to the kitchen and we can talk."

Billy's mood dropped a couple of pegs as he said, "Yes, ma'am."

Billy knew he'd get in trouble now as he followed his mother to the kitchen and took a seat.

Emma poured two cups of coffee, set one before her son and sat down across from him.

"Now, Billy, tell me what just happened that had you so embarrassed?"

Billy kept his eyes on his coffee as he said, "I kissed Cora, but I'm not sure if she kissed me first. We kind of just found ourselves kissing."

Emma was working hard to stifle a smile as she maintained her motherly countenance.

"And is that as far as it went, Mr. Harper?"

"Oh, yes, Mama. Just one kiss, and it was really wet and mushy."

Emma was really struggling now but asked, "But did you like it?"

Billy still kept his eyes down and said, "Um, yes, kinda. Mama, is it okay if I don't talk to you about this anymore? I really need to talk to Joe."

Emma lost her desire to laugh and asked, "I wish you could, Billy, but Joe's disappeared. Deputy Smith was just here dropping off the reward money that Joe gave all of us and I asked where Joe was, and he told me that he just left town and didn't want anybody to find him."

"He did?"

"Yes, and it really has me frustrated. After I read that wanted poster he wrote on, and what you told me earlier, I thought that once this was over, he'd stop by more often and we could spend a lot of time together and he'd ask me to marry him, but instead, he seems to be ignoring me. He even rode right past the ranch without even a wave yesterday. I thought I knew him so well, but now I'm not so sure."

Billy said softly as he looked up at his mother, "I know why he's doing this, Mama."

Emma looked at him in surprise, and asked, "You know? How do you know, Billy?"

"The night that you had that campfire talk with the other ladies, he asked me if I liked any of the girls and I told him I liked Cora. He told me that it was fine and gave me all sorts of advice like you only kiss a girl when she wants to be kissed and to treat all of the girls extra carefully because of what happened to them."

Anyway, I told him that he seemed to know a lot about girls and women, and he laughed. He said he was flying under false colors, whatever that means, but he said because he grew up without a mother or sisters and went to school with only boys, he was afraid of girls. He liked them a lot, but he said he was awkward when talking to girls. I said that he seemed to be able to talk to them fine, but he said that he could talk to them as people, but when if he tried to talk to a girl or woman about something serious, like love or marriage, he'd turn to jelly inside. He said he was afraid to do it. I think that's why he isn't talking to you anymore, Mama. I think he really loves you, and the more he loves you, the harder it is to even talk to you."

Emma asked quietly, "Billy, why haven't you told me this before?"

"Because I made a promise not to, sort of. I kind of said okay, but I said I'd do the best I could. But I think you can help him, Mama. He always said how strong and impressive you are and says that you're the most handsome woman he'd ever seen, too."

Emma sighed and said, "Well, Mr. Harper, maybe tomorrow, I'll ride into Lander to deposit this money and see if I can't find out where our sheriff has gone."

"I think I know that, too, Mama."

Emma laughed and said, "Why am I not surprised? Is there anything that he hasn't told you, Billy?"

"Joe tells me everything, Mama. Even papa wouldn't do that. Joe treats me like a man and I really want him to marry you. I think you'd both be really happy."

"I think you're right, my wonderful son, and when I bring him back, you can talk to him about Cora. So, where do you think he is?"

"When we went to get our wagon back and all the horses, we went to the Larsen ranch just north of the McClellan farm. I know the way now. I can probably draw you a map. Anyway, when we were there, we toured the farm and saw trout in a stream, and he said we should go fishing. I'm pretty sure that's where he is."

"You draw the map and tomorrow, I'll go and find our elusive sheriff."

"From here, it's really easy, Mama. Just follow the …"

———

Joe turned into the Larsen ranch access road after had stopped at the McClellans and told them that he'd be staying there for a few days if they had any questions.

He put the pinto in the barn, unsaddled him and brushed him down.

As he did, he looked at the horse. He was quite a handsome horse, despite, or because of his coloring. His ride was perfect, and he had good musculature and wind.

"I've got to come up with a name for you, don't I? I'll think about it and we'll talk tomorrow."

Then he laughed and said, "I'm glad you're not a mare, or I wouldn't be able to utter a sound."

He carried his two large bags that he had picked up at Johnson's and entered the back door, set the bags on the floor and fired up the cookstove, filled the coffeepot and began to explore the house. There were five bedrooms, some newer than others and one was quite large with a bigger bed than he'd seen before. Maybe Roger and Bertha hadn't been joking about trying to make babies when they were almost sixty.

He returned to the kitchen, had some coffee and some bacon and eggs from his supplies and then walked outside with a coffee cup in his hand.

A few minutes later, he was standing beside the large grave that was the final resting place of the Roger and Bertha Larsen and the Knutson twins. He felt especially bad about the Larsens. They were just two good, honest people who enjoyed life and wished he could have stopped that bastard before he set foot on the ranch.

What was almost as sad was what he knew would happen to the place. The cattle would eventually start wandering off as mavericks, the buildings would deteriorate, and it would eventually be removed from the tax rolls. It was just a sad ending for what must have begun as a life of hope when a younger Roger and Bertha started the ranch almost twenty years ago.

Joe shook his head, turned and walked back to the house to prepare for sleep.

———

"By yourself? Mama, you can't do that!" Annie exclaimed, "It's dangerous!"

"I'll have my Winchester and my Colt. It'll only take me about seven hours if I ride fast, and it's summer, so I'll have plenty of light."

Billy wasn't saying anything as he was the instigator of his mother's decision.

Emma had decided to hold off depositing the money rather than ride south to Lander and then ride north again. Billy had drawn a map showing her how to ride east for an hour then change to northeast and pick up the wagon tracks from the two wagons and follow them east to the Indian Agency store and turn north on the road. The next ranch on the right was where Joe would be. She'd know it was the right one if she saw a really big house and if she crossed a creek, she would have gone too far.

After a few minutes of objections from both Mary and Annie, they finally realized that they wouldn't win the argument and caved in, telling their mother that they knew she and Sheriff Joe would be happy.

———

The morning sun was hard on his eyes as Joe was riding into the eastern pastures to explore the place. The ranch was four full sections and had plenty of grass and that beautiful trout stream. The other stream probably didn't have any fish because of the cattle, who didn't seem to care for the stony ground around the westbound stream. They all stayed near the grassy-banked stream.

It really was a beautiful place. There were pines everywhere outside of the pastures harboring a lot of wildlife, but it was the trout stream that had captured his imagination, not that he planned on doing any fishing. He just thought it was a good spot to just sit and think.

———

Emma had started her journey to the Larsen ranch at seven o'clock after having a big breakfast. She had packed a canvas bag with her clothes, her toiletry items, and other things that she thought she might need. She had some food in her saddlebags and a box of .44 cartridges for her pistol and her Winchester. She had discarded the Colt in favor of the lone Smith & Wesson Model 3 that had been in the wagon after Billy told her that was the type of pistol that Joe used.

She was wearing britches and a plaid shirt instead of her riding skirt and blouse and had tucked her long, light brown hair into her wide-brimmed flat hat as she rode east out of her ranch. She had her horse moving at a medium trot and as Billy had suggested, kept her eyes moving.

Emma may have said she wasn't the least bit worried, but when the ranch house was long gone from view, she became mildly concerned. Her biggest concern was getting lost. Billy had told her that all she had to do was to ride east and then curve northeast after an hour, find those tracks and she'd be at the Larsen ranch within three or four hours.

It sounded simple enough, so, after checking her pocket watch a few times, she turned northwest, or she intended to turn northwest. She really turned more to the north, and as she rode, the wagon tracks didn't show up yet and she began to get seriously worried.

She stopped for an early lunch, and was looking back the way she came, wondering if she had missed something. Emma wasn't regretting her decision to go, she was regretting not buying a compass, even though she didn't know how to use the damned thing.

She shook her head and as she turned to climb back on board, her heart stopped. She thought about reaching for her rifle but knew it wouldn't do any good. She froze in place and kept her blue eyes focused ahead as the Indians rode toward her brandishing Winchesters or spears.

Emma had no way to talk to them unless they spoke English and hoped that one of them did. Suddenly, she realized they might thing she was a man, so she snatched her hat from her head, letting her long sandy hair cascade down her shoulders.

The Shoshone had known she was a woman long before she saw them, and as they approached Emma, she stepped away from her horse showing none of the fear that was bubbling inside, she raised her right hand with the palm flat, facing the Indians.

One of them separated from the others and he walked his horse forward.

Emma said firmly, "I'm looking for Sheriff Joe."

The fierce visage of the warrior evaporated as he said, "Sheriff Joe?"

"Yes."

The warrior pointed at her and asked, "Are you his woman?"

"Yes."

"Come with us," he said.

Emma exhaled and walked unsteadily back to her horse, stepped up into the saddle and waited for the Shoshone to lead. They broke into a medium trot and Emma followed. She took her canteen and took a deep swallow of water, popped the cork back in place and hung it back on the saddle.

None of the warriors looked at her as they rode, but soon, she spotted wagon tracks. The Shoshone seemed to be following the tracks as well and kept going.

An hour later they passed the agency store, but Emma didn't know what it was, only that it was a building.

They rode to the turnoff and the Shoshone stopped and the warrior who had spoken to her, turned his horse and said, "Sheriff Joe, north. Tell him I am sorry for the cut."

"I will. Thank you."

Young Buffalo smiled at Emma and waved her on. Emma smiled back and nudged her horse forward and turned him north onto the road. When she turned to wave, the Shoshone had all ridden off.

———

Joe was standing by the rushing water of the stream just looking at the fish fighting the current and felt a kinship. He'd been fighting against a strong flow of his own making since he walked out of that orphanage. He'd failed with Mary Sheehy, losing her to the butcher, but that was different. He was younger then and had been infatuated with the pretty redhead and had barely even talked to her. In a way, his fear of getting close to women had saved him from making a mistake.

But this was about Emma. Emma was so much different from any other woman, especially Mary Sheehy. Emma was a confident, strong woman who could match wits with him and tell him when he was doing something stupid, but she was still a warm, soft-hearted woman with great compassion for others and a great capacity for love.

Emma was in total control of his heart, but he knew it wouldn't matter unless he faced up to his weakness. He had to ride back to Lander tomorrow and then go to her ranch and ask if he could start seeing her. He couldn't afford to lose Emma. There couldn't be another Emma and it was his last chance to end his perpetual loneliness.

His mind finally set, he turned to go back to the house and was rocked when he saw a rider pass the house and head right for him. He wasn't shaken because he hadn't heard the hoofbeats, it was because riding towards him, her hair flowing behind her, was the one woman he had to talk to about a subject he had never dared to mention to any woman.

She was smiling as she neared, and Joe felt the weight of reluctance descending on his mind despite his earlier resolve. When he had made his decision minutes ago, it was all mental action, but Emma's approach meant it had to be real action sooner than he had expected and he had to fight off those fears.

Emma pulled her horse to a stop and quickly dismounted, left the reins hanging and just strode to a point just three feet in front of him and said, "Joe, I need to ask you something."

Suddenly, Joe knew exactly what Emma was going to ask and couldn't let that happen.

Emma smiled and began, "Sheriff Joe Brooks, will you m…"

Joe put up his right hand and shouted, "Stop right there! No! No! Don't say it! This is all wrong!"

Emma's smile vanished. *No? He was denying her?* Emma felt like a fool. She'd ridden miles across open country thinking Joe would just say yes and wrap her in his arms and kiss her. But he said no before she even got a chance to ask.

Emma said, "No? But I thought…"

Again, Joe interrupted her and said, "No, Emma. It can't be this way. It just can't."

Emma felt tears beginning to well in her eyes, so she lowered her gaze, and began to turn back to her horse, her heart and soul crushed, but strong hands took her by her shoulders and turned her back.

As she lifted her eyes, she saw a tortured Joe Brooks looking at her with his deep gray eyes.

"Emma, it can't be you. I have to do this for myself. I need to do this, so please be patient."

Then she understood that he hadn't been denying her, he was fighting his own internal battle, so she whispered, "I'll be patient, Joe."

Joe nodded and continued to hold her shoulders firmly as he began, saying, "Emma…Emma, I, I think you are the most remarkable woman I have ever met."

Then he took several deep breaths before continuing.

"Over the past week, I have made a lot of excuses for not talking to you, and the more I thought about you the worse it became. I…I have a problem talking to women about anything that might lead to something serious. I've always been this way. I thought I'd live the rest of my life alone and it scared me. It scared me as much as talking to women did, but you have become so important to me, that I told myself that I had to get over my fear or I would lose you forever, and I can't let that happen, Emma."

He paused again, looked over Emma's hat, then looked back down into her loving blue eyes and he knew he could do it. He was so close.

"Emma, my dear Emma, would you, will you marry me?" he asked in a rush, his eyes seeking her answer, hoping that he hadn't gone too far.

Emma reached up with her right hand and laid it gently on the left side of his face.

"You were right, Joe. You had to be the one to ask, and my answer is an unshakable yes. It's why I came here."

Joe felt a flood of relief, smiled, but asked, "How did you know I was here? No one knew."

"Billy thought that you'd be here, so I came."

"But if I wasn't here, Emma, that would be a very dangerous thing to do."

"Well, I'm here and now you can protect me."

Joe dropped his hands from her shoulders, took a half step closer and embraced her, holding her close.

"I'll always protect you, Emma. You are so very precious to me. I'm sorry that I had to stop you from asking your question. It was very important to me that I break out of my jail and ask you myself. It was very difficult, but I had to do it because it was you, Emma."

Emma rested the side of her head on his chest and said softly, "Billy told me, Joe. I understand."

"I asked him not to tell you, but I'm glad that he did. I've never felt so absolutely free and happy, Emma."

Then, without warning, he pulled her from the ground and swung her around twice just to hear her laugh.

Finally, he set her back down and found his face just inches from hers and said, “You are an honest, straightforward woman, Emma. I hope that I never disappoint you.”

Emma smiled at Joe and said, “You could never disappoint me, Joe. Are you going to kiss me now?”

He slid his hands around her waist and pulled her even closer.

She put her hands behind his neck and kissed him deeply as he held her close. Joe felt his toes curl and was still stunned by what had just happened, but he knew it was right.

Emma knew before she even had ridden off to ask Joe to marry her that it was right, but when he was kissing her, she felt her knees grow weak and knew that this was the love she had sought for almost twenty years.

When they pulled apart slightly, Joe exclaimed, “That was wet!”

Emma started to laugh as she cupped his face in her hands and said, “Don’t tell me that you’ve never kissed a woman before! Not ever?”

“No, I haven’t, Emma. You are the first and will be the only one, but I have to admit that I enjoyed it immensely.”

“Do you want the bad news, Sheriff Joe?” Emma asked as their noses remained two inches apart.

Joe wanted to kiss her again, but said, “I suppose you’re going to tell me anyway.”

“Yesterday, I walked in on Billy and Cora. They had shared a kiss before us two oldsters.”

Joe started laughing and said, “He’s never going to let me live that down, is he?”

"Not if we don't tell him, but we can beat him to all of the other good stuff if you want to drag me into the house, or are you a prude in addition to being untested?"

Joe grinned at her, slid his hand across the bottom of her britches and she raised her eyebrows.

"I guess that answers that question. So, do you take me into the house, and I'll show you how this all works?" she asked.

"I'll take care of your horse first, as we may be busy for a while once we go inside."

Emma smiled, kissed him again and said, "Party pooper."

Joe grinned at Emma and said, "Being married to you is going to be an adventure."

"Adventures are always exciting," she said as she pulled him against her even closer.

Feeling her softness pressed tightly against him, a totally overwhelmed Joe barely was able to say, "You are an exciting woman, Emma."

Emma grinned back and slid her hand across Joe's backside saying, "You have no idea, Sheriff Joe."

Joe then reciprocated by grasping her behind with both hands, while Emma slid gently across his torso.

Joe croaked, "I think I might have the gist of it, Emma."

"I'll do anything you ask of me, Joe," Emma said softly as she kissed him on his neck, giving him goosebumps.

Joe replied softly, "And whatever you need, Emma, I'll provide, but I'll need your patience, too. I'm new at all this."

"I'll be more than happy to show you everything, Joe," Emma replied seductively.

Joe kissed her one more time before he stepped back and said, "Emma, let me take care of the horse now before we totally neglect the poor beast."

Emma smiled and said, "Then I'll go inside and wait for you. Is that acceptable, Sheriff?"

Joe grinned and said, "Yes, ma'am," but before he left to take care of the horse, Joe pulled her close again, and kissed her passionately.

Emma responded as each felt the rising passion that couldn't be held back much longer, so they mutually stepped back slightly.

Emma smiled and asked, "Are you sure that you're afraid of women? I'm beginning to think you made all that up."

Joe stopped smiling, grew serious and as he gazed into her eyes said, "I can't explain this, Emma. I've always had this giant dam in my head about love and marriage and I couldn't see past the wall. I don't know if Billy told you the first time that I thought about asking a girl to a social and couldn't do it. She married a butcher and I thought I was doomed to a life alone. I realized later that what I felt then was nothing more than infatuation with a pretty girl, but you were so extraordinary, and I wanted to be with you so much, that all I could think about is how to get past that dam."

But I kept making excuses, so I wouldn't have to try. Excuses like, you needed a mourning period, or I was some sort of heartless killer that wasn't good enough for you, but I knew I was lying to myself. I was just afraid to tell you how I felt about you. But even though I had just convinced myself I had to tell you, when I saw you, I suddenly wasn't sure again. Then, when you started to ask me to marry you, I knew it had to come from me. If I didn't do this, then how could I ever get past that dam wall and make you happy?"

When I stopped you from asking, I saw the first cracks in that dam, and when I was finally able to ask you to marry me, even though it wasn't exactly a perfect proposal, that dam finally broke. And behind that dam was a beautiful, sunlit valley that had been hidden from me for my entire life. You opened my eyes to that valley, Emma. You are the one who showed me that I could have love in my life because that is what was beyond that dam; pure, unfiltered love. Now, I know I'll be able to love you as you deserve to be loved. There will be no walls between us, Emma."

Emma smiled at Joe and said softly, "Joe, you may not have been able to talk to women about love before, but what you just told me is the most beautiful expression of love I've ever heard. I love you, Joe, and I want to spend the rest of my life with you."

Joe leaned over and kissed Emma gently before saying, "I love you, Emma, with all my heart. I'll never stop loving you and will show you how much I love you every day."

Emma sighed and smiled at Joe, then said, "I'll take my bag, and you can take care of the horse, but you'd better make it quick, Mr. Brooks."

Joe unhooked Emma's bag, handed it to her, and replied, "You'll be surprised how fast I can get this done."

Emma just smiled, turned and walked to the house as Joe walked her horse quickly to the barn.

———

Emma entered the kitchen and was surprised how big it was. She hadn't really paid attention to the house as she had been focused on Joe, but it was a much bigger house than hers. She had planned on getting changed into something more feminine, but instead decided to make some coffee, not that either of them needed the stimulation.

Once the cookstove was fired up, and the coffeepot in place, Emma pulled a skillet from the shelf and put it on the cookstove surface, walked into the cold room and found it well-stocked. She took some butter and some basic foods to make a quick supper, not expecting to leave the bedroom for some time.

She had just begun to add ingredients when Joe popped into the kitchen.

Emma said, "I thought it might be a good idea to eat now while we were still dressed."

Joe walked up behind her and said, "Oh, I don't know, Emma. I wouldn't mind watching you cook sans clothing."

Emma turned her head and grinned at Joe, saying, "My! My! You have gotten past your problem, haven't you?"

"Only with you, Emma. But you know, I was talking to you about things that I never was able to say to a woman soon after we began spending some time together. That's when I first knew how special you were, but I'll tell you something that I never told anyone."

Emma stirred her food and asked, "What is this deep, dark secret?"

"Do you remember the first time we ever met, Emma?"

"Yes, I do. You showed up at the ranch because someone had rustled four of our cattle."

"Yes, and I was talking to Wilbur when you walked out onto the front porch. You were wearing a light blue dress, you had a plaid apron around your waist, and you weren't wearing any shoes. When you stepped out and I saw those blue eyes and long, light brown hair, I was a bit shaken. When I returned the cattle two days later, you were wearing a green and white dress with a white sash and had your shoes on. You were standing on the back porch with your arms around Annie and Mary."

Emma smiled at the memory and said, "You kept glancing at me, but not in a greedy, lust-filled way, but more like an innocent little boy. I was amazed that a big, husky man like you could have that look. You really are as innocent a man as I've ever met."

"Not so innocent, Emma. I've killed fifteen men over the past week alone and twenty-seven over the past fourteen years. But you know, I can live with that, but there is one thing that really bothers me still."

Emma turned and looked at Joe, then asked, "What is that, Joe?"

Joe found it much easier now to keep his eyes locked on Emma's as he said, "When I had to go to the McClellan's farm to stop those eight men, there was a big gunfight. The McClellans were shooting from behind cover as the seven men on horseback fired back. After three of their number had fallen, the remaining four bolted to the north to get into some trees. I couldn't let them get there. One was shot by one of the McClellans, and I shot the others."

But one of them, Jean Martin, wasn't killed, but severely wounded. He was lying on the ground in a lot of pain when I found him, and he knew he would die soon. He asked me to hear his confession, so I could pass it on to a Catholic priest, so the priest could give him absolution for his sins, and he could go to heaven. I refused him, Emma. I turned down his dying request and just ended his suffering. I played at being God, Emma. Did I become so important that I felt I could usurp God's right to final judgement? I condemned that man to hell, Emma. I didn't have the right to do that."

Emma pushed the skillet from the hot plate to the warming plate on the cookstove and cupped Joe's face in her hands.

"No, Joe, you didn't do anything wrong. That's not how confession works. Take this from a woman who was raised as a Catholic."

"You mean even if I had heard his and took it to a priest, it wouldn't have worked?"

"No, that's not what I meant. For a priest to absolve sins, the confession must be made with true repentance for committing those sins. You can't just confess to try to avoid punishment. You have to feel remorse for what you did because it was wrong, and you hurt others. Do you believe that the outlaw really felt sorry for murdering the men and boys and raping the women and girls? Or was he just trying to avoid facing God's wrath?"

Joe hadn't thought of it that way at all, and replied, "No, there was no remorse in Jean Martin. He was scared of going to hell for his crimes. I've seen the same look on the faces of men before the hood is dropped over their heads and they suddenly realize that true justice will soon be delivered, and they would finally suffer even more than those they made suffer."

"You are a good man, Joe. The best man I've ever met, and I'm so very happy that you'll be my man for the rest of my life. Don't let all the good you've done to protect the good folks from becoming something less than that."

For the second time in less than an hour, Joe felt a soothing sense of relief, and both times were because of the extraordinary woman standing before him.

"Thank you, Emma. You've chased away another demon. Now, I'll get out of your way and just let you cook. Okay?"

She kissed him quickly, then said, "You can just sit and watch. It's almost done."

"I'll do that," Joe said as he walked to the kitchen table, pulled out a chair and took a seat facing Emma as she stirred the food in the skillet.

As she cooked, Emma found it hard to believe that all of this had just happened. When she had set out that morning, she thought it would be simple, but it had turned out to be much more complex, and so much more intimate. Joe may have felt relief from his own inhibitions and worries, but she knew that all of her own bad memories were being washed away, knowing that for the first time in her life, she was in love and was loved. Soon, she would be making love to the only man she would ever love. It was an amazing outcome from that horrible situation.

Now, she just wanted to enjoy herself with Joe, and that in itself was as redeeming as all of the deep conversations they'd already experienced.

She reached over, took the coffee container down and spooned the ground coffee into the boiling water, knowing that when she stretched out to retrieve the coffee, her form was more pronounced.

"Enjoying yourself, Mr. Brooks?" she asked without turning.

"Absolutely, Mrs. Brooks," Joe replied with a light laugh.

Emma didn't turn, but smiled, nonetheless. Mrs. Brooks, she thought.

Joe helped set the table and soon they were enjoying the food but enjoying each other's company even more.

Emma then asked the big question, "So, where will we live, Joe?"

Joe took a sip of coffee and replied, "I don't know yet, Emma. I was hoping for your wise counsel on that decision. I was thinking about quitting my job as sheriff and just going somewhere, but that was a couple of weeks ago. Then, with all my tortured thinking about you and what I had done in the last week or so, I was sure that I couldn't be sheriff any longer, but now, that's all changed. You've opened up a whole new world to me and I want to do what's good for you."

Then Joe paused and asked, "Do Billy, Annie and Mary know?"

"It would have been kind of hard to sneak out of the house and be gone for a few days without them knowing, but Billy was the one who gave me the directions, and once Annie and Mary got past their worries about my riding out here alone, both of them were ecstatic. You're already their hero, you know. I think Billy worships you as a god."

"A god with a lot of flaws, Emma."

"We all have flaws, Joe. I'm a hard woman that tends to be abrupt."

Joe smiled and said, "This is from the woman that ignored her own pain to help all of the other women and girls when they needed it most. You keep saying you're a hard woman, Emma, but I believe you are the softest-hearted woman I've ever met. You cared for every one of those women and girls and did everything you could to make them better. That isn't how a hard woman acts."

Emma smiled at him and said, "Well, you'll admit that I'm not a wallflower."

Joe smiled back, saying, "No, you are far from that, but I wouldn't love you like I do if you were. Thank you giving me the honor of marrying you, Emma. I'll look forward to waking every morning and seeing your face."

"Pretty soon, it will be all covered in lines and wrinkles," she said with a wry smile.

Then she paused a few heartbeats, looked at her rough hands and said, "Joe, I'm not young anymore, and I can't have any more children. I know you wanted to have your own family, but I can't give you your own children. Does that bother you?"

"No, sweetheart, it doesn't concern me in the least. Emma, I'm almost thirty-five. I don't want any babies, and when we get married, I'll inherit a son and two fine daughters. I'll have a family and a perfect wife."

Emma surprised Joe when she had to wipe away some tears, putting the lie to the whole hard woman self-description.

"I'm far from perfect, Joe. Sometimes, I think I'm more of a man than a woman. I just don't behave in a proper, feminine manner. I'm even wearing britches and a shirt. I should have put on something nice for you while you were unsaddling my horse."

Joe swallowed his last bite, then said, "Emma, you are more woman than any other female I've ever met, and I think it's great that you don't behave in that proper, feminine manner. You just keep being you and I'll be the happiest man on the planet. As far as your choice of clothing goes, I couldn't imagine you looking more feminine than you do. The britches accent your wonderfully shaped backside and having all those buttons down the front of the shirt are giving me all sorts of ideas. You are everything to me, Emma, and that includes that wonderful package that holds your compassionate soul."

Emma almost melted inside as she sat watching Joe. Hearing such heartfelt words of love and praise were so alien to her, but so wonderful, too.

"Do we bother cleaning up now, Joe, or will you finally make love to me?"

Joe rose slowly, saying, "Cleanup can wait."

Emma also stood and they each took a step forward.

Joe took her hands in his and said softly, "I want to make love to you as you want me to make love to you, Emma. Show me how to please you. Tell me what you need me to do. I want to make you happy, my love."

Emma was almost shaking when she replied, "Come with me, my true love."

She turned, and they walked down the hallway. Emma began to turn into the first bedroom, but Joe pulled her further down the hall.

"The third door, Emma. You'll understand in a few seconds," he said softly.

Emma understood immediately when she saw the oversized bed and turned to Joe.

"Why is it so big, Joe?"

Joe pulled her close and when they were pressed together, he replied, "Roger and Bertha never had any children, and it appears they kept adding bedrooms to the house in the hope that they would have a houseful of them, but never did. When I first met them, they said they were still trying to have that first baby, and I thought they were kidding. They were in their upper fifties when they said that, and

I don't believe now that they were joking at all about at least doing all they could to have them."

Emma then whispered, "Then, let's continue the tradition, Joe."

Emma followed her words, by taking his hand and pressing it to her breast. Joe took it from there as they began to kiss and touch each other.

Emma did as Joe asked and began telling him what she wanted and how to make her feel more pleasure, but she also asked him to tell her what he would like, and he told her. Neither slowed down or balked at a request or instruction.

Joe found that he had been right about the anticipation of undoing all of those buttons on Emma's shirt and Emma had just as much enjoyment in unbuttoning Joe's.

Then, as they removed the final vestiges of apparel, things exploded in a frenzy of kissing, touching, grabbing, all accented and improved by words and sounds as they each discovered the complete joy of unfettered love and lust.

Joe was an outstanding student and Emma would have given him straight 'A's if she had been able to remember the letters of the alphabet. Both were totally lost in each other for almost a half an hour, which Joe thought was normal, and Emma knew how far from normal it was.

Finally, after the screaming and demanding echoed through the house in almost a violent crescendo, Sheriff Joe, no middle name, Brooks found that level of absolute passion that he had never come close to experiencing before as Emma felt her eyes roll back into her head while she clutched at Joe and reached her own nirvana.

As they lay on the large bed, bathed in layers of perspiration, and breathing heavily, Emma slid up to Joe, kissed him softly then rested her head on his chest.

"My God, Joe! Are you sure you've never done this before? I've never felt anything close to that in my life. Not even close!"

Joe chest was still rising and falling rapidly as he replied, "Trust me, Emma, if I'd done it before, I'd never stop. I didn't know it was supposed to be like this. I'm sorry I couldn't wait any longer. I'll do better next time. It's just that I had to have you. It was selfish."

Emma laughed and said, "Joe, we took over thirty minutes for our first time. I've never spent more than ten minutes before."

"Really? That's kind of sad, Emma. You deserve much more. I'll never stop trying to make you happy."

"Well, you're certainly succeeding from the start, Mr. Brooks."

"Do you think Annie and Mary are worried about you, Emma?" Joe asked.

"No, I don't think so. Billy will keep them calm. Did you know he wants to talk to you about that kiss he had with Cora? He started to talk to me when I asked but begged me not to talk anymore about it and said he needed to talk to you."

Joe patted her on her wet behind and said, "Well, at least now I know a lot more thanks to his lusty mama."

"I've never been called that before. Lusty sounds good to me when you say it."

"You are that and then some, Emma."

Then Joe asked, "Emma, how are the girls doing on the possible pregnancy problem?"

Emma sighed and said, "We already are sure three of the girls are okay because of the timing of their monthlies. My Mary never had a concern in the first place, and we're sure about Clara Riley and Rachel Foster. We'll know about Annie in the next few days, then Cora Riley and the last one will be Katie Foster."

Then she added, “Annie has another reason to worry, too. She and Ben Hobson are getting close, and she’s afraid that if she becomes pregnant, it will drive Ben away.”

“I can talk to Ben if you’d like, Emma, but I think we should wait until we know.”

“Then there’s the chance that if any of the other three miss their monthlies, it’s because of the stress of what happened to them. Emotional problems can cause that, so if one of them misses her monthly, it will be another four weeks before we’d be sure.”

“I hope that the last three don’t have to worry about that much longer, but we’ll do all we can to help.”

“You’ve already done more than you can imagine when you gave that talk at the campfire. Then, with all the money you gave to the widows, you allowed each of us a lot more freedom to choose what to do.”

“Money is easy, Emma, it’s what you did to give them back their dignity and belief that they could go on with their lives that made the difference. I was worried about making love to you, you know, and not just because I hadn’t done it before. I was worried that it might rekindle memories of what those men did to you and the others.”

“At first, I thought I could just ignore what he was doing to me, but I couldn’t. Then, I thought I could just hate him and let my anger push the memories back, but that didn’t work. But what did work for me was when I began to fantasize about you. I imagined being with you just as we just did, only the fantasy wasn’t even close to the reality. But it was your love, and my love for you, that washed those memories away. They’re still there somewhere, but if they come back, whether it’s in a nightmare or just a random memory, I’ll just ask you to hold me or make love to me again. They’ll be gone eventually, but I’ll need your love to make that happen.”

“I’ll be there for you, Emma.”

Emma let contentment flood her as she closed her eyes and listened to Joe's heartbeat.

———

"Mama's fine, Annie!" Billy said loudly.

"But we're worried," replied Annie.

Billy threw up his hands in frustration and said, "I'll tell you what. If Mama and Joe don't return by tomorrow night, I'll ride to the Larsen ranch the next morning and tell them you're worried. Okay?"

"But then, you'll be gone, and we'll be all alone," Mary complained.

"You could stay at the Rileys while I'm gone."

Alice finally said, "No, I'm sorry, Billy. It's just that we've never had a night without mama being here, and what if she's all alone?"

Billy smiled and replied, "I think that our mother is far from being alone, Annie. I think she's with Joe and they're both very happy. You should be happy for her."

"We are, Billy, but we miss her, too," Mary replied.

"We've all got to grow up soon, Mary. I know Annie has her cap set for Ben Hobson."

Annie flared pink, then replied, "I heard that you and Cora Riley were sparking on the couch when mama walked in."

Billy smiled and calmly said, "We were, and I admit that I enjoyed it, too. So, did Cora."

Then the whole concern thing was forgotten as both sisters sought more information about the whole kissing process.

CHAPTER 10

Joe and Emma agreed that they needed to ride back to her ranch the next morning because they knew that the girls would be worried about having their mother riding off through wild country on her own.

So, after they had spent almost an hour extra in bed, and then had breakfast, cleaned the house and saddled the horses, they departed the Larsen ranch at nine o'clock, reaching the cutoff and heading west just a few minutes later.

They were riding at a medium trot and managed to just exchange glances as they rode along, but it was enough. The only lingering question was where they would live after they were married.

After Joe had gone, the Lander Gazette published a full story of the entire episode as retrieved from court testimony and Joe's reports. They had to print triple the number of their normal run and the story had been picked up by the Cheyenne Daily Leader and then the Rocky Mountain News in Denver.

Sheriff Joe had become famous throughout the West and was completely unaware of any of it as he and Emma rode west.

All of the readers of the stories were impressed that one man had defeated a gang of sixteen outlaws and rescued nine women and girls. It was the stuff of legend, but not all of the readers were happy about the story.

Fast Jack Anderson was sitting in the barber shop in Cheyenne waiting to get his overly long black hair trimmed. The recent copy of the Cheyenne Daily Leader was crushed in his right hand. They'd hanged his brother and made this sheriff out to be second coming of Bill Hickock to boot. Nobody hangs an Anderson. He thought about forgetting the haircut, but knew the westbound train wasn't going to leave until four-thirty, and he'd have to get some supplies anyway. He'd take the train to Green River and then have to ride all the way up to Lander, a hundred plus miles north. Maybe another brother wouldn't care, but Hank was his younger brother and it was his job to look out for him.

Fast Jack knew his brother had been running with Hanger Bob because he had been part of that gang as well, but he and Bob had words and if it wasn't for the backing of those damned frog-eaters, he would have taken him. Hank had stayed with the gang, which had bothered Fast Jack at the time, but he'd gotten over it as he worked to carve his own reputation as a gunfighter for hire. Business had been good with the range wars that had erupted in southern Wyoming and northern Colorado, but this wasn't about business. This was personal.

After his haircut and shave, Fast Jack Anderson pushed his twin Colts down onto his hips, grabbed his hat and pulled it onto his newly-shorn head.

He left the barber shop, mounted his horse and headed to Magoon & Powelson Dry Goods to get his supplies for that long ride.

———

Joe and Emma took a break from the ride, and after hitching the horses, spread out a bedroll and passed a very enjoyable time in the open under the warm Wyoming sun.

"You are doing a magnificent job in your studies, Sheriff Joe," Emma said, punctuated with a long sigh.

"That, ma'am, is because I have the most incredible schoolmarm ever created," Joe replied as he smiled at Emma.

"I suppose we have to get on the horses again," said Emma.

"I imagine, but that doesn't mean I can't watch you get dressed."

Emma kissed him quickly but rose slowly to give Joe the full view. Joe then stood and let Emma's eyes wander as they both dressed again and spent a few minutes kissing before recognizing their adult responsibilities and mounting their horses again. Emma didn't comment on all of the scars since the first time, including the very recent knife cut.

"How much longer, Joe?" Emma asked as she set her horse to a medium trot.

"About two more hours. We should get there before four o'clock."

Emma smiled and just reveled in the utter contentment and happiness that filled her as she rode beside Joe. It was worth the almost twenty years of waiting.

———

"I told you!" Billy shouted when he saw Joe and his mother riding in from the east.

The three young Harpers had been sitting on the back porch for two hours, waiting impatiently for their mother's return. Billy wanted to talk to Joe, too. He had managed a few brief minutes of time with Cora and the kissing had gotten quite intense.

They all stood and waved with both hands high over their heads as Emma and Joe rode down from the pastures.

Their waves were returned, and Annie said, "Maybe we should have made some food. They're probably hungry after their long ride."

"Mama won't mind cooking if Joe stays," Billy said.

Mary was going to make a Cora comment when Annie bounced down from the porch and Billy followed. Mary joined them as the two riders drew close to the back yard.

Annie didn't waste any time when they were within speaking range, and loudly asked, "Are you and Joe getting married, Mama?"

Emma glanced over at Joe, who was already grinning, then grinned herself and looked at her children and said, “If you must know, Sheriff Joe asked me to marry him and I accepted. Does that answer your question, Annie?”

Annie then asked, “He asked you? I thought you were going to ask him?”

Emma and Joe were climbing down when she replied, “I thought so, too, but he stopped me before I could ask him, so he could ask me. It worked out much better.”

Then, Billy stepped up to Joe and shook his hand, asking, “Do I call you papa now? Or do I keep calling you Joe?”

Joe replied, “If you call me papa, I’ll tan your hide. Joe is my name and it’s what you’ve been calling me for a while now.”

Billy grinned and said, “Whatever you say, Papa!”

Joe laughed and smacked Billy on the shoulder before turning to the girls.

“Annie and Mary, you can call me Joe, too, and I’ll always be here for both of you. If there’s anything you ever need, don’t be afraid to ask. Okay?”

They both smiled and said, “Okay, Joe,” in harmony.

“Billy, let’s take care of the horses while your mother and sisters go and talk. I’m sure they have a lot of questions,” then he turned to the girls again and asked, “Or am I mistaken?”

They both continued to smile, and Annie replied, “No, sir. We do have a lot of questions for her.”

“Okay, we’ll take care of the horses, and I’ll answer all of Billy’s questions, including the ones that don’t involve me or your mother.”

Billy wondered how Joe knew he had more Cora questions, and so did his sisters as Emma smiled at Joe, gathered her daughters and walked to the house.

Joe and Billy walked the two horses into the barn and began to remove their tack.

"So, Billy, start asking away," Joe said.

"Are you going to still be the sheriff, Joe?"

"I think so, Billy, but we all have to work out where we will live. Do you want to live in town? I think I can come up with an even better suggestion when we get inside."

"We'll go wherever you want to go, Joe."

Joe smiled and asked, "So, what is your Cora question?"

"Did my mother tell you that I kissed her?"

"Yes, she did."

"Well, we did some more kissing yesterday, and I really like it and everything, but I think Cora is mad at me now."

"Why is she mad at you, Billy?"

"Because all she wants to do is kiss me now, and when I said we should just talk like we used to, she said I hurt her feelings and went home."

Joe thought that Emma would probably know the answer better than he would, but still took a stab at it.

"When you see Cora again, tell her that you wanted to talk to her because she's so smart and besides, you love to hear the sound of her sweet voice."

Billy nodded and then said, “Thanks, Joe. I knew you could figure it out.”

“Glad I could help, Billy. Just remember that I’m just learning a lot of this from the best teacher I’ve ever had.”

Billy grinned, then said, “My mother is your teacher now?”

A sheepish smile flickered on his lips as he replied, “Teacher and a whole lot more, Billy. Anything else you’d like to know?”

“No, sir. I figure we’ll have a lot more time now.”

“That we will, Billy.”

———

Emma had answered a lot more questions from her girls, and as they cooked, Emma noticed that some of the questions from Annie were about the possibility of her mother having a baby again after she and Joe were married. Emma knew that wasn’t possible, but also understood what brought on her question. Annie’s monthly was due today and obviously it hadn’t arrived yet. Emma needed to spend some private time with her older daughter.

When Billy and Joe entered the kitchen, even Annie’s thoughts shifted to the other primary question: where would they live after they became husband and wife?

They had all taken a seat at the kitchen table, when Joe made his suggestion.

“If it’s all right with everyone, I’d like to continue to be the sheriff. A very smart woman that I know helped me make that decision. That means I’ll have to live in Lander. I’ve thinking about this problem for a couple of days now, and when I was out at the Larsen ranch with Billy and with that very smart woman that I mentioned, I thought how wonderful it would be to have our own land, but not for raising cattle. I’d like us to have a home that gives us some privacy, yet still allows me to go to work.”

He had everyone's attention as he continued.

"Just southeast of Lander, about a mile and a half, there's an abandoned ranch. It used to be owned by the Granderson family who tried to raise cattle on the place. It's a full section but they had a hard time of it because there wasn't enough grass to even support a small herd, which is why it's still available. There's a house and a barn on the place, and they're not in great shape, but the land is something else. Just like the Larsen ranch, it has lots of water, in fact, it has three large creeks and a pond, but the same rocks that make it a terrible ranch, makes beautiful scenery. It's got lots of pines around the borders to act as windbreaks, too. What I'd like to do is buy the place, contract with Carlisle Construction to repair the house and barn and then to build a second house nearby. It would only be ten minutes from Lander and we'd still have our privacy. What do you think?"

Emma asked, "What do we do with this ranch, Joe?"

"That's up to you, Emma, but you could sell the cattle and then take your time to decide. We have three young people here that may need their own place in a few short years, so they may want to move in and turn it back into a working ranch. We'd buy some cattle to get it started if that becomes necessary. We'd have to keep up the house and barn, but that's not difficult."

Mary asked, "Why would we need two houses, Joe?"

Emma laughed and replied, "One for us and one for the rest of you, and don't you dare ask why!"

There were knowing grins among the young Harpers as they began to eat.

Joe looked over at Emma and winked.

After supper, the discussions continued in the main room and the idea of living close to town and not have to take care of the herd appealed to everyone.

Around seven o'clock, Emma caught Joe's eyes and indicated that she needed to talk to Annie alone, and Joe nodded.

Joe then said, "Billy, let's go outside for a few minutes. I want to show you something."

"Okay, Joe," Billy replied as he stood.

Then Joe turned to Mary and said, "Mary, why don't you come along. You might like this, too."

"Okay."

Joe, Billy and Mary walked down the hallway and left the house through the back door as Emma walked over to where Annie sat on the couch and took a seat next to her.

"Annie, you're afraid that you might be pregnant. Aren't you?"

"Yes, Mama. My monthly was supposed to be here by now and it hasn't."

Emma put her arm around Annie, and her daughter laid her head on her mother's shoulder.

"That is only one possibility, Annie. The other is that all of the horrible things that happened to us have caused you to miss your monthly. We won't be certain until you miss a second one, but if you are with child, don't let it ruin your life. Remember what Joe said at the campfire? The baby will be yours to love."

"I know, Mama. But it sounded so easy when it was only just a possibility, but now that it might really be happening, it's a lot harder. I'm only sixteen, Mama."

"I know, sweetheart. I was sixteen when I became pregnant with you, although, I'll admit it was under far different circumstances, but here I am holding my baby and I never regretted for a moment loving you."

"But you loved papa, and I hated the man that did this to me."

Emma sighed and said, "No, Annie. I didn't love your father like a wife is supposed to love her husband. We lived in the same house and shared the same bed, but there was always an invisible barrier between us. You and the other children never noticed because it was all you ever saw. I became pregnant with you because I was curious about making love and didn't think of the consequences. It was much more my fault than your father's, and he wasn't too pleased to have to marry me when he was only eighteen, but he never hurt me, and he did love you, Mary and Billy."

"Why didn't you tell us, Mama?"

"I told Billy a little while ago, and I told Joe because he had a right to know. If I had told you while your father was alive, it would have almost made you have to choose which parent to love, and that wouldn't be right, Annie."

"Are you going to tell Mary now?"

"I will when the time is right, but it has to be me that tells her. Okay?"

"Yes, Mama, but what if I am carrying a baby? How can any boy even look at me knowing I have a baby?"

"The common practice is to hide you away during your pregnancy and then pretend the baby was mine, but that's just silly. You'll have to nurse the baby anyway, but I'll care for the child and you can go on with your life. When you marry, and that will happen, Annie, because you are a pretty and capable young lady and you will still have your choice of suitors, including Ben Hobson, unless I'm wrong. When you marry, you can raise your baby as your own, or Joe and I will bring it up as ours. Either way, your child will grow up surrounded by love."

"Unlike the way Joe grew up. Isn't that right, Mama?"

"Yes, Annie. Unlike Joe's childhood."

Annie leaned over and kissed her mother, then said, “Thank you, Mama. I feel better now.”

“Good. Now, tell me about you and Ben Hobson.”

———

After Joe had walked outside with Billy and Mary, it was Mary who asked, “What are you going to show us, Joe?”

“Your mother needed to be alone with Annie, Mary. Annie’s worried and needed your mother’s advice.”

“That’s what I thought. Annie’s worried about having a baby, isn’t she?”

“I’m pretty sure that’s what it is.”

Then Mary surprised both Joe and Billy when she said, “I think I should be a schoolmarm or something. I don’t ever want to get married.”

Billy glanced up at Joe who was knocked off stride by her comment but regained his composure quickly.

“It’ll be your decision, Mary, but I don’t think you should make it so soon after what happened. What happened to you and the other girls was despicable and I know it hurt you terribly. I was worried about your mother being so upset about what happened to her that she wouldn’t want me to even talk to her. But she told me the only way to push those horrible memories away was to be loved. She said that without that, they’d always be there and torture her for the rest of her life. You have a very wise mother, Mary.”

They continued to walk while Mary mulled over what Joe had just told her.

“Do you think I’ll ever be normal again, Joe?” she finally asked.

"You're already normal, Mary, just because you are able to talk about it. All I can recommend is let time and nature, as well as your family, help. And I include myself as part of your family now."

Mary smiled up at Joe and said, "I'm glad you're marrying our mother, Joe."

Joe looked at Mary, smiled and replied, "And I'm proud to be able to call you my daughter, Mary."

Billy just smiled.

———

Fast Jack Anderson sat on the westbound Union Pacific's middle passenger car as the train hurtled toward Green River. He wouldn't arrive until early the next morning, then he'd have that three-day ride to Lander and his meeting with that sheriff.

———

Joe had told Emma about the conversation with Mary and she explained her talk with Annie to Joe when they had an all-too-short amount of private time.

He had convinced a reluctant Emma that it would be better if he slept in the barn, even though all of the teenagers probably knew what had happened at the Larsen ranch. Joe's real reason was that he thought it would be creepy sleeping with Emma in the same bed she had shared with Wilbur just two weeks earlier.

So, after a chaste kiss, Joe headed out to the barn for the night.

After he had set up his sleeping bag in the loft and stretched out, he was arguing with himself about saying the hell with it and going back to Emma when his debate became pointless. He heard creaking from the ladder and in the moonlight from the open loft doors, spotted Emma's head pop out from the opening at the back of the loft.

"I was just about to come and visit you," Joe said as he sat up.

"Well, I couldn't count on you doing that, so here I am. I am not going to sleep alone again, Sheriff Joe Brooks," she said as she stalked across the floor in her nightdress, then, when she reached the bedroll, just knelt momentarily before throwing her arms around him and kissing him.

Joe pulled her down on top of him and they resumed his lessons.

It was no secret among the young people still in the house where their mother had gone. Each of them had heard her footsteps as she padded across the creaking floor to leave the house, and each had to keep from giggling as they thought their mother didn't know that they were all still awake. She did know but wasn't about to let that stop her.

Joe and Emma spent a good night in the hay loft, and somehow managed to both squeeze into Joe's bedroll, making for a cozy night's sleep when they finally drifted off more from physical exhaustion than anything else. They weren't teenagers anymore, despite their behavior.

But they did manage to return to the house before the real teenagers awakened, and Joe watched Emma as she swayed into her bedroom to change while he started the cookstove.

Joe still couldn't fully believe he could ever be so lucky to be marrying a woman like Emma. She was simply amazing. He made the mental comparison between Emma and Mary Sheehy, who was actually a couple of years younger than Emma, and it wasn't even close. Mary had been quite pretty when he first met her, with her red hair and bright blue eyes. She was coy and flirty and had driven Joe to distraction. But he'd never had a chance to really talk to her until almost a year after she married the butcher and was heavy with their first child. Her personality had changed, and she seemed almost resigned and drab compared to how she had been before. By the time she had borne her third child, she had begun to put on weight, which he could understand being married to a butcher, but she had seemed as if she was just going through the motions of marriage and he found himself feeling sorry for her.

Yet, when he contrasted Emma, who had brought three children into the world herself and had still retained both her assertive manner and her figure, the differences between the two women was a wide gulf. But it was more than just their personalities and physical differences that made Emma so special. She had joked about her mannish behavior, but maybe that was it. Not mannish meaning she was masculine in any way, but that she was confident and unafraid to say what she thought and did as she thought was necessary despite what other women, or men, for that matter, would think of her.

Emma was an independent, strong-minded woman who challenged him as no other woman had. It was why he could talk to her even before he had decided that he couldn't live without her. He knew for certain that he never would have broken down that dam for any other woman. Just his Emma.

Emma woke up her charges as she stepped down the hallway to the kitchen, wearing a big smile. Today was going to be her wedding day and she was marrying the one man she wanted to have in her life. As she kissed Joe again before starting breakfast, they both knew that this was meant to be.

By nine o'clock, five riders departed the Harper ranch headed for Lander. They had all nixed the wagon for the trip, preferring the speedier mode of transport. It was a glorious morning and the weather reflected the bright mood of the riders.

When they arrived in Lander just before ten-thirty, their first stop was at the sheriff's office.

After they all tied off their animals, Joe and Emma walked hand-in-hand into the office with Billy, Annie and Mary trailing.

Charlie and Ed had been talking about the possibility of Joe not returning, when they turned to see a grinning sheriff and the Harpers pass through the door.

"Joe! You're back!" shouted Charlie as he quickly stood from behind the desk.

"I'm back and I have all sorts of news for you," Joe began while wearing a big grin.

"First, I'll need you both to come next door with me to act as witnesses while Emma and I are married. Then, we have things to do for the rest of the day. Oh, and I'm going to stay on as sheriff, if for no other reason than to keep you both in line."

"You're gettin' married?" asked Ed with a look of complete disbelief.

"Yes, we are getting married as soon as you both manage to get hold of yourselves. I need two adults to act as our witnesses and you meet that requirement, although I'm not sure about you sometimes, Ed."

Ed laughed and then the two deputies stepped around the desk, shook Joe's hand and congratulated Emma before grabbing their hats.

"Let's go and see Judge Moore, then," Joe said as he looked at Emma, whose blue eyes were dancing to match the polka that was going on inside.

The crowd vacated the sheriff's office and quickly walked to the adjacent county courthouse.

After doing the paperwork, Judge Moore himself walked out to the outer office, and after expressing a similar statement of disbelief that the sheriff was about to be wed, congratulated the couple and ushered them into his chambers.

The ceremony was brief, and Joe had to promise to buy Emma a ring, something she had never worn before, but soon the judge pronounced them man and wife, Joe kissed his bride and Emma became Mrs. Brooks.

They then returned to the outer office, and after signing the paperwork completing the legal part of the marriage, Charlie and Ed each kissed the bride before returning to the office.

As they left the judge's offices, Joe said, "Let's stop at the land office and see about that property."

Emma was latched onto Joe's left arm as she replied, "We can do that, husband."

The three teenaged Harpers all were smiling at their mother behaving like a teenaged girl herself as they crossed the hall and entered the land office.

"Art!" Joe exclaimed as they entered the office.

Art Crowder was filing papers in back and stood to look over the filing cabinet, saw the sheriff and shouted back, "Just a second, Joe!"

After shoving the last sheet of paper into its proper location, Art walked around to the counter and asked, "What can I do for you, Joe?"

"The Granderson place southeast of town. What do I have to do to buy it?"

"You want to buy that ranch? It's not a very good ranch, Joe, but if you want it, all you'd have to do is pay the back taxes on it. It's been abandoned for six years now, but for a good reason."

"I know. I just need to have a place close to town."

Art smiled and said, "So, you're not leaving after all."

"Nope. So, how much are the back taxes?"

"Hold on. Let me pull the records," Art replied as he turned to go back to the same filing cabinet that he had just left.

He removed a folder, brought it to the counter, flipped it open and began thumbing through the pages and pulling one out.

"The taxes on that place were only $11.50 a year, but then there were penalties and such, so it comes to $97.75. I still don't know why you'd want it, Joe. I have a few other abandoned ranches that are better than that one."

"It'll suit us, Art. Emma and I are going to get it fixed up and even add a second house."

"*You got married, Joe?*" asked Art, adding himself to the list of disbelieving questioners.

Joe just grinned and said, "Emma was too special for me to let go, Art."

Art smiled at Emma and said, "Congratulations, ma'am."

Emma said, "Thank you," as Joe began counting out the money to pay the taxes.

Art gave him a receipt and then spent another ten minutes changing the deed of the Granderson ranch to the Brooks property.

After shaking hands, the new family left the land office and then the county courthouse.

"Now, we'll need to make a stop at the bank and then we'll all go to Moody's Restaurant for lunch."

Emma's pouch of money was in her saddlebags, so they decided to ride to the bank, even though it was only a hundred yards away.

After arriving, they stepped down, Emma took the pouch from the saddlebags and with their arms linked she and Joe entered the small building with the young people trailing behind.

Joe guided Emma to the clerk, and said, “John, Emma and I just were married, and I need to have her added to my account and make a deposit.”

John Evans, like everyone else, wanted to shout, ‘*You got married?*’, but he was a banker, after all, and had to maintain his dignity, unlike the county judge.

“Congratulation to you both. Please have a seat, Joe and Mrs. Brooks, and we’ll get that paperwork done shortly.”

John left his desk and walked to the cashier’s window, took out a ledger and some forms, then returned to his desk. Emma had her pouch of cash on her lap.

John wrote on the forms then slid it across the desktop to Emma.

“Mrs. Brooks, if you could just sign here, please,” he said, indicating the line for her signature.

When she had signed, almost signing as Emma L. Harper, she pushed it back to the clerk.

Then he asked, “And how much do you wish to deposit today, Joe?”

Joe looked at Emma, who smiled, set the pouch on the desk and pulled the large stack of bills from the leather pocket and set it in front of John.

He retained his almost distracted demeanor as he began counting the cash and then said, “Is two thousand three hundred dollars the same amount that you expected, Mrs. Brooks?”

“Yes, that’s right.”

John then wrote out a receipt and handed it to Joe. On the receipt was the new balance of $16,765.40. For a financial institution the size of the Lander National Bank, it was an enormous amount.

Joe gave the receipt to Emma whose eyebrows lifted significantly as she saw the balance.

"I'll need some blank drafts, John."

"I've already brought some with me, Joe," the clerk replied as he slid six of the drafts across the table, adding, "I thought you'd be needing some."

"Thanks, John. Now we've got to do some more errands."

They shook hands, John congratulated Emma again and they left the bank.

As they crossed out onto the boardwalk and turned toward the restaurant, Emma asked, "How on earth did you ever get so much money, Joe? I thought I'd be more than doubling the size of your account."

"Frugal living, Emma. They're paying me a hundred and ten dollars a month now and even when they were paying me seventy dollars a month plus room and board, I never spent much. Then, there was the reward money added onto that. And now that I'm married, and they're not paying me room and board anymore, my salary is going to go up another twenty-five dollars a month."

"Joe, why is it so much? Ranch hands only make thirty dollars a month and I don't think the clerk in the bank makes forty."

"When I first took the job, nobody else wanted it. At least nobody that was honest. They had upped the salary from fifty to seventy dollars to lure in a peace officer from another jurisdiction, which is why I came here. Then, over the years, as I showed that I could do the job, they'd increase my salary every once in a while. When I hired Charlie Wheatley four years ago, I convinced them to give him eighty dollars a month because of the size of the county. Ed is paid the same amount, too. We earn it most months, but I'll be honest when I tell you that I really earned every penny this month."

Emma squeezed his arm and said, “I’ll say that you’ve earned your year’s pay this month.”

Joe smiled at her as they reached the restaurant and walked inside.

———

Fast Jack Anderson had unloaded his horse in Green River and walked him to Hooper’s Dry Goods to get his supplies, including two more boxes of .44 cartridges for his Colts and his Winchester. He didn’t use the carbine much, preferring his twin pistols for most of his work.

He valued his reputation highly, as it was the driver for the amount he could demand from his employers. With all the stories being published about this Sheriff Joe Brooks, killing the lawman would only enhance that reputation and drive up his pay, but only if he was identified as the one who killed him. That meant he had to do it legally in front of witnesses.

He was proud of his skills with his revolvers, being able to use both hands with speed and accuracy. He didn’t doubt that he could beat this sheriff. The stories all agreed that he’d shot the gang with his rifle and not his pistols. Fast Jack wasn’t even sure he carried a pistol, although the drawing in the Cheyenne paper showed him with a six-gun at his waist. It didn’t matter. Fast Jack was confident in his own skill and knew he didn’t have an equal in Wyoming Territory.

As he rode out of Green River, he was looking forward to his arrival in Lander.

———

“Can we go and see the new ranch now, Joe?” asked Billy as they left the restaurant.

“I think that would be a good idea now that it’s ours. I want to be able to tell Homer Carlisle where we want the second house built.”

“What about furniture, Joe?” asked Emma.

“We’ll see how bad the furniture is in the old ranch house, and then after we get the plans all set up for the new house, we’ll stop over at Johnson’s and have Henry place a big order. It’ll take a while to get here, though. It’ll have to be freighted in from Green River, and they might not have it there, either. So, it could have to come from Laramie or Cheyenne, maybe even Denver or Omaha.”

———

Just thirty minutes later, they turned down a barely-recognizable access road towards a rundown ranch house and an equally dilapidated barn.

No one commented as the five riders reached the house and stepped down. Up close, it wasn’t nearly as bad as it looked from the road, which was opposite of what was usually true.

“Watch out for weak boards,” Joe said unnecessarily as they stepped carefully onto the porch, but as it turned out, the porch was made of thick, whitewashed pine boards that withstood their weight without protest.

They entered the house and were surprised again that the furniture that they didn’t even expect to find, although dusty, would be serviceable with some cleaning and oil.

The fireplace was in good shape and as they inspected the rest of the house, they met with more surprises when they found a clawed bathtub and pump in the bathroom, and a rusty, but complete cookstove.

“This isn’t too bad at all, Joe,” Emma said when they finished their tour, “we can make this house livable again.”

“I’m just surprised that all of the furniture is still here. I know this place has been abandoned for six years, but usually these places are emptied by scavengers after a few months.”

"I don't know why they didn't, but it's a good thing that they didn't. Now, let's go look at the barn and then we'll decide where to build the second house," Emma said as she hooked her arm around her husband's waist.

Joe put his hand around Emma's waist as they left the house and headed for the barn. When they arrived, they could see that it needed work, and the corral needed fixing, but was mostly intact.

"What's that, Joe? A bunkhouse?" Billy asked as he pointed to a small building.

"I think it's a smokehouse, Billy."

They mounted their horses and toured the property, and everyone agreed with Joe that it was a very scenic property, despite its inability to support livestock. The streams and the pond added to the overall visual impact of the land.

"Now, where do we build the new house?" Joe asked.

Emma pointed and replied, "Over there. On that flat area near the pond," and no one argued that it was an ideal location.

They returned to Lander and met with Homer Carlisle and explained what they wanted. Joe let Emma handle the design and just sat back and grinned at Billy and the girls while Emma explained her requirements. Joe was impressed that she even remembered to add a gun room and an office. Once the design was finalized, Joe left a large draft to pay for refurbishing the old house, barn and corral, and building the new house. At the last second, he had them expand the barn significantly and add a wooden floor. When it was all done, it subtracted over twenty-five-hundred dollars from their bank account, but like Joe told Emma, that's what the reason was for having the money in the first place.

Their last stop of the day was to go through catalogs with Henry Johnson, who was very pleased with the sizeable order and after leaving another not-quite-so-large draft with Henry, the family left the dry goods store and walked down the boardwalk to the sheriff's office.

Joe just stuck his head inside and asked, “Is anything going on, boys?”

Ed grinned and said, “Only that we’re tellin’ everybody that you’re stayin’ and you and Emma just got hitched. Cole Lipscomb at the Herald is gonna write up a big story about it. He figures on sellin’ twice as many papers as usual.”

“Well, if you need anything, we’ll be out at the Harper ranch. I’ll be in tomorrow morning.”

Charlie had a grin on his face as well as he said, “Well, don’t come to work too tired, boss.”

Joe just grinned back, waved, and closed the door. He turned back to his new family, who all were holding back laughter at hearing the comments.

“Okay, let it go,” Joe said as they began to laugh, including Emma.

She grabbed his arm and said, “I wonder what Sarah and Jennie will think when they get the news.”

They began walking back to their horses and Joe replied, “They’ll probably be thanking their lucky stars that I asked you to marry me and not them.”

“Oh, really? I’ll have you know, Sheriff Joe, that I had to stake my claim on you before they tried anything, and I’m glad that I did.”

Joe gave her a light squeeze as they reached and then mounted their horses. It was just four-fifteen when they rode out of Lander to return to the ranch.

Fast Jack Anderson was riding a little faster than he had planned but was a bit sleepy after the train ride. Still, he had managed to put more than sixty miles behind him. The road to Lander from Green River was better than he expected but shouldn’t have been surprised because of all the freight traffic and the daily stagecoach runs between the two towns, one in each direction. He'd passed the southbound stage earlier and wondered if the northbound stage would thunder by him soon.

He'd learned that there was a stage station in another five or six miles ahead and planned on staying there overnight. That would leave him about the same distance tomorrow, getting him into Lander late in the afternoon.

He was still trying to come up with some way of getting the sheriff to challenge him to a showdown. It rarely happened that way, even in places like Dodge City or Deadwood. Most shootouts were just quick, angry, and often drunken, brawls with handguns added to the mix. But there had been a few of the face-to-face meetings and Fast Jack knew that they had been widely covered by the newspapers, even back in the East. That would be the added bonus to killing the sheriff. Everyone would know and fear the name of Fast Jack Anderson, and he'd charge a big fee to anyone who wanted to hire his guns.

After another half an hour, he spotted the way station and pulled up to the corral on the side. He walked inside the building and had to wait for the station manager to acknowledge his existence before saying he needed a place to sleep for the night. As he wasn't a paying coach passenger, he was told he'd have to wait until all of the passengers were accommodated. The driver and shotgun rider had their own room.

"Mind if I get my horse watered and fed?"

"Not at all. The stage should be comin' in about an hour from now. Usually they only have two or three passengers, and we have four rooms, so you should be okay."

"I appreciate it," Fast Jack said as he tipped his dark gray hat to the manager and left the building to take care of his horse.

Fast Jack was never rude to folks as it served no purpose.

He walked out to his tall black gelding. The horse was his prized possession, even more than his Colts, which were a close second.

"Let's go get you some water and some feed, Jake," he said to the horse as he took his reins and then led him to the trough.

When the stage pulled in forty minutes later, Fast Jack counted just two passengers, and they were a couple, so he re-entered the office and paid for a room after the couple had gone to their room to freshen up.

"We're servin' supper in a couple of hours," the manager said.

"Sounds good," Fast Jack said as he picked up his Winchester and headed back to the room.

Emma, Annie and Mary were cooking supper as Joe and Billy walked outside toward Wilbur's grave.

Joe had planned on making the visit on his own, but when he and Billy had finished taking care of the five horses, Joe had said he'd be paying a visit to the grave and Billy asked if he could come along.

When they reached the grave, Joe and Billy removed their hats, and Joe said, "Wilbur, we killed all those bastards who hurt Emma, Annie and Mary, and murdered all the menfolk at the Riley and Foster ranches, but I'm sure you know that. I'm sure that none of them are up there with you, either, but I wanted to let you know that I married Emma today and I know I'll do all I can to make her happy. I'll take care of Billy here and make sure he turns out to be as good a man as I think he's already become. You did that, Wilbur. You showed him the way and I'll continue that. I'll take care of Annie and Mary, too, and when they decide to marry, I'll do all I can to ensure that they're happy. I think Billy wants to talk to you, too."

Billy looked up at Joe, then back to the grave, then said, "Papa, mama told me that you didn't love her, and she understood that, but told me that she was pleased that you loved me, Annie and Mary anyway. So, thank you for that and helpin' me with growin' up. I know Joe isn't my father and he doesn't pretend to be takin' your place, and that's the way it should be. But Joe's a good man and he's right for mama and he'll make her happy, like he already has. We'll be movin' to a new house soon, but we're gonna keep the ranch here, too. Maybe I'll marry Cora in a few years and move back. I don't know, but we're not gonna sell the place because you're here."

Billy paused, then choked out, "Goodbye, Papa."

Joe put his hand on Billy's shoulder, and they turned, put their hats on and headed back for the house.

Supper was a much lighter time for everyone now that things seemed to be settling down. There was no more uncertainty about the future, other than Annie's possible pregnancy, and even that seemed less stressful to her than it had been just yesterday.

"How long before the construction work is done, Joe?" asked Emma as they ate.

"Homer said six to seven weeks. He'll have both of his crews working on the job. One will repair the house and barn, and the other will do the new construction."

"When will the furniture and things arrive?" asked Emma.

"They'll be here before that, but Henry Johnson will hold them in his warehouse until the house is ready. We'll probably have to add some things that we forgot anyway. Then we'll have to fill both pantries and cold rooms with food, too."

"You mean that I'm going to have to cook now?" Annie asked.

"Only if you want to. We'll probably all eat together in the new house, but in the winter, you might not want to make the trip and cook in your own place."

“Mary is a better cook than I am,” Annie said as Mary nodded.

Joe glanced at Emma who was smiling at the idea of having a house all to themselves.

———

After supper, Joe was showing Billy and the girls how to play poker, and they each had a pile of pennies and nickels in front of them. Emma was kibitzing.

Mary was winning, and Billy was aghast that he was losing to his sister.

Then, Mary asked, “Mama, are you and Joe going to sleep in the barn again?”

Emma looked at Joe, and both adults exploded in laughter as did Annie and Billy when they realized that Mary wasn’t about to get her butt paddled. Mary joined in, having been fully aware of the potential consequences by just asking the question.

When they finished laughing, Joe said, “Emma I do believe that Mary is a miniature version of another straightforward woman that I know.”

Emma looked over at Mary and replied, “I’ve known that for years, Joe, and despite my best efforts, I can’t drive it out of her.”

“Don’t even think about it, Emma. The world needs more women like you both. I think Annie is going to be one, too,” he replied as he turned and smiled at Annie.

Annie smiled back and was glad that Joe was married to her mother. The house was already a lot livelier than it had been before, and she almost wished she were younger, so she could enjoy it more.

———

That night, Joe and Emma shared the bed rather than the loft, and tried to subdue the volume of their lovemaking, but failed to a large degree. Emma kept telling Joe that he shouldn't concern himself with the teenage audience, but Joe was a still worried about it until Emma took total control of his mind and just about everything else.

CHAPTER 11

Fast Jack Anderson was on his big gelding before the stagecoach left that morning. The coach was due to arrive in Lander at three-thirty, so he figured if he left a couple of hours earlier, he'd arrive by one o'clock or so. He wasn't planning on meeting the sheriff today, though. He needed to do some groundwork first and make sure he got a good night's sleep, too. He'd seen idiots who'd stay up late and spend the night in a saloon or a bawdy house before a gunfight, and each of them had paid the ultimate price. Fast Jack was nobody's fool. He wasn't about to give anyone an advantage.

———

Joe and Emma walked out to the barn that morning, so Joe could saddle the pinto, who still hadn't been named yet.

As he tossed the saddle over the pinto's back, Emma was leaning on a stall support post.

"We've been married less than a day and you're leaving me already," Emma said as she looked out the barn doors.

Joe didn't look at Emma as he replied, "Yes, I'm leaving you. I found another woman and I intend to woo her and take her to Mexico. Then, I'll divorce her, leave her there and come back in time for supper. You'll never even know."

Emma laughed and said, "This marriage is a lot more fun than I deserve, Joe."

"And, Mrs. Brooks, I haven't told you the good news yet."

"You can't give me any more good news than you've already given me. It's not possible."

“Then I won’t tell you that after I tell the Underwoods that I’ll be leaving their boarding house, I’ll be stopping at Lee’s Laundry and getting a contract for laundry service. They have these large baskets and whenever we fill them with clothes, I’ll carry them with me to work, drop them off and then two days later, I’ll return them to you all clean and folded. Now if that’s not good news, then what is it?”

Emma stood from her stall post, walked up to Joe threw her arms around him and kissed him.

When she thought he got the message, she leaned back and said, “My Lord! That is the best gift I have ever received. The girls will be tickled pink, too. No more laundry! My hands and back thank you more than you can imagine, my glorious husband.”

Joe grinned, ran his hand across her backside and said, “I can’t have this being used for such drudgery, now, can I?”

“Don’t get me going again, you, lust-crazed man. What manner of creature have I created?”

Joe kissed her softly and replied, “The kind that will love you until his dying breath, Emma.”

Emma kissed him back just as gently and replied, “And that had better not happen for another fifty years, Sheriff Joe Brooks.”

“I promise, Emma. I’ll be careful.”

“Please, Joe. I need you.”

“Don’t worry, Emma. Things are quiet now.”

Emma smiled as she stepped back to let Joe finish saddling the pinto.

“Did you name the pinto yet?” she asked.

“Nope. I’ve been too busy lately.”

Emma smiled as Joe climbed into the saddle, then looked down at her and said, "I'll see you at suppertime, sweetheart."

Emma nodded as Joe walked the pinto out of the barn, down the access road, and set him to riding south to Lander.

Emma sighed and walked back to the house.

———

Later that morning, Emma was visited by a crowd of riders from the north who had heard the news. The entire Hobson, Foster and Riley clans arrived in waves before ten o'clock, requiring two coffeepots.

Cora and Billy went for a ride in the pastures while Ben Hobson and Annie just strolled down the access road talking.

———

"So, Joe, what's this I hear about you buyin' some land south of town?" Charlie asked as he sat with a cup of coffee in his hand.

"I bought the abandoned Granderson place and I'm having the old ranch house and barn fixed up and a new house built for me and Emma."

"I have to tell you, Joe, you have the whole town talkin' about how fast you and Emma decided to tie the knot. You disappointed a lot of ladies around this county."

"I doubt it, Charlie. I thought I'd have to wait for Emma to go through some time of mourning or something, but she didn't want to wait, and I'm glad she didn't. I'm really happy with Emma, Charlie. I thought I'd die an old bachelor, which is one of the reasons I was thinking about quitting."

"We figured as much. So, when you see Emma later, tell her we both appreciate it."

Ed said, “I don’t think I woulda stayed if you quit, Joe. I’m still learnin’.”

“Well, I’ll be here to show you what you need, Ed. Anything going on?”

“That new Indian agent is supposed to be arriving tomorrow. He’s askin’ for an escort to the agency store. I don’t know if he’s afraid of the Shoshone or all those outlaws that he’s been hearin’ about,” Charlie said as he handed the telegram announcing the pending arrival of the agent.

Joe read the telegram and looked over at Charlie, “Phil Larsen? Is he related to Roger Larsen, who owned that ranch just east of the reservation?”

“Beats me. You can ask him tomorrow. Do you want me to escort him up there, Joe?”

It was the first time Joe had to consider his own needs as he said, “I’d appreciate it, Charlie. Depending on how much baggage the guy has, it might take you two days.”

“I figured on two days from the start. It’ll be interesting to see how this one works out. I guess the army is delivering a large stock of supplies to the agency store in a few days, too,” Charlie said as he handed Joe a second telegram.

“I’ll tell you what, Charlie, let him stay in town until the army arrives with that wagon train of supplies, then they can escort him to the agency store. It’ll only cost him three days, and it doesn’t sound like he’s all that anxious to be out there on his lonesome.”

Then Charlie said, “Maybe he’s bringin’ his wife.”

“That would be a first. But if he’s related to Roger Larsen, maybe that’s why he took the job. He’d inherit the ranch and live there. It’s not a long ride to the agency store.”

Charlie shrugged as he took his seat behind the desk and Joe went back to his office to catch up on the paperwork while Ed walked outside to do rounds.

———

Fast Jack Anderson passed a sign that read: LANDER 10 MILES. He was making better time than he had expected. He'd even stopped twice and now he was a little over an hour away from Lander and he'd begin to find out what he needed to know.

———

"I got a pair of size twelves, Joe. You should have asked," Henry Johnson said as he walked to the back room and soon returned with a pair of boots and set them on the counter.

"Why were they in back, Henry?" Joe asked as he examined the boots.

"I don't have unlimited shelf space in here, Joe. You should always ask."

Joe had already found a Stetson hat that fit, although it wasn't his favorite color. It was a tan hat with a black band. He took the boots, took a seat on a barrel, and pulled off his old boots.

After setting them aside, he yanked the new ones on and walked around the store. They fit, but they sure were stiff.

"It'll take me a while to break these in, Henry. But I'll take these and the hat. I hope this new one doesn't get any bullet holes in it any time soon," he said as he walked stiffly up to the counter.

"Well, you might as well start breaking those new ones in. You dropping your old ones off at Brewster's to get resoled?"

"Yup. I'll do that on the way back. I don't think I can get that hat repaired, though. I'll still wear it when I'm working around the ranch, though. It's a good hat."

Henry took Joe's payment, gave him his change, and Joe left with his old boots in his left hand and his holey hat in his right.

He dropped the boots off with Pete Brewster who said he'd have them ready tomorrow.

Joe was in a good mood when he left the cobbler's shop, and as he walked on the boardwalk, he exaggerated his lean to accelerate the boots' breaking in period.

As he stepped along in his unusual gait, his old hat still in his hand, he spotted a rider coming into town that looked familiar, but he couldn't place the face exactly. The horse he was riding was one of the best he'd ever seen, and he noticed the man was wearing twin Colts.

Joe had never seen another man with a two-gun rig besides himself and pegged him as a gunfighter. It didn't take a genius to figure out that there was only one reason for his being in a town the size of Lander. He half-expected it after that damned story about how he'd killed all those outlaws hit the newspapers. It was the biggest concern he had about the article, and now it was happening.

He kept an eye on the man as he parked his horse in front of the hotel and stepped down. The hotel was next to the Underwood Boarding House, where he had to go anyway, so he just turned, crossed the street and stepped up onto the opposite boardwalk.

He turned into Underwood's Boarding House and spotted Mattie Underwood as she was dusting in the parlor. She heard him enter and broke into a broad smile.

"I hear that you'll be leaving us, newly married Sheriff Joe."

Despite the newly-arrived problem next door, Joe couldn't help but smile back. Mattie was just a happy person.

"That's true, Mattie. I'll be by to collect my things later, but I wanted to let you know."

"We'll miss you, Joe. You've been our guest here for a long time, but it's the best reason I can imagine for your departure. I'm very happy for you."

"Thank you, Mattie. I've got business next door, so I'll be back when I can to pick up my things."

"Take your time, Joe. We've got three vacancies."

"Thanks Mattie," Joe said as he turned and quickly left the boarding house.

He turned right on the boardwalk and then slowly entered the hotel. The gunfighter was signing the register log when Al Newton looked past his new guest and said, "Well, good afternoon, Joe. What do you need?"

"Oh, I just thought I'd come and talk to your new guest for a moment."

Fast Jack put down the pencil, and slowly turned to face who he knew for certain to be the sheriff.

Joe looked at the man and asked, "Do I know you? You look familiar, but I can't place the face."

Fast Jack drawled, "Probably because you hanged my brother Hank Anderson a little while ago."

Joe nodded, then said, "So, you must be Jack Anderson, his brother. I've heard about you. You go by the nickname of Fast Jack. Is that right?"

Jack leaned against the counter and replied, "I've been called that. I can't help what folks call me."

"Well, they call me Sheriff Joe, because the good folks of Fremont County have chosen me to protect them. It's my job and I try to keep the peace. If you're here to just honor your brother, his grave is in the town cemetery."

Jack tilted his head to the side slightly, and said, “I’ll do that in a little while. But I really came here to kill you, Sheriff.”

Joe didn’t blink but said, “I thought as much. I didn’t think you had a reputation as a back shooter, though.”

“I’m not a back shooter. Every one of the men that I shot had the holes in front. From what I read, a lot of yours had their holes in the back.”

Joe knew he was trying to rile him up, so he answered, “Some did, but every one of them had already fired a few rounds at me first. Maybe you still think that I should have waited for them to reach cover and let those four men use me for target practice, but I wasn’t in the mood. Your brother wasn’t shot in the back, or the front either, for that matter. He was tried, convicted and hanged for murder and rape. I don’t feel the slightest bit of remorse for bringing him in. Or do you believe I should have just let him go?”

“What he did doesn’t matter to me. You’re the one who had him killed and it’s going to cost you, Sheriff.”

“I’m not going to get into a gunfight with you, Jack, so you may as well ride out of here right now.”

“We’ll see, Sheriff. We’ll see,” Jack said as he turned, slapped two silver dollars on the counter and waited for the key to his room.

Al Newton glanced at Joe for permission, and Joe nodded. Al handed Fast Jack his key, and Jack grabbed his Winchester, turned and walked away.

Joe watched him disappear into the hallway and then said, to Al, “He won’t give you any trouble, Al. He’s here for a purpose.”

“Joe, he said he was going to kill you.”

Joe just nodded and said, “I know,” before he turned and left the hotel, still holding onto his old hat.

He crossed the street to his office, walked inside and found both deputies leaning on the desk, looking at him.

"Who was the gunny, Joe?" asked Ed.

"Fast Jack Anderson. Hank Anderson's brother. He seems to blame me for his brother's hanging and not his brother," he replied as he walked inside and pulled off his new hat and hung it on a peg.

"What can we do about it, Joe?" asked Charlie.

"Nothing. He's not wanted anywhere that I know of, and he hasn't broken any laws."

"Did he tell you he was going to kill you, Joe?" Ed asked almost breathlessly.

"He did, but there's nothing I can do about it. He's not a drygulcher, so he's kind of stuck. He needs to try and get me to face him in the street, but I'm not going to give him that opportunity. All we do is just go about our business as usual and ignore him. If he was a normal outlaw, it would be different, but this man is a professional killer. The only difference between him and those men in the gangs was that he's smarter, uses the language better, and hasn't been charged with murder. And he has patience, which is always a problem. He looks cleaner, too."

"So, we're just gonna let him walk the streets?" asked Ed.

Joe walked past Ed and Charlie toward his office, replied, "Yup," then walked inside wearing his new boots and carrying his old hat.

Fast Jack sat on his bed, his twin Colt rig hanging over the post as he thought about the recent meeting with the sheriff. He wasn't as easily rattled as he had expected, and that meant that this sheriff wasn't going to be an easy target. Men who had tempers were always anxious and sometimes they were clumsier because of it, or they'd take a snap shot instead of waiting that fraction of second to make sure that bullet went where it was supposed to go.

Jack needed to find out if the sheriff was any good with those pistols he wore and was trying to think of the best place to get that information. He'd have to find out soon, because he didn't doubt for a moment that the word would get out soon that he was in town to kill their sheriff.

Fast Jack Anderson then stood, pulled on his gunbelt, and left his room to get something to eat, and maybe smile at the waitress and get some information.

———

Joe trotted the pinto into the barn and stepped down. He didn't think anyone had seen him ride in, and he hadn't seen anyone out in the pastures or the yard, which was a bit odd.

He quickly unsaddled the gelding, brushed him down and left him in his stall before walking back to the house. Since returning to his office, and during the ride back to the ranch, Joe debated about telling Emma about Fast Jack Anderson. His only argument for not telling her was that she would worry just having the gunfighter in town, but before he reached the ranch, he had decided to tell her, but stress that he didn't believe anything would come of it.

When he crossed the back of the yard, he noticed the large number of horses in the corral with their tack on the corral fences. He recognized the horses and knew that most, if not all, of the women from the other ranches were visiting Emma, which would postpone any private talk for a while.

So, when he opened the kitchen door, he wasn't surprised to see the four widows, three of their daughters and Billy in the room talking. As he stepped inside, they all turned to him and smiles broke out on every female face, including the one he admired the most.

"Your husband is here, Emma!" shouted Sarah.

"I suppose we ought to let you two run off to the bedroom now," Jennie said, working it into her giggles.

The rest of the daughters and Ben Hobson emerged from the hallway as Joe stood red-faced in the doorway, most of them giggling after hearing Jennie's comment. Even Ben was laughing.

Joe looked at Ben and said, "You're a traitor, Ben Hobson," then noticed Billy snickering and just shook his head.

Then, the crowd approached Joe and began congratulating him. Emma was in the mix and soon reached Joe and kissed him in front of everyone, creating a new wave of giggles and laughter, but Joe didn't care anymore.

While Joe had Emma in his arms, he asked, "What are the chances that your husband can get something to eat?"

Emma smiled and asked in reply, "We have a houseful of women and you're asking me if we have any food ready?"

"What? None of you eat at all?"

Emma took Joe by the hand, led him through the feminine sea, parting as they reached the kitchen table. Joe took a seat and not thirty seconds later, a plate with a steak, a baked potato and biscuits was passed from hand to hand until Emma set it in front of him. Then, the coffee was passed along, and Emma set it down and took a seat next to him.

"I'm not eating in front of everyone, Mrs. Brooks. Have you eaten?"

Emma didn't reply as a second plate matching Joe's arrived by the human conveyor belt and thirty seconds after Emma's supper arrived, Joe and Emma were alone at the kitchen table.

Joe looked at his wife and smiled as he cut into his steak.

"That was pretty impressive, Emma."

"Everyone showed up this morning and we've been waiting for you to come home. They're all leaving now. Ben and Billy are saddling their horses for the younger girls, and Annie is just out talking to Ben."

Joe cut into his steak put a big chunk into his mouth and began chewing as Emma did as well. Joe watched her take a big bite of her steak and wanted to smile. There was nothing dainty about his bride.

After she swallowed, Emma innocently asked, "Did anything exciting happen today?"

Joe put down his knife and fork and replied, "This afternoon, a man rode into town that looked familiar. He was wearing a two-gun rig and had the look of a professional gunfighter; the first one I've ever seen. I followed him into the hotel and had a chat. He goes by Fast Jack Anderson, and he's Hank Anderson's brother."

Emma stopped the forkful of baked potato as she asked, "Why is he here, Joe?"

"He said he was going to kill me for having his brother hanged, but I'm not going to give him the chance."

"How? Are you going to arrest him?"

"No, I can't arrest him because he hasn't broken any laws and isn't wanted anywhere. I'm going to deny him a chance to draw those two Colts he wears by ignoring him."

"Ignoring him? How is that going to stop him from shooting you?"

"Men like him don't backshoot their victims. He operates in a different realm than outlaws like his brother. His reputation is what makes him money. He may say he's here for revenge, but I'm sure it's just as much to build his reputation. I've been concerned about this since they published those newspaper articles and had already decided what to do. I'm not going to have Charlie or Ed keep an eye on him and I'm not going to even look at him. He'll make noise when he can, but sooner or later, he'll have to leave."

"But if he leaves, won't that hurt his reputation?"

"There is that, but the longer he stays, the more that reputation will be damaged. He'd be better off leaving tomorrow. I don't want you to worry, Emma. Word will get around what his purpose is, and he won't be welcome in Lander. It'll be okay."

Emma wasn't so sure, and said, "Of course, I'll still worry. I won't rest until he's gone, but I'll just hold my nagging until then."

"Thank you, sweetheart. The other advantage of doing it this way is that once he's gone, word will get out and we won't see any more of his kind."

Emma nodded and returned to her potatoes while Joe took another bite of steak.

———

A frustrated Fast Jack returned to his room at seven o'clock. He'd asked that chubby waitress, and hadn't learned anything, then spent over an hour at the bar. He'd bought four beers for different men and all he'd found out was that no one seemed to know if he was any good with his pistols. They all seemed to be really impressed with their sheriff. Sheriff Joe they all called him; every single one of them. It was as if they all read those newspaper stories and believed every word. From personal experience, Jack knew that the stories were always exaggerated. Still, after his conversation with the sheriff, he wondered how much embellishment had been inserted in those newspaper articles.

Tomorrow, he'd get that sheriff to face him, one way or the other.

———

Joe had met the same kind of reaction from Billy, Annie, and Mary that he had received from Emma, but had eventually convinced everyone that ignoring Fast Jack was the best defense.

That night, as Joe and Emma lay in bed, not letting a minor threat like a potential killer waiting for Joe interfere with their love life, Emma listened to Joe's heartbeat.

"Joe, I don't want to lose you after waiting so long to find you. Please be careful."

"Do you think I'm going to be careless after finally finding the one woman that forced me to confront my problem? No, Emma, I'll be extremely careful. The only other choice I'd have is to face him, and I wouldn't come out ahead."

"I thought you were good with your pistols."

"I am, but I probably don't practice nearly as much as he does. For him, accurate, fast firing is his life. To me, it's just a job."

Emma sighed and said, "You're the very best at that job, Joe. I'll never be selfish enough to ask you to stop doing it just because I'll worry about things like this. You're just too important to the people in this county."

Joe kissed his wife on the top of her head and hoped that he was right about ignoring Fast Jack Anderson.

Joe entered his office the next morning at eight o'clock and discovered he'd been beaten to work by both his deputies. The coffee was even made already.

"Morning, boys," he said as he hung his new hat on a peg. His old hat was in his office.

"Morning, Joe. What are we gonna do about that gunny?" asked Charlie.

"Nothing. I'll explain what I want to do about him after I get a cup of coffee."

They both watched Joe walk to the cup shelf, take his down and fill it with steaming, black coffee before he half-sat on the edge of the desk, took a sip and said, "I don't want either of you to pay one bit of attention to him. I'm going to ignore him as well. We'll go about our duties like we always do. I think he'll get frustrated and leave."

Ed said, "Lizzie Pinter at the restaurant told me he was askin' how good you were with your pistols. He asked Lou Early and John Harvey over at the saloon, too."

"That's good. It means he doesn't know, and he'll be a bit nervous. After a couple of days, I think he'll just leave. He's not making money staying in Lander."

"Are you sure about this, boss?" asked Charlie.

"It's the better of only two options, Charlie. Now, is anything else going on?"

"Just that the new Indian agent is supposed to be arrivin' on this afternoon's stage. Are you gonna explain about his havin' to wait for the army?"

"I'll talk to him. Let's start our routine day, boys," Joe said as he headed for his office.

———

Word had spread like a prairie wildfire about Fast Jack's purpose for coming to Lander and when Joe made his rounds, tipping his new hat to the citizens, they all looked at him curiously, wondering why he wasn't arresting that nasty man in the hotel who was planning on killing him.

He stopped by the cobbler and picked up his repaired boots when he was returning after completing his morning rounds, which were really more of a way of showing that he was on the job. Today, it just seemed to mean much more to the good folks of Lander.

Joe returned to his office and set his old boots next to his desk and carefully placed his new hat on the desk.

Fast Jack walked along the boardwalk, searching for the sheriff. He had waited until nine o'clock to have breakfast, not wanting to get into a gunfight with anyone early in the morning and having to worry about the possibility of being blinded by the low sun.

He continued to prowl the town until noon, getting bored and frustrated by the sheriff's failure to show his face. He hadn't seen either of those deputies, either.

He went to the café for lunch and took a long time eating, expecting the sheriff to show up, but after having his third cup of coffee, he left a silver dollar on the table, pulled on his hat and left the eatery.

He scanned the streets and the boardwalks again and didn't see the sheriff. Finally, he walked to the barber shop and took a seat on the bench. He pushed his hat back on his head, folded his arms across his deep red vest and just watched.

Joe hadn't eaten lunch, which wasn't unusual for him, but it was intentional today because he expected Fast Jack to be sitting in the diner waiting for him.

He sat in his office, cleaning his Smith & Wessons and checked his loads. When he put them back in their holsters, he didn't put the hammer loops in place. He'd hook them back into position when he rode home that evening.

His other big preparations were to change to his old, still-more-comfortable boots, and would wear his old hat, just in case.

At three-thirty, he heard the stage arriving at the depot, so he grabbed his old hat and walked past his deputies saying, "I'm going to go and meet our new Indian agent."

"You want us to come along, Joe?" asked Charlie.

"No, but you can watch through the window if you'd like," he replied as he left the office and stepped out onto the boardwalk.

As soon as he exited his office, Fast Jack snapped from leaning back with his legs stretched out before him, to a straight-up sitting position. He yanked his hat on tight and rose from the bench and began to walk in the sheriff's direction.

Joe had seen him out of the corner of his eye but kept walking toward the depot. As he watched the coach, the door opened and a heavily whiskered, heavyset man of about fifty stepped down and held out his hand to assist a woman of about thirty from the stage. Then, the driver handed down luggage to the station manager, who began stacking the bags and cases onto the ground.

Joe wondered if the woman was married to the Indian agent, and assumed she was. He didn't recognize her, and she was the only other passenger. He was also curious about the quantity of luggage.

Joe reached the depot before Fast Jack reached him, so Joe approached the Indian agent and offered his hand.

"Mr. Larsen? I'm Sheriff Joe Brooks."

He shook Joe's hand and replied, "Pleased to meet you, Sheriff. May I present my wife, Irene?"

Joe smiled, tipped his hat, and said, "It's a pleasure to meet you, ma'am."

Before she could reply, she looked past Joe and her face told Joe what had grabbed her attention.

"Sheriff, you've been avoiding me, and I don't appreciate being ignored," Fast Jack snarled behind him.

Joe continued to ignore Fast Jack as he looked at the new arrival and asked, “Mr. Larsen, are you related to Roger Larsen who lived near the reservation?”

Phil Larsen glanced at Fast Jack before looking back at the sheriff, wondering if he had a hearing problem.

“Um, yes, yes,” he finally replied, “he was my older brother. Did you know him?”

Joe smiled and answered, “Yes, I did. I thought he and his wife, Bertha were exceptionally good people.”

“I’m talking to you, Sheriff!” Fast Jack shouted from less than twenty feet away.

Larsen then asked, “Sheriff, are you aware that there’s a man shouting at you just behind you?”

“I am, and I am not about to give him the satisfaction of acknowledging him. Anyway, I was wondering if you wouldn’t mind staying in Lander until the army supply train comes through in a couple of days? You and your wife could relax, and they’d provide both escort and transportation to your destination.”

Phil Larsen was growing more nervous about what appeared to be an impending gunfight, so he replied, “That will be fine. Irene and I will check into the hotel. Thank you.”

“I’ll talk to you later, then,” Joe said as he smiled at Mrs. Larsen, tipped his hat and said, “Ma’am.”

Then he turned on his heels and began to walk slowly back to his office as both Larsens watched with wide eyes as the man with the red vest followed. They weren’t the only ones as residents began to cluster on the boardwalks anticipating the same fusillade of gunfire that the Larsens did.

But Joe continued to walk as Fast Jack followed, shouting insults and daring Joe to face him.

Joe stepped up onto the boardwalk and entered his office, closing the door behind him.

Fast Jack found himself standing in the middle of the dusty street with dozens of eyes all staring at him. He felt like a fool as he turned and walked with as much dignity as he could muster back to the hotel while everyone continued to gaze at him.

"Did you notice that the sheriff had a bullet hole in his hat, my dear?" Phil Larsen asked his wife.

"No," she replied with a smile, "I never looked at his hat. That was something I don't believe we'd ever see in St. Louis, Phillip."

"I should hope not!", her husband replied as the porter began loading their luggage onto a cart.

———

"You sure made him mad, Joe," Charlie said as Joe poured himself more coffee.

"I know, and maybe that was a mistake. I didn't think he'd get angry. I was a bit surprised that a man like him began throwing those insults at me, too. He was calling me yellow and a back-shooter and a few other names that I'd be embarrassed to repeat even to you two."

"We heard 'em, Joe. I don't like this one bit."

"I'm not too happy with it, either. Well, it's too late now."

Then after taking a drink of coffee, he said, "That was the Indian agent, Phil Larsen and his wife. She's about twenty years younger than he is, if I had to guess. He was Roger Larsen's brother and I'm sure there's a story in there somewhere. He'll be staying at the hotel until the army comes through."

"Are we still gonna ignore him, Joe?"

"May as well. He didn't shoot me," Joe replied as he finished off his coffee and returned to his office.

Fast Jack was fuming as he sat on his bed. This wasn't working out as he expected at all. He had never shouted at an opponent before, but the frustration of being totally ignored had set him off. Nobody ignores Fast Jack Anderson, and he knew he'd have to act fast now. He couldn't allow word of this humiliation to leak out. Now, it was a matter of pride.

He stood, pushed his twin Colts down hard onto his waist, grabbed his hat and walked out the door.

"I'm going to head home, Charlie. You guys may as well lock up and head home, too."

"We're right behind you, boss," Charlie said as he and Ed began cleaning up some paperwork.

Joe grabbed his old hat and stepped out the door, spotting a very angry Fast Jack Anderson walking towards him and noticed that the gunfighter's Colts were untethered this time, which was a sure sign that he meant business.

Joe took a deep breath and turned right to head to the livery, acting as if he hadn't seen the man striding towards him, then after five steps, he realized that he was putting people in jeopardy by walking in front of businesses, so he hopped down into the street and angled toward the center as he continued to walk toward the livery.

Fast Jack picked up his walking pace to close the gap between them, but that damned sheriff still had his back to him as he walked in front of him a hundred feet away. It looked like he was heading for the livery just another sixty yards away, so Jack had to do something to get him to turn around.

He pulled his right-hand Colt, took quick aim and fired.

Joe was more than just startled when the ground exploded eight inches outside his right foot but managed to keep his stride.

Jack was enraged when Joe continued to walk as if nothing had happened. He aimed to the left and squeezed the trigger again. The Colt bucked in his hand and flame and a cloud of gunsmoke blew out of the muzzle before the dirt road next to Joe's left foot blasted into a small volcano of dust.

Joe continued to walk, the livery now only forty yards away. He knew heads were appearing in the windows and that Charlie and Ed were probably running from the office, pulling their pistols to come to his assistance, but he wished they just stayed out of the way. He made the mistake of believing that Fast Jack wouldn't shoot him.

Fast Jack then screamed, "Turn and face me, you, damned coward!"

Joe didn't turn but should have as Jack, now in full fury, suddenly stopped, raised his Colt a third time, but didn't aim at the ground. He'd get that damned sheriff's attention one way or the other.

He aimed at Joe and squeezed the trigger.

Joe felt the .44 slam into his left upper arm, hitting the humerus as the bullet's force spun him to the ground. But the moment the bullet hit, he felt as if time had slowed and things seemed so incredibly clear. He saw everything in extraordinary detail and seemed to have all the time he'd need to return fire.

He dropped his right hand, carefully pulled his Smith & Wesson from its holster, cocking the hammer as he drew it level, hearing the metallic click as it locked in place. It was like child's play as he drew the revolver level, and as the world slowly passed by his all-seeing eyes, he waited until the pistol's front sight hypnotically intersected with Fast Jack.

He took what felt like ten seconds to notice the gunfighter's wild eyes, clearly saw the hammer of Jack's Colt being leisurely drawn back by Jack's right thumb as Jack's mouth was working and unintelligible sounds flew out with a shower of spittle.

Joe felt a smile forming on his lips as he willed his right index finger to contract, pulling the trigger back to release the hammer. He welcomed the ballooning cloud from his pistol's muzzle and swore he could see the .44 caliber round spinning away toward the man who had shot him. He never saw his bullet strike its target as time suddenly returned to its proper tempo and he lost sight of the gunfighter when his spiral to the ground carried his eyes away from his target.

As he plowed to the dust, he finally felt the massive amount of pain in his left arm and the warm flow of blood soaking his left sleeve. But he knew he couldn't forget about Fast Jack, even in his reduced physical capacity, so he swung his smoking revolver and his head back to where the shooter should be standing but didn't see him. The blood was dripping from the fingers on his left hand as he struggled to gain his footing as he searched for the man who had shot him. *Where did he go? Did Fast Jack run away, thinking he had killed him?*

He was able to get to his knees when hands pulled him up and began wrapping his arm with a cloth. *Why were they helping him? He only had a flesh wound in his arm.*

"Joe! Joe! We've got to get you to see the doc!" a voice shouted at him.

Joe heard a familiar voice say, "I'm okay, Charlie."

Without knowing how it happened, he found that he was walking down the street, wondering how he had managed it so easily. Then, he felt his knees buckle and he almost fell on his face.

Joe was confused now, because he wasn't walking anymore but saw the sun in the sky and faces peering at him as he continued to float along. It was as if he were flying, but on his back. He closed his eyes against the bright sunshine and felt the warmth on his face. The heat felt soothing and he thought of Emma, and how she comforted him just by her smile. Emma. *Where are you, Emma? Are you in our new house waiting for me?* His last conscious thought was of Emma standing on the porch of their new home by the pond, and he smiled.

"He should be home by now, Billy," Emma said as she looked down the access road two hours after Joe had been shot.

"Mama, he probably just got busy."

She glanced back at her son and said, "I'm getting changed. Go and saddle my horse."

Billy didn't argue, he just trotted off the porch and jogged to the barn.

Emma quickly returned to their bedroom and hastily opened a drawer and began tossing aside clothing until she found a riding skirt and then a blouse. She almost ripped her buttons off her dress in her rush to get changed but was soon pulling on her riding boots.

She ran from the house and almost fell as she quickly went down the porch steps, missing the last one, but she recovered from her stumble and then ran to the barn, her fear rising.

Billy had saddled his mother's horse as fast as he could, but still hadn't finished the job when she entered the barn.

Emma helped Billy finish the job, quickly mounted and walked the gelding from the barn, then broke into a fast trot, cutting diagonally to the road, and headed south to Lander.

Billy then began saddling Irish as Annie and Mary entered the barn.

"Mama thinks that Joe is hurt, doesn't she?" Mary asked.

"Yes. I'm going to Lander, too."

Annie quickly said, “Wait for us,” as she rushed to start saddling her horse.

Mary had never saddled her horse before but began the basics as she threw the blanket over her mare’s back.

Fifteen minutes after Emma raced off the ranch, her three children all reached the road and turned south at a fast trot.

———

Joe remained unconscious as Doctor Riddle repaired the extensive damage to Joe’s torn left arm. The bone, while fractured, hadn’t been cracked all the way through or displaced, which was a big help. The bullet had passed through the bicep after ricocheting off the humerus. It was the ricochet that had caused the most damage to the soft tissue and the loss of so much blood. If his deputies hadn’t gotten to him so quickly and applied the shirt-tourniquet, Joe would have died in the street.

But as soon as Charlie and Ed had heard the first warning shot fired by Fast Jack, they had bolted from the office, reaching the boardwalk when the gunfighter fired his second shot. Both were pulling their Colts as they ran to help Joe and watched in horror as Fast Jack aimed his Colt and fired, spinning Joe to the ground.

As they watched in normal speed, they witnessed Joe’s incredible feat when, even after being shot, spun clockwise, pulling his pistol as he turned and fired at Fast Jack before Jack could fire again. Fast Jack went down, and Ed momentarily stopped at the gunman while Charlie plunged his pistol back into his holster to help Joe. He saw the blood spreading across the ground, and before he even reached the sheriff, he began ripping his shirt off. He knelt by his stricken boss and finished yanking his shirt off and spun it quickly into a cotton rope, wrapped it around Joe’s upper arm above the wound and tightened it, stanching the flow of blood as Ed arrived.

By stopping the bleeding, the doctor was able to not only save Joe’s life, but the arm as well, although it did require all of his skill. All that practice in the War Between the States served him well.

Charlie and Joe had paced outside for the hour and a half that it took to finally close the wounds and wrap the arm.

When Dr. Thomas Riddle finally exited the surgery, he looked at the anxious lawmen and said, "He'll be fine, but that arm is going to take some time to heal. You did a great job, Charlie, but I think you'll need to go home and get a shirt on."

Charlie nodded and replied, "Thanks, Doc. I'll do that."

Then he turned to Ed and said, "After I get a new shirt, I'll ride out and tell Emma."

"Okay," Ed said, then asked, "Doc, is there anything else we can do?"

"No, he's still out, but he shouldn't be much longer. I'm sure Emma will be here when he wakes."

"Okay, Doc. Thanks again," Charlie said as he and Ed left the office.

They split up when they reached the street, and Charlie turned for his house while Ed headed back to lock up the office.

It was Charlie who first spotted the rider blasting down main street from the north with her long hair flying behind her. He stopped and waited for Emma to arrive, knowing she'd better slow down soon or she'd pass through Lander entirely.

Emma saw Charlie in the street without a shirt looking at her and knew that something bad had happened. Her heart was already hammering against her ribs when she had started the ride and now it threatened to explode as she brought her horse to a sliding stop twenty feet in front of Charlie who had danced aside not knowing she'd be able to stop in time.

"*What happened, Charlie?*" she shouted as she dropped quickly to the ground.

"He'll be okay, Emma," Charlie replied as he walked closer to her lathered horse, "He took a shot in the upper arm that must have nicked an artery or something because he was bleeding a lot, but the doc says he'll be fine."

Emma didn't ask why Charlie was shirtless, but instead excitedly asked, "*Where is he? Can I see him?*"

"He's in Doc Riddle's office, but he's still out."

Emma didn't care for the horse or even answer Charlie but took off running to the doctor's office.

Charlie took her horse's reins and led him to the livery.

Emma burst into the doctor's office and Marie Riddle, who was leaving the surgery carrying some instruments that needed cleaning, almost dropped the tray to the floor when she was startled by Emma's explosive entrance.

But she recovered and said, "He's in here, Emma, but he's still unconscious. He lost a lot of blood but should recover completely. My husband will be in to talk to you shortly as soon as he finishes eating."

Emma finally regained her composure and said, "Thank you, Marie. Can I wait in the room with him?"

"Of course, I'll bring in a better chair for you," she replied before she walked down the hallway toward the kitchen.

Emma reached the doorway and slowly entered the surgery seeing her shirtless husband lying peacefully on the examination table, his head on a pillow and his left arm heavily bandaged, but she noticed that the other bandage on his lower arm had been removed.

She stood beside Joe and kissed him on the forehead, then stepped back slightly and slowly exhaled a long breath. She wished now that Charlie had stayed so she could find out what had happened and if that bastard brother of Hank Anderson was still around or had run away.

Mrs. Riddle arrived with a chair for her, and Emma asked, "What happened, Marie? Is that gunfighter still around?"

Marie set the chair down before answering, "No, he's dead. Charlie and Ed told us the story and they said it was the most extraordinary thing they'd ever witnessed. The gunfighter was walking behind Joe shouting at him to get him to turn and face him, but Joe kept walking to get his horse. Then the gunman pulled his pistol and fired one shot at the ground near Joe's foot and then another. They were in the jail when the first shot was fired and had reached the boardwalk when he fired the second. But Joe kept walking as if nothing was happening."

Then they said that Fast Jack aimed at Joe and shot him, but missed and hit Joe in the arm, and as Joe was spinning from the shot, pulled his revolver, took his shot while he was turning and killed the gunfighter with one shot right between the eyes. They ran to help Joe, and Charlie made a tourniquet out of his shirt and that saved Joe's life. Some of the other men took the gunfighter's body to the mortician."

"Why didn't Joe drop to the ground or run behind cover?" she asked.

"You'll have to ask Joe about that. No one knows why he did what he did. It surely wasn't because he was afraid. Nothing scares Sheriff Joe."

Emma knew better, but didn't say anything more than, "Thank you for the chair, Marie."

Marie smiled at Emma and left her alone with Joe.

Emma took Joe's hand, held it in both of hers and examined the rough texture as she said, "Joe, why did you let him shoot you? You never even turned around until after you were shot. Are you so anxious to make me a widow again so soon?"

She wasn't expecting an answer, yet she heard a very soft, "I'll never make you a widow, Emma. You are my life."

Emma began to cry as she quickly stood and looked into his barely open eyes and then kissed him gently on the lips.

"Why, Joe? Why did you let him shoot at you?"

"I screwed up, Emma," he replied hoarsely, "I didn't think he'd actually shoot me because he wasn't a back shooter."

"But if he hadn't missed, you would have been dead, Joe," Emma said as she kneaded Joe's hand.

"I don't think he missed, Emma. If he did, he missed by maybe an inch. I think he wanted to nick my left arm, so I'd turn, and he'd be able to shoot me in the front."

Emma was confused and asked, "Why would he even attempt that, Joe?"

Joe was struggling to keep focus, but answered, "He'd lost control, Emma. I could see it in his face when I turned. He had wild eyes, was still shouting, and spittle was shooting from his mouth. Where did he go? Did he escape from Lander?"

"No, he's at the mortician. Marie told me that you shot him right between the eyes."

Joe took in a deep breath and then exhaled before saying, "I missed then. I was aiming for the middle of his chest. But he's gone and now everything is okay again."

Emma's tears had stopped, and her accumulated worries and concerns took over as she said, "It's far from okay, husband. You almost lost your left arm. You need to get better now, and that means you will take time off and stay with me until you are healed. Is that understood?"

Joe managed a weak smile as he tried to focus on Emma's fiery blue eyes.

“Yes, ma’am. Now, this is the woman I fell in love with and married. I’m going to sleep for a little while now, Emma.”

“You go right ahead, and I’ll be here when you awaken a second time.”

Joe wanted to say more, but his eyelids slowly closed, and he drifted into sleep.

CHAPTER 12

The next time Joe opened his eyes, the room was still dark, and he noticed that he wasn't on the hard examination table anymore. He was in a normal bed. He looked around slowly without lifting his head and saw a tiny sliver of sunlight to his left. It took another minute to realize that the room was only dark because heavy drapes had been pulled across the window.

He slowly sat up and let his head clear before he looked to his right and found a sleeping Emma in a cot beside his bed with a blanket pulled up to her chin. Joe smiled at her peaceful face, and then realized he couldn't stay in bed much longer. His left arm was pulsing with pain as he swung his feet around to the floor on the side of the bed away from Emma.

He waited for a more than a minute to make sure he was stable, and tried to stand, but sat right back down. He was still weak, but he wasn't dizzy, so Joe tried again and managed to make it to his feet, but he must have been making enough noise to waken Emma, because he was suddenly being told to sit back down in firm Emma commands.

Joe dropped back to a sitting position on the bed as Emma walked around the bed's foot to face him.

"And where, Mr. Brooks, do you think you're going?" she asked as she stood before him with her hands on her marvelous hips.

"I need to get to the privy, O' Great Goddess of Authority," Joe replied with a grin.

"You'll do no such thing. You'll use this can provided by the doctor. If you can't hold it in position, then I will."

"Um, if you don't mind, ma'am. I have only one hand and I need that one to hold onto other things."

Emma held back her smile and said, "Then, grab your other thing and I will hold the can where it needs to be."

"Thank you, Wonderful Woman of Compassion," Joe said as he unbuttoned his pants and did as Emma suggested.

When he finished, Emma set aside the can and sat on the bed on Joe's right side and kissed him on the cheek.

"We need to get some food and water into you, Joe. The doctor said you need to drink a lot."

"Okay. What time is it?"

"I have no idea. I'll open the drapes and go and get you some food and coffee. I'll pour you a glass of water right now."

After he'd drunk a full glass of water, Emma had him lay back down while she headed for the kitchen, with a brief stop at the privy to empty the can and use its facilities herself.

She had sent Billy, Annie and Mary back home after explaining the situation and they said they'd be back in the morning but hadn't arrived yet. Marie had given Emma free reign in the kitchen while Joe was there, but she had told Emma that he could probably leave today if he didn't ride anywhere.

Joe was sitting in the bed, supported by four pillows as he ate his breakfast and Emma sipped her coffee nearby.

Doctor Riddle had stopped by and explained the extent of his injuries and his prognosis for a full, but lengthy recovery. He said he'd also removed the stitches from the knife wound while Joe was unconscious but would have to return in two weeks to have the new sutures removed.

"So, I can leave today?" Joe asked Emma between bites.

“Only if you ride in a buggy and not on a horse,” she replied.

“Can you go and buy a buggy and horse from Carpenter’s Wagon Works this morning, Emma?”

“I think that’s something I can handle. You’re going to have a lot of visitors this morning. Billy, Annie and Mary all followed me into town by fifteen minutes, but after I told them you’d be all right, I sent them back to the ranch. They should be showing up soon. I imagine your deputies will be stopping by as well.”

“I’m looking forward to hearing the whole story. You know, Emma, it was so strange. When I felt that bullet hit my arm, everything seemed to slow down. It was like time began to stretch out for me. I could see everything so clearly, as if I was looking through giant field glasses. It seemed so easy as I pulled my pistol, cocked the hammer and then waited for my rotation to bring Fast Jack into view. I could even see him drawing back the hammer of his Colt and those insane eyes as I fired. I even saw the bullet spinning away before time resumed its normal speed and I lost sight of him. After that everything was like I was an observer.”

Emma said, “If anyone else had told me that, I’d tell them they were full of horse manure, but I believe you, Joe. I don’t pretend to know how that happened, but I believe you.”

Joe then set his fork down and said, “When they were carrying me away, I felt the sun on my face and closed my eyes, just letting the warmth fill me. It was so soothing that all I could think of was you, Emma. You are my sun and you always calm my soul. I was floating on my back with my eyes shut thinking of you and I smiled.”

“Charlie said he and Ed were wondering why you were smiling,” Emma said softly.

“It’s you, Emma. It will always be you.”

Before she could say anything else, there were the sounds of hurried footsteps and Billy, Annie and Mary popped into the room, saw that Joe was awake and broke into smiles.

“Glad to see you’re awake, Joe,” Billy said.

“Awake and ready to leave, Billy. Your mother needs to go and buy us a buggy and a horse, so I can come home, though.”

Emma took that as a signal, stood and kissed Joe gently before kissing each of her children on the cheeks.

“I’ll be back in an hour or so,” she said before stepping out of the room.

Joe spend a half an hour answering questions as he drank one cup of coffee after another. He didn’t explain the bizarre time slowdown or the out of body sensation as he was being carried to the doctor’s office, though. Most of the questions were the now standard, ‘Why did you keep walking away?’ and ‘How did you make that shot?”, which he attributed to luck. No one would ever believe that it was luck that had guided Joe’s extraordinary shot, but amazing skill.

When Charlie and Ed arrived, the Harper teenagers stepped aside, but listened as the deputies talked to Joe.

“Charlie, I want to thank you for saving my hide,” Joe said, “if you hadn’t been quick on your feet, I wouldn’t be here talking to you. I owe you one.”

Charlie waved off Joe’s thanks and said, “We have his horse and tack in the livery, and we put his two-gun rig in your office. We went through his saddlebags and found two hundred and twenty-four dollars. We left that in the safe.”

“I’ll tell you what, Charlie, the county owes you a new shirt, so why don’t you and Ed divide that money between the two of you.”

“Joe, it’s your money. Those are the rules that you gave us, remember?”

“Okay, so it’s my money and I’m giving it to you and Ed, and that’s the last I want to hear about it. How’s his horse?”

"He's a keeper, Joe. He's a lot better than the pinto you're riding now. I think you should keep the black gelding and give the pinto to Emma to ride. I think she'd like it better than that boring brown that she's riding now."

"I may do that, Charlie. Doc tells me I'm going to be laid up for a few weeks, so you'll be in charge. If anything comes up, let me know."

"The only thing that's come up so far is that our new Indian agent has returned to Green River already. He and the missus took the morning stage. I guess this part of the country is too violent for him."

"That's strange. I would have thought that he'd just move into the ranch house on the Larsen place."

"Nope. He did put it on the market before he left, though."

"He'll have a hard time selling it, but he should be able to get something out of that herd before they all wander off."

"I don't believe he thought that far ahead. He just checked out, stopped at the bank, then he and his wife got on the coach."

So, the Larsen ranch was going to be abandoned, Joe thought. Maybe he'd mention it to Al McClellan. With all of those sons, one will probably be marrying soon and need to start his own place.

After Joe got the full story from Charlie and Ed, who were both apologetic for not putting a couple of rounds into Fast Jack before he got that third shot off, Joe told them it would have been impossible anyway. He answered their questions about the whys by admitting he had erred in his judgement of Fast Jack and had pushed him too far by humiliating him in front of the townsfolk.

By the time Charlie and Ed left to go back to the office and open the safe, Emma had returned with the new buggy and horse. She had written the first draft she had ever used and told Joe it gave her a sense of relevance she had never experienced before. She felt independent and a full partner in the marriage.

After paying the doctor's fee and thanking him and Mrs. Riddle for taking care of him, Joe left the doctor's office with his left arm in a sling.

He climbed on board the buggy with its fresh leather smell and Emma took the reins.

"Can we stop at the livery and get our three horses, Emma?" Joe asked.

"Three?"

"The brown you rode in on, the pinto, and Fast Jack's black gelding. I'm giving you the pinto because he's got such a smooth gait and he's a handsome boy. I never did name him, either."

Emma smiled and said, "I'll take care of that," then she flicked the reins and the buggy made a U-turn to go to the livery as Billy, Annie and Mary rode alongside.

Thirty minutes later, the three trailed horses were strung behind Billy's Irish as they headed north out of Lander, arriving at the ranch seventy-five minutes later.

Billy took care of the buggy and, with Annie and Mary's help, unsaddled all six horses. Billy was impressed with the big black gelding and deemed it worthy of Sheriff Joe.

For three weeks, Joe was reasonably well-behaved as his arm healed. The sutures had been removed and Doctor Riddle was pleased with the progress but cautioned him about doing anything strenuous.

Emma ensured that Joe didn't do anything strenuous at nights as she took charge of their bedtime activities, and Joe had no complaints.

Annie's monthly arrived which created a great sense of relief. None of the girls had become pregnant, but in a surprise development, Sarah Foster did. It might have presented a problem, but although the expected locus-like invasion of unmarried men had never happened, more than a few men made it a point to offer their help to the three available widows in managing their ranches.

In fact, one of Joe's most important duties while he recovered was to talk to the widows about each of the men that drew their interest. He knew most of them, and those he didn't know, he interviewed as if they were being hired as new deputies. The result was that Sarah Foster was married just three weeks after Joe and Emma had tied the knot and Abby Hobson was wed a week later. Jenny Riley was a little more particular but announced that she was going to get married soon.

Joe began returning to the office just three weeks after he'd been shot but was limited in his duties. He still couldn't saddle his horse, which embarrassed him to no end.

He'd sent word to Al McClellan about the availability of the Larsen ranch at a bargain basement price, so he bought the property for his son, John, who was already married and had a baby on the way. It was good timing.

While all of the marrying and healing was progressing, so was the construction of the new house south of Lander. Joe, Emma and the young people would ride out to the site once every few days to watch the progress. The old ranch house was the first job to be completed and with the old furniture restored, new mattresses and bedding in place and the cookstove cleaned, the place was ready for occupancy, but they held off until the second house was done.

Joe returned to full time work five weeks after the shootout and no longer wore the sling or had any restrictions. It still reminded him of how close he had been to dying when he lifted the saddle onto Mars, the name he had given the big black when he found that he wasn't a true black, but a reddish black that only showed itself in the bright sun.

Emma had named her pinto Scraps because she said he looked almost like a quilt made of leftover material.

Finally, six weeks after the shootout, it was time to move into their new home. They had sold the cattle to the other three widows' ranches at a discount price as their new husbands all wanted to increase the size of the herds, leaving the Harper ranch devoid of livestock.

Billy, Annie and Mary moved into the old, but now almost new ranch house while Emma and Joe moved into the new construction. It was a well-appreciated separation by both parties.

All of the horses had been moved to the new property, which, while unable to support a decent-sized herd of cattle, had more than sufficient grazing for a dozen horses.

Billy and Cora had drifted apart as teenagers are wont to do, but he wasn't without a girlfriend long as an older woman, Rachel Foster, who was nine months older than Billy, became the new focus of his attention. Annie and Ben, the worry about her pregnancy over, resumed a normal teenager relationship, leaving only Mary without any attachments.

With the new privacy granted by their new home, Joe and Emma continued their never-ending explorations and the bond between them grew stronger almost daily. Joe was becoming more of a father to the teenagers and it wasn't uncommon for them to come to him with their problems, which was almost non-stop, as it is with most young people taking their first tentative steps into the adult world.

Mary was sitting with Joe on the front porch of the new house in one of the five rockers that they felt was necessary while Emma prepared supper.

"Joe, remember when I said I wanted to be a schoolmarm and you told me that I should wait to make a decision?"

"I remember."

"Well, I don't think I want to be a schoolmarm, but I was talking to Mrs. Riddle and I think I'd like to be a nurse."

Joe looked over at Mary and said, "It's a very hard job, and nurses can't get married, Mary, unless they're like Mrs. Riddle and they marry a doctor first and then become his nurse."

"I know. But when I watched Mrs. Riddle helping you, I thought that's what I'd like to do. I haven't talked to mama about it yet. Could you talk to her?"

"I will, but I don't think she'd object at all, Mary. She'd be very proud of you."

"I thought she'd be upset because I decided that I wouldn't get married and have babies."

"She won't be. Your mother is a very considerate and understanding woman. Besides, Mary, you still have a few years to make your choice."

Mary smiled and said, "Thank you, Joe."

"You're welcome, sweetheart."

That night, as Joe and Emma were wrapped together, Joe told her of the conversation he had with Mary, and her only negative reaction was a bit of hurt that her daughter would think she'd oppose her desire to become a nurse.

"Why wouldn't she ask me, Joe?" she asked softly.

"Just because she thought you'd tell her she should get married and have her own family. It's just a misunderstanding, Emma. You know how much your children love you."

"I know. I'm just being maudlin."

"Yes, you are. You're turning into a squishy, weepy woman who is afraid of her own shadow."

Emma lifted her head from his chest, glared at him, then saw his grin and started laughing.

"You, sir, are an evil man," she said as she rested her head back where it belonged.

"I am, and the only man who will ever love you, Emma."

"The only one who ever has and ever will."

———

The summer was coming to an end and a new Indian agent had arrived and taken up residence in the back of the Indian agency store. He wasn't any better than the recently deceased Mort Forrest, which was no great surprise.

It had been a quiet couple of months after the shooting, and Joe began to believe that it was going to stay this way from now on. It was a poor assumption on his part.

On September 7th, 1881, a cool Wednesday with a cloudy sky overhead Joe was in the office with Charlie and Ed, playing a game of poker while the heat stove did double duty keeping the office warm and the coffee hot.

The door opened, and Henry Johnson stepped in quickly, closing the door behind him.

"Joe, there's some feller down at the store who's been askin' about you. He looks like one of those gunfighters again, only this one has just one pistol. He says he aims to meet you in the street. He said is name is Owen Green. Does that name ring a bell?"

"I've heard of him. He's come a long way to be disappointed. You go ahead and head back to your store, Henry. I'll deal with Mr. Green."

"Okay, Sheriff Joe," Henry said as he quickly left the office.

"You're not going to ignore this one, are you, Joe?"

"No, not this time. We're going to try something different this time."

"*We?*" asked Ed.

"We," replied Joe as he pulled on his new hat and walked back to his office. He returned with his Winchester '76.

"Each of you grab a Winchester," he said as he strode to the door.

Charlie and Ed grinned at each other, dropped their cards and snatched a Winchester from the gunrack.

The three lawmen left the office and Joe stepped out into the street, spotting the gunfighter walking in his direction a good eighty yards away.

"Afraid to face me, Sheriff?" Owen Green shouted.

Joe didn't want to shout, but cocked his Winchester, and said to his deputies, "Don't fire unless you have to, but I don't think you'll have to."

Neither deputy answered as the three lawmen continued to walk down the street.

"Need your deputies to protect you, Sheriff?" Owen yelled as he drew within sixty yards.

Joe's answer was sudden and emphatic as he quickly brought his Winchester to bear and squeezed off the first round. He was already levering in his second .50-95 Express when his first heavy lead slug traveling at supersonic speed slammed into the ground in front of Owen Green, who didn't believe that the sheriff had just fired.

He was grabbing for his Colt and turned to his right to get out of the sights of the powerful rifle, as he started to run, Joe shifted his aim to his left and fired again.

As the ground in front of him erupted from Joe's second shot, Owen pivoted and began to sprint in the opposite direction, but a third bullet blasted the dirt in front of him and he instinctively ducked and ran back the other way again.

Joe and his deputies had continued to walk quickly toward the panicked gunfighter as Joe kept him in the street with large ground bursts, emphasizing the power of the Winchester and his readiness to use it.

0wen finally was able to pull his revolver from his holster and was cocking the hammer when Joe squeezed the trigger for his sixth and final shot.

The heavy missile crossed the forty-one yards and blew Owen's little toe from the rest of his foot, causing him to scream and fall to the ground, grabbing his right leg as his open boot began to ooze blood.

"Now, let's go talk to Mr. Green," Joe said as he lowered his rifle.

They all crossed the forty-yard gap to the wailing gunfighter in ten seconds and when they arrived, Charlie snapped up Owen's Colt Peacemaker.

Owen looked up at Joe and snapped, "You ain't got no right to be shootin' at me!"

"Sure, I do. You've got a wanted poster on my desk, Owen. It said, 'Dead or Alive', and I was a good enough person to let you live. Now, we're going to take you to see the doctor and he'll patch you up. Then, we'll contact the folks that want you and arrange for you to be taken away and hanged."

Joe nodded to Charlie, who handed Joe the pistol and then he and Ed pulled Owen Green from the ground and walked him away. Joe looked at the pistol and noticed the three notches carved into the wooden grips.

"What a nasty thing to do to a nice weapon," he said as he slipped the pistol into his waist.

By then, citizens who had watched the shooting from their windows began filtering out into the street.

Joe just smiled at them as he returned to his office and write his report.

But he had forgotten that the sounds of gunfire could easily reach his new home, especially the loud Winchester '76 firing those heavy cartridges.

Charlie and Ed had returned from Doc Riddle's office, and Joe was in his office when Emma arrived, quickly tied off Scraps and trotted into the jail.

Charlie and Ed both looked up and without a word, just pointed back to Joe's office.

Emma stepped quickly past the smirking deputies, entered Joe's office and closed the door before taking a seat.

Joe had heard her footsteps and wasn't the least bit surprised when she arrived.

"Hello, beautiful wife," he said as he leaned back from writing his report.

"Were you shot this time?" she asked.

"No, ma'am. I treated this one quite differently. I took my Winchester and had Charlie and Ed behind me as we walked into the street. I fired first into the ground and had him bouncing back and forth with more shots until I saw him cock the hammer and then I shot his toe off."

"*You shot his toe off? On purpose?*" Emma asked with big eyes.

"On purpose. I had to stop this from happening, Emma. I've been thinking a lot about it since the Fast Jack shooting. I didn't want to put you through that again, but I had to send a message to any others that would come to Lander. It's not only dangerous to me, and very worrying to you, it's hazardous to the good people of Lander who might get hit by a stray bullet. So, I decided to humiliate the next one and I'm going to be sure that the story gets out that if they come here, they won't get the chance to face anyone. If you think you can come to Lander to enhance your reputation, you'll be driven out of town, with or without a toe."

Emma leaned back in her chair, looked up at the ceiling and said, "I'm always going to worry about you, aren't I, Joe?"

Joe looked at his wife and realized the burden he was putting on her.

He waited until she looked back at him and asked, "Emma, you are more precious to me than life itself. I'm not going to put you through this any longer. I'm going to resign today, and we'll just live a quiet life together. Okay?"

Emma tilted her head and replied, "You can't be serious. I am always going to worry about you, Joe, because I love you so much. It's just part of life, but I would never dream of asking you to quit."

She stood and walked around behind the desk and perched on his lap, putting her arms around his neck.

She kissed him and said, "You are the best lawman in the entire West, my beloved husband. You protect the good people from the bad and I cannot tell you how proud I am to be known as the wife of Sheriff Joe."

EPILOGUE

The shootout in the streets of Lander, resulting in the lost toe of Owen Green, was the last time that Joe had to fire a gun inside the town, although he did have four more shootouts in the wild country of Fremont County over the next six years before turning over most of the out of town jobs to Ed.

The Harper ranch was kept in pristine condition and was occupied in July of 1883 when Annie Harper married Ben Hobson. The ranch was repopulated with a small herd from the other ranches and Annie became pregnant the first month of her marriage, giving birth to a baby girl on April 7th, of 1884. They named her Lauren Marie.

Despite Mary's stated desire to become a nurse, she met a young man who arrived in Lander in June of 1885 and set up his dental practice. Six months later, after working as his assistant for four months, Mary married John Winters and had their first child, a little boy they named Joseph William.

Billy and Rachel Foster continued as boyfriend and girlfriend, and after Billy became the newest deputy sheriff in 1887, they married, and moved into the ranch house that he had recently shared with Annie and Mary.

Over the next ten years, Joe and Emma continued to watch their grandchildren multiply, and by the time they celebrated their tenth anniversary in 1891, they had nine grandchildren.

In fact, all of the six girls who had been taken by the Hanger Bob Jones gang were able to find fulfillment in their marriages and their motherhood. It had become a tradition that each of the young women, before they accepted their beaus, would ask for Sheriff Joe's approval.

On that tenth anniversary, Joe corrected a shortcoming when he finally slid a wedding ring over Emma's finger, and she slipped one over his.

Joe finally stepped down from being the sheriff when they celebrated their twenty-fifth anniversary, and he'd reached the ripe old age of fifty-nine. Charlie was too old to take over and Ed had left Lander to become the sheriff of Laramie County, so Billy Harper succeeded his idol and had his badge pinned on by Joe while Emma stood by with tears in her eyes.

As Joe and Emma lay together on the evening of the swearing in ceremony, the first night that Joe hadn't been the sheriff in thirty-eight years, he kissed Emma on her forehead and let out a deep breath.

"Remember I told you about how I thought it was funny that Roger and Bertha Larsen were still trying to make a baby when they were almost sixty?"

Emma smiled as her head lay on his chest.

"Yes, I not only remember it, I saw it as a goal."

"Well, it's not so funny anymore, is it?"

"It was never funny to me, Joe. I thought that if two people loved each as much as they must have and as we do, how could we stop making love? I think it's ironic that they never had any children and neither did we, but we still keep trying."

Joe patted Emma on her damp behind and said, "You told me from the start that you couldn't have any children, Emma, but you showed me how it worked. I've been learning for twenty-five years and we still have at least another twenty-five years to go."

Emma kissed her husband, then resumed her normal position before saying, "Don't think for a moment that I haven't forgotten that promise you made to me twenty-five years ago when you told me that you'd love me with until your dying breath and I said it had better not be for another fifty years."

"And I intend to keep that promise, Emma. You do realize that we're talking about 1931, don't you?"

Emma said, "That does sound so far in the future, doesn't it? Maybe we'll all be flying around by then rather than riding horses."

"I'll stick to horses, if it's all the same to you, ma'am."

"Whatever we're doing then, Joe, it doesn't matter as long as we do it together."

Joe gave Emma a gentle squeeze for an answer.

Joe always assumed that he would die before his Emma. He didn't know why he thought it would be that way. Maybe it was because Emma was always the center of his world.

They had great-grandchildren and great-great grandchildren at their fiftieth wedding anniversary on June 14th, 1931. Emma was so weak from the cancer that was draining her strength and her vitality that she had to be pushed into the barn where the celebration was being held.

Despite protests from Billy and just about everyone else, Joe insisted on pushing the wheelchair himself, and as the couple arrived, the barn was stuffed to overflowing with their children, grandchildren and great-grandchildren. All of the girls from that almost-forgotten horror in 1881 were there to pay their respects to the two people who had saved them from the terror and then helped them return to normal lives. Each of the other widows had already passed on.

Billy had retired as sheriff and presided over the affair, which wasn't very long in deference to Emma's pain and failing health.

But when Billy finished his speech about Joe and Emma and what each meant to him, his sisters, his wife and the other women who had survived that ordeal, Joe stepped forward, and in a surprisingly strong voice spoke to the assemblage of family and friends.

"Each of you know how much my Emma means to me. As I look out among you, I know how much she means to each of you as well. There has never been another woman like my Emma and there never will be again. I count myself the luckiest of men to have shared my life with her. She is my life."

Then Joe stepped over to the wheelchair, and looked into Emma's now cloudy blue eyes, smiled and kissed her softly.

Emma looked up at her husband and said, "Come to me soon, my love."

Joe nodded and whispered, "Very soon, sweetheart."

He then wheeled Emma from the silent room and crossed the three hundred feet to their house. As he pushed her, he felt the pain in his chest grow stronger, as he knew it would. He struggled to push her up the ramp, but finally got her onto the porch, opened the door and pushed the wheelchair inside.

He closed the door and pushed the chair to the kitchen table, planning on making his Emma some cocoa. But when he asked her if she'd like a cup of hot chocolate, he received no reply.

He pulled a chair close to his wife's wheelchair and saw her head bowed. His beloved Emma had finally left him, but she was at peace now and he knew she was waiting for him.

Joe took in a deep breath as he held back the tears that he knew would never come. Then he stood and pushed the wheelchair into their bedroom.

He carefully lifted his wife's terribly thin frame from the wheelchair and gently laid her on the bed, the sharp pain radiating down his left arm. *Soon, my Emma, soon*, he thought as he straightened, and pushed the wheelchair away from the bed.

He slowly stepped around to the other side of the bed, having difficulty breathing, and lowered himself slowly to the bed beside his beloved wife, then leaned over and gently kissed her on the lips.

Joe knew it would be seconds now, but still managed to say, "Emma, you were the only woman I've ever kissed and that was the last one I will ever give you. I kept that promise I made to you fifty years ago. I loved you for every minute of those fifty years and now, I'll keep the second promise I made to you. The one I made in the barn. We'll be together again soon, my love, my Emma."

He then stretched out on the bed and took Emma's thin left hand in his right and closed his eyes. Sheriff Joe was going to join his Emma.

SHERIFF JOE

1	Rock Creek	12/26/2016
2	North of Denton	01/02/2017
3	Fort Selden	01/07/2017
4	Scotts Bluff	01/14/2017
5	South of Denver	01/22/2017
6	Miles City	01/28/2017
7	Hopewell	02/04/2017
8	Nueva Luz	02/12/2017
9	The Witch of Dakota	02/19/2017
10	Baker City	03/13/2017
11	The Gun Smith	03/21/2017
12	Gus	03/24/2017
13	Wilmore	04/06/2017
14	Mister Thor	04/20/2017
15	Nora	04/26/2017
16	Max	05/09/2017
17	Hunting Pearl	05/14/2017
18	Bessie	05/25/2017
19	The Last Four	05/29/2017
20	Zack	06/12/2017
21	Finding Bucky	06/21/2017
22	The Debt	06/30/2017
23	The Scalawags	07/11/2017
24	The Stampede	07/20/2017
25	The Wake of the Bertrand	07/31/2017
26	Cole	08/09/2017
27	Luke	09/05/2017
28	The Eclipse	09/21/2017
29	A.J. Smith	10/03/2017
30	Slow John	11/05/2017
31	The Second Star	11/15/2017
32	Tate	12/03/2017
33	Virgil's Herd	12/14/2017
34	Marsh's Valley	01/01/2018
35	Alex Paine	01/18/2018

36	Ben Gray	02/05/2018
37	War Adams	03/05/2018
38	Mac's Cabin	03/21/2018
39	Will Scott	04/13/2018
40	Sheriff Joe	04/22/2018
41	Chance	05/17/2018
42	Doc Holt	06/17/2018
43	Ted Shepard	07/13/2018
44	Haven	07/30/2018
45	Sam's County	08/15/2018
46	Matt Dunne	09/10/2018
47	Conn Jackson	10/05/2018
48	Gabe Owens	10/27/2018
49	Abandoned	11/19/2018
50	Retribution	12/21/2018
51	Inevitable	02/04/2019
52	Scandal in Topeka	03/18/2019
53	Return to Hardeman County	04/10/2019

Made in the USA
Columbia, SC
08 November 2019

82951058R00217